the breaking

DODSFELL

BOOK ONE

MAVE HATHAWAY

Cover Design by Jess at brushtoblades

Map Art by Mave Hathaway

Interior Art by Marta Riva

Initial Edits: Ash & AL at Splitleafsaturdays

Formatting: Lofty Wings Press LLC

Paperback ISBN: 979-8-9907814-1-2

EBook ISBN: 979-8-9907814-2-9

Published by Lofty Wings Press LLC

I wrote this with the encouragement of those close to me, but it is dedicated most to those living with their own monsters. They take many forms and the storm is always darker before the rainbow. May you find it in the end.

BAELIAN EMPIRE

The Breaking

Death of the Wolf (Publishing 2025)

...more coming soon...

DRAGON LEGACY

The Apprentice

...more coming soon...

trigger warnings

TIXDARR

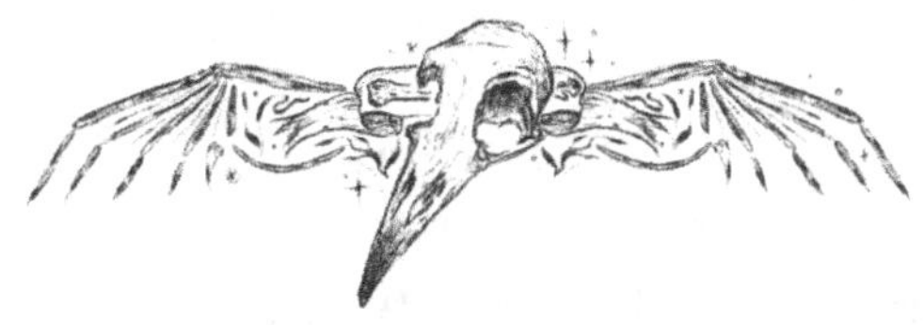

The rumor amongst the Gods residing in the Void is that the mortals that may have the opportunity to read this are concerned about their own mental well-being. As the Lord of the Dead I will never understand. Regardless here are the terrors you may encounter on the page, a mere slice of what I specialize in.

- Physical abuse
- Implied Child Abuse (not shown on page)
- SA violence (seen through a vision, not explicit on the page)
- Death
- Torture
- Gore

I shall see you at the end of this story if you enjoy it, do proceed with caution.

~ Tixdarr, Lord of the Dead

The Baelian Empire
Balthor
Dulvak
Dodsfell
Palion
Temple
Drakore
Longspire
Meltem
Fae

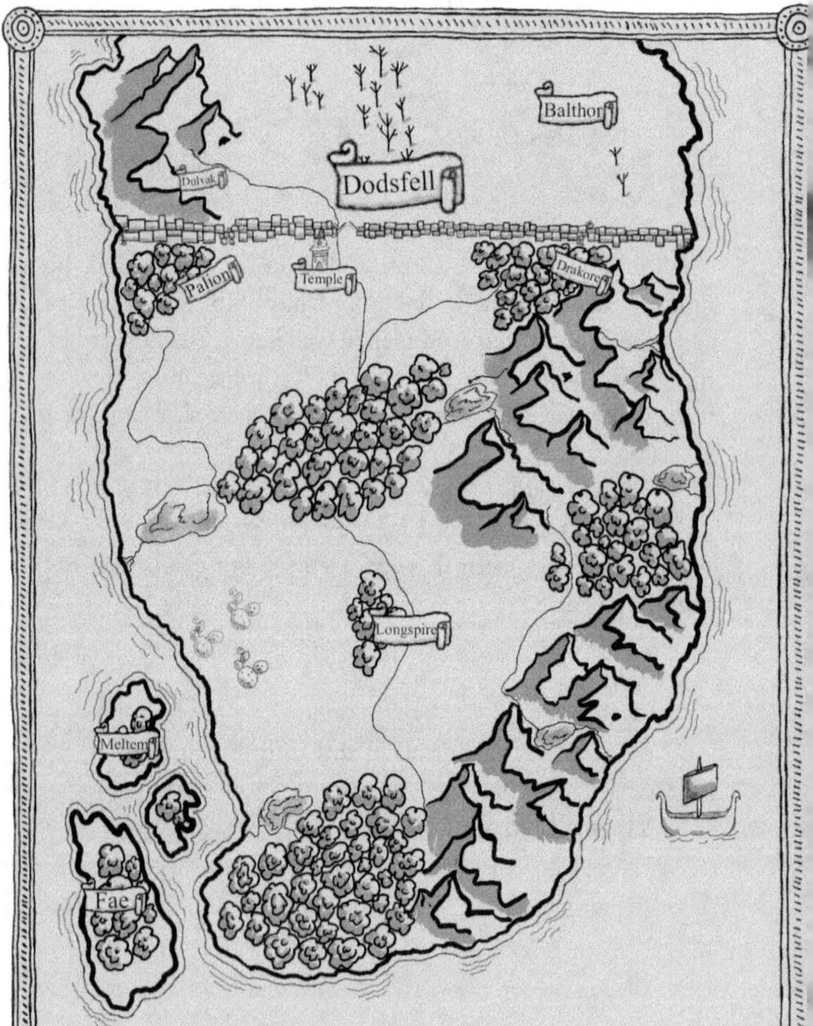

book blurb

Darling Mortal Readers,

A mortal's psyche is flexible, varying from being to being. Yet, how much pressure does it take to snap it? I thought I held all the knowledge one needed to destroy a psyche, but it seems that my talents have dulled. It started when a force unknown to the Gods locked us up in the dratted Void. A dismal, boring place for any of us but especially for me. I grew used to traveling back and forth from my own realm, toying with those I encountered. Snapping the psyches' of my demons has always been one of my favorite pastimes. Mortals are no more than snacks for me, the occasional treat that wanders into the realm. The stronger they are of will, the smokier of flavor. The recent boredom of the Void has led me to begin testing the true reach of my powers. Aurelia Berrid, Princess of Drakore and heir apparent, is the current focus of my newest experiment. I can't imagine I will be unable to break her with all that I have planned. I am a God and no one can deny a God in the end. I won't stop at her either, I shall see all around her crumble into dust blowing on their precious wind. Perhaps in the end if she proves difficult I could attempt to mold her. Though I don't know if once I do that anyone could ever call her a mortal again.

    ~Tixdarr, Lord of the Dead

the enigma of time

TIXDARR

Time passes differently for every being living and dead. I hear rumors that you mortals follow a very specific calendar and it's important for the contents of this and many stories to come that you know the calendar that exists within my world. I have kindly deigned to break down the months in order of the year and even added the associated festivals celebrated throughout Baelia. I have limits to my patience however and have not added in every single festival that may be celebrated within Baelia. Be grateful I decided to help at all.

~Tixdarr, Lord of the Dead

Drak - Festival of Dragons *(Secretly Celebrated)*
    Bura - Festival of New Life
    Tiv - Festival of the Mother
    Anit - Festival of Water
    Byr - Festival of Fire
    Duele - Festival of Harvest
    Osi - Festival of Protection
    Riari - Festival of Healing
    Bene - Festival of Wind
    Xita - Festival of War
    Oxi - Festival of the Father
    Tix - Festival of Death

religious hierarchy

TIXDARR

It's important moving forward wayward mortal visiting our world, that you have a full idea of how our Pantheon functions. The Gods within the Pantheon each get a temple, but only if the people of the land choose to honor them with one. The temples can be simple or complex. For our purposes we will review the more complex of our temple structures, I would hate for you to be confused. The powerful Gods such as my sister Tiva have multiple temples throughout the continent. Be advised moving forward in our universe, this is not an exhaustive list of Gods worshipped in Baelia. That would take far too much of my precious time.

~Tixdarr, Lord of the Dead

TEMPLE POSITIONS

Oba: The head of the temple. One main Oba covers many smaller temples, only the strongest of the Gods warrant multiple Obas. This position has only ever been held by a woman, chosen by the God in question.

Abbot/Abbess: The right hand to the Oba in the temple she resides in. In smaller temples this individual will run the temple and report issues to the God's chosen Oba.

Acolyte: A member of the Gods order. Serves the temple and spreads the word of the God they all worship.

THE PANTHEON OF BAELIA

Gods:
    Goddess of Tiva ~ Fairy ~ Goddess of Motherhood
    God Oxius ~ Minotaur ~ God of Fatherhood
    God Tixdarr ~ Demon ~ God of the Dead and Afterlife
    God Burasil ~ unknown species ~ God of Animal and Hunt
    God Benmes ~Winged ~ God of Air and Wind
    Goddess Deulla ~ Centaur ~ Goddess of the Earth and Harvest
    Goddess Byra ~ Dwarf ~ Goddess of Fire
    Goddess Anita ~ Merfolk ~ Goddess of Water
    God Xitar ~ unknown ~ God of Fighting and War
    God Osin ~ unknown ~ God of Protection
    Goddess Riarin ~ Elf ~ Goddess of Healing and Medical

pronunciation guide

TIXDARR

The other Gods have suggested that you may want to know how to pronounce the various names of things presented in this story. So here you go mortals parse through these words and figure out how to enter my world completely.

~ Tixdarr, Lord of the Dead

People:
Maledic - (Mal-e-dic)
Kygoss - (Ki-goss)
Aurelia - (a-Rey-li-a)
Hesperdae - (hez-per-Day)
Cerial - (See-re-ul)
Faziel - (Fæ-z-el)
Balthor - (Bal-th-ar)
Areth - (Air-th)
Recin - (Re-sin)
Dulvak - (Dull-va-k)
Estrez - (S-trez)
Aewenna (Awe-win-a)

Dalro - (Dal-ro)
Allith - (Al-ith)
Feginth - (Fe-g-in-th)
Spréach - (Spree-ach)

Place:

Baelia - (Bay-lee-a)
Palion - (Pal-ee-on)
Drakore – (Drr-a-k-ore)

Gods:

Goddess of Tiva - (T-ee-va)
God Oxius - (Ox-ee-us)
God Tixdarr - (Tick-star)
God Burasil - (Brr-a-sil)
God Benmes - (Ben-mis)
Goddess Deulla - (Do-el-a)
Goddess Byra - (Bi-ra)
Goddess Anita - (A-ni-ta)
God Xitar - (Zi-tar)
God Osin - (Aw-sin)
Goddess Riarin - (Ree-are-in)

Months:

Drak - (Dr-æ-k)
Bura - (Brr-a)
Tiv - (T-i-v)
Anit (Æ-nit)
Byr - (Bi-r)
Duele - (Do-el)
Osi - (O-see)
Riari - (Ree-are-ee)
Bene (Ben-a)

Xita - (Zit-a)
Oxi - (Ox)
Tix - (Ticks)

contents

I suppose to start our tale I will give you a background of the Gods. We used to wander the mortal realms poking our noses into their business and causing chaos. Then an imperceptible shift became apparent within the Void. The middle ground a place devoid of color, sound, or ultimately any stimulus its intention to allow us to create new masterpieces without the interference of mortals.

It is important to note at this stage that a select number of Gods view themselves as 'Upper'. My darling sister Tiva and her mate Oxius like to tout that they rule the rest of us. Sometimes it is more beneficial to just allow them this small erroneous thought. After all, while they are distracted trying to manage the others I am free to create mischief where I will it. Anyway, they had called a meeting which wasn't unusual within the Void, the neutral ground for all Gods. However, when they were done running their mouths, no one was able to shift back to the Mortal Realm. I was naive and certain that my own realm of Dodsfell would be exempt from this oddity, yet no matter how much of my own power I sunk into the attempt, I couldn't shift home either.

Since then we have been stuck. It has taken a long time to rebuild my power reserves, especially when I can still be sucked dry by the over eager demon who knows how to access my power. That time has been spent plotting and planning. While I suspect that I am not alone in being able to circumvent this lockdown the extent of others success is unclear. I will figure out how we got locked up here no matter what mortals I must use to get there.

one

QUEEN HESPER

DRAKORE - BYR - YEAR 7557

Silver vines curled around emeralds of various sizes, golden rosebuds peeking around the glittering rocks. Her ghostly hand delicately traced the metal vines, a shudder radiating through her mind as she realized razor-edged thorns dug into the scalp of the head that bore it. Maroon ichor dripped down the head of the bearer, a trickling splash echoed through her mind. Yet, eerily no indication of distress appeared on the slightly glowing figure before her.

The intricate crown seemed to be embedded into the four strand braid, additional diamonds pinned into the raven hair. The diamonds drew Hesper's eye around the head of the mysterious woman. She attempted to focus, pushing at her magic, willing it to shift. Finally the face belonging to the inky haired beauty became the focal point.

Shock rippled through Hesper recognition reverberating through her soul at the older Aurelia staring unseeing back at her. The glow of the vision made Aurelia's pale skin glow in an ethereal light, the blood dripping down from the crown appearing black. The blue eyes once full of love now appeared hardened. *How had she become so darkened?* The crown however posed one irrefutable fact, Aurelia had wed the Palion pup. A fact that made little sense considering currently he was betrothed to Cerial, Aurelia's older sister. *How did this come to occur?*

Her eyes ached as she stared at the vision's rendition of her youngest daughter, memorizing the differences between the girl asleep down the hall and the version she peered at in her mind. New lines appeared on her face, a smile that failed to reach her formerly joyous eyes. Hesper glanced down past Aurelia's fake smile and saw another glint of metal. She plied her will as one may wield a sword, forcing her unruly magical sight downward. Her chest burned as slowly the vision shifted once more, exposing a familiar necklace.

The last Queen of Drakore had gifted Hesper the necklace upon Hesper's Rite of Inheritance. The Rite when she and her soulbond partner Aydan took their rightful place as ruler's ages ago. The necklace passed down through the females that belonged on the Drakore throne. Since Aydan had been the only offspring of the last ruling couple, the necklace had come to her as Aydan's soulbond. The fact that it rested upon Aurelia's neck foretold more than her mind could fathom.

The necklace was a dragon caught in flight, a delicate chain connected to the outstretched wings, the intricately detailed lower claws clasping a glowing red gem. Hesper brought up a phantom hand and traced the dragon's wings delicately as if touching it would help her figure out how it might end up on the neck of her youngest daughter, earlier than Hesper and Aydan had planned for.

It had become apparent that the impossible task of unification would rely on Hesper and Aydan. Drakore and Palion had never been united, though the kingdoms had worked hard to maintain positive enough relations. When Hesper and

Aydan never managed to produce a male heir, only two daughters living to majority, their roles were clear. One destined for Palion, the other left to rule Drakore. It had taken many years to decide which girl to send, yet when Cerial's loving and peace giving personality became clear she was the obvious choice.

Thoughts of her first born, Cerial, triggered a change in the vision, the older version of Aurelia disappearing leaving Hesper in the dark. Her heart racing at the revelation that something ill could be coming. She urged her magic to release her back to consciousness or show her what she needed. Gradually a glow began in the distance, the magic allowing her to float closer. Her mind stuttered. The figure illuminated by the eerie light had to be Aurelia, perhaps from a different stage of life since the crown was now missing yet the physical resemblance remained so strong. The eyes the same stunning blue, that of the sky on the clearest day. The hair at first sight appeared dark, dark enough to be Aurelia's.

Still, some forgotten maternal instinct gnawed away at her insides, something wasn't right. The magic allowed her closer and the hair began to lighten at least in spots. A gasp left her as the hair that seemed lighter suddenly glowed blonde, an unseen light source shining down on the body, the magic tired of waiting for her to understand. The body that of her eldest daughter Cerial.

Cerial and Aurelia, sisters frequently mistaken as twins. They had a two year age difference, but their matching eye color and similar slight builds caused constant confusion. The defining feature always came down to their hair. Hesper squinted and realized why Cerial's had looked so dark from afar, it was matted and thick with a rusty brown substance. Someone, blurred out by the magic, intended to remain a secret even from her, let fly a whip and Cerial's back bowed a scream leaving her throat that cut Hesper to the bone.

Blood.

Her hair was matted. Fresh blood oozed out from beneath the crusted locks. The question of how she had come to be in such straits became evident as a blurred figure took a fistful of Cerial's once gorgeous blonde curls and pulled her head back no mercy in his punishing grip. Hesper, unable to look away from her daughter's face, saw as she contorted in pain, Cerial's cheeks had clear tracks where the tears had scrubbed the grime away.

Hesper felt as her body fought her magic, her breath shallow, not reaching her lungs. Her ghostly hands clutched at her chest as pain seared hot and sharp, tears flowing down her face, her ears filling as her physical body remained prone. The magic paralyzed, preventing her from leaving the vision no matter how hard her consciousness fought. The magic required that she watch the eternity of torture inflicted upon her beloved Cerial. Some part of her mind registered that Aydan rolled over and touched her shoulder, his rough hands bringing more awareness to her physical form. The screams coming from Cerial echoed in Hesper's mind, lodged there unlikely to fade while Hesper walked Baelia.

The expulsion she craved so deeply came with a jerk. Her mental consciousness sent pinwheeling back into her body. Hesper's own scream stuck in her throat as her heart galloped under her skin desperate to escape the cage it lived in. She surged upward, desperate to distance herself from the helpless position of sleep. Aydan moved closer, gently rubbing her back as she slowly tried to bring her body's functions back under her own control. As her heart rate slowed and her breath began to send oxygen to her deprived lungs, her mind put together the pieces of what her magic had shown her.

The gift of vision was a unique one. Those with it had to work within certain constraints, such as being unable to see the futures of anyone directly reliant upon her. Thus, she had never seen the girls' future and she had ceased seeing Aydan's when they wed. That was what Goddess Tiva decreed, yet now she had seen not just one but both of her girls in their future. Perhaps it should be seen as a gift and not an unspoken prophecy of its own.

Determination filled the gaps left behind by the waning panic. For reasons she would never understand, Goddess Tiva had given her a window into the future of her children and she would try as hard as she could to not waste the opportunity. Her mind drifted inexorably to the darker reasons this gift may have been bestowed, her flesh rippling at the possibilities.

Her death.

If she died before the events her gift had deigned to show her, it would explain why. Someone somewhere had made a decision that solidified her ending, thus making it possible for the Goddess Tiva to reveal the futures of those closest to her. She shook her head, pulling her mental self up out of the dregs of the darkness, rolling her shoulders the mental reprimand readily available. *Forewarned meant forearmed, if they were armed they could fight.*

It would be complicated to ensure Aurelia's readiness to take on Palion's throne in Cerial's place. The roadblocks that stood in the way would fight against the change. Aurelia would undoubtedly fight against the plan, mostly from a lack of trust in Hesper's motives. The second complication would be Palion's own King Harold, who would make them pay for the privilege of switching the agreement. His wife had been his grounding force of kindness, with her death any shred of decency had perished within him. Hesper could understand the personality change even when it brought complications to her own doorstep. Should anything take Aydan from her she would cease to exist as well.

She looked over her shoulder, the blanket pooling around her waist, taking in the strong jaw and kind eyes that were patiently waiting for her to fill him in on what she had seen coming. She gave him a weak smile, "Thank you for being here my love. We have a hard path ahead I fear, but together anything is possible." She turned from him, closing her eyes and just basking in his warmth, letting it banish the darkness she had waded through.

Aydan curled against her, the places where their skin touched, setting off sunbursts of warmth, his heartbeat reassuring on her shoulder. His arms encircled her stomach as he secured them tightly together. "My darling, if you are dedicated to walking the road, I shall be there right at your side to aid, however I am able to." He nuzzled into his favorite place just under her ear and left a trail of kisses down to her shoulder.

"You must write to Harold. We need to change the union between Lucian and Cerial. It must be Aurelia." She winced, waiting, grateful he couldn't see her face.

She held her breath as she felt his body stiffen in shock. Her own anger spiking deep within, a fire she could never really suffocate. He wasn't supposed to have a favorite. No matter how many times she tried to talk herself out of it, Hesper knew Aurelia was the favored child in Aydan's eyes. The spit fire daughter who asked forgiveness and never even considered asking permission, whose greatest desire in life was the day the Great Power granted her wings.

"Hesper." Aydans voice hitched, "I know you are rarely wrong. How are you so sure you are seeing their futures? You've never seen them before so perhaps this glimpse is something else. Perhaps it's someone else who needs their future to be changed. How sure are you?"

She sighed, her head suddenly very heavy. She pulled her knees up resting her chin on them. "I am as sure as I can be Aydan. You know how fickle my magic can be but it was directly influenced by the thoughts of the girls." It came out more like a whisper knowing the implications for Aydan. He had hoped for Aurelia to be the one guarding Drakore in his stead when the time came. "She wore Palion's crown, older obviously but quite clearly in Palion regalia. She..." Hesper paused hesitating to tell him about the necklace, the implication world shattering. On an exhale she rushed it out. "She had on her neck my necklace." Her hand lifted to the dragon in flight around her neck as she toyed with it.

Aydan's hands gripped tighter on her arms as the news sank in. He cleared his throat, "You can't know Hesper. Perhaps you gifted it for her marriage day. Perhaps Lucian is her soulbond partner and she lives a happy life." Hesper knew his hope for Lucian to be the soulbond partner of Aurelia was a fantasy built on twigs, but it helped him so she let it be.

Tears gathered in her eyes. He was too damn good, reaching for any possibility of positivity, a pang of pain stabbed through her at the thought of leaving him too soon and being without his positivity. The signs that she may die soon were clear. She wished with all her heart that she could spare him the pain that may come. With a halting voice, she relayed the rest of the vision. Part of her was grateful she couldn't see Aydan's reactions as he listened to her describe the condition Cerial had been in. Hesper struggled containing her own emotions and if she saw the shuffle of them across his face she would be unable to explain it all.

The inky shadows of the predawn light filled the bedroom, the sun not yet risen past the trees as she pulled herself out of the bed and away from him. He needed space to accept what had been seen and make his plans for the future. A lot needed to be accomplished to protect Cerial and to prepare Aurelia for her new fate. At the end of the day, Hesper knew she would follow that foreign gnawing instinct that had been awakened during the vision, listening to it would, she hoped, lead to happiness for those she loved the most.

two

KYGOSS

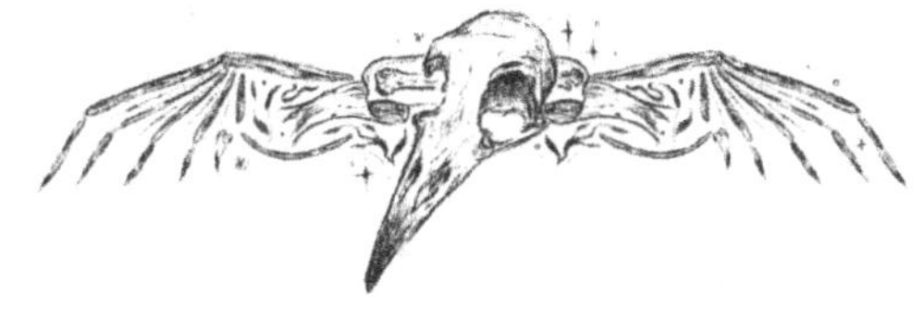

DRAKORE - BYR - YEAR 7557

The warmth of the sun sank into his skin, burning away all concerns that may have been in Kygoss' mind. The large windows reminiscent of those in his home in the Crowlands warming his heart even when the sun lay hidden away. A side benefit of this particular study came in its seclusion from the main traffic of the palace. This isolation came because he was located at the top of a turret in the most disused corner of the palace.

Roughened leather boots rested on the thick oaken desk that ate up much of the small room. Kygoss rubbed at his stubble beard, his mind wandering over his role within the nation. When he accepted his post he had expected his job to be action-packed. *Spymaster* elicited a certain expectation of closed doors and dagger fights in the alleys, or at least for him it had. He had kept the post for as long as he had despite consistently being forced from his family, due to his friendships with his King and Queen. The court of course had no idea of his job, instead seeing him as an old friend turned advisor, which nowadays was closer to the truth.

Peace-time led to a different reality however causing Kygoss to frequently wrestle with if he should keep the job regardless of his friends. Drakore had been at peace for nigh on a century, the minor tiffs between itself and Palion hardly warranting a second thought. It was a common occurrence now to receive intelligence about so and so's significant other screwing around with someone they shouldn't. A small secret side of him wished for exhilarating thrills in his day to day while the larger part of him was grateful that the generations after him would know only peace and prosperity.

Rapping knuckles on his open door had him almost falling out of his chair jarred from his thoughts. He stood in a rush when he realized who loomed in the doorway, the bow clumsy as he almost fell over shooting a sly grin at the Queen. "Your Majesty! I would have come to you had you but summoned me. I never want you to feel like you have to track me down."

Kygoss had known Queen Hesper since they were both hatchlings, having grown up in neighboring houses in the Crowlands. She hadn't forgotten her childhood friend when it became clear her destiny lay with the Royal family as Aydan's soulbond and became the future Queen. Once secured on their throne Queen Hesper and King Aydan had ensured that he had a place at court. His sly grin faltered as he assessed her closer, the dark circles, rushed appearance, and restless pacing in the hall all so unlike his stately Queen.

A seriousness draped over him as he ushered her to a chair, stuffing his natural tendency for joy and mischief deeper within himself. He used his wind magic to secure the door shut behind them. "What happened? Is it Aydan? The girls?"

Hesper shook her head sharply. "I've had a vision, Kygoss.

A terrible one. I have been working with Aydan to take steps to change it. I need your assistance though."

His eyes widened as shock ricocheted around his chest. The Gods were the bestowers of visions and would not take kindly to them being changed. Never in the history of their long friendship had Hesper felt the need to challenge the divine beings who gifted her this magic. Whatever she had seen must have truly been terrible for her to risk godly retribution. "What was the vision? Change? How?"

She shook her head, causing more hair to escape her hastily assembled updo cutting off any further questions. He watched as she patted the hair trying to tuck the wisps of hair back where they had escaped. "It was a vision of the girls. I can't stand to rehash it once more. I am not exactly sure how to change it. As I figure it out I need to entrust Aurelia to you. She will need to be trained just as I was. She's now going to Palion. You know the Pup is unlikely to be of much help in their rule. His father is difficult to say the least."

Kygoss let out a breath sorting through the massive influx of thoughts that flew around his mind before asking, "The Gods gave you a vision of what is to come for the girls?!"

"They did." A breath escaped Hesper's tightly clenched lips as she rubbed at her temples.

"That should be celebrated. No one with the gift of future sight gets to see the futures of their loved ones, at least it's not documented. Yet you want to insult the Gods by changing it? How will you know you've changed it?" The words died in his throat at the look of anger that radiated from Hesper.

"Celebrate. I shall take that under advisement." Ice dripped from her words as the Queen he so admired came through her tone and demeanor, replacing the frazzled friend who had appeared at his door.

Kygoss swallowed the additional questions regarding the vision she had, focusing instead on the topics that would affect him the most in his official position as spymaster. "In regards to Palion, I was under the impression Cerial would take that throne? She has a way with difficult souls after all. Our spies have informed us that Lucian is one of the more difficult added to that his father is a complex individual all on his own. Look at what she accomplished with Darius."

Thoughts filled him of the teenage Darius who had been filled to the brim with anger, his soul so broken that his only response was to fight the world. Yet somehow his kindhearted niece had stepped up and befriended the frothing, frenzied, maniac of a teen that frequently damaged things before ever speaking. All the damage that Darius' father had caused seemed to be gone now, Rayner a distant and dark footnote in the story of how Darius grew.

Rayner Svenston, the Military General, had been a terror to his only son, frequently sending the boy to the palace bleeding or bruised. Hesper had worked out an under the table deal, one that left Kygoss with a nasty taste in his mouth. The disgusting man would keep his position, while she took full guardianship of Darius. As far as Kygoss was aware it had been an agreement sealed with an oath, binding Rayner to stay away from Darius directly. Try as he might Kygoss had been unable to figure out the exact terms, but immediately upon the conclusion of the meeting Darius had joined the girls in the royal nursery.

Kygoss watched as the friendship between Cerial and Darius blossomed from afar. Clearly Darius had suffered through Cerial's constant attention, while she had taken an instant unshakeable liking to him. The physical injuries that his father had inflicted healed quickly but the invisible wounds, those that lay within Darius' very soul were clearly still a problem. He vacillated between rage and sorrow often in situations that made little sense for those emotions to be portrayed. Cerial quickly became relied upon to calm Darius down, redirect his emotional outbursts, and for reasons no one could figure out it worked. Which led to the decision that when she wed Lucian, the Pup of Palion, Darius would be assigned as her protector.

"Yes well, it wasn't Cerial wearing their crown, it was Aurelia. Perhaps it's the sign we needed from the Gods decreeing that she should accept Darius officially. You and I both suspect they are soulbonds. Honestly I am surprised she's waited to tell me, she would have found out on her birthday when they saw each other. The connection is undeniable as you well know with Maie. It's possible that Goddess Tiva has decided our plan for Cerial to reject Darius formally in order for her to unite the kingdoms and marry Lucian is untenable. Regardless of the reasons Aurelia will push back on the decision I am sure. However, I can't see a downside of her ruling Palion versus ruling here in Drakore. She was promised the throne three years ago but time changes things. Palion can use her kind soul." Hesper shrugged her shoulders, the decision clearly made.

Kygoss considered this reasoning. Aurelia was indeed rather kind, but he believed it wouldn't be accurate to call her a kind soul. She was no kinder than anyone else. In fact he found her rather crow-like, mischievous with a penchant for sass.

"I refuse to deal with a snarky teenager by myself when I know that Aydan will take her side and try to change the agreement back to Cerial. I will have my hands full attempting to prepare Cerial for taking my position as Queen here in Drakore. Let Aurelia explore more of my homeland before she leaves us for Palion. After all, she's always been drawn there, may as well indulge her while we can." Hesper raised an imperious eyebrow, Kygoss knew it for the challenge it was her own crow tendencies showing.

Kygoss nodded the movement jerky as his brain processed

her words, refusing to rise to the challenge. Instead he stuffed his own feelings down. There would be time enough to assess them. He couldn't stop the stream of words that came out, sounding too close to his true feelings. "So you want Uncle Kygi to deal with the petulant teenage tantrum that is coming, while also teaching her the ins and outs of ruling, religion, and magic?"

He slapped the desk, forcing a sense of joy and excitement out, his hand hitting just a tad too hard. He knew his smile was forced but there was little he could do to fix that right now. "Bring it on! She can't be worse than Maledic. He was terrible at her age, so bad in fact I couldn't stand being home for longer than a week because no matter what I said he just argued. In fact if I didn't have Maie in my corner I don't think we would have survived."

Hesper cracked a smile breaking her Queenly mask and nodded. "Thank you Kygoss. I knew I could count on you. Is there anyone who can take on your duties here? We can't have the inner secrets and rumors falling into the void without you here to catch them." A part of him was glad she accepted his false enthusiasm but it also sliced deep, pain radiating within his heart, his dearest friend didn't see his truth only her own.

Kygoss raised a dramatic, bushy eyebrow as he clutched his breast, a mock look of shock on his face. "Replace me? Perish the thought." Kygoss shot her a wink and reassuring smile. "My birdies will know how to find me if I'm needed. I can also be back in a few wing beats if I need to be should something important arise. Are you expecting trouble?"

A shadow crossed his friend's face, one he hadn't seen before and it made his skin crawl.

"Something is coming. I, I just can't see it."

Realization struck him like the lightning he knew she wielded. If she couldn't see it, her future was involved as well. His chest constricted at the possibility, "You will be fine, Your

Majesty. I shall see to it and I will tighten up my patrols. You will see. Forewarned is forearmed, remember." He threw her another wink doing his best to calm her mind, using the humor he relied on.

"I think it's my job to say that as the resident seer." Her voice was dry but the smile that curled on her lips told him that he had been successful at calming her.

He followed behind her to the door grabbing the roughened edge to stabilize himself as internally he reeled from the idea that something was going to happen that may impact the life of his best friend. "Well when you forget to say it someone else has to, do they not?"

As Hesper strode down the hall toward the stairs, her hair still falling out of her hasty updo, Kygoss slowly closed his study door. He leaned his back against the worn wood.

Why is it that during the toughest time this child has seen in her life she was being given to someone else to see her through it? He shook his head upset that his friends had once more failed at parenting. Neither of them had shown any real talent for the job but this reached new lows.

He closed his eyes and let his consciousness drift toward the land of memories that existed within his mind, the boxes he hid thoughts inside. As he relaxed, deep breaths calming him as he focused on Maledic and Maie, the two loves of his life.

A large box teeming with memories tipped over releasing a plethora of mental sustenance that he could spend months reliving. Instead he focused his attention on one in particular. The memory of Mal's sixteenth birthday, the day hell erupted inside his own household.

Maie stood at the kitchen counter kneading a loaf of bread, flour covered every surface of her clothing, so much so that the powder danced upon the air glimmering in the sun.

Kygoss walked up behind her and encircled his arms around her waist resting his chin on her shoulder. "My darling is this the famed birthday loaf?"

Maie's melodic laughter danced through the room echoing off the tiled walls. "Of course it is. You know as well as I do that Mal loves this brown bread more than cake so this is what he shall get."

Kygoss chuckled. "He is an odd one, our little bird."

Their joy was destroyed as the sound of a slam ricocheted around the entire manor, dust floating down from the rafter beams. It seemed as if even the walls quacked at the intensity, a shudder going through everything.

Kygoss stood straight, turning, searching. Maie released the bread dough half turned, wide eyes scanning for the threat to their family home. He leaned down, almost mechanically and whispered low. "Stay here. Stay quiet. All will be well. I will go get Mal." He kissed her temple refusing to stay and listen as she erupted in whispered protests, the flour skittering around her in clouds of disgust.

Kygoss moved with stealth, keeping to the shadows, sliding his feet onto the hardwood floor testing for squeaks and imperfections before shifting his weight. As he got to the second floor, the home of their bedchambers he still couldn't sense any particular threat.

Nothing appeared to be amiss. Nothing was broken. None of the windows were open that shouldn't be. Everything appeared calm and quiet. Just as that thought had left his mind the very house seemed to shift on its foundations with the impact of another thud. This time he happened to be closer to its place of origin and fear settled into the pit of his stomach as his eyes landed on the door of his newly minted sixteen year old. His very quiet and calm sixteen year old.

Kygoss swallowed hard as he stared at Maledic's door and considered his options. He could pretend that he had heard nothing, go back to Maie and distract her or he could open the door and face down the teenager.

He rolled his shoulders and took a few more steps towards Mal's door when another echoing thwack sounded. He practically jumped out of his mortal skin as Maie shoved his shoulder, "Go on. Open the door."

Kygoss turned sheepish eyes to his wife, "Maie." He stressed her name. "He is making noises far larger than he should be able to. Perhaps this is one of those hormone moments we should leave him be with. Check on him later."

"Oh pish posh. Move aside Kygoss. Or grow some balls and do it yourself."

He half turned and glared at her. "Fine."

He closed the distance between himself and Maledic's door. His hand gripping the handle and pushing it open quickly. He dodged to the side and not a second to soon as a miniature bronze statue went whizzing out the door and embedded itself into the wall directly across from the opening.

"Maledic Mercer Corvus!" Maie's voice cracked like a whip through the air as Kygoss hid out of the way avoiding any flying projectiles.

He watched, shame coating his throat, as his tiny wife moved into the opening, her flour coated arms on hips, a stern look on her freckled face. Kygoss stood straighter, the urge to tackle her to the ground before their errant teenager could impale her with some flying nonsense strong.

"Maie?"

"Get your ass in here Kygoss or find a new place to sleep

tonight." He swallowed. She frequently threatened to kick him from her bed when her anger was directed at him.

Kygoss slunk into the room before more could happen. His mouth falling open at the sight of his son's room. Every movable object from shelves or drawers had been removed and tossed around.

Thrown.

Broken.

Destroyed.

"Why?"

Maie shot him a silencing look and turned to Mal. Maledic was hunched and appeared to be barely breathing on the center of the bed, his bedding a shredded nest around him.

"Maledic." Her words held less sharpness but no less demanding of an answer, a gift with language that he himself was still learning.

Maledic looked up at his mother, his dark brown eyes glistening with unshed tears. "What's happening to me?"

Maie strode through the room, stepping carefully over the various detritus and climbed up onto the bed, sitting as close as she could without touching him. "You are feeling the bond take hold."

"Bond? What bond causes this pain?" Mal's voice cracked with pain.

Kygoss thought back trying to remember what bond could have taken hold of him and caused himself this same amount of pain. Yet try as he might he couldn't remember feeling this when he turned sixteen, so he leaned in curiosity peaked. Maie sighed heavily and with a delicacy only shown from a mother she stroked Mal's hair away from his sweat streaked face.

"You my darling boy will have a Soulbond Mate in this lifetime. You are also clearly the oldest in the partnership." She shot a look at Kygoss and he realized why he didn't have this experience, she had. Maie was older than him.

"As the oldest you are the foundation of the partnership, the Gods embed the link within your heart, and your soulbond's heart will already carry the other end. Once she, or he is of the appropriate age the chains will connect. Unfortunately, the foundation holders carry the pain of creating the bond."

Mal shot them both a heart wrenching look. "When does the pain stop?"

Maie looked down in her lap avoiding Kygoss' gaze. "It will always ache, and when your partner experiences trauma and pain you will as well."

Kygoss took a deep breath, his eyes fluttering open. Perhaps Aurelia's entrance to her teenage years wouldn't be as dramatic and eye opening as Mal's had been. It had taken weeks for Mal to understand the new feelings that flooded his body and mind. Emotional outbursts, violence and sadness had been so common Kygoss had often fantasized about returning to his duties in the palace proper, yet he had ridden the storm out with Maie guiding Maledic through it all.

He sent a prayer to Tiva that Aurelia wouldn't be the foundation of her soulbond partnership. She would have a hard enough life being bound to Palion, hopefully her entrance into the next stage would be gentle, helping her focus on what would come next.

three

AURELIA

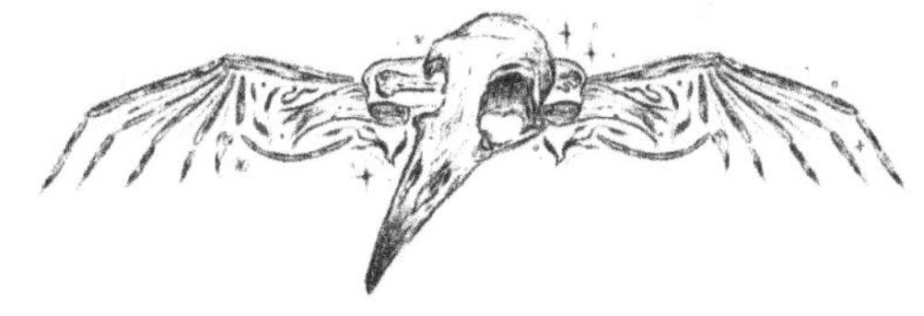

DRAKORE - DUELE - YEAR 7557

Cerial's blonde head bobbed through the crowd making its way out of the palace gates. Aurelia did her best to keep up, desperation clawing at her to see where Cerial snuck off to everyday. Her overcoat stuck to her skin, the heat of the day having built up despite the cooler temperatures that existed in the shade.

Cerial's actions sparked deep curiosity due to the suffocating rules they lived by. Just the act of heading toward the gates leading out to the city beyond was suspicious. Their parents had strict rules about leaving the palace grounds making Cerial's choices interesting. Aurelia noticed a dark headed man step near to Cerial draping a red colored scarf over her blonde curls. She watched as Cerial tipped her head up, a smile just visible from Aurelia's vantage point. Cerial secured the scarf and nuzzled in under the protective arm of the man. It hindered Aurelia's view. The scarf had the unfortunate side effect of allowing Cerial to blend in with the crowd as many women who were married used them to protect their hair from the wind and sun.

A muttered curse escaped as she wove in and out of the crowd drawing nearer to the huddled pair. Her angle shifted just enough so she was able to see the face of the man with an arm draped possessively over her sister's shoulder.

Darius.

Their foster brother? That's what her parents called him anyway. Aurelia had always been standoffish around him as his violent unpredictable nature caused her to be wary. *Why would Darius be walking with Cerial out toward the city? Why would he be holding her like that?*

A crash sounded from the stable followed by muffled shouting. Cerial pushed Aurelia behind her trying to keep her safe from whatever was happening. Aurelia peered around Cerial watching, holding her breath.

"What is it Cer?"

Cerial hummed in her throat as she assessed the sounds coming from the stable. "It's nothing you need to worry about Aurelia. Go on back to your rooms. I'm sure your governess is waiting for you."

Aurelia opened her mouth to argue but Cerial had already moved away, heading toward the stable and the source of commotion. An idea sparked within her, she would just follow and see for herself rather than sit and wonder.

The stable door stood open and after her eyes adjusted to the darkness she noticed that Darius, the new boy in the nursery with them, stood in the middle of the tack area screaming. Throwing things that he could reach, and being physically intimidating to the stable hands that tried to calm him down. It rocked Aurelia. She had never really been exposed to violence in such a manner.

Her shock grew as Cerial strode determinedly toward Darius. "Darius?"

Darius stiffened at her voice and Aurelia watched as he turned his rage filled face toward Cerial. He roared, sounding animalistic. Aurelia could feel her blood growing cold with dread. Her own power as meager as it seemed flared to life desperate to protect her sister. Air rose whipping around everyone, the horses whinnying in protest.

Cerial took a few more steps forward her entire focus on Darius. "Darius. Come back Darius. Focus on my voice."

He staggered as if stricken, his steps wobbly and unsure as he closed the distance. Aurelia took a deep breath a scream at the ready. If he tried to hurt her sister she would come unglued.

Once Darius reached Cerial he lifted a hand, Aurelia's breath lodged stifling out the scream as Cerial reached out and gently traced Darius' hand.

Darius grunted. His face transforming from anger to fear and nervousness. "I didn't, did I? Please tell me I didn't."

Cerial shook her head emphatically. "You didn't. You aren't him. You are safe. Come let's get you a cup of tea."

Aurelia tucked herself into a shadowed corner watching as Cerial led Darius out into the courtyard beyond. She could remember the confusion, why would Cerial care about some strange boy whose favorite pastime was to throw things and scream?

Cerial's eighteenth birthday had happened a few weeks past and ever since that day she had been disappearing from lessons on the pretext of being ill. Yet, after a few hours she would return to the lesson disheveled, a smile covering her face no illness to be seen. Aurelia, who had a natural penchant for mystery, got suspicious after the first two occurrences. Somehow none of their teachers had figured it out when it seemed so glaring to her, Cerial's birthday and this mystery illness were connected.

It hurt most because they had been so close throughout their entire life, with only two years separating them, they faced most experiences together. The sting of betrayal spurred on her investigation, she would do what she could to close the rift that had begun to appear between the two of them.

The heat finally reached an unbearable level, so she popped open the top two buttons revealing the hint of her undershirt beneath the intricately embroidered overcoat. This had been the compromise with her mother to avoid being constantly trussed up in dresses. She wore breeches and heavy overcoats which hid most of her femininity and let her be free to run wild. Her mother hadn't even fought her that hard, merely groused a few times and demanded the coats get more and more elaborate as the years wore on.

Her distraction was so complete that the lessons she had received on keeping an eye on those around her became non-existent. She didn't notice those around her had started to take an interest in the crow that hopped along in her shadow pecking at the dirt and straw. She stood up on a small crate just behind a wagon, peering with all her might over the crowd edging up onto her tiptoes for just a few more inches of lever-age. There she could just make out Cerial's red scarf covered head and Darius' broad back as they exited out the gates taking a right into the city beyond.

Aurelia shrieked as pain radiated from her ear lobe. Instinct took over, slapping the side of her head sharply, the movement tipping over her precariously placed body. She fell off the crate to the ground, a loud thump echoing up followed by a cloud of dirt and dust, effectively covering her entire dark outfit in grime. Desperation bubbled within her still unsure what had injured her. There was a titter of exclamations around her, especially by passing women. Aurelia whipped her head around searching for the source of what made her ear ooze blood. She could feel the seeping blood trickle between her fingers but the sight of it smeared across her pale skin enraged her. She popped off the ground turning once more before her eyes caught and held onto the crow that now perched atop the cart she had been peering around. She rubbed at her ear glaring daggers as her foot beat a fast tempo into the dirt.

He gave a squawky caw right before hopping into the air, with two wing beats and a popping noise Kygoss landed on the crate she had vacated, leaning against the wagon his mouth tilted in a knowing smirk. He waggled his finger under her nose, "That's not how I taught you to spy, young one. That's how an agent gets caught."

Her magic swelled within her, the feelings of tiny bubbles popping within her bloodstream as it filled her body. Clouds began to emerge from her fingertips as her emotions crested wave after wave of frustration, embarrassment and anger. "Uncle Kygi!! You aren't supposed to hurt your nieces. You distracted me. I was doing just fine until you bit me." She stomped her foot clawing at her magic trying to stuff it back down. She hated not being able to keep her emotions to herself instead, broadcasting them into the world for all to see and judge through her magical slips. It was getting worse as she got older and no one seemed capable of helping her or explaining why.

"My little bite was merely proof to you that you were in serious danger. What if an enemy of your parents had been in my place? You wouldn't have been able to just walk away, I can promise you that Short Stack. I may be training you to be one of my birdies but, you aren't showing me that you're actually ready for it. Your lady mother has requested an audience. Perhaps you could pretend to be the Princess you were born to be in between spying sessions." Kygoss cocked an eyebrow in challenge, "Later we can review how to recognize a tail, that way you don't get bitten again."

The urge to scream filled Aurelia. "I haven't done anything to warrant a meeting with her! Whatever nonsense Cerial is up to I am trying to stop her not help her." She scuffed her foot on the ground kicking up dirt as she rubbed her ear. "Why is it that I am the one always getting into trouble while Mistress Perfect gets to go into the city with Darius without any consequences?" Her question muttered and barely audible but she noted that Kygoss' body had stiffened.

"Off you go Short Stack." Kygoss shooed her back toward the palace, a smile plastered on his face. Aurelia trudged toward her mothers study, only throwing back one look toward Kygoss. She was curious perhaps he would go and find Cerial. He appeared to be staring in the direction Cerial had left. She shrugged mentally preparing for the undoubtable battle that was to come with her mother.

<hr>

Her mother's personal office was a large and airy offshoot of the library. As Aurelia neared the door the nerves set in, her heart thrumming in her chest. Around the age of thirteen she had been told she was destined to take over the Drakore throne, one day wearing the crown that sat upon her mothers head. It was daunting to consider, but she used the knowledge and time to study her parents with the hope of understanding how to do the job they both lovingly embraced, in the future. As the thick wooden door swung inward the large desk greeted her, deceptively carved to look dainty and delicate but bore an inner strength that rivaled most furniture in the palace.

There was a time shortly after being told her future that Aurelia had stood upon this desk pretending to direct troops into battle. She had stomped and jumped gesticulating wildly and the desk hadn't moved at all, no shuddering, or quaking, just stood ramrod straight holding all of her. Oddly that had been the moment she had felt confident in undertaking the daunting task even though she was so young and life had yet to unfold in front of her.

Since then it had occurred to her that her mother had a lot in common with the desk in question. Delicately beautiful, frequently touted to be the most gorgeous in the land but her inner strength rivaled even her father's. Her parents didn't hide the fact that Hesper made the hard decisions for the kingdom and the family. Aurelia did her best to think like her mother even though they didn't exactly get along. It was a fascination, the twin personas that existed, the delicate female fond of pretty things and particular fashion matched with the strength of a warrior's will.

She knew that she should approach her mother with a clear head, devoid of excessive emotions but her mind seemed incapable of clearing aside the clutter. The internal battle for control from her emotions was lost as she crossed the threshold and threw herself into the delicate wooden chair across from her mother.

The antique chair, one that was usually reserved for the adornment it afforded the room, groaned in protest to her weight. The slight wince that came from her mother at the sound caused an inward smile, lightening some of the darker emotions swirling just under her skin. She wouldn't go down without a fight, the time of letting Cerial get away with mischief had ended when she decided to hide it from Aurelia.

Hesper cleared her throat, her voice strained. "Aurelia, you will be going on a trip."

Aurelia blinked. The words ricocheted around her head,

struggling to find a landing place. Her thoughts bounced from the reality that taking a trip couldn't be seen as a punishment, to how they could let her leave the palace grounds given their overprotective nature. After a few minutes of stunned silence her mother continued.

"The Gods have gifted me a window into the future, and due to that you will be sent to the Crowlands for a bit. I hope you take this time to get acquainted with my homeland and the places I grew up around."

Aurelia straightened, her mind jolted out of its cycle of thoughts. "What! You are letting me go to the Crowlands? Why now? I have asked for years to go."

On a sigh her mother rubbed at her temple a clear sign to anyone within their family that something had been *seen*. "The Gods choose when the time is right to show me the future and you are well aware of that. Go. Have fun while we are still in the position to give you what you want. While you are too young to understand the intricate details, you will be wedded to Lucian Ronnet the heir to Palion, not becoming the Queen of Drakore instead the Queen of Palion. I am giving you their throne at the Gods behest. Be grateful."

Aurelia surged to her feet, the chair toppling behind her. The magic searing hot in her veins, like liquid fire. Her mouth tasted of metal as her entire body shook with the effort it was taking to control her emotions on top of her magic. "I don't want that throne! I want this one. You've always told me I would rule Drakore with my soulbond, Cerial would get Palion with those disgusting dogs." Her words were clipped, but luckily she managed to get them out without screaming.

"The only constant in the world is change Aurelia. I need you to take a deep breath, I can feel your magic escaping your hold."

"You're surprised!? My magic speaks more to this land than Cerial's ever has. You are punishing me! What could I have done to warrant you taking my birthright away and giving it to her? Is it because of Darius?" A lump began to form as she swallowed against tears that were threatening to rise within her despair swamping her mind.

Despite the agitation roiling in her gut she didn't miss her mother's sharpening gaze. "This is what the Gods have decreed Aurelia. You are the one destined for Palion's throne. What is this business about Darius and your sister?"

Aurelia exhaled a deep breath and struggled to control the lightning that had begun dancing just under her skin causing tingles and excruciating zaps throughout, begging to be let out. "I don't know yet. I was interrupted. They are spending a lot of time alone together. That much is clear. I was going to find out why but *now* I will be in the Crowlands."

She didn't wait to hear anything her mother may want to add. The burning in her eyes overwhelming her senses, she ran before the hot liquid could fall and cause more shame. Desperate to avoid people she ran up the servants stairs to her rooms. The Gods were supposed to give people what they asked for, what they needed not completely destroy lives.

four

AURELIA

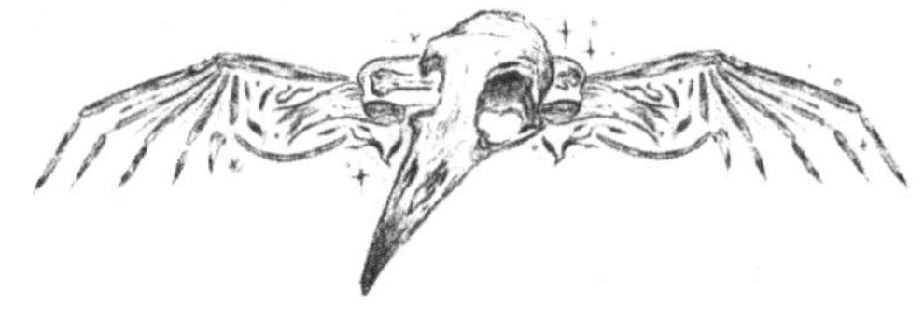

DRAKORE - DUELE - YEAR 7557

> A soulbond is not guaranteed. If a creature is lucky enough to be chosen to connect with another in such a way it does not mean that both individuals will choose to honor the bond. Rejection is rare, but it does happen. The Gods do not after all take away free will. Those that reject will pay whatever the Gods deem worthy of such blasphemous decisions.
>
> ~The Archives of the Tiva Temple

A few days ticked by before the dreaded loud echoing knock sounded at her bedroom door. Her eyes met Kygoss' through the crack in the door. She scanned him head to toe noting a small pack he had thrown over one shoulder. She looked around him and noted the guard that had been posted outside her door ever since her mother's decree was now absent. "The moment has come, Short Stack. We need to make good time to get to my manor for our midday meal." He patted his round belly and grinned, "I sent a letter to your Auntie Maie last night so you know she will have something quite delicious waiting for our arrival."

She couldn't stop the groan as it escaped, in a vain attempt at evasion she tried to close the door in his face. Kygoss however must have anticipated that reaction because his foot slid into the way. She rolled her eyes and began to kick at his foot in vain, "Just wait out here. I'll be out in a minute. I still need to talk to Faziel." Aurelia couldn't contain the sigh of relief as Kygoss removed his foot, even as frustration reared its ugly head at the entire situation.

Kygoss' laughter echoed into the hall as he turned away, "Alright, alright. Five minutes Short Stack and then we are off."

"Yeah, yeah." Aurelia closed the door with a snap and turned to see Faziel, a twig of a girl, watching her dull brown eyes wide in shock.

"Lia you just kicked the spymaster! You can't just do that. You have to listen to him, *he's an elder*."

"He's merely Uncle Kygi. Once you've been here longer you will see that for yourself Faziel." She waved away Faziel's concern, heading to her wardrobe to get the things she would need for the days to come. Her mind sorting through ideas on how to get Faziel to pick up where she left off.

Faziel interrupted her scheming, "Lia where are you being forced to go? Your parents hate you and Cerial going out and about."

"Oh if you only knew," Aurelia muttered under her breath shaking her head before glancing quickly at her foster sister. "My mother claims the Gods require me to go to the Crowlands. She was rather vague on the particulars though. I was actually wondering if you would be interested in helping me while I am away."

She watched Faziel out of the corner of her eye pleased to see acceptance on her face. The less prying questions the better. "What's the favor?"

"Well I need you to watch Cerial."

"Watch Cerial? She's a grown adult though. Why would I watch her? Why are you watching her?" Faziel had scooted closer to Aurelia practically falling off the edge of the mattress.

Aurelia turned and studied her. *So much for not asking prying questions.* Aurelia was grateful to see that the bruises from her past were gone but Faziel's eyes were still so hollow. Sadness filled Aurelia as she remembered the little girl, only fourteen, who had been deposited into her room a few months ago, barely more than flesh and bones, the discolorations disguising the true paleness of her skin. Aurelia shook her head slightly, dispelling the memory as she refocused on her clothes. Aurelia's mom rescued Faziel from parents who had beaten her one too many times.

"Haven't you noticed her odd behavior? She's always sneaking out." She couldn't stop her hands from twisting the clothes as she shoved them into the pack. "I have tried to figure it out, but now that I am being sent away I obviously can't be in two places at once." She took a deep breath trying to harness the snapping tone that had just slipped out. "That's where you come in. You know sisters always look out for one another, even when the one being watched doesn't enjoy it. We have to protect our own."

Faziel scrunched her face obviously working through her thoughts while Aurelia finished shoving in a few more clothing bits. She tied the top of her pack even as bits of clothes hung out at odd angles. She tossed the pack on to the bed next to Faziel as she leaned against the bed frame. "She won't make it easy. It will require you to sneak around and try to not be caught."

"Why do I have to be sneaky? Is that because she doesn't actually like me?"

"No, no of course not. It's because whatever she's doing she knows it's wrong. I think it's connected to her birthday but I seem to be alone in that theory. I don't have a lot of time to really debate the point. Will you?" Aurelia fiddled with her pack strap meeting Faziels eyes.

Faziel nodded haltingly, "I suppose I could. I haven't had a lot of experience being someone's sister but I want to try. I can show you I will take care of her even if I don't know much about sneaking. If I get caught though, what am I supposed to say?"

Aurelia pulled the pack on one shoulder and gave Faziel a small smile. "You have to rely on your ability to create a story. All sisters do it to get what they want. Think of it as an initiation. Weave her a story just as you did with your own parents, when you got caught doing something they didn't like. Cerial is kind enough that even if she figures out the lie she wont hold it against you. I know I've been caught often enough."

Faziel's smile didn't seem to completely reach her eyes, doubt floating across her face. Aurelia stepped forward in an attempt to distract her giving Faziel a big hug. "Just know that once I return, you and I will get the time we need to become sisters of the heart as it should be. Just remember to stay safe!"

Faziel squeezed a bit tighter than what Aurelia was used to from others, adding to the pit of darkness that had opened up in her stomach. Aurelia noted the tears that glistened in Faziel's eyes as they parted.

As she crossed the threshold Aurelia took a deep breath, noting that Kygoss stood arms crossed over his chest watching her. Those feelings filling the dark pit in her stomach morphed, turning into anger, fire and indignation. She shoved her way past him, forcibly catching his side with her much smaller shoulder despite the wide corridor in which they stood. She glared daggers at him, or at least her best imitation of her mother's disdainful face as she dropped the haphazard pack at his feet.

Refusing to speak she stomped down toward the stairs to the courtyard. Kygoss whistled annoyingly just behind her, the entire way to the horses waiting for them at the front of the castle. She turned to him and held out her hand imperiously.

She could have sworn that there was a twinkle of amusement in his eye as he raised a bushy brow, while strapping his pack onto his horse. "Yes, Your Highness?"

Aurelia let out a huge sigh, the use of her title was never a great sign from her Uncle Kygoss. "I need my pack Kygi." His name came out as a whine despite her best efforts to clamp down on the sound.

"Oh right, that. I am guessing you will find it exactly where you left it, Short Stack. In the hallway outside of your room."

Aurelia gaped as Kygoss mounted up. As her brain caught up to her mouth she began to sputter. "But.. but. You were supposed to bring it for me. I am after all being shipped off in preparation to be a Queen. Queens don't carry their own bags."

Kygoss pulled his horse around to face her, she balked at the sight of an emotion Uncle Kygi had never shown her, *anger*. It caused the lines in his face to become more prominent, his eyebrows angled and sharp. She took an involuntary step backward as he began to open his mouth to respond, interrupted by the familiar sound of a throat clearing from the palace steps.

The blood coursing through her hot and ready to fight chilled to sludge as she turned and saw her parents standing in the doorway. Dread filled the corners of her mind as her eyes latched on the familiar lumpy pack hanging from her mothers delicate hands. She glanced between her mother and father, swallowing hard. This would not go well for her, it was rare that both her parents were mad at her at the same time.

Her mother led the way down the steps holding the pack, her eyes blazing in anger. "Did I just hear my daughter declare that Queens do not carry their own bags? *My daughter*, a girl who was raised by a Queen who frequently carried all assortments of bags and things when the time called for it."

Aurelia felt herself shrinking. Her shoulders beginning to touch her ears as she wished herself anywhere but here, while her mother got closer. "Did I not Aydan?"

Aurelia's father, stepped up behind her mother placing a hand to her lower back, responded his voice colder than she had ever heard it before "Hesper, you have never been one to shirk from helping. Aurelia, we raised you better than this. You were raised to help those in need and to work hard regardless of your title. That hasn't been erased just because we believe you will inherit a different throne than the one we prepared you for. I expect better from you."

Aurelia stared into the dirt encrusted cobblestones, the stable hand still holding the reins of her mount beside her. Shame filled her as she realized how rude she had been to someone who, while a member of the court, also held the title of family. "I'm sorry." It was a muttered admission as indignation joined the shame whirling together to create a mental haze inside her mind. Her cheeks began to heat as the haze morphed into an incessant buzzing that dulled out the world.

"Speak up child." Her mother's voice came from directly behind her, causing her to jolt a bit. The internal buzzing had begun to make it very difficult to hear.

Aurelia stood straightening her shoulders and looked at nothing in particular as she spoke loud, loud enough that even she could hear herself over the sound of her mental buzzing. "I offer my sincerest apologies Uncle. I should never have assumed you would carry my things. If I was unable to complete the task, the appropriate way to get assistance would be to ask for help." The words sounded mechanical even to her, the speech having been drilled into her by her mother during the frequent times she had been in trouble.

Kygoss' voice sounded from her left, to her own ears it sounded far off and muffled by her shame and self loathing. "It's alright Short Stack. Get that pack bound and mount up. My belly is urging us forward to my beloved's rabbit stew."

She could make out her mother's chuckle at Uncle Kygi. Her father must have come nearer but she hadn't heard him move. Her body moved of its own accord, her mind still frozen with the buzzing overload of emotions. She turned, taking the pack from her mother and bound it to the saddle, avoiding eye contact, her hands moving by memory.

She made a move to swing into her saddle when her father's smell of pine and leather filled her nose. He leaned around her, "Don't leave just yet my little bird. We all make mistakes, please don't let your emotions rob us of a proper goodbye. I want to see your smile once more before you leave us for the Crowlands." It was whispered into her ear and as he rested a hand on her shoulder, his magic twining with hers. Her mind began to clear as her father's magic aided in clearing the clouds of shame and self loathing quicker than Aurelia would have managed on her own.

She thought she heard a sigh of distress coming from her mother but it happened so quickly it was possible she had misheard. She blinked and then turned, grabbing her father into a bone breaking hug. She snuggled her face into his chest as she always had growing up, his embrace being the only place she felt safest, even her magic stayed docile.

"Thanks Papa. Are you sure I have to go?" She couldn't keep the whine from her tone as she whispered her request.

"Yes my little bird. It's imperative for you to go to the Crowlands, however, I make you this pledge. When I can share exactly why, I will. For now though you will have to trust me."

She pulled back and studied his face. His blue eyes and black hair so like her own. She nodded, not sensing any ill intent, "Alright Papa. I will go and learn."

He nodded back a sadness that she couldn't understand in his eyes. Her mother interrupted their moment by tapping her shoulder. "Alright love, up you go."

Aurelia rolled her eyes at her father as her mother hoisted Aurelia's slight frame up onto the horse, as if proving Queens did indeed do more than nothing. Her father shot her a discreet wink before arranging his own face in a mask of disapproval that matched her mother. Aurelia smiled and took the reins pulling the horse alongside her Uncle. Turning back in the saddle and sending them one last wave of farewell before she leaned into this sliver of freedom she had been presented with, taking the lead. She spurred her horse off to the main road, listening to Kygoss' yell of consternation as he imparted his farewells and attempted to catch up.

five

KYGOSS

SLANA - DUELE - YEAR 7557

It didn't take long for Kygoss to realize the extent of just how temperamental Aurelia had become. He loved his friends, Hesper had after all seen him through a tumultuous childhood and Aydan had become the brother he had always yearned for. Their lackadaisical approach to parenting, however, left a lot to be desired.

He preferred to take the four hour journey to his home at a leisurely pace, never one to rush when there wasn't a need. Aurelia didn't seem to be of the same mindset. Somehow she managed to trim at least an hour if not two from their journey. Foam oozed out between the lips of his brown mount's mouth, her breathing a visible puff in the humid dense air. Gratitude swamped him as he noticed that Aurelia had finally pulled her young steed to a halt in front of him. They had reached the end of the road.

Aurelia turned in her saddle, meeting his gaze as he dismounted and led his mare to the river, the horse trampling on the small bits of greenery that grew along the edge of the water. "Uh. Uncle Kygi is this the right way? Perhaps I missed a turn?"

Kygoss smiled at her, "Well, if you did it would be due to your irrational need for speed. However, luckily we are right where we need to be."

He let his horse get as much water as she needed before scooping up the cool liquid and rubbing it along her hot sides, hoping to cool her off before the final leg of their journey.

He watched out of the corner of his eye as Aurelia began scanning the area, confusion clearly evident on her face. "Right. Well this land looks great. I guess." She shrugged and dismounted to join him at the river's edge.

Kygoss began laughing. "Short Stack, we aren't there yet."

Aurelias head came up quick as she once more observed their surroundings. "How is that possible? The road is gone. There's a cliff on one side and this massive river on the other."

Kygoss' grin widened. "You are observant aren't you. Well, most often those who come up here do so in the air. My ancestors were paranoid that two-legged demons or Palion creatures may sneak in and try to steal the land. It is very difficult to get to where we are going on our feet." He saw her blanch a bit, "Difficult, but not impossible."

He walked the river's edge, it had been a few years since he last had to traverse to the manor in his mortal shell versus just shifting into his crow form and flying home. Yet he had trained the sentries to ensure that the way was maintained just in case.

In the gravel there was a small rock formation, something that could be perceived as normal, no taller than a few inches that marked the spot where the river was its shallowest. He tugged on his horse's lead and slowly, steadily trusting in the signal he walked across the four foot expanse of river. The current tugged at his boots the chill penetrating the leather, but the water never got deeper than his calf enabling him to walk carefully through the deadly water.

Aurelia studied him, but before he could explain it to her she began to walk. At his angle it was clear that she had veered from his exact path, fear spiked through him. "Aurelia stop!" He had to shout over the sound of the rushing water barreling over the road heading for the cliff beyond.

Perhaps she hadn't heard him. Perhaps she had seen something that drew her in the direction she went but she zigged and zagged, not walking a straight line seeming to hop along the water. He watched horror filling him as it got deeper and deeper, quickly covering her knees and riding up her thighs to her waist.

He tried again. "Aurelia!! STOP!" *Would it be better for her to stop now or should she just push through?*

As far as he knew her experience with water had been limited to the small lake in the back of the palace grounds. Knowing her parents as intimately as he did, the likelihood that they hadn't seen the need to teach their daughter to swim doubting its usefulness was high. This cruel twist of fate may change everything.

Panic built within his mind, whirling with how to explain to his friends that their youngest daredevil had died because he hadn't been overly explanative in the plan to cross the river to the Crowlands. A river both Aydan and Hesper were aware of. They trusted him. As his thoughts spiraled, Aurelia swirled in a circle as if dancing in the water, a look of wonder and joy on her face. She moved farther into the river, the water now firmly up to her waist, lapping higher as if it eagerly tasted her young flesh ready to suck her under with its mighty current. Still she moved steadily forward.

Calm began to infiltrate his senses as he realized how far she had achieved. The water was beginning to lessen and against all odds she still moved forward, unbothered by the river's internal pull. She hadn't died, she wasn't drowning. He glanced behind her and noticed her horse still standing stomping on the ground, clearly unwilling to follow his mistress into the depths of the quickly moving river.

After securing his own mount to a branch he headed back across the river, using the safe route to gather her mount. As her horses hooves landed safely on the gravel river bank, Kygoss breathed a sigh of relief. Aurelia reclined on the river bank, a look of serene happiness on her face.

"Short Stack, it's time to keep moving. Perhaps this time you can wait to hear the directions before blindly moving forward. You could have died in that water. Many have tried to cross and been swept away by the current." He couldn't help counseling her. They were family in name but not blood, which made it a difficult line to see when he was overstepping and when he was fine.

She glanced up at him and blinked, processing "I'm sorry Uncle Kygi. I felt a pull, something I don't really understand but I knew everything would be fine."

He filed it away in his mind to debate the meaning of later. Instead he turned to face the many trees awaiting them, gesturing widely. "Welcome to Slana, Aurelia."

Outsiders to Slana knew the land only as the Crowlands, his ancestors opting to keep the well-known name bland. It aided in keeping curious eyes away from their small sliver of oasis that had been cultivated in the peaks of the Falrath Mountains. Slana's position in the range butted up against the border with Dodsfell, making them one of the last vestiges of mortality before one reached the Realm of the Dead.

The original intention behind Slana involved creating a haven for those who preferred their shifter bodies over their mortal ones. As the years progressed however times changed and buildings were crafted both in the canopies of the trees and at the base, designed to be camouflaged. Someone who wandered in would have a hard time finding anything useful between the ingenious engineering of buildings and the magic that had been used to hide the thriving world of the Crows.

They couldn't make out the buildings just yet but Kygoss could smell the campfires. That mingled with the fresh water of the river rushing behind them and the clean mountain air, Kygoss' blood began to sing a song of joy. Excitement thrummed through him at the prospect of seeing Maie and Maledic once more, their time apart having been too long.

"The way forward is a small track so it's not something that can be run down by your horse as you did on the road here. I am going to lead the way and you can either walk behind or mount up and follow on your horse." Aurelia nodded and shrugged a bit, her face losing the peace it had gotten in the water instead the pensive whirlwind took its hold once more. Surprise filled him as he realized she had yet to start shivering. He neared her and it dawned on him she had begun to exude heat. *Interesting*.

He began the trek into the trees gently leading his horse down the path. Kygoss scanned everything taking note of the sentries stationed in the tree canopies, they had gone to the trouble of attempting to camouflage their black wings making it a tad harder to pick them up in the shadows and light snow fall the mountains could receive. Each crow gave him the wing signal to pass, and he threw back a welcoming hand gesture. "I think I can smell your Auntie Maie's famous stew. She always seems to know exactly what I am craving and has it ready and waiting when I get there."

Aurelia stayed silent, she had mounted her horse and steadily followed him into the quiet of the forest beyond.

Kygoss shot her a sidelong look, "I know that parents are

hard, I can still remember the arguments my Papa and I would get into over the simplest things." He took a guess plowing on, "Mothers are a different story." He caught her sudden flush, he nodded careful not to look her directly in the eye. "My Ma was known all around these parts as the kindest soul you would ever know. Yet no one but Hesper and I saw her when she was angry or worse *disappointed*. I found that the best balm for a disappointed Ma is time. She will forgive you Short Stack, never fear."

He glanced at her once more and saw the stubborn set of her jaw and gave a half shrug allowing her the space to be silent and upset. He took the time to assess the path he led them down. He had created it, once more tasking the sentries with its maintenance. One of his initial acts as Leader of the Crows created the pathway where approved flightless individuals could access Slana. He had done so with great care ensuring that the land between the path and the city was impassable for the average flightless, ending the path at his manor and his alone. The manor wasn't far, situated on the edge of Slana. This made his duties easier and allowed for his spies or birdies to find him with anonymity.

The journey would take no more than a half an hour or so but they had to be careful as the land had various holes some mud filled, easy for the horses to injure themselves if they pushed too hard.

Eager to pull Aurelia from her thoughts and bring back his goofy niece he cleared his throat, "How much of the history of this land did your mother tell you, Short Stack?"

"She told me that the Crowlands or I guess Slana as it's really called could only be accessed with wings, which is why only Cerial has been allowed to visit. Once the power manifested her wings Mother brought her out here. I always wanted to come too." He could hear the disappointment and buried anger in her voice. "Turns out she lied."

"Your lady mother didn't lie per se. When we were children that was the only way to get to Slana. It made visits from outsiders difficult especially after my own Papa issued a decree that only the royal house would be allowed to visit Slana. He suffered from paranoia, convinced that anyone else would try to steal our lands for themselves.

When I took control with my beloved Maie I knew we had to change at least a little bit. So I created this path, your mother is aware the path exists but hasn't had the opportunity in her busy schedule to assess it herself. We agreed when it was completed that only those who absolutely needed to know about it would, in an aim to keep Slana as safe as possible. Someday I aim to open this beautiful land to more people but it's a slow process. I can't lose the faith of my people and as I am sure you are aware, crows tend to hold grudges."

He heard a snort of laughter from behind him.

"A different way to look at this, Short Stack, is that you are now old enough to hold this precious secret." He heard a familiar caw from high above him and he waved in acknowledgement.

"Who is that?"

"Ah, that is my son, Maledic. You two met a long time ago when you were nothing more than a babe. He is your sister's age though just celebrated his eighteenth birthday a few months back."

"Has he had any weird habits pop up since then?"

Confusion flooded Kygoss, *weird habits.* A memory of Aurelia sneaking around the courtyard flitted through his head and he turned to meet her eye, his eyebrow raised. "Maie hasn't spoken of any. Is this about your sister and why you were spying?"

Aurelia fiddled with the reins unsure what exactly to tell. "Well she had her eighteenth birthday a few weeks ago, and now she's off and disappearing for long stretches of the day without explanation. She doesn't include me in anything anymore. I think Darius has something to do with it. I saw them." She huffed a loud sigh. "I saw them leave together that day you caught me. I can't figure out what they are up to though."

Alarm bells began to go off in Kygoss' head at that. Eighteen, the age that soulbond partnerships were able to be cemented. Foundational partners would know of the bond at the age of sixteen and beyond but those that they partnered with would be blissfully ignorant until maturity at eighteen. It was never guaranteed to form a bond and some shifters didn't even believe in them at all, however when those pairs were formed it needed to be declared and proper ceremonies performed. Especially considering the fact that Cerial came from royal blood. Aurelia would have to wait to find her soulbond another two years at least if she found him at all. Aurelia could be wrong, nevertheless her story sparked the flame of suspicion. Perhaps Cerial had found her soulbond in Darius. *Yet, why would she keep it a secret?* They had been close ever since Hesper brought him into the Palace to live, probably paving the way for the bond to click into place.

He shrugged his shoulders keeping his face carefully carefree. "You know you both are entering a difficult life stage. In a few years you yourself will have more power, and a whole lot more hormones swirling around you. I am sure Cerial will come back to you before too long. She just needs to take some time to discover herself again after so much change." Aurelia nodded her face glum.

"Besides, didn't Hesper bring in another fosterling, that little girl Faziel. Perhaps you can create new friendships just as your sister has. It won't take away from your unique sisterhood, but it will help you while she finds herself again. She will reach out to create mischief with you once more, Short Stack. Never fear."

He turned and lengthened his stride, giving her some space to consider all that had been spoken as they finished what short distance that lay between them and the manor in relative quiet. Concern that he had further upset her began to set in as the silence lengthened. A girlish giggle washed his concern away.

He turned slowly, just enough to see her from his periphery unsure what could possibly be causing her to giggle so carefree after such hard topics. He slid on a mask of neutrality as he watched incredulously as his son still in his shifted crow form gripped the pommel of Aurelia's saddle with his talons. He knew it was his son by the ever so slight silver crescent shape formed where the tail feather began to emerge, a match to the birthmark Maledic had on the base of his spine.

He walked in an awkward sideways gait watching as Mal hopped off her saddle and soared into the air overexaggerating his wing movements, swooping and careening through the air. Suddenly Mal arrowed down making a beeline for something hidden in the grass, Kygoss glanced toward Aurelia and noticed that she was watching Maledic raptly, turning in the saddle to keep eye contact.

Mal had a purple snowdrop flower clutched in his beak, more of a weed than a flower. Kygoss watched the flower arc through the air and land on a pile that had begun to be formed on Aurelias lap. His son seemed to be observing the pile and then measuring the joy he could glean from Aurelia before flapping off and returning with yet more of the pesky flowers snapped off from the grounds around them. Kygoss studied Aurelia who seemed to be enamored by this display. All sadness having been swept away on the petals of snowdrops.

He turned his attention to his reclusive son, the son who hated interacting with strangers and shunned visitors as if they carried the plague. Perhaps he was being overly sensitive especially after the revelation about Darius and Cerial. Maledic had undoubtedly seen the sadness that rolled off Aurelia and was trying to cheer her up with some pretty flowers.

It didn't have to mean more.

It didn't.

Six

SLANA - DUELE - YEAR 7557

Once they cleared the forest path the manor house filled his vision. A vigor reminiscent of his youth filled his mind, the knowledge that his beloved dwelled within, cooking and running their lands while he attended to his spymaster responsibilities. He bound onto the saddle, whooping as he spurred his horse into a gallop toward the stables. The concern over Aurelia and Mal forgotten as his mind focused solely on reconnecting to his other half. The teenagers could mosey in at their own pace the threat of danger incredibly low.

He leapt from the horse's back, rushing through the chores to secure his steed. He tried to avoid running, yet he couldn't completely control his speed, his steps more of a skip through the house towards the one place he knew Maie loved the most. He rounded the corner and halted his breath catching in his throat as his eyes landed on her.

She stood at the counter, her arms flexing as she kneaded some dough bound to become a delicious treat. Flour floated in the air making her appear to be covered in glittering stars, almost as if she was in another place and time completely removed from the hectic life he juggled. Her bound up brown hair, just now starting to streak with grey, covered with a head scarf. True to Maie fashion it was upside down and askew to better scoop the hair off her neck, or so she liked to claim. She had chosen to wear his favorite colored dress, purple. Somehow once again she had known he was coming today, and chose it to make him smile, and smile he did his grin filling his face.

Slowly moving in such a way that she wouldn't be aware of his presence he came up behind her and slowly slid his arms around her waist. He leaned in his face nuzzling in under her ear inhaling her unique scent of bread and strawberries. She started, but relaxed into him a girlish giggle escaping as she tucked the dough into a linen lined resting basket.

Her haven exuded relaxation and comfort, flower pots full of herbs bordered every available windowsill, a constant smell of comforting food accosting one's nose. She turned in his arms, her blue eyes twinkling with joy meeting his. He marveled at how well they continued to match one another even after twenty years of being together. She was his perfect partner, able to show patience in the times when he lacked it. This skill had been needed while Maledic navigated his teenage years; he hoped that Maie would be open to navigating them through the storm that Aurelia would bring.

Maie laughed, the sound honey sweet to his ears, as he pressed his cold nose to the hollow behind her ear. He felt her reach behind to the counter where undoubtedly her dish cloth was resting. He braced himself as the damp cloth made contact with his shoulder, swallowing his chuckle.

"Get off you great buffoon. What's happening beyond Slana in the rest of Baelia? How are the girls doing?"

Kygoss laughed as Maie twisted out of his hold, "You can see for yourself Maie my sweet. Aurelia should be settling in her stuff upstairs, I left Mal to help her."

He watched as Maie's eyebrows shot up, "Mal? He avoids newcomers. Why would you leave him to do it?"

Kygoss took a deep breath. *What to tell? How to explain?* "He welcomed us into the territory and seemed to take a shine to her. I didn't see a need to interrupt them."

Maie gave him an assessing look nodding once and his eyes rolled up into his head. He had forgotten her unnerving ability to read his face as easily as she read one of her recipes. She squared off with him, her chin jutting out stubbornly, "I see. There's naught to do about that for at least two years. She can't accept nor reject him til then anyhow so may as well let them enjoy each others company."

A wave of fear rolled through Kygoss, he kept his voice light, refusing to give in despite all he had to lose should something go wrong. "I can send him away. Gossek needs an apprentice, he would learn clan leadership there. Perhaps the distance will stop the process."

Maie hesitated her turn toward the stew and shot him a look. "You've known he was to get a soulbond for the last two years. Just because you wish it were a different female, one perhaps in an easier position doesn't mean your actions will actually change their fates. Instead, you could curse him to a life of always searching, wondering and waiting. He will always feel her at least echoes of her, that will get stronger if they acknowledge the bond. Regardless even if they had never met he would still feel her."

"She's destined for Palion, Maie. I can't steal away a royal daughter just because she's the supposed soulbond for my heir, as much as I may want to help. Perhaps it's better if he doesn't feel his side of the bond strengthen at all."

Maie exhaled deeply, "You, my wonderful man, are forgetting one very important detail. His bond is already feeling things. He is the foundational partner. His path was chosen, to be the grounding force for them by the Gods. I know you don't have that experience, but I can tell you, I felt when you broke your arm as a teenager despite us not having met. Hurt like hell. I had no choice but to feel you Ky and Mal has no choice either."

Kygoss flushed, sadness filling him at the pain he had inadvertently caused her throughout their lives. Before he could put words to his sorrow Maie had continued on, not dwelling.

"It's to be Palion, after all. Hesper couldn't face the grief this change will cause either so she has shoved her parental duties on to us once more." Maie had once more faced the counter and was busily preparing the next stage of her scrumptious creation. "At least Aurelia will get to see some beauty before being exiled to that wasteland."

She sent a sidelong look at Kygoss pointing her knife at him, "I won't approve of you interfering with the God's work Kygoss. It's impossible to know what is correct in this situation without the Gods telling us directly. Since that isn't likely to happen we can take solace knowing she won't be able to make her choice in the matter until she's eighteen. Heaven forbid she rejects the match entirely. Leave it be and we shall see what happens."

Their conversation was interrupted when Kygoss began to hear the chatter of voices getting ever closer, most likely on the central stairs. *Odd.* Maledic was a very quiet individual choosing to administer his mischief in silence rather than loudly. Kygoss settled himself into the small family table they kept in the large airy kitchen. Reserved for just his family, when guests were in the manor for official business, meals were taken in the much grander dining hall. Aurelia however could never be classified as just a guest so he gestured her to a seat across from him when she cleared the kitchen's threshold. "Well now Short Stack all settled in?"

Maledic snorted at the nickname and cocked his raven haired head observing the small princess. "Short Stack? Due to your severe lack of height I am guessing."

Aurelia blushed beet red and rolled her eyes as she took the seat he indicated, "That is neither here nor there. Someday my height will come or I shall excel at wearing ridiculous shoes like my mother. Anyway, that name isn't for you, only Uncle Kygi can call me that."

The ever quiet Maledic smirked but nodded.

Aurelia looked at Kygoss and nodded. "Yes I did. Thank you for the nice rooms overlooking the waterfall. It's so gorgeous. I've always wanted to see a waterfall up close."

Kygoss threw a sharp look at his son and then at his wife who was still stirring the, by all accounts finished, stew. "Overlooking the waterfall you say? Yes, that room does have an excellent view. I had no idea we had changed it over to a guest room though. Maledic?"

"Yes Pops?"

"Where are you sleeping if your room is now a guest room?"

Kygoss caught the sound of Maie's muffled laughter as she stayed resolutely facing the other direction, stirring her concoction.

"Oh no worries. I have taken to roosting in the attic." Maledic pulled out the chair next to Aurelia and straddled it, draping his lanky limbs over the small sturdy chair.

Kygoss folded his hands atop the table to prevent further reactions, doing his best to respect his wife's wishes, "I see, roosting in the attic. Interesting. Aurelia, we have to discuss what your parents want you to study while you are staying here."

Aurelia looked down, slumping into her chair. "Right. The job at hand...Palion."

Maledic stiffened at her words, his chin resting on the back of his chair as he tapped the frame. Kygoss raised an eyebrow at him. "I don't suppose that when you changed your room you also changed your name?"

Maie chose that moment to make her presence known once more, walking behind Kygoss and discreetly, disguising the action as a loving caress pinched the back of his neck. Quick and sharp as an adder's bite. Kygoss flinched heavily, the need to rub out the pinch unavoidable.

Maledic blushed fiercely as he faced his parents before he shook his head. "No, but she needs a friend right now. If she will let me, I will be that friend." Kygoss noted that Mal's tapping had increased in tempo, assessing the fervor with which he tapped.

Aurelia looked up at Maledic and gave him a small smile, "You can stay and listen," she began to tap the table top an off key echo to Mals chair tapping. "Alright Uncle Kygi. What do their Highnesses want of me now?"

"Well they want you to learn in-depth religion, magic control, and the art of ruling a kingdom. That last part will be taught with the assumption that your *partner*, Lucian will be uncooperative. One class is all about him and his family so you can see just how unsupportive we expect you will find him. You will also learn the history of their royal lineage so you are prepared to take your place." Kygoss leaned forward and placed his hand over Aurelias tapping one. "I will make sure and I am positive Mal will help me. You won't drown in work and responsibility. We have time and we shall have fun as well."

Aurelia looked between them both and gave a watery smile. Kygoss thanked the goddess that Maie took this moment to bring over bowls of steaming stew placing them around the table along with a platter of steaming bread. "Your Auntie here will also ensure you have plenty of great food to eat as well."

Maie smiled indulgently and they all dug in mentally preparing for the work ahead.

$Seven$

AURELIA

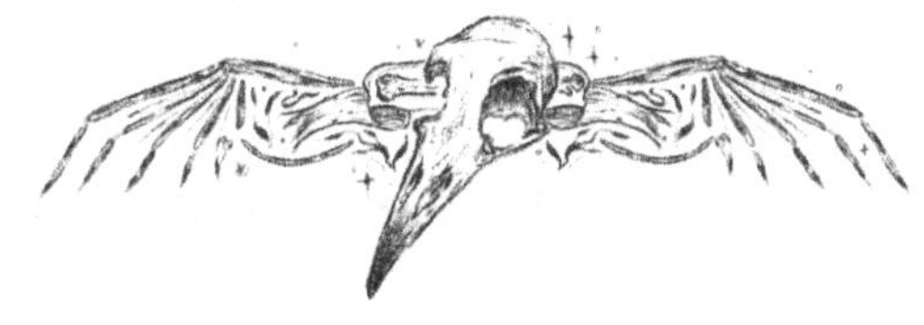

SLANA - OSI - YEAR 7557

As Kygoss neared the kitchen doorway following Maie out, he turned back giving a steely look at both Mal and herself. "Your lessons will start up in a day. I expect you both to behave. Which means," he seemed to aim the next words at Maledic causing questions to fill her already busy mind. "You stay together or you don't go. No mischief or pushing the rules my boy."

She caught the firm nod Mal sent his father right before being engulfed in a warm hug. The smell of herb stew and fresh bread mingled with the spice of her Uncle's normal scent. "It's nice to have you here Short Stack. Take the time you have away from the high expectations and relax for once. I won't tattle on you to those who may disapprove." He shot her a wink ruffling her hair before he left taking the steps two at a time up the central staircase.

She giggled, wiping away the stray tears that he had evoked with the embrace that felt so foreign and so comforting all at the same time. As a Princess of the blood the only one who could truly embrace her was the immediate family. Yet, when she had been little she could remember the hugs and the flying rides her Uncle would do over his head. All before her mother deemed her too old for such antics. Now the only embrace came as an occasional one from her father.

She let out a deep sigh, shaking out her shoulders, determined to not let the past ruin her present. Maledic interrupted her mental ruminations by clearing his throat. He shot her a grin laced with mischief the second they were alone. "Wanna go see Slana proper?"

"Isn't it impossible?"

Mal scrunched his nose before a laugh emerged. "You mean your lack of wings?" He mimed wings by flapping his hands.

Aurelia chewed on her bottom lip. She felt her face flush first the burst of heat spreading out to her fingertips. Oddly though, her magic stayed silent despite numerous past embarrassing situations leading to a flare of wind or steam.

"I've been told quite clearly that this place was designed for the winged only. Those of us trapped in a mortal shell..." She crossed her arms keeping the hurt she still felt locked deeper within. Though as Mal began to laugh the hurt began to climb within.

"Now wait a minute." Mal raised a hand struggling to catch his breath. "I am not laughing at you, I'm laughing that my father thought I would stick to the obvious lies you've been fed." He draped an arm over her shoulder leading her out the kitchen side door as he continued. "Slana is somewhat unapproachable on foot unless you know the right people." He threw her a saucy wink. "Once you get here everything becomes walkable. There are more interesting things up high perhaps, but that's why the Gods created ladders."

She shoved at his shoulder, rolling her eyes. Joy washing

away the apprehension and embarrassment. "Maledic, do you want to be my friend?"

He glanced back, his brow furrowed, "Yes."

"Let's start our friendship with a promise. No lies. No matter the gravity of the situation, you and I will tell the truth."

Mal turned to face her, his face covered in dappled shadows due to the trees they walked amongst. She almost ran directly into him. She skidded to a stop not expecting his abrupt change of pace. "Wanna make an oath out of it? I don't mind because, I know I won't lie to you, no matter the circumstances."

She gnawed on her lip thinking it through. Oaths were serious business and held lasting consequences if broken. "I think I'll take your word for it." He waited, watching her, leaving thoughts of why in the wake of his brown gaze. "Go on, lead us to Slana. I've heard so many stories from my mother and father."

His face brightened as he turned, continuing to walk down the beaten path.

The path led them deeper and deeper into a forest with trees that reached heights defying Aurelia's imagination. It would take six or seven individuals her size to even hope to encircle the width of the trunk. The farther they went it became clear some of the trees were hollow, used for dwellings for the crows of Slana. As they walked she noticed Maledic become some sort of a spectacle every time the people noticed him, embracing him with a smile and greeting.

Soon the path widened encompassing a large fountain in the center. The trees ringing it seemed to be more shops and restaurants instead of dwellings. The hustle and bustle clearly indicative that this had to be the city center. Aurelia paused looking around watching all the people wandering on the ground level before looking up above her. There were rope bridges at various levels of the canopies connecting the trees, each had people and crows flitting from place to place.

Maledic directed her to some spindly chairs and tables motioning her to sit. "Wait here. I'll be right back."

She opened her mouth to protest but in a blink he was swallowed by the random swarms of people wandering to and fro. Just as quickly as he left he was back in front of her holding two steaming mugs, a plate of bread balanced on top. She blinked. *Bread? Why is bread so important?*

He deposited the mugs on the table first, careful not to tip them over before placing the plate down. Tantalizing scents wafting up from both. "Okay, close your eyes." She watched as he took his seat pulling it closer to her.

Aurelia raised an eyebrow but complied. She could feel steam caressing her face, the smell confronting her nose an enticing mix of chocolate, cinnamon and something she couldn't quite place. "Can I open my eyes? What is this?"

"A well kept Slana secret. One ingredient grows only here and therefore we alone can create this combination." Aurelia's mouth quirked into a smile, the excitement pouring out of Maledic contagious.

She took a tentative sip. Her taste buds danced as chocolate flooded her mouth. She let the drink fill her mouth warm and comforting. Then as she swallowed a new flavor emerged onto her tongue.

A flavor so close to cinnamon it could be easy to confuse the two. Hints of an earthy nutty flavor swirled amongst the spice of cinnamon. It echoed along her taste buds as the chocolate flowed down her throat.

She couldn't contain the joy that the flavor explosion

evoked inside her mouth. Before she could open her eyes Mal spoke. "Wait! Keep them closed. Inhale."

She did, giving in to his weird experiment. *What could it hurt the drink is amazing?* What else could he have to top it off.

The new smell was subtle, just a hint of chocolate, the main smell being that odd cinnamon that she had tasted in her drink now overpowering her nose. She scrunched her nose, "That smells like a lot."

Maledic's guffaw filled her ears, drowning out the buzz of those around her. "Fair. Just try it when you're ready. It's the perfect companion to liquid chocolate." As her eyes opened she had to blink several times, surprise filling her to see that half the bread was already gone.

A smile alighting her face she took the time to relax, looking around at all the people. An elderly woman sat across the way, their eyes met and the woman waved cheerily at her causing Aurelia to blush. Her attention quickly captivated by a group of children probably around ten years of age. As she watched they were huddled together as mortals but as if a signal had been given all but one child flew off in their crow shape. She did her best to track the fliers before accepting she could never keep them all in sight. Settling instead on watching the lone child on the ground. They had their hands over their eyes spinning in a slow circle.

Suddenly they stopped, eyes turned up toward the canopy. They pointed shouting names and laughing. As each name was called the crow belonging to it flew down shifting with a small pop looks of joy and chagrin filling the faces.

She turned to Maledic. "What are they playing?"

He studied the children as they began a new round. "Hide and seek with the added aspect of identifying their friends in crow form."

She scrunched her nose. She knew hide and seek, a child's

game that she herself had played but identifying the shifted crows? "Why is identifying the crows so important?"

He gave her an assessing look before answering, "It aids in building visual acuity as well as training the crow participants to camouflage in plain sight."

She watched the children for a few more minutes, her mind wandering to her times at play at the palace.

The blonde curly head of Cerial weaved in and out of the courtyard, dodging around all the different detritus that littered the cobblestones. "Cerial! Stop cheating!! I found you fair and square!"

Cerial looked back at her laughing, "New rule. You have to find me and catch me. Then you win."

Aurelia groaned "Just because you're older doesn't mean you get to make all the rules. I'm gonna go tell papa about this, just see if I don't."

Cerial turned and glared. "Aurelia you can't do that. We are sisters, we can't just tattle on one another. We have to support each other."

Aurelia laughed, "Fine." She used Cerial's indignation and skipped forward a few steps tapping Cerial's arm before dancing back.

Cerial shrieked. "Seriously!! Aurelia."

"Its your turn to count." Giggling Aurelia sing-songed away from her sister as she scoped out the area for a new place to hide.

Mal pulled her back to the present by clearing his throat, "Does the royal house not have a shifting game? To hone your skills in your alternate form? I know the owls and sparrows do."

"Oh." Sadness filled her as she considered how to explain. Their fledgling promise echoing in her mind. "As the royal heirs only the eldest gets a shifted form. Mine will come when Cerial takes the throne or when I take my own throne in a different kingdom."

She didn't want to look at Mal the next words coming as a whisper. "Some call it the curse of the spare. Destined to watch those around fly but not able to feel my own wings till much later in life if at all."

She buried her nose in her cup drinking deep from the calming concoction. She expected pity when she met Maledic's eyes but instead saw only determination. Her mind reeled at the possibility that he actually believed in her. "Then get you a throne we shall. First you must try the bread. I promise you it's the best. It's my birthday request every year."

She laughed at his insistence complying, picking up the heavy bread that held a generous swirl of creamy melting butter. She took a bite marveling at the texture, it felt more like cake, moist melting against her tongue leaving behind a decadent flavor. It out stripped any bread that she had ever had in the palace.

A small groan escaped. "Mal, you have to give me the recipe. I want this for my birthdays too! It's rich in flavor without that sickly sweet frosting the palace chefs insist on coating everything in."

Mal laughed. "You'll just have to come here on your birthdays. The recipes are top secret."

She rolled her eyes. "Yeah right, after the two years of training are done my mother will ship me away and I'll be locked behind another gate. One I have no control over."

Mal turned contemplative. "I bet we can get you in

control. It'll take some work but, if I come with you I'll be able help from the inside."

Aurelia scoffed. "I don't think anyone will agree to that, especially Uncle Kygi, you're his heir. Then old King Harold has to approve my retinue." She chewed her lip, shaking her head as the negatives mounted inside drowning out her desires.

Mal touched her hand giving her fingers a small squeeze. "Stick with me and we shall find a way." Aurelia sat back letting the bustle and flow around her relax her stiff shoulders, nodding.

Eight

AURELIA

SLANA - RIARI - YEAR 7557

> It's said that shifter's descend from when creatures mated with a God. Gifting the future generations with the ability to transition between a mortal form and that of the creature in question.
>
> ~Archive of Tiva Temple

"The Goddess Tiva is the high mother, responsible for every living mortal. She of course rules the Great Gods..." Aurelia's head hit her chest with enough force that the words fell straight out of her brain. The abruptness left her gasping a bit as she straightened, once more trying to focus on the Acolytes words. She began pinching her thigh hard, the continuous lancing pain keeping her awake through the monotonous droning.

The intricate complexities that came with religion had always been a sure fire way to put Aurelia into a sleepy trance, no matter what she did to try to stay awake. Aurelia had always wondered why she felt so sleepy. Logic dictated that her issues stemmed from not believing in the Gods. Yet, it could also be the boring instructors. Whatever the reasoning, Aurelia had never found the subject interesting.

The majority of those living within Baelia worshiped a pantheon of Gods, despite no one having heard from the Gods directly in any known time. The younger generations seemed to be deviating from the blind faith, outwardly questioning if the Gods had ever even been real. The religious complexities that ruled their world never made sense to Aurelia, who resolutely believed they never would.

The lessons in Slana were worse than the ones she had been forced to participate in at the palace. There she had been surrounded by familiar people, Faziel or Cerial, to distract her. In a pinch even grumpy Darius would be better than this stifling solitude. She enjoyed Slana more than she had ever enjoyed her time at Drakore, the loneliness of her lessons however caused her mind to jump around, eager for anything to distract, unable to settle on the monotonous droning happening in the front of the room.

Her mind drifted back to a time when Cerial and Darius had stood up for her when the Acolyte had been particularly difficult. Sadness filled her as she realized that now no one would intercede on her behalf if the Acolyte was mean.

The lesson droned on and for the life of her Aurelia couldn't understand the difference between the God Xitar and the God Osin. She tried to ask a question but the Acolyte had merely given her a derisive look and continued with the lesson focusing her attention on Cerial and Faziel in the front of the room.

She released a deep sigh resigned to fail the assignment yet again when Darius' meaty finger poked her roughly on the shoulder. "Do you understand what she just said?"

Aurelia just shook her head, dejection filling her. She hated failing.

She didn't realize what was happening at first as Darius stood. "Hey. You need to teach better. This is ridiculous." He threw down his charcoal stick dramatically before stalking intimidatingly up to the Acolyte.

Cerial had turned, surprise and something else on her face. She stood and intercepted Darius, a hand on his chest as the Acolyte cowered at the front. Darius leaned over and whispered in Cerial's ear emphatically gesturing. She leaned back, her eyes flitting to Aurelia before a smile filled her face. She nodded once and turned toward the Acolyte.

"I need you to review the differences between the Gods Osin and Xitar."

A muscle ticked in the Acolyte's jaw as she considered the request. "You appeared to have a great handle on all the concepts, Your Highness."

Aurelia shrank into her chair knowing that this Acolyte was excluding her because of her lack of shifting abilities. Some individuals had huge issues with it despite the fact that it was completely normal for royal families. Cerial however glared haughtily. "Looking around I don't think I am here alone now am I?"

The Acolyte's eyes flitted around the room but she stood her ground. "I suppose I can alert the Oba to your complete incapability to teach every child in the way of the Gods. It's best she knows that way they can send you to a different task. Perhaps cleaning the temple? I am sure she shall have an idea where you would be better suited."

Cerial turned to the rest of us shrugging simply. "I suppose classes are canceled until the Oba gets us a new Acolyte to teach."

The current one stomped her foot. "Your Highness that is extreme. I shall review the requested material."

Cerial rounded on her eyebrow raised. "And take the questions from all in this room?"

Darius had stepped to Cerial's back, the muscle behind the question while Aurelia straightened pride filling her. Cerial always had her back. Faziel would learn that she to would be protected by her. She had only recently joined them in the Royal Nursery and appeared relatively confused over all.

As if the universe had heard her plea, a slight rustling came from the rafters of the airy study drawing her out of her memories as she glanced up. The construction of this manor appeared to be highly unique, especially when compared to the solid stone palace she had grown up in. All the ceilings were made from open rafters, welcoming avian shifters of any variety to roost or rest as they saw fit. Delight bubbled up from some hidden place within her at the sight of the crow. The crescent moon tailed Maledic in all his feathered glory hopping from talon to talon. She suppressed a giggle as he cocked his head and sent her a beady eyed wink.

Aurelia glanced up at the front of the room, the Acolyte appeared to be busily drawing on a massive board describing different Gods and their responsibilities to the residents of Baelia. Maledic, having undoubtedly noticed the distraction, glided down and landed on her desk depositing a note. Once safely delivered he nipped at her fingers before hopping down to the floor. She stuffed her hand over her face while watching him maneuver under her chair, determined to stifle the giggles that bubbled within. Crows would never be seen as graceful on the ground.

As quietly as possible she unfolded the paper.

Bored yet? Scrawled the small cramped writing.

Delight sang through her blood as she grinned, using her charcoal stick she scribbled. *Yes.*

Aurelia glanced at the Acolyte nodding along to the words being spoken, not actively retaining any of it. On a yawn she leaned back spreading her arms wide over her head, casually dropping the note as she settled back in her seat.

A black beak snuck out from under her chair and pulled the note back under with him. She wondered how he would respond as he didn't have hands in the crow form.

Her musing ended with the sound of a throat clearing imperiously from right next to her desk. "Mistress. Did you hear a word I just said?"

"Of course."

"If that's the case you can explain to me who the God Tixdarr is." Aurelia swallowed back her nervousness, as she took in the Acolyte's crossed arms and glowing eyes. Her foot tapping pretentiously waiting.

Aurelia opened her mouth with the ready made answer, "He rules..." Before she could finish the Acolytes hand was gesturing for her to elaborate. Aurelia inwardly groaned.

Aurelia swallowed hard her mind struggling to reach any of the random facts that had been shoved inside about Tixdarr throughout her life. "He rules the Realm of the Dead, Dodsfell. Which is our neighbor beyond the Great Wall Barrier and is overrun by demons and ghosts."

"Yes, yes and why is it we only have one Tixdarr temple in all of Baelia?"

Aurelia blanked. *Only one? Didn't every kingdom have one?* Her mind refused to recall the words the Acolyte had just explained despite her inner turmoil.

Aurelia's face flushed, "I don't know ma'am."

The Acolyte rolled her eyes. "Listen closely, young miss. There is one central Temple dedicated to Tixdarr as he is the only God we are aware of who took up living within the Mortal Realm we call Baelia long ago. What we know of as his temple is in fact his old palace and because it was his home, we don't try to replicate it in other kingdoms. In fact it stands alone, not in any kingdom, although Palion is the closest to it. The farther reaching kingdoms of Baelia such as Stagspire or near the Meltem Islands have to ship their dead to the temple, which is why the Acolytes of Tixdarr get to travel more than any other order."

Aurelia nodded along, the words not really sticking. *What did it matter?*

As if reading her mind the Acolyte continued. "I know you don't see the importance yet. But ruling one of the kingdoms neighboring Dodsfell means you need to know all you can of what happens inside that place. It will arm you with knowledge you may need to protect Baelia, the Godly order left to both Palion and Drakore."

"Yes, but isn't it true once a long time ago Baelia was protected by one kingdom and then it was split into two. Probably due to some weird power play. As it stands I know for a fact that Drakore protects the air while Palion the land. What will knowing the history of Tixdarr do for either kingdom? No one has heard from the Gods directly for easily a century. Perhaps they aren't even there anymore." Aurelia swallowed the rest of her words at the look she was getting from the Acolyte.

It was clear her heretical statement would lead to a punishment. Aurelia took a deep breath, her nerves on fire at the tension building. Suddenly as if the quiet had lured him into a sense of complacency, Maledic chose now to hop out from under her chair, the note clutched in his beak. "Your lack of attention makes more sense now." She glanced down at Mal, "It's time to shift young lordling. *Now.* Do not make me use my magic against you."

Slowly Maledic hopped to a clearer section of the room and with a few pops he was back to his lanky male frame. Aurelia was still surprised by how tall he was, at only eighteen he towered over her five foot two frame. Uncle Kygoss and Auntie Maie were not at all what anyone would consider tall but it appeared that their son would make up for that.

The week she had been in Slana Maledic hadn't been far from her side. He had done what he could to make her feel safe and comfortable in a foreign city, the makings of a true friend. She stood and put herself between the boy who had done nothing but welcome her into his life, and the Acolyte. "Leave him be. He didn't do anything wrong. He merely tried to bring some excitement to your lessons."

"Regardless," she said dismissively, ringing a small bell to summon the servant, "I must inform his parents of his distractions." Aurelia watched as the Acolyte scribbled a note.

Rage filled Aurelia, her blood singing with lightning as she surveyed the Acolyte. She could feel her body heating from within as the magic boiled, her anger the fire it needed. Before she could give words to the anger, or rashly release her pent up magic Maledic touched her shoulder gently. He leaned down and whispered. "It's fine Spréach."

His touch diffused the magic before it could overwhelm her control leaving her cold and oddly empty. She slowly shook her head, returning his whisper with one of her own tears forming in the corner of her eyes. "No it's not. You shouldn't be punished for being my friend." She couldn't keep her voice from breaking with emotion, her face flushing as a result.

His hand tightened on her shoulder "No matter the punishment I will be right here Spréach never fear."

She huffed a breath. The questions were too many for her brain to properly process. *What was with this newest nickname? Why did he want to be her friend so badly?* Her only experience with eighteen year olds seemed to show they wanted to leave younger ones behind. Yet, the evidence was right in front of her, an eighteen year old determined to be her friend.

The servant entered the room and the Acolyte handed over the missive. "See that this young man and the note are delivered directly to Lord Corvus."

Aurelia stepped forward ready to follow, but the Acolyte shook her head pointing to the desk Aurelia had vacated. "No. You have a lesson to finish."

Aurelia glared daggers at the woman trying to stop her, the rush of magic coming faster this time. Steam escaped from her hands as she clenched and unclenched her fists. "You can try to stop me but I wouldn't suggest getting in my way."

Maledic grabbed her steaming hand, squeezing hard, shaking his head as he stepped around her. As he released her she grabbed his wrist forcing him to stop. "No. We face it together, we were both at fault."

The Acolyte threw up her hands. "Princess or not you need to learn your place, this is not suitable behavior. It is not appropriate to threaten to use your magic when you don't get your way." Aurelia just glared at her, refusing to comment further.

Mal met her gaze and nodded once a smile on his face as he gave her a mock bow. "After you Spréach."

"You all have to stop with the nicknames." She huffed as she stepped around him, rolling her eyes.

ninε

KYGOSS

SLANA - RIARI - YEAR 7557

He wasn't surprised by the stark differences of emotion that stormed through his door on the heels of the servant. He didn't bother reading the note, since he could already hear multiple footsteps in the hall. It took merely a few breaths for Aurelia, her face a mask of anger and indignation, and Maledic quiet and subdued, to enter. He steepled his hands in front of him at the desk and waited for the impending explosion, firmly expecting Aurelia to erupt with passion.

Maledic took a seat in one of the two chairs, meeting Kygoss' gaze, a goofy grin evident. "Hey Pops."

"Maledic." He kept his tone serious and foreboding, making it clear to his only child that a goofy grin wouldn't erase the mistake. Aurelia watched the two of them, the cogs turning in her brain contemplating what the next step would be. Once it was clear to Kygoss that Aurelia would be silent, standing next to Maledic's chair with her arms crossed, he looked down at the note skimming the contents, his ire growing.

"Why is it that my son and only child feels the need to attend lessons that he accomplished years ago? Why are you attending them in your shifted crow form?"

"Well, Pops. I have had a renewed interest in the religious hierarchy of our land. I knew that would be the first thing taught to Aurelia so I popped in discretely to monitor and learn." Maledic met his gaze unwaveringly, seemingly unperturbed by the anger simmering within Kygoss' mind.

"I see perhaps I should have petitioned for you to be an Acolyte." He did his best to keep his emotions tamped down.

"Ah well. If the Gods had intended for that then you would have had more children." Mal shrugged indifferently. "As it is, they only blessed you with me. Destined for the role of Lord, sadly not a role devoted to the word of the Gods." Kygoss stomped on the flare of frustration that surged within him. Mal knew all the right buttons to press.

Kygoss slid his gaze to Aurelia and noted her attention volleying between the two of them. "On to you, young lady. Why are you here exactly? You have lessons. My recalcitrant son is the issue, as far as I can tell you are not part of the problem." He gestured at the note still crumpled on his desk.

Aurelia flushed looking at the carpet. Her gaze lifted to his, a fire burning in the depths. "I came to help Maledic. He only came into that lesson to make me feel better, I was clearly lonely. He shouldn't be in trouble for helping." Her chin lifted in challenge.

"He isn't in trouble for being your friend Short Stack. *He* is in trouble for interrupting your vital lessons and skipping out on his own." He paused studying the serious looks on the teenagers faces. "I was young once and can understand how boring lessons can be. Sometimes having a friendly face amidst the discomfort helps the time pass. This calls for a change of plans however, I want to make it clear you are not getting rewarded for bad behavior."

He shot a glare at Mal. "Since it appears you can't be separated, you will attend each other's lessons, meaning you will have double the workload. I expect that you," He pointed at Aurelia, "can keep up with the level of rigor that Maledic is held to despite the age difference." He turned to Maledic, "You are expected to help her study, but *not* give her the answers."

Kygoss didn't miss the quick grin Mal and Aurelia shared. He subtly rolled his eyes at the nonsense and turned to Aurelia once more. "Now young miss, I need you to go back to your religion lesson. It will be the last solo lesson, but I need a word with my son in private."

Aurelia nodded and turned toward the door, only stopping once as if contemplating saying something but instead she straightened her shoulders, opened the door and was gone.

———

Kygoss turned and met his son's mischievous gaze. "Do you realize what's happening Mal?"

"I have made an educated guess." Mal tapped his fingers erratically on the arm rest.

"You are by all accounts a man, and one ready for his soulbond. She is not."

"I know that Pops."

"You know that you are not allowed to tell her of your connection or more accurately possible connection until she reaches eighteen." Mal nodded once. "Do you also realize that she is destined to be someone else's wife? She might be your soulbond, *maybe.* It is impossible to get confirmation for two more years. Regardless of that fact, she will have no choice but to marry Lucian." He watched Mal's face carefully trying to understand his son's mindset.

Mal fidgeted and straightened. "I know she is expected to

marry Lucian, at least for now. But as you always say we don't truly know what the future holds. The only person I know who has even a window into the possibilities is Auntie Hesper and she can't see her own children's futures."

Kygoss groaned a bit, "Mal, she has seen it. Her latest vision consisted of Aurelia in Palion regalia. The crown of the land rested on her head."

He watched as the color drained from Mal's face. "The Goddess Tiva will show us the way Pops. She wouldn't give me a soulbond only to yank her away. I have to believe that the Gods aren't that cruel." It came out as a whisper, as if his belief in them wasn't solid enough to make the thought ring true. Kygoss stood and walked around the desk pulling Mal into a hug. "I hope not my son, I hope not."

ten

AURELIA

SLANA - BENE - YEAR 7557

She walked out of her room and gasped, almost running into Maledic. "What are you doing here?"

"I thought today could be fun, let's slip away and go look at that waterfall you have been so fascinated by." Maledic said as stood up off the wall he had been leaning against.

Her mouth fell open, excitement filling her. "I would love to! I have never seen one up close only ever in paintings."

Mal nodded, returning her wide smile with one of his own before leading her out of the manor house, toward the forest that lay behind.

"Do you often get visitors to Slana?" Aurelia picked her way through the forest. In the palace she had teams of servants to do her washing and care for her clothes, here it had been made clear to her that regardless of her title she would be responsible for her own cleaning and repair. Auntie Maie would help her if she hadn't the skill necessary but it would be Aurelia's responsibility. This left her carefully plotting her next steps, avoiding the truly muddy parts hoping to come out of this adventure with minimal additional chores.

Mal didn't have the same worries, it became apparent as he would stride ahead and then stop turning to watch her slow process. Once they met up together he would shake his head a silent laugh present before trying to go more slowly. "We don't really have many visitors. Everyone in Drakore knows the crows have the Crowlands, that's obvious but the exact location is not freely given. My ancestors were wary of other avian clans coming in to take what is ours."

"Oh. I guess wandering in the woods isn't too frightening then. If no one comes up here." She had said it more to herself but Mal shot her a grin over his shoulder.

"Well there are still wild animals, the non shifters do exist even if they are rarer. It is also possible that some of the avian clans happen across our lands. It's always wise to be vigilant."

Aurelia nodded, doing her best to internalize the warning. It may appear safe but one never knew what lurked around the corner.

They rounded a large tree putting them close enough that the roar of the waterfall finally reached her ears. It thrilled and scared her, the sounds of water crashing against the river bed. Maledic stopped and held out his arm across her path, halting her. She looked at him, confusion filling her, at least until she began to hear it too. Someone or several someones were screaming and laughing up ahead.

Mal looked at her, assessing. "That's probably my friends. We like to hang out here but they can be rather annoying to the uninitiated. We can always come another time if you don't feel up to meeting them." He turned away as if to lead her back to the manor.

She made her decision in a split second, a wicked grin lighting her face. She dodged around his arm and danced out of reach before sprinting around the big trees ahead eager to see what his friends could be like. She thought she heard him mutter a curse behind her before running to catch up.

She skidded to a stop in the muddy ground as she came face to face with two lanky males, dressed only in shorts half submerged in the water, their bodies on full display. Aurelia's cheeks heated. Her mother had ensured she led a sheltered life, never viewing an unclothed male body in any state. She had snuck off and seen a few in the practice yards but that had been from afar. Suddenly she had no idea where she could look. Their skin much darker than hers fascinated her, the water glinting off of them made the males sparkle. She awkwardly raised her arm waving before clearing her throat, her eyes looking at the river beyond them. "Hello."

The males in front of her waded closer, their facial expressions almost predatory. "Hello gorgeous." The taller of the two, his jet black hair plastered to his head said reaching the shore line first.

Aurelia wasn't going to back up and show her discomfort, her magic thrummed within her limbs reminding her she wasn't powerless. Yet she didn't need it. Mal appeared out of nowhere stepping protectively out in front of her his hands tucked into his pockets.

"Stulten that's no way to talk to a lady, your mother taught you better than that." His voice sounded strained. She didn't realize that she would be this grateful she had someone to look at who had a shirt on.

The black haired Stulten took a half step back assessing the situation before a sly grin curled from his mouth.

"Well, well Maledic Corvus has found a backbone. Interesting." He half turned toward Aurelia and bowed his nose grazing the river water, "My lady, my humblest apologies for my manners I beg you for your forgiveness."

His waterlogged companion, a red head with a look that spelled trouble stepped forward and bowed to both her and

Mal. "Mal, it's been far too long. Would your new friend like to join us in the water? We promise to be on our best gentlemanly behavior, not a hair on her head will be harmed."

"Recin..." It emerged as a growl from Mal.

Aurelia stepped around Mal, a hand on her hip as she assessed all three males in front of her. "I thought you all were supposed to be friends." She turned to the redhead, Recin. "I am going to go explore by myself, I no longer want to deal with whatever this is." She waggled her finger between the three of them before turning once more to Recin. "I speak for myself, keep that in mind next time you have a question."

She promptly turned on her heel ignoring whatever nonsense the boys were talking, heading directly toward where the waterfall met the river. She felt an undeniable joy fill her as she neared the flat rocks. The climb invigorated her, blood singing in her ears as she crested the top. She laid on her stomach reaching a hand out as far as she could, feeling for the first time in her life the rush of falling water. Something spoke to her soul, louder than what had called to her when she had crossed the river with Kygoss. This was purer, a shout within her lifesblood, her magic rising to meet it reveling in the magic of the rainbows that glittered off the water's foamy spray.

A sudden desire filled her so completely that it couldn't be ignored. She rummaged at her boots, unlacing them with quick efficiency, shucking off her over coat. The under shirt clung to her, the lack of arm coverage causing a shiver to move through her.

She swam during the summers in the palace lake, it wasn't a completely foreign experience, however she had never dived into a rushing river with water flowing onto her. She didn't even bother looking around for the boys instead diving blind, giving into the feelings of wonderment that filled her.

Cold. The first feeling to penetrate deep into her consciousness. Cold and the suffocating need to breathe. She tumbled end over end. It wasn't clear where the bottom of the river lay and where the blessed life giving air flowed. She sank into her power, trying to find the thread that called her into the river that had risen up to meet the joy in her blood. *There.*

Suddenly she felt a calm rush over her. A pain zapped at her neck lasting no more than a few seconds, then her lungs inexplicably carried on expanding and contracting despite being surrounded by water. *Breathe water. How? What?* She swam away from the crushing fall of water and found swimming much easier than she ever had before.

The world finally righted itself. She could see a flicker of sparkle just out of the corner of her eye. She turned her head, excitement filling her as fish of various colors came into view, all swimming along the bottom of the river bed. They darted in and amongst the rocks and plants carrying on with their daily lives. It took a few minutes to adjust to how the water dragged against her clothes. Her hair swirling around her creating clouds of raven strands that the fish had begun to dart between. Her mind filled with joy as she swam further her pale hands looking oddly translucent in the water, rainbows of color dancing upon her skin. She turned to dive deeper and curiosity about the world under the waves when something snagged her roughly around the waist hauling her up.

Up and out.

The world spun. Her back made contact with the bank abruptly. The sky suddenly filled her vision as she blinked river water from her eyes. The air had been knocked from her lungs as she made contact with the river bank. Aurelia doubled over coughing desperately trying to breathe.

"What? Why?" The words came out between coughs as she desperately tried to bring air back to her lungs.

She opened her eyes to see blurry images, Recin and Stulten leaning over her. She shoved at the ground putting distance between herself and them. She looked around and only then could she see Mal. Panting at the edge of the river looking at her pain clearly evident in his face. Pain that quickly began to morph into anger.

Her own anger rose to match it. She sat up, air finally filling her lungs properly.

"What in the Goddess were you thinking! A sudden death wish perhaps? The final payback against your parents?" Maledic yelled at her as he advanced. *Yelled.* In the weeks she had been here he had never raised his voice at her.

"I wasn't doing anything wrong! You never said I couldn't swim in the river. Your friends were in the water. What's the harm for me?" She refused to back down, instead rising to her feet standing chest to chest with him, their breath mingling as they both attempted to control their anger. Her blood heated causing the water to steam off her in clouds.

"They don't stay under the water long enough to kill themselves." Mal glared daggers at her.

"I... I ... I didn't." Yet a niggling thought poked through her quickly disintegrating anger. She felt the need to breathe and then something inside of her had shifted and she hadnt had to think about it.

She could feel her blood draining down her face as she contemplated what that might mean. *What had happened?* It was too much, she turned away from him heading back up to the rock where her shoes and overcoat were piled.

She could hear raised voices behind her, Mal she was pretty certain was calling her name. She plowed on though grabbing the overcoat pulling it on roughly. She didn't bother to put her boots back on instead carrying them as she stomped away. Recin stepped into her path, his hands raised.

"Look. I know we started off on the wrong foot. I may not know exactly what happened while you were in the water but perhaps we could talk it out. He, Mal that is. He doesn't get this upset like, ever. I swear. I've known him since we were born." Recin scratched at his hair looking at the ground, a plea in his eyes. "Come and talk. I think you stomping off will make it worse."

Aurelia shot a glance at the bank where Mal was standing and talking to Stulten his hands wildly gesturing. Stulten seemed to be nodding with understanding. She gave a measured look at Recin. "I don't know you. I don't trust you. After the talk when I got here I don't think you're really his friend. Why should I listen to your advice?"

Recin groaned, rubbing his face, "We have a weird relationship I admit. Yet, he is my brother. Brother of the heart. Please help him. He needs you to talk to him." Recin swallowed hard rubbing the back of his neck.

Aurelia took a deep breath searching his face, it felt like Recin truly wanted to get Mal help. "How long was I under the water really?"

"Easily double the length of time I can spend under the water. He went a little crazy the minute you went under though, especially where you went under." He glanced back over at Mal, "The waterfall is particularly dangerous due to the rocks that lie in the river bed. It's possible to be pushed under with such a great force that you can hit the rocks and never surface again. He thought that had happened. He jumped in searching for you amongst the foamy water. I found you first but he is the one that tossed you on the bank. He was desperate."

Aurelia turned to stare at the back of Mal's head and sighed. She could feel a fragile string being formed between her and Mal, a thread of friendship. *Friends work together, they fight but they also heal together.* "Fine."

She made her way toward Mal, silently debating how to navigate this aspect of friendship. She never had to bother admitting wrongdoing to her sister, not even to Faziel or

Darius. They just got over it or didn't. Aurelia hadn't truly cared either way, yet this felt different.

Mal turned as if he could sense her standing behind him. A shock rippled through her at the pain and hurt on his face, something deep within her yearned to comfort him to grab him up in a hug and show him that she was fine. Yet her stubbornness won out. She crossed her arms in front of her, "I was fine Mal. You were busy with your friends."

Mal took a visible breath before nodding slowly. "I'm sorry if I hurt you. I was afraid you had gotten injured in the current, there are a lot of big rocks down there. We never talked about you diving in like that and I wasn't, I wasn't prepared."

She screwed up her face, *prepared for what,* pain lancing through her. "Something called me in, it couldn't be planned for. I also know that you would probably get in a great amount of trouble if you killed one of the princesses in the river, even if it had been an accident." She stared at the ground rubbing her arms cold, suddenly filling her despite the heat of the day. "I'll be careful next time." She made to turn but Mal grabbed her elbow, tipping her chin up so their eyes met. A pit opened up inside her, nerves that she didn't understand or comprehend began to flutter from the depths of her soul.

"I was more concerned that my friend Spréach was in danger. My life would be much darker with her drowned at the bottom of the river." His brown eyes held hers.

Her nerves growing within her she cleared her throat, "Why do you call me Spréach?" Her voice was more of a whisper, her throat having gone mysteriously dry.

He released her a grin spreading across his face. He reached up and ruffled her still damp hair, "It means spark. You my friend are sparks given life if anyone is. Can I ask you a question?"

She stuck her tongue out before shrugging, "Always. Friends can ask questions."

Mal chuckled "When did you take an oath?"

Aurelia raised an eyebrow. "What are you talking about?"

He tapped her shoulder. "You are oath marked on your back by your shoulders. From what I could see it's probably taken the shape of dragon wings."

So that's where it settled. "Ah that. Well, my father and I have an oath. I did it when I was much younger." She shrugged. "It's not a big deal."

Mal nodded as he slung an arm across her shoulders leading her back towards the manor house for food, the near death experience forgotten.

Eleven

KYGOSS

SLANA - BENE - YEAR 7557

Kygoss strode into the small lesson room having dismissed the afternoon instructor for the day. Satisfaction filled him when neither Mal nor Aurelia seemed at all perturbed by his presence or the change in schedule. The ability to modify their plans at a moment's notice with calmness would be needed as they aged into the chaos that life had in store for them.

He thumped the folder down on the desk and faced them. "Palion. What do we know?"

Aurelia visually stiffened, her relaxed nature gone in a blink as she stuttered, "Ruled by King Harold and home to land shifters."

He shot her a warm smile. "Correct. What else?"

A frostiness escaped from Mal as he added, "Lucian Ronnet is set to inherit as the only child of Harold and his deceased Queen."

Kygoss nodded again and flipped open the folder pulling a rendering from within. It was a recent artistic rendering of Lucian. One of his best Palion birdies had gone to a lot of trouble to make sure Drakore knew exactly what Lucian looked like, making it impossible for Harold to substitute another during marriage talks.

The chiseled blonde head sneered from the paper as Kygoss tacked it to the board at the front of the room. "This is Lucian. It's vitally important that you," He gestured at Aurelia "know all there is to know about this individual." He waited a beat but Aurelia continued to stare stubbornly at the table top. He shot a glance at Mal noting his own struggle to contain volatile emotions.

Kygoss clapped his hands dramatically. "Okay." Everyone jolted at the sudden noise. "This is a topic neither one of you is particularly fond of. Yet, you are both forgetting something."

Mal, his fists tightening on the table grunted, "What would that be?"

Aurelia still maintained her downcast eyes but Kygoss barreled on. "Knowledge on anything leads to power. It may be power over a situation, such as the impending match Aurelia is to make. It can also lead to power over a person, such as being able to manipulate this sorry excuse for a Prince." Kygoss gestured dramatically at the drawing. "Without taking the time to learn about him, his court, his family and his kingdom you are going to be thrust into a situation where you are asking to be hurt. If you allow me to help you then you will walk in and own them."

Aurelia finally looked up a dark gleam in her eye, one that had Kygoss internally flinching. This was going to be a very interesting match in the end. "Alright Uncle Kygi. Teach me. Make it easier for me, because easy or not I will win, one way or another."

Kygoss picked up the threat, he wasn't however sure who was being threatened. *Would she hurt herself? Hurt Lucian?*

The Gods would know and hopefully lead her to the correct path.

He cleared his throat of the emotion gathering there. "Lucian Ronnet. Do you know his powers?"

They both shook their heads but luckily they also had writing supplies out and appeared ready to take notes. "He is a wolf shifter, the reports are he has a very weak mastery of fire as well. It is rumored that if he doesn't secure the match with Drakore he will be removed from the line of succession."

Aurelia gasped her head snapping up finally looking at the drawing, "How can a father do that to his only son? A product of a soulbond mating?"

Kygoss shifted and pulled another rendering from the folder placing it next to Lucians portrait. His dark haired, dark eyed father Harold glared out from the paper. "This man." Kygoss tapped the paper, "Is King Harold and he became something truly twisted when his Queen died. While he was never a standout individual she brought the light and positivity out of him. When she died in childbirth shortly after Lucian was delivered, his goodness died with her. The Great Power did not heal her due to not running strongly within her veins." He glanced at Mal, "Do either of you know why she didn't have a strong connection to the power?"

Mal cleared his throat. "You told me this once. It's because their match occurred after Harold took the throne. She couldn't access the Great Power. If they had met and matched before he took the throne she would have been introduced to the power through him. It's also why soul-bonded royal couplings where both people are tied to the Great Power are rare. One exception is Auntie Hesper and Uncle Aydan. They met while he was still Crown Prince."

Kygoss nodded, his chest swelling at Mal's knowledge retention. He looked at Aurelia. "Do you understand why you must match with him before he takes the throne?"

"I would assume I will get shipped over there sooner rather than later so they can train me to be the Queen they want. They undoubtedly want to erase whatever influence Drakore has in my Queenly makeup. They would also want to see if I am Lucian's soulbond mate."

Kygoss cleared his throat not quite able to meet her eyes. "No worries there. Reports have come in that his wolf mate has been located, while the reports are conflicting, it is believed she will be denied a spot by Lucian's side."

Silence met his words. The air became heavy as tension grew. He finally lifted his gaze to meet Aurelia's as he felt the beginnings of stinging electric shocks in the air. Her eyes were wide and wild as she stared at him. "You're saying that there's no chance I am his soulbond mate?"

Kygoss couldn't help his glance at Maledic who looked rather smug despite the pressure in the air, "No, there is no chance of that. However a match is still expected due to both of your respective titles." It dawned on him suddenly why her anger would be so white hot.

He held up a finger, stopping her outburst as it rose to the surface. "Your mother is unaware of Lucian's wolf mate. That piece of information has been found rather recently and it is more pressing to teach you about it, given the Gods' edicts about your future, than to await your mother's guidance."

Aurelia let out her pent up breath with a loud exhale. Kygoss watched as she glanced at Mal and snapped. "What are you smirking about? Is my impending doom entertaining asshole?"

Kygoss lifted a hand stopping Mal's retaliation. "Alright we are getting off the point. We don't need to continue to insult one another. Refocus, the other very important aspect is that there is no trust between the people and the rulers in Palion. It's something that can be exploited if you think about your actions and don't act rashly." Aurelia huffed loudly, turning her head away from Mal. Kygoss studied his son who looked just as pained as she did. Mal however rallied and spoke a question. "Is she going to be forced to go by herself?"

Kygoss considered. "It's common for a Princess coming to a kingdom as a bride to arrive with an entourage that then returns to her home after the wedding. So in short, she would spend most of her time there away from Drakore individuals, yes."

Mal's face closed up at that. Aurelia straightened. "If Lucian needs me as bad as he seems to, I will have some conditions. Firstly I want my own court. Whom I get to appoint. If." and she threw a long calculating look at Mal, "There's anyone I want to appoint from Drakore they shall come. Other conditions will get added as I think of them, but I will not go there to be powerless Kygoss."

He smiled largely, orchestrating a bow. "That is the goal of these lessons, Your Highness."

twelve

QUEEN HESPER

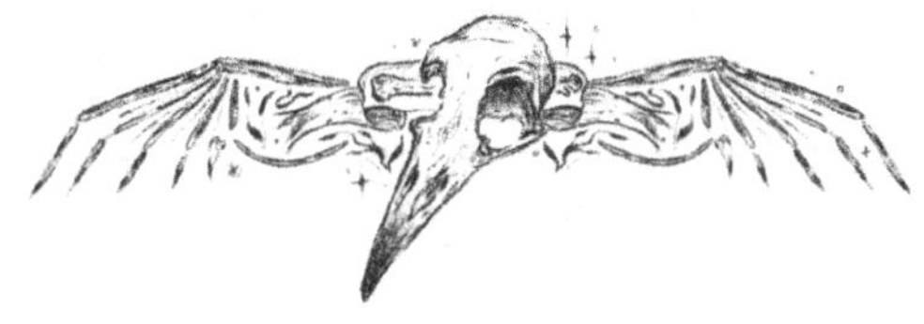

DRAKORE - OXI - YEAR 7557

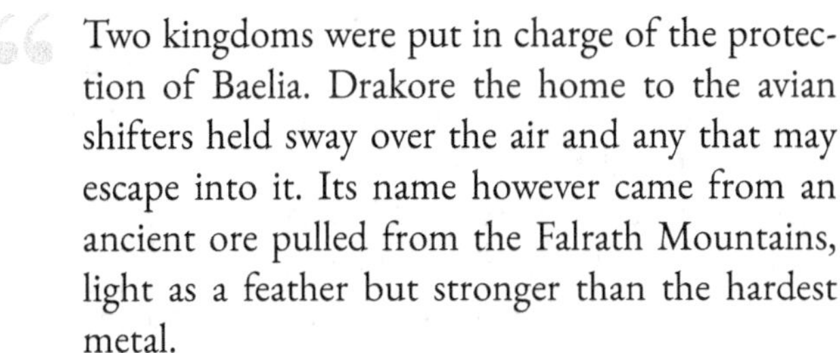

Two kingdoms were put in charge of the protection of Baelia. Drakore the home to the avian shifters held sway over the air and any that may escape into it. Its name however came from an ancient ore pulled from the Falrath Mountains, light as a feather but stronger than the hardest metal.

~Tome dedicated to the Founding of Drakore - Located in the Drakore Archives

Hesper smiled as banners snapped in the light breeze that seemed to always be blowing within Drakore whipping down off the Falrath Mountains. The city surrounding the palace was festooned in the gray and blue of the royal house, streamers flying from the rooftops. Children swarmed the streets and alleyways waving makeshift Drakore flags. This particular festival marked the day Drakore was founded all those years ago, the day the Gods declared it a kingdom with a purpose; the betterment of Baelia. Hesper had her doubts that Aewenna the current Oba of Tiva even knew the exact day, instead picking a random day to celebrate during the high fall.

According to tradition the royal couple lead the parade, something that Hesper and Aydan treasured taking part in. They enjoyed handing out bags of provisions to those in need, seeing their citizens up-close and in person. Today began just the same as every other year they had participated, the greeting of cheers and smiles a balm to her soul. Proof to her that the people loved them as much as Aydan and Hesper loved the people they were stewards of.

Before her vision this year she had planned to introduce Aurelia as the heir to Drakore, finally allowing the public an up-close interaction with one of her daughters. She and Aydan had always strove to keep the girls away from the public's eye, hoping to only introduce the heir. Hesper sighed knowing it was one aspect of their rule the people didn't agree with. She however didn't want the people of Drakore to fall in love with one daughter only to have her shipped off to Palion. The vision had come just in time for her to change the plan with the public none the wiser. The girls however were less than impressed. Cerial saw it as her right to be introduced this year as an adult, formally recognized as the heir apparent in a grand ceremony. Yet, she couldn't, not until Aurelia was secured within Palion just in case. Aydan begrudgingly agreed to support her decision with Cerial but she knew it would be a continuous yearly fight.

Hesper attempted to keep her smile in place as the sight of some young people centered her thoughts on Cerial. She had put up quite a fight this morning, when they had informed her that she would be forced to wait for her younger sister to reach maturity. It made Hesper quite grateful that Aurelia currently resided in Slana, as she would have undoubtedly added to the argument.

While Hesper and Aydan led the crowd through the city their council members were also present. It gave those new to the city a chance to meet those in charge of their wellbeing. Hesper took great pride in the opportunities to approach the civilians, introducing herself, playing with the babies, and handing out treats or toys to the kids running wild in the streets.

The only person who had pushed back on this tradition year after year was Rayner Svenston, The General. Perhaps his displeasure came as an unfortunate side effect from her interference with Rayner's own family at the insistence of the Gods. She had been sent vision after vision leading her to step in and save Darius from the untimely death he would have endured from his father. Yet, clearly it held a cost. Despite being excused from attending Rayner had accompanied them today, displeasure radiating off of him with enough intensity those nearest flinched from his presence. The deal she had made with him all those years ago still rankled her but she had been desperate, for the visions to stop and for Darius to be safe. Even if it ended with the asshole still clutching at his measly semblance of power, she had stripped the power from the title as soon as she was able, instilling it to another. Hesper also ensured that Darius stayed out of sight, determined that they keep him out of reach of his abuser. She felt a sense of responsibility for Darius now and would do her best to keep him safe.

She took a few more steps but a sudden and inexplicable pain rippled through her head, it lanced from the back of her head toward her eye. She lifted her hands to her temples dropping the bag at her feet. Despite her concentrated effort to keep her magic in check, to keep the vision from happening a strangled cry escaped her lips. She felt her body fight, it seized up tensing suddenly. She managed to lift her eyes to Aydan's worried ones before her knees gave out and the world went black.

She clamped down on her magic, trying desperately to make her mind return to her body. The only result from her attempts was her vision going from a hazy gray to black as night. The shadows receded slowly revealing Aurelia on the ground. Hesper positioned above her, watching as the rag clad girl hunched on the ground. Aurelia's skin glowed unnaturally, pale as a phantom, her eyes practically glowing in her sunken face. Hesper concentrated her power wanting to get closer, to try and understand why Aurelia would be dressed in rags after the last vision had her in a crown. *Something must have changed. What though?*

She could hear the screeching and clicking of talons growing closer. From the sound of it there had to be hundreds of talons scraping the ground. She began to chant to her youngest, her voice getting louder trying to drown out the sound of the talons that kept coming closer.

"Run Aurelia Get up and Run. Don't let them catch you. Rise GIRL! RUN RUN RUN RUN."

As Hesper's voice died off having gone hoarse, the demons arrived at Aurelia's side. Aurelia's body soon became surrounded by the lesser creatures, green and blue bodies all jostling for a chance to see her. Hesper watched as her daughter dragged her head up, a gasp escaping her scratched throat. Aurelia bruised and beaten, dried blood coating the front of her rags. Hesper could feel the tears gathering at her eyes, falling filling her ears, "No not her too. Please Gods!"

Yet, it was happening. In front of her eyes demons were

grabbing and stroking her daughter, manipulating Aurelia's body, forcing their way into her. Hesper began to beg her magic to release her, to let her leave this vision. It took too long but eventually she felt her mind released into waking consciousness once more.

As her eyes fluttered open she saw Aydan kneeling over her, his face swimming in and out of focus as the tears dried up. The blue of the sky was gone, replaced by a brown thatch, the panic and fear of the vision didn't subside instead it latched on to the new place. "Where are we?! What's happened? How long have I been out?"

Aydan's face scrunched in confusion. "Hesper. It's okay. Mistress Hakimi, Keeper of the Tavern on the Hill saw your distress and offered a place for you to rest. Rayner is making sure everything is safe. I told them nothing major happened, you just experienced one of your visions. You did have a vision right?"

She let out a sharp exhale, her voice cracked with the emotion from the vision still strong in her veins. "Yes. I did. Where are we?"

Concern flashed in Aydans eyes, "Mistress Hakimi graciously offered a room at the tavern for you to recover in. I didn't think you would want your vision to be a spectacle."

Hesper sat up slowly nodding, she threw a grateful smile towards the Mistress of the Tavern who stood wringing her hands in the doorway. "My gratitude, Mistress. Please if you ever need anything we are in your debt." Hesper turned her attention to Aydan, "The vision showed me things I could never have imagined. We need to get Aurelia home." She shot a glance at the Mistress and back to Aydan, "We need to head back to the palace."

Aydan nodded understanding, settling in. "Are you sure you won't forget anything important?"

"I wish I could but what I just saw will live in my memory forever."

Aydan worked quickly once he saw Hesper secured on her own steed, borrowed from a guard. He firmly directed the council members to carry on, finishing the route handing out the sincerest apologies as they went. Everyone including Rayner would be expected to report to the palace at the end of the day, noting any signs of ill or disturbance within the city. Hesper eyed Rayner who was sneering at the change of plans. She shook her head slightly, turning her attention back to Aydan as he issued orders. She swelled with pride as he mounted up on his own commandeered mount. He ruled with a kindness that often was seen as weakness against her harsh personality, yet, when he did take charge it thrilled her.

Upon entering the housekeeper rushed out of an alcove near the entrance, distress evident on her face. Hesper fastened on a bland smile, knowing Rana something must have gone wrong. "What has happened? How can we help?" She could feel the frustration at the distraction radiating off Aydan, his eagerness to hear her vision and learn what it showed evident.

Rana hastily bowed. "Cerial ma'am. She's been missing since you left for the festival. There's also a representative from Palion waiting in the audience chamber; he claims it's vital he sees you both." She inclined her head to Aydan.

Hesper blinked her mind processing everything that had happened. "Alright. We will send out the search party for Cerial if she hasn't returned by supper. My guess is she's sulking. I need to freshen up and then we shall meet with Palion's representative. Does he have a name or rank we should take into consideration?"

Rana shook her head shrugging a hint of anger sparking

from her. "He didn't say and once he made his needs known he refused to talk to anyone but you."

"I see." Hesper could feel her tone getting colder, she hated when people she trusted were treated poorly. "In that case let's have him stew a bit in his thoughts. We shall return in three hours to deal with him. Send my sparrows immediately to the Crowlands. Aurelia and Kygoss need to report back. Now."

thirteen

QUEEN HESPER

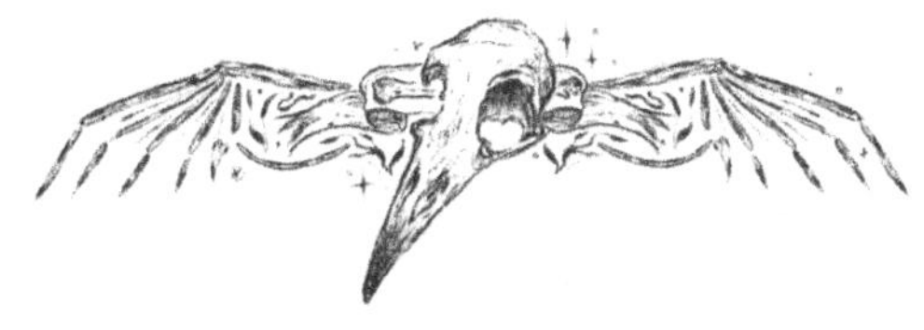

DRAKORE - OXI - YEAR 7557

Her neck itched as Aydan's eyes bore holes into her during the walk back to their quarters. She didn't allow the discomfort to show however, focusing instead on her need to clean her face and spruce her hair. They needed to portray a self assured ruling couple, especially a Queen that radiated confidence. Harold always tended to doubt her capability after his own wife died, seeing women as a weak necessity. She refused to give his representative any ideas that Harold could be correct.

Once the door of the room shut Aydan leaned against it ensuring that no one interrupted them as he turned demanding eyes in her direction, "Hesper. You owe me an explanation."

She met his eyes in the looking glass, "I saw horrible things Aydan. Demons doing their worst to Aurelia." Shame swamped her as the words left her mouth. She had never been very good at treating her youngest with kindness, the tendency to punish first and praise last. Aurelia always seemed to be a natural no matter what task was presented to her, a skill

Hesper herself lacked. Each time Aurelia raised her chin in defiance, confident in her choices, Hesper felt torn internally between pride and indignation. Indignation came easier, that a child could skate through the injustices of being royal using pure determination to pave her way, while Hesper slogged through issue after issue. It was stupid, she knew she should bask in pride over her daughter actively changing royal expectations, yet she couldn't manage it.

Aydan cleared his throat, arms crossed in front of him as he leaned back on the door. "We aren't leaving this room until you give me more of an explanation Hesper. You just recalled her and Kygoss from Slana, arguably one of the safer locations within Drakore after seeing her at the hands of demons. Why did you bring her home? What exactly is your plan?"

"*We* are recalling Aurelia. *We* are the best option to protect her, Aydan. Also perhaps her being in Slana is what led to this. Perhaps something she encounters in Slana leads her to this situation. Perhaps the demons are on their way right now. It was incredibly difficult to tell her age, there was so much blood. If Aurelia is here you can fly her out. The crows can't do that."

She could hear the repressed anger in his voice as he ground out, "Have you considered your constant changing of plans is doing nothing but ensuring the outcomes you are seeing?"

She turned, a flush beginning on her chest and overtaking her face indignation at his audacity. "Are you questioning my gifts now? What happened to trusting me Aydan? You've never questioned my magic before!" She approached him menacingly, her voice rising despite herself. "I have never done anything to endanger our children or our kingdom. I have put all my faith in my gift and the Gods. Perhaps you should reevaluate your priorities and what you believe in." She stabbed his chest with her finger, her control on her anger snapping. *Like I can control the God's favor, stupid man.*

Aydan rubbed at his temple. "Whose future were you focusing on when the vision came?"

Hesper found herself crossing her arms and turning slightly away, opening her mouth to retort the obvious but stopped as she considered what had been going through her mind right before the vision struck. "A lot rolls through my mind during the festivities. It's hard to tell which thought triggered the vision."

"I see."

Hesper groaned loudly. "You don't get to say that with that tone. The God's send the visions when they think it's appropriate. I can't control it. It's possible that it had nothing to do with my thoughts." She turned from him pulling her hair out of its intricate updo the pain of pulled hair singing down her scalp, a welcome distraction from the frustration swelling within her.

Aydan moved away from the door heading to their liquor cabinet, pouring a hefty drink before taking a seat. "You see, here's the thing Hesper. I have been watching you have visions for nearly twenty years at this point. Each time you have a vision it's related to when you think deeply about a certain person, place or thing. Each and every time."

Hesper walked over and poured her own drink. "You can't remember each time it's been so long."

Aydan shrugged. "You believe what you want, my love. I have seen this time and time again. Whatever you thought of right before your vision is what triggered your magical sight of Aurelia being tortured, meaning that person or situation will undoubtedly be involved with it."

Hesper swallowed her drink quickly, holding out the glass for another one. Aydan obliged, striding over and filling it. She sipped this one. "You may have a point. After all I can't think of a specific time where I can disprove your statement. However, I had so much happening inside my mind right before this that I don't know that we could pinpoint it to one specific moment even if I could spout all my thoughts verbatim."

Aydan nodded understandingly, a spark of the positive man she loved so dearly visible through his mask of anger. As she casually braided her hair pinning it up once more, they hashed out the different possible leads, doing their best to consider all the avenues she could remember thinking about. It didn't seem to be productive; it wasn't like an answer came from the give and take. It felt as if no time had passed when the servant knocked twice on the door reminding them of their obligations downstairs.

Hesper regarded Aydan and could still see the tension of anger in his shoulders and his mouth. Yet, regardless of his own emotions directed at her she trusted that he would support her in the confrontation to come.

As they entered the room they noticed that the Palion representative dwarfed a chair that Rana must have procured for him, the look he shot at them as they walked to the thrones radiated pure boredom. The impatient tapping of his foot the only tell of his internal stress.

Hesper straightened her already straight shoulders and turned a glare of pure venom at the interloper, charging the look with the anger she felt at Aydan's doubt, "I see Palion doesn't train its dogs to show actual deference toward royalty. I shall make a note of this custom for when I next visit Harold."

The stranger chuckled darkly as he slowly gained his feet. Hesper realized this was one large male, standing a tad taller than Aydan's 6'2" frame, built of pure muscle making his body overwhelmingly large.

"Interesting you bring up visits to Palion. I am here to

send a warning from King Harold. He has been notified of a coup being planned here in Drakore and tasked our spymaster with verifying the claims. After finding it credible enough they sent me." He bowed low.

Hesper stood in front of her throne using its height to aid in staring down at the man in front of her. "And who are you exactly?" She found her seat first, Aydan deliberately waiting to take his, only after she settled, a game of deference they played with all potential enemies. Never allowing them to know who truly ruled the roost of Drakore.

"My name is simply Ulfur, Beta of the Palion Wolves, Head of the Palace Guard and a trusted member of the Prince's inner circle." He met Hesper's gaze impudently.

Aydan leaned forward, his tone biting, "What proof did your spymaster provide to King Harold?"

"Your military has been conducting some very interesting maneuvers in the neutral lands." Hesper reigned in her shock, only allowing a blink to betray her. The neutral land lay between Drakore and Palion, home to Tixdarr's temple and a small support village. Traditionally Palion cared for these people when needed but Drakore interceded if called upon. Something that hadn't been formally requested in generations.

The lie left her lips before she had fully decided upon it, her brain flipping through the possibilities. "While I appreciate Harold's concern, those maneuvers were pre-planned. We opted to use that land in order to avoid raising the concerns of our people. All is well here and I do hope you convey that back to your King."

Ulfur stared at her hard, his beady eyes seemingly missing nothing, "Right. Do you plan on giving him an explanation on what they were practicing? It may save me a trip, you understand."

She slid him an icy smile. "If he requests an explanation,

feel free to inform him we are merely training a larger than normal recruitment class. Nothing more and nothing less."

Ulfur's answering smile had Hesper grinding her teeth at the predatory nature. "Of course Your Highness. One more thing though. He would love to know why all of the sudden your eldest daughter, by all accounts your prettiest flower, has been removed from the betrothal talks. On top of that we were unable to even locate your youngest, to ensure that she is a suitable match for our Prince."

Anger flashed hot through Hesper, the audacity unthinkable. "Aurelia is alive and well." She ground out, her jaw clenching so hard it sent shooting pain into her neck. "She is getting trained in the Crowlands where she will be safe and sound until the time arrives for her to marry your, *Prince*." She sneered the title not bothering to hide the disgust from her voice. "Cerial has been released from the betrothal due to her finding her Gods chosen Soulbond. Who are we, mere mortals to stop what the Gods deemed important." She threw an icy smile that didn't reach her eyes.

Ulfur showed no outward reaction to any of the news. Managing to infuriate her with how calm he seemed to take it all in. "That would in fact change things. It's rather nice that you had a spare daughter to rely upon. King Harold wants to offer Aurelia a safe place, perhaps when she returns she can come to Palion." Ulfur bowed once more.

"That won't be necessary until the marriage is ready to be solidified. Is there anything else? Perhaps you want to stay. I can have Mistress Rana set up a guest suite for you." She lifted a hand and the housekeeper appeared as if out of nowhere.

Ulfur gave a sneer. "No offense meant to you or yours but you couldn't pay me to stay here. There is too much pointing to an oncoming storm for my liking."

"You are dismissed then. Be sure to notify your King we appreciate the kindness he has shown us." Hesper flicked her wrist dismissively, turning her full attention toward Rana ignoring Ulfur.

Rana leaned forward and whispered, "I was just notified the council members have arrived to debrief the parade."

Hesper sharply inhaled thoughts of the coup swirling in her head, "Is Rayner with them?"

Rana shook her head her forehead puckered in concern. "No ma'am. Should I send the guards out to find him?"

Hesper shook her head looking around the room, noting Ulfur's absence she began to rub her temples hoping to stem the flow of anxiety and stress. "Not yet let me discuss it with Aydan first."

Rana nodded curtsying low before going to let the council members into the chamber.

fourteen

AURELIA

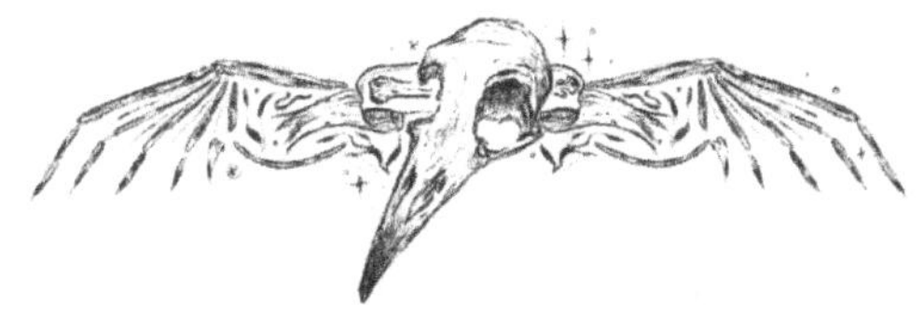

SLANA - OXI - YEAR 7557

The day dawned like many others, bright and cheery the wind at a minimum. Aurelia itched for an adventure instead of endless rounds of Queen lessons. She dressed hurriedly hoping to cross Maledic's path before breakfast and sweet talk him into taking her on an adventure.

She exited her room and yelped in shock as she came into direct contact with a chest. She took a step back and made eye contact with amused brown ones.

"Oh I was just going to look for you. We should go on an adventure, leave this musty manor for the day."

Mal's grin widened. "I had much the same thought Spréach. Let's go saddle the horses and explore the mountain trails."

She nodded looking forward to the fresh air and new sights.

Once they left the manor's immediate grounds following a horse trail, which required them to ride single file. When she spoke she had to do so a bit louder than she would normally in order for Mal to hear her.

"What is it that the great son of Kygoss Corvus wants for his future?"

Mal whipped his head back to meet her gaze expression unreadable. He turned back around causing anxiety butterflies to take flight in her stomach. *Had she touched a nerve? Was something wrong?*

"I want more than anything to live happily in peace. The title of Lord won't offer me that."

Aurelia hummed in her throat considering what to say next. "If you weren't a Lord's son what would you do?"

There was a long pause before he met her gaze again. "You'll laugh."

"No I won't! In fact I'll go first. If I wasn't a Princess I think I would be a teacher. I've always been fascinated by kids, not that I have much experience. Maybe I would teach in a village." she trailed off her mind filled with the reality that her dream would never happen.

Mal had turned once more facing her, letting his horse amble aimlessly forward through the forest. "Seriously? A teacher? That's interesting."

Aurelia flushed. "I mean I may not be the smartest, but given the opportunity I would have done my best."

Mal's face angled in anger, "That's not what I meant. You shouldn't talk about or even think about yourself like that. You are smart, the smartest. I just thought that it sounded interesting and I bet it would be pretty peaceful." His face grew contemplative as the silence stretched. "I would work as a stable hand or perhaps own my own horse farm to teach racing and breed perfect racers."

Aurelia felt a shiver down her spine, as her magic started to boil within her veins. She glanced around looking to see if something would have caused her magical senses to go on alert. Not seeing anything she internally shrugged, "Why horses?" Mal had turned back to help navigate his horse around some fallen logs as he hummed in his throat. "They calm me. My magic has been erratic after I turned sixteen, hard to get it to listen to my demands. Caring for the horses used to be a hated punishment but now it's the task that keeps me in control."

Aurelia nodded understanding issues with power, her own erratic on a good day and completely unreliable on a bad one. As if thinking about it called the problem forth the winds began whipping around them.

She took stock of where they were and realized the horses had come to fork in the trail. One led up the mountain while the other continued on a relatively flat land at the base. As they moved forward a few more feet lightning began to dance down her hair dripping onto the saddle.

"Uh. Mal. Something's wrong."

Mal turned around and his mouth fell open in shock. "What are you feeling? What is triggering the magic?"

"At the moment I am feeling rather panicked. Before that I was calm, happy nothing to be concerned about." She tried to take a deep breath but it got caught in her throat causing her to cough and splutter.

He dismounted, throwing the reins over a low lying branch, rushing to her side. She reached down allowing him to help her, impressed that he didn't shy away from the lightning now dancing down his shoulders where her hair brushed.

"I don't think this has ever happened. It's like something is calling to the power within me." she whispered. She felt a surge within her and water rose from the ground in answer creating tiny rivulets that streamed away. They both stared dumbfounded at the water.

"Have you ever been able to call forth water?"

She swallowed against the thickness in her throat merely able to shake her head as her body began to quake in fear. She let out a whimper as she felt the power flex once more beneath her skin, this time feeling as if it was reaching up and out. Heat followed in its wake pouring out of her skin. Mal's face contorted in pain before he was forced to drop her hands.

"When did this start?" His voice demanded edged in panic.

Gritting her teeth as once more the wind swirled around them whipping hard enough they both braced against a trunk, the horses whinnying.

"It just happened a few steps ago. I started to feel off but I couldn't tell why."

Mal grabbed her hand as small flowers began to sprout at her feet dragging her back the way they had come. After five steps the magic seemed to calm. Her breath started to reach further into her lungs. Mal dragged her another five steps before leaning her now exhausted body against a tree trunk.

"Do you still feel it? The magic?"

Aurelia felt within shaking her head as it became clear that her magic had resumed normal levels of annoyance. "Nothing."

Mal nodded his look of panic receding. She watched as he headed back to the horses they had left tied to branches. *Odd. His magic wasn't affected but hers went insane.*

He released the horses with a smack to their hind ends, sending them back towards the manor. Her mouth fell open.

"What? I could have used the ride!" She felt indignant and a bit frustrated.

"We need the walk. I want to see what else if anything in this mountain sets you off. The horses know the way home."

She rolled her eyes. "Great for the horses. I am not an experiment Maledic Corvus!"

He sent her a devilish smirk. "I know Spréach but I can't help protect you if I don't know what the hell happened. You don't even know what's happening. We'll talk and walk and if you feel your power freak out you'll tell me."

She sighed heavily knowing there wasn't much in the way of options since he already sent the horses back. "Fine." She propped herself off the trunk standing tall glad that it was a relatively warm fall day.

"Since you can't be a teacher, what is it that you want most when you take the throne you're destined for?"

Her mind reeled at the seriousness of the conversation. "I want to take care of whatever people I am ruling. Though my father is convinced it will be the Drakore people. Well he was. I don't know how the oath will work now."

"The oath on your back?" She could hear the curiosity in his voice.

"When I was thirteen I was told by my parents I would inherit the throne here at home. They had finalized an agreement with Harold for Cerial's hand, you see. That night he came into my room and asked me to perform an oath with him for the betterment of our people. It was something his mother did with him when he was named heir." She took a deep breath before modulating her voice in a mocking semblance of her fathers deep baritone. "Will you Aurelia Berrid take it upon yourself to see that the Drakore people live in peace and harmony in the years to come as you grow and come into your own power?"

She chanced a glance at Mal who looked rather stoic. "However, if I am on the Palion throne I won't have power here. So perhaps it becomes null and void?" She hoped it would.

"The marks remain on you though. The dragon wings etched into your back. I saw them at the waterfall. I'm guessing it's a lifetime Oath Aurelia."

She sighed heavily. "Yeah I suppose so. It makes the future very complicated to say the least."

"He should never have put you in that position as your father."

A spike of protectiveness flared within her. "He's also a King Maledic. Those lines are blurry at best. I've gotten used to it. He wouldn't have done it if he didn't see the strength in me. He's the closest thing I have to a best friend."

Mal cocked his head curiously. Aurelia kept quiet for a few more steps her breaths coming in pants at the exertion. She paused on a rock turning to him. "He always goes behind mothers back. She's rather mean at times but he softens the consequences when he can. He also has never treated me any different even though I am currently shiftless. On clear nights when I was much younger he'd even take me flying. I can tell him just about everything as long as mother isn't around."

Mal nodded. "I still think he should never have done that. King or not. You are his daughter. That supersedes everything."

She felt tears gathering at her eyes as she stared at her naive friend. "If only that were true. I hope you have the ability to put your future younglings ahead of everything, but I know that for me the priorities will always be: The Kingdom and then my family. It's how royalty works, Mal." She shrugged defeat echoing through her.

He gripped her chin forcing her eyes up to his. "It doesn't have to. Keep me around and you shall see."

A laugh bubbled up. "You are strong enough to take on centuries of traditions?"

"By myself no. But I will come with you. I will work to make sure you have a strong circle around you for your future and for whatever throne you sit. That way you have many to rely on. You shall see."

She rolled her eyes. "Promises, promises."

He stepped back throwing a wink at her. "Come along Spréach, let's get home before lunch. I'm guessing your magic spike had to do with the mountain peak. We shall talk to father about it some time."

She stood nodding. "Just not today okay?"

He grinned. "Whatever you say."

fifteen

KYGOSS

SLANA - OXI - YEAR 7557

Kygoss' feet were up on the desk, lounging as he perused the cryptic note he had received this morning. His feet hit the floor as a sparrow flew in the open window, shifting in mid air. Dread washed through him as he noted the blue and silver livery on the sparrow shifter's uniform. It was far too soon for Hesper to have recalled them unless something terrible had happened.

Kygoss nodded at the shifter, keeping his face passive, taking the scroll from the shifter's hand. "Sir, the Queen has requested you and her daughter return to the palace as quickly as possible. A note has been sent to the Princess directly." Kygoss dismissed the sparrow shifter with a wave and a nod.

He made his way to the lower level of his manor in search of Maie. He sighed deeply, calm washing through him at the sight of her in her favorite place. Regardless of what may be happening in the world at large his world still turned so long as she thrived. The healing concoction she sang to smelled quite pungent and powerful, "My love."

She turned the smile slipping as the tune she hummed died off, "It's time then huh? Seems rather fast if you were tasked with preparing Aurelia. She promised you two years, much longer than the six months or so that she's been here. I wonder what changed."

He approached her slowly knowing how deeply it hurt to be parted from each other. "Yes, my love. I have to report to the palace by tonight. Perhaps you can come visit soon, but before you do let me make sure everything is safe for your travel. I have a feeling."

She went to embrace him but stopped looking at him quizzically. "A bad feeling?"

"Something very ominous this way comes my love. I am hoping the feeling is stemming from the way Hesper decided to recall us to the palace and when I get there all will be fine but it's better to be safe. I need you and Mal to live through whatever happens."

The color that lighted Maie's heart shaped face slowly sank from sight leaving it hollowed and dark. "He has to let her go. He has to let her leave him behind. That's not going to go well."

"No, it's not."

After kissing his soulbond he shifted into his crow form and headed out the window doing a cursory assessment of the grounds, seeing no evidence of the teens in the forest that surrounded he swooped back into the house through his own open study window. On silent wings he flew through the rooms, stealthily searching for the wayward teens.

He could hear talking emerging from Aurelia's room. The door had been left a jar, enough room that he could ease through it before hopping into the rafters. He sent a thought of thanks to his long dead father, for the well constructed manor ensuring that avian shifters would have roosts no matter the room they found themself. The exposed rafters beams while providing those perfect roosts also made spying on his teenage charges a bit easier.

Kygoss hopped forward peering down his crow eyes a bit sharper than his mortal ones. Aurelia paced, Kygoss could feel her power spiking inside her skin, yet the physical evidence of her power spikes were now absent. Her work with Mal had gone far in giving her control but she still brimmed with power, more so than he sensed in all but her parents. Mal sprawled out on his bed, laying on his stomach picking at the covers with his free hand while the other held his chin up. His eyes however were tracking Aurelia's every movement.

Kygoss tuned into their conversation, a bit shocked at how far they had developed in such a small amount of time.

"Mal, if I go back I will just be locked back up in that palace with only small bouts of time in the palace gardens. From the sound of her note I won't even be allowed to do rides anymore. I can't do that. I can't just forget what freedom tastes like. Plus what about you! I have to leave you behind. You're my best friend. Cerial and I weren't even on talking terms when I left." Aurelia paced as she ran her fingers through her raven black locks.

"I can promise you we will see each other again." Maledic sounded almost bored as he stated what he knew to be obvious.

She huffed and Kygoss caught the eye roll. "You keep saying that. But you can't see the future can you?"

Maledic threw her a grin which Kygoss knew spelled trouble on the horizon. "Not really but I can tell you for certain I won't let anything stand in the way of seeing you again."

Aurelia halted and faced him, her head cocked as if studying his expression and dissecting his words. "What are you planning, Mal?"

"Simply that I will see you again."

"What will you do if my mother says no? Or if your father says no?"

"I will remind them that I am an adult now and make my own choices." Kygoss watched as Mal sat up folding his long legs gracefully under him as he got near the edge, nearer to her.

Mal held out his hands and Aurelia slid hers into his. "I promise I will be there when you need me. I am but a few wing beats away and while you are still grounded," Mal tweaked her nose causing a giggle "I will fly to you to aid in entertainment. Even if I have to stand up to our parents."

She sucked in a breath. "What if she ships me to Palion without giving me enough time to tell you. It could be a trap."

"Remember what you told my father? You have your own conditions for the marriage. Stick to that and my father will send word to me if you are sent away. I will just fly to Palion instead of the palace. Easy solution."

Aurelia let out a deep breath. "I don't want the Palion side of things to get in the way. I am scared I will truly have no power there."

"Why is that? We have learned Queen's get their own courts and advisors. I shall be yours. I shall advise you on Drakore. Perhaps I'll be your spymaster as my father is to your parents. We will find a way to stay friends no matter the distance and I won't let you be alone."

Aurelia threw her arms around Mal's neck. As Mal's face went over her shoulder he brought his gaze up and met Kygoss' stare. Kygoss could see the challenge gleaming there. It was a promise to Aurelia and a gauntlet thrown at Kygoss and the Queen. Kygoss however just nodded confirmation to his son and hopped out of the room as silently as he had entered it.

He shifted back into his mortal shell and waited in the hall giving them a few more minutes to plan and scheme on how they would stay friends despite all the odds that would be thrown into their path.

Eventually he knocked on the door, Aurelia opened it, her chin held a stubborn tilt and her eyes were red rimmed betraying her emotions. "It's time, Short Stack. Grab the important things and Auntie Maie will send the rest of the stuff up to the palace later."

Aurelia merely nodded and grabbed a bag that sat next to the door. She didn't look back into the room, instead forging ahead toward the stables.

Kygoss glanced into Mal's room and saw him curled around a pillow, a sadness deep and dark emanating from him. Kygoss felt torn for the first time in a long time between duty and what he knew would be best for those he loved the most. He spoke to the prone form, "Mal, I will do what I can to protect her and make sure you are not separated for too long. While I am gone you need to protect these lands and your mother for me while I protect Aurelia."

Kygoss turned and trudged to the stables finding Aurelia already mounted, her face a mask of anger and sadness as she watched the trees surrounding the house. Once more it threw him with how much control she had managed to learn in such a short amount of time.

Kygoss mounted in silence and watched as she led him down the path they had come in on. A deep sense of foreboding and alarm filled him. He scanned the trees and sky but saw nothing but the back of Aurelia's head. *Would he ever see this version of the children again, where they were so full of fun and joy?* He could feel a change from deep within him radiating through the land, but what could be causing it? His deepest darkest desire was to turn the horses back around and protect Aurelia within Slana. Mal would be happy, Aurelia would be happy but her parents wouldn't. He had a job to do and his friends were counting on him, without proof he risked the royals accusing him of kidnapping their youngest daughter. He shook his head feeling lost and disconnected from the Gods for the first time in his nearly forty years of life.

sixteen

QUEEN HESPER

DRAKORE - OXI - YEAR 7557

> Ancient magic dwells within Slana, incapable for any one being to understand. Yet if a creature finds themselves in need they will be taken care of. Help will always be there deep within the Falrath range for those in need, they must only search for it. Stories swirl over what form the magic actually takes, each more ridiculous than the last.
>
> ~ Slana Archives

She tried, she really did, to wait in order to give Kygoss time to settle in from his journey back from Slana. Yet there had been another Palion representative just today, repeating the ominous words from Ulfur. Her dress felt tighter, her breath shallow incapable of reaching the entirety of her lungs. Aydan had left her to go deal with their wayward eldest who had decided to now be a rebel. A pain began to grow behind her eyes as her thoughts grew to encompass everything that had begun to unravel.

Her mind raced, unable to keep up with the various possibilities that may occur if Drakore's military were really running operations in the neutral lands. It threatened their kingdom's peace with Palion, it also indicated that unrest really was occurring within her kingdom. Right under her nose, despite the work that they did for her people. The person she had given the power of General appeared to be nothing more than a puppet. Incapable of actually swaying any of the military.

Her mind raced with possibilities ranging from the disastrous to the innocent, regardless of what she did to control the terrors her mind created she couldn't look at the situation logically. Ever since Rana had told her that Kygoss had returned home the itch beneath her skin grew. An hour had passed and the irritation under her skin, the one she couldn't seem to reach had become unbearable.

Hesper's long legs ate up the distance between the throne room and the spiral staircase leading to Kygoss' lonely study. The sound of paper rustling, and a low murmured muttering greeted her before she opened the door.

"Kygoss. What is happening in this kingdom? What is coming?" Desperation broke through her carefully constructed Queenly mask despite her attempts to harness it.

Kygoss stopped rifling through the papers that had been stacked haphazardly on his desk, his skin paling as he registered the tenor of her voice. "What did you see Hesper? Why is it you have recalled us?"

Her head buzzed, the importance of knowledge temporarily outweighing the terrors that had occurred within her mind. "What is that Kygoss?" Her finger trembled as it pointed towards the piles of papers strewn across his desk. "You told me reports would come to you in Slana."

"They did."

She glared at him, paranoia getting the better of her, "Then why is there a ridiculous amount of papers piled here, there and everywhere. What are they reporting? What is happening?" The shrillness echoed through her own head, as panic set into her mind. Her magic as if sensing her lack of control spiked under her skin, an echoing bolt of lightning cracking across the clear afternoon sky. Clouds soon followed thunder rolling, her grip on everything unraveling before her.

"HESPERDAE!" Kygoss shouted, breaking her free of her downward spiral. In a calmer but no less firm voice he demanded, "Enough! Sit down." He gestured rather violently at his door and with his grasp of wind powers he slammed the door shut.

Shock became her guiding force. Shock at his tone, rather than the direct order, had her sinking into the chair. Grabbing the pillow from the chair next to it she buried her face and screamed, releasing the tight control she had maintained on her emotions and magic. The smell of must suffocating her, she shoved aside the disgust, as she focused on releasing her built up emotions. Lightning continued to strike outside, thunder rolling reflecting the inner turmoil that writhed within marring the once beautiful winter day.

As her outburst dried up she slowly dropped the pillow into her lap dragging her eyes to meet Kygoss' gaze. He had swept the majority of the odds and ends paper scraps out of sight, crossed his hands over his belly staring at her waiting for her to speak. She had been in many standoffs with him throughout the years and knew he had far more patience than she did.

"A lot has happened. I have had a vision, a terrible terrible vision and we had a few visits from representatives of Palion.

The vision so unspeakably horrible I had to bring her home, so Aydan can fly her to safety if necessary. You know as well as I that crows can't carry a passenger." She glanced at Kygoss and saw he had donned a neutral mask, one that even she couldn't read.

She pushed on, "Palion believes a coup is in the works and their evidence is rather damning. Rayner is running mysterious operations in the neutral lands. He disappeared after the festival last month. Everything I have seems to be unraveling." she inwardly groaned at her inability to control the crack in her voice. The admission of weakness tasting of ash in her mouth.

"Have you sent a patrol to find Rayner?"

She rolled her shoulder the tension building again. "I can't know which guards are on my side and which are on his. How do I send someone out without knowing where their loyalties lie? I am hoping that my spymaster may have an idea on where he would hide so I can spook him out before he realizes I am on to him. Though it's possible he's already figured it out."

She met Kygoss' gaze and caught one of his few tells. He had shifted his eyes to the pile of papers and back to her. The movement subtle, only his eyes but after the length of time they had known each other secrets were nearly impossible. "Kygoss. What is it?"

"Palion may be correct. I have been getting whispers all fall." he openly flinched at his own admission knowing he should have told her long ago.

Her blood ran cold. "Whispers of what exactly?"

"The military of Drakore is discontent." He raised a hand stalling her immediate flood of words, "It's important to note that this happens every few years. Never before have we taken the rumor seriously, nor has there ever been a need for a strong response to the gossip. I don't understand what would have changed between this instance and the last time it happened."

"Perhaps it's time we ask the man who runs the military. Potentially he can explain the difference or give us a reason to not believe in the rumors." She rubbed at her temples the beginning of a deep ache taking hold in the depths of her skull. "If we have Rayner locked away it's reasonable to believe that the rest of the military will calm down."

Kygoss nodded slowly. "I agree but it will be difficult to find him. I shall exercise my network and see if we can flush him out. However, if he is at all suspicious he will undoubtedly take refuge in the neutral lands until it's time for his plan."

Hesper continued to rub her temples, "So the next thing we need is his timeline *if* it's even him. Right."

She met Kygoss' gaze, "how did Aurelia do out there?"

"She learned a lot." Hesper caught an odd smile of pride emanating from her friend, "I partnered her with Mal and they have become fast friends. He took charge in teaching her control over her powers. The amount of magic dwelling beneath her skin is astonishing. I informed her of all the relative information on Palion I have, but I didn't really have time to show her how to use it to her advantage. If we can, she should finish her training out there. She needs to learn self defense, and the finer details of ruling." Kygoss took a breath causing Hesper to bite her lip as her anxiety spiked. "You do know that those in Slana have other ways of protecting her if it came to it. She need not be flown anywhere. There is a lot of old magic, magic you yourself have intimate knowledge of."

Hesper sat up and thought over Kygoss' words. "Aydan and I would rather not rely on something ancient and unproven. As to her training, we shall consider the possibilities and make a decision when life resumes its normal patterns." She hesitated, "Though I appreciate your opinion."

Kygoss cocked his head, "I am just here to help when she's on the precipice of a teenage meltdown, but when all is well my thoughts are dismissed. Good to know." He gestured at the door removing the air sealing it shut. He stood leaning against the desk. "I will have an answer to where Rayner is later today, Your Majesty. I shall send a coded message your way once the knowledge is secured."

Hesper stood awkwardly, unaware how exactly she had misstepped but the coldness emanating off of Kygoss was obvious. She walked slowly, and as she reached the door she glanced back at Kygoss. "Kygi?" He shot her a look of pure anger. "What else can I do for you, Your Majesty?"

"It's fine." Her mind reeled, not understanding his emotions, meekness filling her. She turned away, her feelings in turmoil. She slowly made her way down the spiral stairs running through the entire interaction with Kygoss, trying to find where it all went sideways.

Seventeen

AURELIA

DRAKORE - OXI - YEAR 7557

The idea of joining Faziel and Cerial somewhere in the palace, forced to endure a stuffy lesson without Mal left her feeling numb. Her emotional overload required time to find calmness once more. The concept she may have to manage another's emotions left her nauseated.

She shooed away the stable hands, opting to spend her time brushing the horses and cleaning tack that they used on their journey from Slana. Undoubtedly it was an occupation her parents would balk at, considering her status, while they wanted her to carry her bags, dirty jobs were to be avoided when possible. Mal had used this particular chore to find his inner peace, perhaps it would help her. The monotony of brushing caused her to access a meditative state which did indeed help to better control the flood of feelings that swelled within. It also had the unique benefit of helping her keep Mal with her despite the physical distance.

Maledic presented an entire tangle of emotions and feelings all by himself. She did not understand their sudden and complete friendship. Words weren't even needed in the beginning, a feeling of safety had filled her when he had landed on her saddle. The feeling had been so complete that she had opted to trust it throughout the last six months. A decision she had yet to regret at least until now, when she missed him as though she had left behind a piece of her.

The slamming of the stable door broke her reverie, a man filled the doorway, a rather large male. His entire stature screamed that he wasn't from this kingdom, that he was different. The hair on the back of her neck rose as she assessed him, peering around the horse, the brush in her hand going limp. Instead of wiry muscles and a lean frame he presented the exact opposite. Bulging muscles filled a broad frame, his movement closer to the ground and lumbering where men she was familiar with seemed to glide. A bubbling presence gurgled within her mind, as it floated through her the sensation of pops, more surprising than painful as they burst. This unrecognizable magic spoke deep within her mind, telling her that this man she stared at belonged to the wolves of Palion. She blinked and dug around her own mind searching for how she had known and where the bubbling magic had come from but no answers appeared.

She figured he hadn't seen her, after all she stood behind a horse. Yet he paused outside the stall, returning her gaze. "You from here?" His voice rough and gravely. Refusing to be intimidated however big he was she squared her shoulders and held his gaze.

"Yes."

"I would run if I were you. It's about to get bloody around these parts. A coup is in progress and the idiots in charge will not stay in power for much longer. They won't listen to my King." He shrugged his beefy shoulders and gave her a once over. "You are too small for them to listen to, get out while you can Pipsqueak." He stomped off toward his horse and valet that were waiting on the far end of the stables as Aurelia gaped in disbelief.

It took a few minutes for her brain to catch up with what the strange man actually said. She needed to tell someone, but who. Who would believe her? Who would help her? Her first instinct screamed to find Mal, get his advice and come up with a plan together. She couldn't wait for his response though it would take time, time she didn't think she had.

Her next instinct was to find Kygoss. Perhaps he could find a way to get word to Slana, or explain to her what could be happening. She raced through the courtyard and into the palace heading straight for Kygoss' study. It took a few minutes the sound of her feet pounding on the stone before she reached the staircase. Round and round she went up to the top, her pace slowing as her side began to ache a stitch starting to burn. She looked at the closed door any hopes she had that he would hold answers falling.

She couldn't help herself, her knocking, echoing across the empty corridor. She held her breath, hope flaring. Yet her chest began to burn aching for a new breath before she accepted he wouldn't be the answer she needed today.

She sat on the top step breathing deep debating where to go next. Her parents would seem like the obvious answer. Her father favored her more often than not but unfortunately finding him alone was nigh on impossible these days. Her mother would insist that Aurelia keep to her lane, not worrying about things above her station. She knew her father well enough that he would grudgingly agree, unwilling to argue. He would battle for Aurelia but those happened behind closed doors when she wasn't around to witness it.

She forced a deep breath in. Her last hope in Drakore rested with Cerial. She looked down the tower staircase dreading the run from here to the temple where Cerial took private lessons for her own ascension. She stood wrapping her arms around her middle holding in the terror that rested on the edges of her mind. She closed her eyes and took another deep breath centering herself as she squeezed her sides.

She released her held breath slowly and reminded herself that Cerial would listen. They had always been close growing up and in the face of danger that would matter more than whatever Cerial currently juggled.

She ran down the stairs heading back out to the courtyard and the large imposing temple that sat opposite the palace. She fumbled against the handle of the imposing door. It took a few agonizing seconds of pushing for there to be a slight budge, emitting a loud groan. Finally it opened enough for her to squeeze her tiny body through. She knew where the private lessons were held, ignoring the looks of confusion she harnessed what energy existed within herself and ran up the stairs heading for the correct room.

Door after door flew by and she skidded to a halt sending a prayer up to Tiva that Cerial was where she was supposed to be for once. She opened up the door and blew out a breath of relief. In the front of the room Cerial sat at a desk copying down notes, with an Acolyte instructor at the head of the room. Both of them turned to stare at the mussed Aurelia, mouths wide in shock.

Aurelia turned to the Acolyte, the lie ready on her lips, "You're needed by the Oba miss."

The Acolyte blanched fear and shock evident on her face. She bowed exiting swiftly. Aurelia rushed to Cerial's side, kneeling next to her speaking quickly. "Cerial I don't know how much time we have. I need you to come with me so much has happened and I need to talk to you. Palion wolves have been here, he threatened us, the Berrids, Drakore. We need to figure everything out."

Alarm bells began to ring inside her skull as Cerial's face remained impartial, no hint of surprise evident. Aurelia watched as her sister's eyes hardened and the fakest smile she had seen displayed became present on her face. Cerial grabbed Aurelia's hands and squeezed, hard enough that Aurelia winced and tried her best to tug them free. Her voice sounded devoid of emotion, "It's fine Lia. We will be just fine. Who told you this terrible rumor?"

Desperation to get free swelled in Aurelia's mind, her magic seeking a way to force Cerial to release her hands. Another lie slipped past Aurelia's lips before she even realized she had decided to do so. "A stable hand as I brushed the horses, we only just got back."

Cerial smiled wider, more genuine than before, releasing Aurelias hands as she ruffled Aurelias hair, reminiscent of so many times in the past. "Lia. I don't know what they taught you in the backwater slums of Slana but you can't trust just everyone. Go on back to the palace and wash up you smell of the road." Cerial's nose wrinkled in disgust.

Aurelia stood slowly, her mind reeling at the woman who sat in front of her. The sister she knew and loved appeared to be gone, replaced by a cold and calculating stranger. Aurelia gave her a half smile, nodding. "I.. I am sorry for interrupting Cerial. I will clean up and that will make me feel better, I am sure."

Cerial nodded at her, but before Aurelia made it to the door Cerial's lilting voice filled her ears once more, "Never fear Lia. If you come across any other disturbing rumors be sure to come tell me. I would be honored to explain the truth to you."

Aurelia didn't look at her, merely nodded as she pulled the door open. A new plan forming in her mind as she made her way to the palace. Her first stop was her rooms, where she quickly wrote a note to the one person she had no reservations about.

Somethings wrong here. I will do my best to

come back to where it's safe. Keep Slana
safe.

She signed it with a feather embedded with an A.

Using her wind magic she swirled the note up, the magic ensured that it would be deposited in Mal's spindly fingers and no one else's.

She changed into her darkest clothing and made her way down the hall to the one place she might be able to glean any semblance of true information. Her parents' joint study the one place where all important decisions were made between them before it became law.

She knew the room well and tended to as a small child hide in the many cupboards that bordered the room. Her increase of height made that option untenable. However a tall cabinet that held various robes of state caught her eye, a perfect place, she could settle in for hours waiting for the various arguments that were sure to ensue.

eighteen

QUEEN HESPER

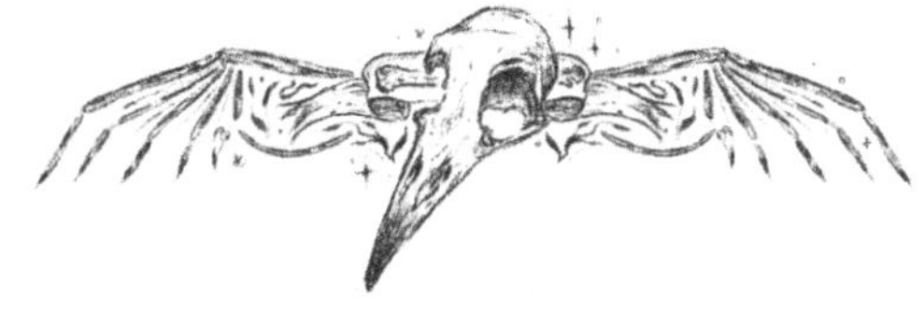

DRAKORE - OXI - YEAR 7557

Hesper spent most of the night tossing and turning, before deciding the time had come to give up pretending. After dressing in a simple gown, she padded barefoot into their study using a candle to illuminate her way. She set the flickering light down gently on the desk before pacing, wringing her hands. As she walked through the room she took deep breaths rolling her shoulders and shaking out her limbs, doing her best to reign in the panic and fear that beckoned her into the darkness. She jumped a bit as Aydan eased the door open and slipped inside the planes of his face illuminated by his own candle.

Air expelled from her in a rush as she shook her head sadly, "I tried to let you sleep love."

Aydan threw a cocky grin at her, "like I could sleep without your warmth cozied up beside me. Plus you need me here. We will shove all our current issues to the side and focus right now on how to survive."

She sent him a small smile. "Setting aside has never been

something either of us is very good at. Did you see Kygoss' message last night?"

Aydan shook his head.

"He claims Rayner is most likely stationed in the neutral lands, near the temple village. He suspects that Rayner is in his shifted form, making it nearly impossible to truly locate him." She rubbed her temples and stared into the darkness.

She turned to face him suddenly, "Should we just release her to them? Perhaps they are right. Perhaps Palion can keep Aurelia safe while we figure out Rayner's nonsense. Harold may even take Cerial behind his gates if we grovel."

Aydan shook his head, "You know as well as I do we can't trust Harold to keep his word while we are distracted. Once our backs are turned I could see him marrying Lucian and Aurelia before she is truly ready."

He took Hesper's hand and led her to the wall behind their desk, where a large map of the lands of Palion and Drakore bordered the edges of Dodsfell hung. He pulled over the candle sticks illuminating more of the map.

He pointed toward the temple and the neutral lands and traced the path that would lead them into Drakore. "If he is truly stationing all those working for him in the neutral lands it will take at least a day for them to reach our palace if they decide to move now. If he was in any way tipped off by Kygoss' search it's likely he's moving on the sooner side."

Hesper nodded heat and rage flooding up her cheeks. She couldn't stand the idea of waiting for him to strike. "Do we sit and wait or do we take the fight to him?"

"Are you suggesting we release her?" incredulity filled Aydan.

"Aydan, it's written that she will be released if Drakore is in danger." Hesper stomped her foot indignantly.

"Hesper. I know you see it as in danger, but this isn't what the Gods were talking about and I think that you know that deep down. We must instead rely upon our mortal fighters. I will approach the head of the palace guard and give him the power to order fighters out. As for other options, you won't enjoy my next idea."

Hesper took a few steps away from him knocking into the cupboard where they kept cloaks of state. Fear ricocheted around her, "Aydan it won't work and you know that."

"I know that you need to try, not just for me but for our people and our children. You need to see how you can better aim the visions. Let's try." He took a few steps towards her.

Hesper shook her head taking a few more steps backward, "Do you think Darius is working with him? Perhaps we should just talk to Darius."

Aydan closed the distance quickly grabbing her hands staring deep into her eyes. "What are you scared of? Why is the idea of finding the truth through vision so terrifying? You may be able to tell us what is happening, or we are no worse off than where we are now. There is no harm." She could feel his increase of pressure despite her body flashing hot and cold.

"Aydan." His name came out on a whine. "I may see the worst things possible, things that I can't unsee. Things that will never be able to be erased." She turned away from him, throwing herself onto the study couch. She curled into a ball pulling her limbs in close trying to hide within herself.

"Hesp you need to do this. Close your eyes, I will be right next to you the entire time." He climbed behind her wrapping his body around her back, ensuring that she could feel him.

Hesper closed her eyes, taking a deep sigh. Her body growing heavy, relaxing. Aydan whispered into her ear, his voice low. "Focus on Rayner, Hesper. What is his future, who is involved? When will he make his move?" He murmured the questions on repeat continually while her mind began to whirl.

Her mind went blank and darkness covered all thought,

laying atop her mind like a heavy blanket. Suddenly with little warning images began to fly past her mind's eye. They flipped through at such a high rate of speed it was remarkable she was able to discern any of them clearly.

Darius stood tall, wings black as night over a pile of bodies within the dungeons of her palace, a sickening smile carved into his face. An older Faziel flapped through the sky, her face shining with a smile. Hesper's own necklace clutched in the hands of a stranger. Cerial speaking with Rayner in a darkened alley Darius at her side. Darius thrusting a dagger through Rayners neck. The crumpled forms of Cerial and Aydan. The people of Drakore, within the city the once bustling streets now silent.

As the magic released her another image shuttered past clear and defined. The last image hardened her resolve, thrusting her toward her future with a precision that wiped away her fears and insecurities.

She glanced at Aydan, determination burning in her eyes. "It isn't something we can stop. We can however make it more difficult for them afterwards. We can make them regret choosing the side of pain." An unspoken understanding passed between them, one born from years of marriage and ruling a kingdom.

The blood drained from Aydan's face as he nodded slowly, a seed of determination taking root within his own eyes. "We can make them pay, my love. We will alert only those who can aid us and won't betray what time we have left. Kygoss will need to know, we will need to entrust the girls to his care. We can also remove all documents and valuables to the safe houses. Anything we want the girls to have in future."

Hesper nodded a sadness in her heart, Cerial played a part in this somehow. She wasn't sure to what extent but it became clear she wouldn't be the inheritor of the Drakore crown. She reached into the cupboard without looking, feeling around to get a robe, covering up her nightgown. Once it was donned she blew a kiss at her husband heading toward Kygoss' room to begin to make the necessary changes. She would try her best to prepare the girls but the last image glared within her mind highlighting just how little time they all had.

nineteen

QUEEN HESPER

DRAKORE - TIX - YEAR 7557

Time continued to tread ever forward leaving Hesper grateful for that final vision. It had left her just enough information to create her plan and focus her energy productively. It aided her in narrowing her goals from saving everyone to ensuring the integrity of the kingdom. She and Aydan took the opportunity to gather all the crown jewels and family heirlooms they could sneak away, reliant on Kygoss' help to utilize the safe houses he had created throughout Drakore.

Those deemed trustworthy, the ones that had stood strong with the Berrids from the beginning, were warned of the coup and when possible snuck out of Drakore's borders toward Palion in the hopes that Harold would open his gates to those in need. Hesper had even approached the Oba of Tiva's temple, Aewenna hoping that the temple could grant sanctuary for those in need in case the Berrid rule fell. Everything Hesper could hope to accomplish she had, even with as little time as she had.

Between Kygoss, Aydan and herself they created a simple

plan to win the day. Hesper would distract, using her power to kill as many as she could before they breached the castle. If she fell in the process the crown would still be safe in Aydan's hands. Aydan held a different task, focused on sneaking away their heirs, once they were safe he would return and secure his place as King, all to ensure that the Great Sky Power stayed within his family line. His wings were better up to the task as they took the form of the legendary dragon.

The girls had been informed that Aydan would come to fetch them in the case of an emergency. In an effort to keep them calm when the time came. Kygoss held the job of ensuring Faziel was safe, using back corridors to shield her until it could be considered safe.

She had spent the last hour selecting her armor, that of a true Queen. Queens waged wars with words and magic, the uses of blades often deemed too violent for the one entrusted with keeping the kingdom grounded in peace and kindness. She stared out the window and watched as the sun slipped lower in the sky, the blue so reminiscent of the girl's eyes swept through with a purple and then pink. The closer the colors were to the sun as it shifted lower the more reds and oranges were present. Gratefulness surged within her that the Gods had made this sunset so gorgeous.

As the sun lowered further she donned her best gown, a glorious golden color, high necked with crystals and beads cascading down making it almost unreasonably heavy while also being impossibly regal. Perhaps it would make those who had rebelled rethink their choices, turning on the Gods chosen rulers as they had. She reached into her jewelry case, oddly sparse for the first time since she inherited it from Aydan's mother. She had chosen the crown for this evening carefully, one that wouldn't make a huge difference to the kingdom if it went missing. A favorite for her, it felt the most representative of the land that she loved even if it was not a traditional regalia of Drakore. The traditional crown with the citrine crystals arrayed in honor of the long lost sun god would have complemented her gown perfectly. That crown had been stashed for their heir's future.

Instead she wore a golden crown, dragon wings creating the silhouette of the crown itself, with jewels encrusting the dragon scales. The jeweled scales created glimmers throughout the room as the dying sun's rays hit the gems just right. In order to save as much as she could of the legacy of the Berrid family she had opted to keep the rest of the jewels at a minimum the risk that what she wore would be stolen. Her fingers only held the ring Aydan gave her on their marriage day. A delicate wire braided ring with no end and no beginning. The one she cherished most.

Aydan walked into their rooms and gaped. "My, my, the most beautiful woman in the world and she chose me. I shall never understand why." The smell of him as he got closer had her blood pumping faster, a need filling her. A need that would have to go unanswered the time to move swiftly approaching.

Instead she shot him a smile, stepping around him careful to keep an arm's length between them. "No, you stay over there mister. There isn't much time and you know that."

Aydan returned her smile, a shade sadder than usual perhaps but he at least was trying to act as normal. "Just one kiss my love. Just one. Then when we win the day I shall have my reward."

She found herself chuckling despite the butterflies beating a war drum that echoed through her body. Her hands trembled a bit as she lowered them allowing him closer, her heartbeat getting louder filling her ears. "One." It came out breathy as emotions clawed their way up her throat.

Aydan wrapped her in his arms, his eyes seeming to study every aspect of her face, carefully committing it to memory.

Slowly taking his time, he lowered his lips to hers. The spark, as alive as it had been all those years ago, sang through her, just as it had the first time they had kissed. She nipped at his lower lip and on a chuckle he let her in, their tongues toying with each other.

She broke the kiss, her breath coming in short bursts as she looked up at him. His eyes were half lidded and his face held the desire that she could feel swamping her. He still held her close, his hands roaming up her back, leaning in to take another kiss, she gently pulled back putting her finger against his lips, whispering. "Only one, remember?

He gently bit her finger and then kissed the digit removing any pain left behind. "Yes, yes." He released her.

She stepped away from him, a coldness sweeping in banishing the heat he had brought to her, and did a small twirl. "What do you think? Regal enough?" Sadness filled her the farther she got from him. It caused her voice to roughen but she managed to clamp down on the tears.

"My love you are the embodiment of the crown. Just remember whatever happens I won't be far behind." She smiled at him, her jaw clenching with the effort at keeping the tears at bay.

"I shall be waiting, my love." The rawness of her voice made even her soul feel like it was ripping in half.

She stepped to the door and blew him a kiss before stepping out of the room and exhaling a deep breath.

She reached inside, focusing not on the deep well of sadness that threatened to overwhelm her, instead opting to focus on the anger that roared within. It took all the mental fortitude she possessed to move away from the door that held her beloved, or away from her children all tucked tidily away in their beds. Her face hardened into the imperial mask she wore only during the highest of ceremonies. The sun had all but disappeared and with its absence the warmth had fled. If she failed it would be up to Aydan to take the reins and stop them using the Great Sky Power, once the children were safely spirited away.

The Great Hall flickered in the candlelight of sconces spread throughout the entryway, an eerie ambiance in which the coming bloodbath would occur. Hesper paced, waiting for a sound to announce their arrival, the scrap of boots, indolent speech of the unsuspecting but no sound occurred. Her skin itched, the tiny hairs on the back of her neck standing at alert. Her magic would be better suited if she could be aware of them before they came inside. That way she didn't have to risk harming any innocents inside the palace.

Her plans flew apart as the doors opened without sound, only a gust of wind announcing the entry of the man they had all suspected, The General Rayner Svenston. Ranged behind him were various members of the Drakore guard and most surprisingly Darius stood just behind his father looking ashamedly at the floor. Appearing as if he wanted to be swallowed up by the ground beneath him.

Hesper folded her hands in front of her and stared Rayner in the eyes. She dug out her most imperious voice, the one reserved for the most recalcitrant courtiers, "What's the explanation of this? It's a little late for a formal visit. I am afraid I don't have any of the guest suites set up for you or yours."

She watched as the expression on the General's face flitted between shock and anger. "I am here to relieve you of duty."

Hesper laughed harsh and sharp, "Last I checked that position is beyond you, in both wit and charm."

Rayner growled in anger, pulling a satisfied smirk from Hesper. "Proof right there." She turned to the men gathered around Rayner, "It seems you have all gone to such trouble for no reason. As the door is still standing open I suggest you all turn and leave." She released a bit of her power letting lightning to strike just outside. Aiming blind made this much more difficult than originally planned, thunder rolled shaking the palace windows.

"That wasn't an offer Hesper. It's an order." The General unsheathed his sword. "You seem to believe you can parent better than anyone, yet we all know differently. You had no right to continually steal children from those you deemed lesser. You stole my son. I hear you also stole another little girl just this past year."

Hesper feigned surprise. "Rayner you must work on the way you issue orders if you fully intend to do what you seem to be after, it most decidedly seemed to be a mere suggestion. Honestly you need more power to your words." She took half a step toward him fully opening her mental shields and unleashing the power within herself, "In regards to Darius, had I not interceded he wouldn't be here today. If anything I saved him, solidifying his ability to turn on my family it appears. I found out not too long ago something very interesting about your son. Did you know he's found his soul-bond?" Her voice became colder, if she had been blessed with the power of ice she didn't doubt that ice would have begun to gather.

Rayner growled. "Darius doesn't believe in that. He's here for me, to support my rule on the throne."

Hesper nodded in understanding, "That is disappointing. I am sure Cerial would be heartbroken to hear it." She stared hard at Darius noting the flush of embarrassment or perhaps shame.

Hesper took another deep breath fully releasing her iron grasp on the storm-fueled powers, aiming the target for her unruly lightning to be outside the palace doors. Her visual field was obstructed so she relied heavily on her memory on the courtyard and the haphazard nature of lightning. The power hummed and simmered up her arms. She could feel it taking hold of her entire being as she loosed it onto the men standing outside. The guards began to scream as she took out more and more of them, the sky lighting up to a gray smoking fog as the wooden structures around the palace entrance took hits intended for the guards.

A voice rippled within her, speaking doubt into her mind. Someone had alerted Rayner and his leaders that it would be safer from inside the palace. It became clear to her amidst the cracking of lightning how her end would come.

Rayner's footsteps were silent on the stone floor, she watched him approach as if from a different body, her attention focused solely on releasing her power as steadily as she could. His face a mask of fury and satisfaction. Hesper didn't have the mental attention to really tense at the entrance of the blade as he neared, yet its painless slide through her gown and flesh shocked her. The crystals rubbed against the metal creating a clanging that echoed through the entry hall. There had been an expectation of pain yet, as the blood oozed out around the blade no great pain overwhelmed her senses. Fearing what else could be done to her she forced the last bit of magical strength into a volley of lightning, screams and the smell of burning flesh wafting through the open door.

She coughed, tasting copper and feeling a cold dribble of blood slide down from her lips. The Great Sky Power rushed through her veins filling her with the feeling of fire, "Kill me if you must, but I know what happens in the future. You forget General, I can see what you cannot." Another cough ripped through her despite the power trying to heal her, more blood bubbling up, "You will never be King."

A moist slurping filled the air as the blade exited her abdomen, pain flooding the hole as blood began to pour from her. Her hands dropped of their own volition attempting to stem the flow, protecting the precious organs laying within. She groaned as her knees wobbled. She turned from Rayner looking at Darius, "Honor the bond with Cerial. Use whatever emotions you have for her for the betterment of our kingdom."

She had barely gotten the words out when the blade crushed more gems on her gown forcing its way into her chest, she could feel the cold metal as it slid between her ribs slicing away at vital pathways. The floor seemed to be coming closer at an alarming rate as Rayner leveraged his sword out of her. The result more damage than even the Great Sky Power could hope to heal.

The world became an odd sensation of flashing scenes, her body crashed to the floor the impact causing more blood to gush forth. She suddenly saw Rayner standing over her, his boots stained with her blood. His face came ever closer, his putrid breath clogging her nose, "You can't see your own future Hesper even I know that."

She coughed again, the blood bubbling out of all the holes that now riddled her body. She took twisted pleasure as the blood droplets seemed to land upon his face. She plastered a smile on her own, she wasn't able to track his face but she could feel his eyes still on her. "I wasn't looking at my future Rayner," more blood dribbled from her mouth. "I was looking at yours." As if the Gods granted her one more small parting gift her eyes were able to focus fully on his face as her words sank in. Horror filled it.

He turned away without another word and Hesper's world became one of sensation. The sounds of boots filing down the hall, some stopping undoubtedly taking in her dying body. The smell of blood, mud and death filled her nose as her eyelids grew heavy. *Aydan would stop them. He had to.*

Her mind filled with images of her past, undoubtedly sent by the Gods to comfort her in her final moments. The first sight of Aydan, awkward as he had been as a young prince still learning his duties. The lace wonder of a dress she had gotten to wear when they wed. The stressful scary process that had been the Inheritance Rite. The gifting of the Great Sky Power blessing their rule of Drakore. The final images were of her daughters freshly wrapped up as newborns. There had been moments in the beginning she had thought it possible to be the mother they needed. As they aged it became obvious that wasn't to be.

Her memory laced visions were disrupted by a throat clearing, "Hesper, I am so sorry. I didn't want you to die, you were always so kind to me."

Her eyes fluttered and she realized Darius sat next to her head whispering fervently into her ear. She vaguely felt his hand at her shoulder and using more mental effort than should be needed she raised her hand to cover his, consoling him one last time.

"It's fine, take care of my girls Darius."

He nodded slowly. The world beginning to finally fade.

twenty

KYGOSS

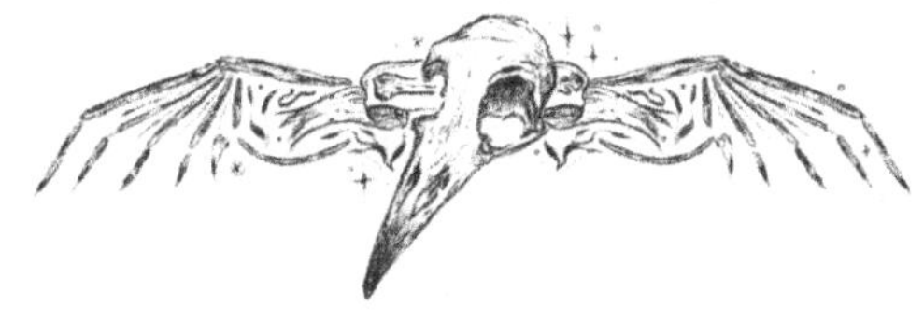

DRAKORE - TIX - YEAR 7557

> Once the shifters all lived together. Air, land and water creatures living amongst one another happily. A time came when the gods demanded that the water shifters band together to save the islands. That the land shifters band together to protect the land. The air shifters band together to protect the air. All in the name of safety for all.
>
> ~ Archives of Tiva Temple

His hands were shaking as he heard the unmistakable sounds of metal entering flesh. The crunch of the jewels, the clattering twinkle they made as the crystal bits hit the cobbled floor. He could hear a breathy gasp that had to have emerged from Hesper causing his heart to fall in his chest. A large ravine had opened up somewhere inside, and his heart seemed to have fallen into it. How could she be dying on the other side of the door? His friend, his companion since he was a lad. Kygoss cursed that he had come unarmed, as much as Hesper had told him tonight would be the night, he had hoped she would be wrong.

Once he realized what occurred on the other side of the door the plans they had made went out the window. Kygoss should be helping Faziel to safety, yet his feet were glued listening to the horror happening beyond. As the lightning streaked across the sky he had been filled with the urge to come and make sure Hesper got away as she had assured him she would. He counted trying to wait to interfere until the boots had all filed past. The only thing keeping him rooted to the spot was the idea that he needed to keep Maie and Maledic along with the crows of Slana safe.

He pulled the door open a little more revealing a wider sliver of the entryway, his only visual confirmation that she lay in dire peril, the sight of her blood pooling around her at an alarming rate. Soldiers still filing past made it hard to see Hesper's face.

Once silence fell he pushed the door open wider, grateful that the hinges weren't squeaking. Yet, before his boots crossed the threshold his ears picked up the sounds of blubbering, and whispered words. He dared a glance and saw Darius hunched over the Queen's prone form. Sadness over took the shock as nausea rippled within him, Darius the lost lad had somehow been involved. He wanted to feel anger, anger that she lay dying far too soon but he knew Darius. He knew that this boy had been once more misled by his disgusting father. She reached up, taking Darius' hands in hers. Her voice, far too faint for Kygoss to make out.

Kygoss stood in the doorway unafraid of Darius, watching the tableau happening in front of him. Darius too taken up with his emotions never glanced up instead running away undoubtedly after his own father. Kygoss moved swiftly to Hesper's side, clamping down the tears that threatened to fall as he stared at his friend as she faded away.

"Hesper?" He whispered softly stroking the sweaty hair tendrils away from her face.

Hesper appeared to rally all her remaining strength as she opened her eyes, focusing her golden irises on his. "Kygi?" She gave a half smile blood continuing to ooze out of her mouth.

"Yes my friend."

She lifted a hand weakly and he patted her shoulder not caring about the blood that had begun to coat him. "Don't worry Hespy. It's fine I'm here I won't leave you. You are with a friend, not alone."

Her face grew grave. "No, no." She struggled against him, her words coming out breathy and choked as more blood bubbled up. "Save Faziel and then you have to go help Aydan. He's supposed to take on the rest but I didn't manage to kill as many as I had hoped to. Help him get the girls away." She pulled at the high neck of her gown, exposing her dragon necklace, the one that could only be allowed to leave her neck upon her death.

"Kygi, I need this to go to the heir."

He blinked immediately noting her lack of naming the heir. *Why wouldn't she just say Cerial?* His fingers felt too large, oddly numb as he fumbled his way to removing her necklace placing the blood stained trinket in his pocket. "I will do what I can for your family Hespy."

The nickname triggered a flood of images in Kygoss' mind, a brash blonde girl, all legs running through the forests of Slana. Her crow form which hadn't been used very often since she took the throne had been an unusual gray color, a sign to all the elders that she was destined for big things. They had learned to fly together racing the sunsets of their childhood.

A sob worked its way up his throat. "I will miss you. Thank you for all you have done in this life."

He leaned forward and placed a kiss on her forehead, noting the small smile on her face as he felt her soul release its grip on her body.

twenty-one

AURELIA

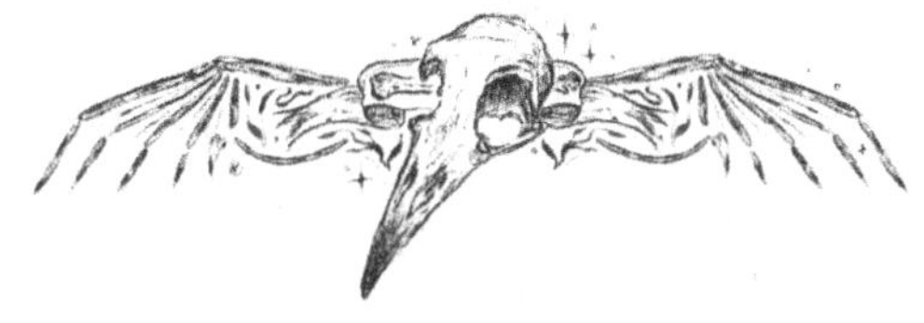

DRAKORE - TIX - 7557

Water rushed by as she sat on the rock dangling her feet in the river below. Little rainbows arched from the foam created where the waterfall met the river. Birds chirped and she laughed as the crow form of Mal hopped around rock to rock gathering tiny pebbles and tossing them at her.

Her blood ran cold as a scream rent the air. Aurelia stood turning in a circle trying to find the source. Her entire self began to shake, her dream self began to quiver as fear took over. She circled back towards the river, muffling her own panicked scream as the mortal form, tall and gangly, of Mal appeared in front of her, "Wake UP!"

The order forced her body into action, her eyes flying open to the utter madness occurring within her conscious world. The first thing that registered in her panicked mind was the sight of Faziel curled into a ball in the corner of the room. She no longer laid on her bed where Aurelia had last seen her.

Faziel rocked her body, hands over her ears, eyes clenched

shut tight, the muttering getting louder, "No, no, no, no, not me. Not me. I haven't done anything. Not me."

The noises began to infiltrate her sleep riddled brain. What at first her brain had dismissed as just a busy start to the day around the palace took on its true sounds.

Screaming.

She stood rushing to Faziel intent to get her calm so they could go and find her parents, where safety undoubtedly lay. The door to their room crashed open. It was her turn to scream, scrambling backwards against Faziel. A gray wolf standing, snarling, blood dripping from its mouth growling as it inhaled deeply the sides of its chest retracting. As Aurelias body made contact with Faziel, Faziel's screams grew in earnest with intermittent whimpering.

Aurelia scrambled to her feet, placing herself in front of the smaller girl, knowing she had to do her job to protect the younger more helpless people, even though she lacked weaponry. She reached inside and pulled some of her power loose from the ties that held it in control. The winds began to whip around the room, smaller detritus taking flight.

A popping filled the air and in the place of the large gray wolf stood a somewhat familiar man. The man from the stables now stood in black fighting leathers, clearly not clad in the gray of the Drakore fighters. She crouched, keeping her hands loose, better able to try and fight.

She had no idea who he could be or who could have sent him. He unsheathed a sword he carried at his back along with a dagger from his belt. He threw the dagger at her feet causing it to land point first in front of her bare toes.

"Who are you?"

"We don't have time to discuss that but I am here to get you to safety. The palace is under attack. Come with me and be rescued or stay and die. Choice is yours, either way at least now you have a dagger to aid you." His voice gruff, but survival instincts kicked in. She gripped her power deep within, feeling a calming sense of safety emanating from him. He did not belong to the source of this problem. Aurelia leaned down and pried the dagger out of the floorboards. Once she stood again she realized he had pulled another dagger from his belt.

"This way."

The stranger, one she knew had never been to her room before, led her with a surety that had her wondering who could have sent this man.

"What about Faziel?" She whispered the question as they stumbled down the stone staircase, unsure how wise it would be to shout at the dangerous man.

"Who?" The man didn't even bother glancing her way.

"The girl who lay crying and screaming in the room! Didn't you see her?"

"I had one job and that didn't include her. I am to get you to safety. Thats all." Perhaps he had realized how crass that sounded because he paused on the stairs for a brief second and glanced at her. "Someone will be along to help her I am sure. After all she does live with a Princess of the Blood and you will be searched for at some point by someone."

Aurelia turned to go back to her room, "They will not. We have to get her now!"

An arm curled around her waist and she squeaked. Her world swirling around her.

"We are going now. The girl stays."

"You big brute!" Tears pricked at her eyes. "She needs help. I'm supposed to help her."

"Pip you are in more danger than she is. Let's go. Now!"

Aurelia nodded sadness filling her as she sensed that she would never see Faziel again. "Where are we headed exactly?"

"There's a coup happening right now. I am trying to get you away from the soldiers who were sent to kill your family."

Aurelia trudged on, her steps feeling heavy with each movement, following as close as she could. She had heard about the possibility of a coup from her place in her parents' study, yet they had not specified the date or at least hadn't before she fell asleep in the cupboard. She wanted to run, but the bodies and bloody trails littering the servants corridors had her reevaluating. She couldn't protect herself with a sword and without it there wasn't much hope against soldiers. While she didn't know this stranger, he currently held her best chance at survival.

He proved her instincts correct as they neared the bottom of the servants corridor and came upon two guards wearing the uniform of the Drakore guard with one minor change. They had red bands wrapped around their upper arms signi-fying their allegiance with someone else.

The man leading her threw an arm out catching her around the midriff halting her progress. She watched on in horror as he used his sword and dagger with wicked efficiency ending the lives of the men who stood in their way.

He motioned for her to step around the bodies as they continued. They could just make out the door that they would need to use to exit when more guards stepped in the way. These she recognized, and they recognized her.

"That's the little twerp. They want her alive. Kill the mongrel and take the girl. Perhaps she will make her father cooperate."

Aurelia instinctively took a few steps backward placing her stalwart stranger between her and the guards. She utilized the seed of power she had loosened to bring the winds up around them all. Aiding the stranger as best she could with the little training she had received so far.

She had only really focused on control, actual combat with

her powers was a skill for future study. Winds however were a long time friend of hers, one she had played with since she was born and as she had grown so had her power over them.

The stranger tilted his body minutely aiming his voice over his shoulder at her, "When the opportunity presents itself, run outside. I will use my wolf to find you." He squared off with the guards, the odds were not great at four to one and anxiety spiked within her, bouncing from foot to foot as she waited and watched.

The dagger she still held in her hand heavy and unwieldy, the reality that she was unaware of how to use it echoing through her bones. The stranger knocked two of the assailants off their feet with a sweep to one side and then the other. Before moving to engage the others, refusing to give them the opportunity to attack her. She realized that if ever there was going to be an opportunity to run for the door the time would be now, two incapacitated and the others engaged with her stranger.

Using the wind to aid her in speed she dodged around the active fighting, coming rather close to one of the men still gasping for breath while attempting to regain his feet. Falling back on years of dance training insisted upon by her mother she skittered across the flagstones twirling away from the hands that reached for her as they realized she escaped.

The door a welcome relief once her hands finally made contact with the rough hewn wood. A pang of sadness echoed into her as she pushed the door open and left the steps of the servants entryway.

After a quick scan of the area around the side of the palace she made her way at a run toward a grove of trees. From her limited knowledge of the grounds due to her parents overbearing nature this grove of trees butted up against a half wall that separated the royal lands from the immediate city that encircled it.

She hadn't ever had an opportunity to explore the city, her parents striving to control who the public grew to love. The sheltered nature however stood in her way now. She went to the row of trees closest to the wall and clambered up the branches waiting, fingering the dagger, hoping the stranger survived long enough to aid her in finding true safety.

twenty-two

AURELIA

DRAKORE - TIX - YEAR 7557

The tree shook with each gust of wind that whipped through the orchard. She tried her best to tamp down her magic and its natural call to the winds hopeful that would calm the branches. Her breath caught each time a branch snapped, or the ground covering rustled. She whipped her head around twitching with every paranoid thought. *Would they find her here?* She could feel phantom hands grabbing at her ankles as if to pull her from her sanctuary in the tree.

Her thigh tensed, exuding an intense stabbing pain that echoed throughout her muscles. All she could risk was a gasp as she shifted precariously to allow one hand to rub out the offending muscle. A flicker of movement had her rigid, tears stinging her eyes as her muscles screamed in protest. A group of soldiers, their arms striped with the red arm bands, fanned out into the orchard, peering behind every tree, stabbing recklessly into the bushes.

She clasped both hands over her mouth as she forced deep breaths desperately shoving her magic into the deep recesses of her soul. She couldn't risk anything dragging their attention up into the branches of the tree itself. A solider stopped just beneath her hiding spot, tears streaming down her face as fear crested in her mind. *One, two, three..* As she reached thirty the soldier finally began to move off joining the other armed searchers.

She finally peeled her hands off her mouth clutching the tree trunk, deep breaths escaping in pants. She did her best to clamp down on the sobs, time would come for completely dissolving first she had to survive.

Eventually the door she had exited opened and out came the stranger, moving stealthily and obviously searching for her. He lifted his nose and sniffed. Somehow he was using the power of smell to find her. *Must be a wolf thing.*

She slowly and painfully extricated herself from the tree by the time that he got close enough to defend her. He took stock.

"Do you have a plan?" she whispered at him.

"I do but it didn't account for there being this many defectors against your parents. Never mind, there's always a way the Gods ensure it." The stranger turned her around at her shoulder and pushed her gently toward the half wall leading toward to the city.

When they reached it, still attempting to stay quiet and out of sight he hoisted her up to the top, "Stay in the shadow of the building."

She nodded and dropped into the city, stepping carefully into the shadow waiting. There were clangs of swords hitting one another and fear spiked in her blood causing a pounding to take up residence inside her mind. She stumbled backwards until her back hit the wall behind her. Sweat coated her hands as she held her breath unsure who would follow her into the darkness.

The large stranger leaped with ease over the wall, more

blood dripping down the sword than had been there previously. She swallowed against the fear that bubbled there and walked into the open to meet him. Her steps halting against the cold cobbles.

He led them through the city's streets sticking to the darkened alleys and utilizing the shadows of the buildings to keep them safe. Hidden from the bright illumination of the moon.

Aurelia's mind whirled, torn between the terror of the night and the newness of her surroundings. The cobbled streets in this area of the city were rough and ill cared for, bricks poking up haphazardly. What she could see of the buildings were that they were run down. Yet her savior seemed to know exactly where he was going, leading her with confidence through the dilapidated area.

"Have you been here before?" She hissed keeping her voice low.

"Missions such as these require some planning Pip. My employers are not stupid or wet behind the ears. They want to ensure you live, thus precautions were taken." He whispered the words almost to low for her hearing alone to catch, luckily they danced upon a breeze flowing toward her ears and hers alone.

Three streets of increasingly broken buildings later and the stranger stopped her in the shadow of what could only be described as a shack. She opened her mouth to argue but stilled as she caught sight of the movement ahead of them. Ten men with bands across their arms were in the process of destroying all barrels in the yard of a tavern. Aurelia's heart leaped into her throat as she saw the tavern keepers family huddled to the side crying at the loss of their livelihood. *Why would they do this? Why was she so important?*

The stranger pulled her back the way they had come his steps quick and quiet. Once he determined they were alone he leaned down whispering as low as possible. "We have to do something drastic. How brave are you, Pip?" Aurelia hadn't realized she held her breath to try to hear him better his voice so quiet in the darkness.

As she pulled the needed oxygen into her lungs she scrunched her nose, her mind racing. She glanced down at her threadbare nightgown. It took a moment to realize she couldn't even feel the cold that should be penetrating her skin, her magic having risen to the surface to aid her in keeping her warm. "I want to live, so what do I need to do? Where are you going to take me?"

"Our final destination is Tixdarr's temple, the way we get there however is going to be significantly different. We are about two streets from the barrier separating Baelia from Dodsfell. I've heard a rumor there is some stone missing, large enough I'd wager for one as skinny as you to squeeze through."

Thoughts whirled around Aurelias mind, her instinct screaming at her to run to Slana, steal a horse, find a way, anything but go into the Realm of the Dead. "Look I don't know who you are, I'm guessing you're from Palion given your wolfish habits but I don't know your motivations. I can't go through the barrier. There's magic there. Everyone knows the magic prevents unsanctioned crossovers. If you try to go without Tixdarr's permission then you will get roasted."

The stranger chuckled, "Fairly observant little bird aren't you. I do hail from Palion. The stories of magic are told to keep curious children from playing in the Realm of the Dead. Never fear my employers want you delivered unharmed and if there was risk of you dying just by crossing the barrier I wouldn't be allowed to send you now would I?"

Aurelia gave him a once over. Assessing if what he spoke was true, stroking her magic hoping it would illuminate the answers she wanted. "If you want me to believe you, who sent you?"

"I can't tell you that."

She rolled her eyes. "Typical. I don't know about you, but I am going to Slana, not Tixdarr's temple."

He cocked his head. "Slana? I don't know a place called Slana. I have to get you to the temple where it's safe. Who knows, perhaps your sister will be there waiting. After all, it's where all refugees are gathering at the moment."

"Then let me go with you not through the barrier alone!" She stomped her bare foot frustration clawed at her chest.

"It will be impossible. You haven't tapped your shifter powers yet have you?"

She looked down at the ground, not wanting to admit her weakness to this unknown individual. "We just need to steal some peasants clothes and I will blend right in."

He laughed at that, keeping the sound low. "Have you ever looked in a mirror Pip? You wouldn't blend in with anything. Your very face is the echo of your mother's, the most well known woman in this area of Baelia. I'm sure as you get older the resemblance will only strengthen. There's no way of changing your face. No, the only option is Dodsfell."

Fear roiled within her gut as they began to move once more, their destination now clear as they trudged through the chaotic streets. Eyes alert for the armband wearing rebels. They made it to the barrier with little upset, and it took a little time to find the hole the stranger had spoken of. She would fit, it would be a tight squeeze but considering she had few curves it wouldn't be too difficult. Dread spiked causing nausea to boil up her throat. She looked at the stranger who had taken up a guard stance, his back to the wall, waiting for her to enter.

"Explain the plan one more time." she whispered emotions causing paralysis to strike her, preventing her from moving forward.

"Once you are inside Dodsfell, you will follow the sloping ground downward toward the temple. Once you reach the bottom of the slope you will see the large Dodsfell gates and be able to see the temple through them. I'll meet you there, it will take you a day or two, I shall have provisions waiting. While you are traveling through Dodsfell I will shift once more into my wolf form traveling to the temple myself. As a wolf I will be better able to evade capture and death."

Aurelia nodded slowly, her mind understanding but her instincts still screaming for her to run away from the barrier. To leave.

She took a stumbling step forward, her feet scraping against the dirt. Her head swiveled around taking in her surroundings, the kingdom of her birth and blood. Her parents faces flashed through her mind, their vague reassurances of safety feeling hollow and confusing. *Why did they lie to me? Why did they pretend this would have a different outcome?* The place that had always been home and safe, now tainted with blood, destruction and lies.

A sob worked its way through her throat as she scanned the skies hoping against hope that someone would wing their way to her and save her from this impossible decision. She closed her eyes and pictured the one bird she wished would appear. *Mal.*

Her hands shook as she gripped the stone of the barrier wall. Her magic pushed against a strange physical shape which seemed to bend and conform against her hands as they tried to push. The foreign magic, one that felt evil and predatory, suddenly cracked allowing her hand in, coating it in an oily evil that began oozing up her arms. She glanced a final time behind her at the stranger standing guard, he caught her eye and nodded once "Go on Pip. I'll meet you on the other side near the temple. The big steel gates, you've seen them before right? Just head down toward them."

Aurelia took a deep breath and nodded once pushing her head into the hole. Her mind reeling. *A big iron gate. Seems easy enough.* She had never seen it herself. Though if it was as big as he claimed it should be an easy task.

The feelings that filled her were sudden and painful. Starting at the crown of her head as it pushed against the magical barrier that encased the wall separating Dodsfell and Drakore, it felt like a thousand needles pricking every bit of skin regardless of the nightgown she wore. Pressure set in the farther into the hole her body went. It bore down on her entire being squeezing her from the bottom and the top. Her bones themselves could feel the pressure.

She couldn't help but groan as her legs and feet still in Baelia on the cobbles of Drakore gave one last push from the land of the living forcing herself fully into the land of the dead. The pain reached a crescendo echoing throughout her body. The world went black as her feet fell through removing all connections she had with the land of the living.

The Realm of the Dead was dark, much darker than Baelia and the temperature she hadn't been feeling was now biting her through the thin nightgown. She reached inside of herself attempting to access her magic to bring the warmth she so desperately needed but the place inside herself where the magic was located felt empty, hollow. Her magic gone. Slowly she stood, the underbrush and sparse plants amongst the dirt looked painful. It was a lucky thing she had missed falling on them when she came through the hole.

Fear set in as the silence echoed around her. The everyday sounds, leaves rustling in the trees, birds chirping, small rodents scurrying, all gone. The moon not visible through the clouds covering the sky above. Her only light source coming from the faintly glowing wall that separated her from the land of the living.

Fear and sadness welled within her and she forced it down, swallowing the tears, turning to face the downward slope that led hopefully to the gate and her stranger who would save her. She sent a prayer up to Tiva hoping that the Gods that she had been taught to have faith in would protect her.

twenty-three

KYGOSS

DRAKORE - TIX - YEAR 7557

Kygoss stood, the knees and legs of his pants soaked in the blood of his best friend. He knew there would be a time for grieving, for now he had to content himself with swallowing the tears that clogged his throat.

He moved swiftly down the hall shifting as he went aiming for the girls' rooms. The first priority had now become to save the daughters of his best friend, then he would work to save her soulbond from whatever terrors may be on the way to him.

His promise to Mal ringing in his mind, he swiftly winged his way to Aurelia's room. Fear gripped his insides as he saw her door had been forced inwards. Upon landing he shifted back searching the room to see if perhaps Aurelia had hidden herself.

He muttered a curse as he noticed that Faziel, a mumbling mess of tears and piss in the corner of the room while Aurelia appeared to be gone. He walked over to Faziel and bent in front of her, putting his face close to hers. "Where is she?"

"Woolf. Big Wolf."

Kygoss' mind raced as he considered what she could have meant by big wolf.

"Wolf. Man. Stairs."

Kygoss glanced toward the stairs and realized in a blink as his mind struggled to keep up with the adrenaline pumping through his body. Palion, the home of the wolves, the home to all land based shifters, had come and attempted a rescue. Knowing their ultimate goal was to wed her to Lucian he made a split second decision to let that worry settle into the back of his mind. She didn't appear to be in Rayner's clutches so he would refocus on her fate after checking on the others. He shifted without warning causing Faziel to yelp in fear, falling backwards into the puddle she had created.

He winged his way back into the hallway down to Cerial's rooms. Interestingly, the door hadn't been broken. Instead the door hung open, no obvious sign of struggle. He shifted again landing in the room studying the evidence before him. Her bed appeared crisply made, no wrinkle to be seen in the bed linens. No dent in her pillow and the blankets were still in place where the maids had left it early in the morning, her nightgown laid out on the bed. Cerial despite what her mother had thought had never in fact been in this room for sleep. *Had she been taken before she could ready for bed? How then did Aurelia and Faziel sleep so soundly for what time they did?*

Kygoss winged out of her room by the window and made his way to his own study, shifting and changing into a clean set of pants. Before throwing the ones marred with Hesper's life blood he palmed her necklace, tracing the dragon reverently. He went to the exterior wall fingering the bricks carefully until he found the one he was after. It had been loosened most likely due to age but now it posed the perfect hiding hole for the trinket that held such deep significance. He replaced the brick as he waited knowing it wouldn't be long before the Rebels came for him as well.

He considered how to play it, innocent and malleable opting for a chance at life and the ability to see his family again or to fight which would undoubtedly be a suicide mission. The idea of going to fight and stand with the Berrids flitted through his mind. He squashed it as quickly as it flittered through. Ultimately he had to stay strong for the crows for they held the last vestige of the ancient Drakore magic safe. Come what may he had a duty beyond that to his friends. He watched his window convinced that any moment his door would be shoved open and guards would flood in to take him by force. Yet time continued to pass the moon falling in the sky, the sun beginning to rise dawning on a new Drakore. Those who survived the night realizing just how drastically things had changed overnight, illuminated in the harsh light of day.

At some time during the night he had taken up his vigil at his desk. The first guard wearing the red armband of the rebels stormed into the room, sword drawn, slowly Kygoss rose from his seat, raising his hands, innocence emanating from every pore. A guard he recognized shot him a predatory smile. "Ready to die old man?"

Kygoss raised a bushy eyebrow feigning confusion. "What are you on about? What has happened?"

The guard appeared confused and gruffly ordered his companions. "Take the old bird down to Rayner. He can decide what to do with him."

The two underlings stormed in and took Kygoss by the upper arms forcing him down the corridor and spiral staircase. Kygoss complied in silence waiting to see what Rayner had done in the hours after Hesper's death, his mind racing over where Cerial and Aydan may have ended up, he shot Tiva a prayer that Aurelia got to Palion safely. He suspected he would be forced to watch Aydan be tortured but the girls seemingly got away.

The guards made the walk through the palace much more complicated than wholly necessary. As Kygoss did his best to maneuver tight corners and comply with the death grip on his arms, his guards unnecessarily tripped him tugging roughly. Pain radiated with every step, his prayers to Tiva continued on a loop in his mind as he kept his focus on surviving to see Maie once more.

They finally arrived at the audience chamber, where the thrones were situated, once the place where Aydan and Hesper received peasants and courtiers. Rayner now lounged on the throne Aydan should have been sitting upon. Kygoss scanned the room and his blood ran cold.

In the center of the room crouched Aydan recognizable by his leathery scaled dragon wings fully shifted out and chained to the ground. Chains wrapped around each wing chiseled into the stone of the ground, another length of chain was secured around his neck ensuring that Aydan stayed in the very painful position on his knees. His wrists and ankles were secured as well making it possible for Aydan to only move his head around, Kygoss focused on Aydan's head and swallowed the nausea that erupted. Aydan's once chiseled and handsome face was now full of bruises, swelling beginning to set in.

To some extent Kygoss had expected this, though to be confronted with it in person made nausea boil continually in the pit of his stomach. The world stopped spinning for a few minutes as he focused on the hunched form across from Aydan. Cerial, her wings a smaller version of her fathers and similarly chained, was situated in such a way that Aydan had to watch as Cerial endured whatever Rayner desired. Kygoss did a once over and realized that she had already been on the receiving end of many sessions, to what end he wasn't sure. Her face and body appeared bruised, the clothes from the day before torn and hanging off of her exposing her body to the room at large.

Kygoss turned his attention to the room scanning the assorted individuals standing around. His eyes caught and held on Darius. It was clear that the bumbling crying buffoon that had whispered to Hesper in her last moments had disappeared, he now stood breathing hard, hands fisted as his eyes stared unwaveringly at Cerial. *Interesting.*

Kygoss fought his own mind, instinctually fighting the shove that came from the guards. Yet he made himself comply, finding himself on the floor in front of the throne, his head forced into a bow, both guards shoving at his shoulders. He heard the chains rustle behind him, and a groan he thought emanated from Aydan. He could do nothing to comfort him but he sent a prayer that Aydan's torment wouldn't be for much longer.

Kygoss lifted his eyes meeting Rayner's, Rayner looked at him curiously, "Where have you been you old bird?"

Kygoss blinked, keeping his mind carefully blank, helping him in feigning ignorance, he lowered his eyes back to the ground. "Well General, I have been in my study, up in the Southern Tower."

Rayner assessed him, before directing his words to the guards who had dragged him here. "Is that correct?"

The guards took a step back releasing Kygoss' shoulders executing their own signs of deference. "Yes sire."

Rayner nodded. "This poses an interesting dilemma then. You have been marked as a Berrid sympathizer. Someone who loved their rule. The question remains, do I kill you or do I let you live?" He turned back to the guards. "Did he fight you at all?" Kygoss kept his head down waiting.

"No sire. He was compliant."

"Interesting. You hear that Aydan? Your long time friend just accepted the removal of your line. Kygoss how do you feel seeing Aydan and your beloved little niece in chains? Does your heart hurt? Wanna know what happened to the great bitch?"

Kygoss swallowed hard, shoving his emotions into a tiny box inside his mind, sealing it shut for another time when he had the privilege to examine them in detail. He looked toward Rayner sitting up on his knees, "The Berrid's were interesting Rayner, but I have to be honest, they were rather a bore. I befriended them once I knew Hesper could pave the way for me to get somewhere in life. I've always wanted more for myself after all."

Rayner assessed him, and right when he thought it hadn't worked a large grin split across it. "That's an interesting take. A snake in the grass indeed. I could almost say you were better at hiding your intentions than me. Now to prove your allegiance you will have to do something. Something a true lover of the Berrid line would never do."

Rayner descended the steps and clapped his shoulder in excitement. "Come along Kygoss."

Kygoss stood slowly turning careful to keep one step back from Rayner, showing deference in front of his men and preventing any minute facial expressions from being detected. He watched Rayner go to a small table, which held a whip and a knife both bloody and gory from recent use.

Rayner grabbed the whip and strode back to Kygoss handing it over glee bubbling over in Rayners eyes and movements.

Kygoss gripped the whip handle surprise flaring at the weight, staring at the darkened leather in disbelief. He eyed the two hunched forms of Aydan and Cerial beyond the whip, his mouth going dry as his heart plummeted.

"Now which one should you whip? Hmmm." Rayner left Kygoss not seeming to notice his disbelief to walk around the hunched figures and laughed gleefully, practically skipping back to Kygoss. "I know. I think I will have you do both! Five lashings for each. You can choose which one to do first."

Kygoss walked over to the figures and caught Aydan's glazed gaze. It was small and to those around them he knew it went unnoticed but Aydan's finger began tapping the chain. He tapped out in the code that the three of them had created before Aydan took the throne, 'Cerial betrayed me. I forgive you.'

Kygoss mentally steeled himself and stopped behind Cerial.

Rayner laughed a bit, "How fascinating the child first. Most unusual. A true Uncle would resist hitting a child."

Cerial must have regained consciousness at this point and began to struggle against the chains. Kygoss shot a look at Darius and saw him tense, his fists rising as if preparing to battle Kygoss himself.

Kygoss prepared himself for the potential of getting hit and brought back the whip and let it fly, once, twice, a third time and then two more quick ones as Cerial screamed and thrashed.

Aydan winced but he didn't react beyond that. Darius however, had come across the room standing right beside Kygoss, his breath hot and rancid, fist raised. Rayner's demeanor shifted in an instant, the glee and excitement turning into anger as he advanced on his son. "What are you doing? Get back in line!"

Darius seemed like he fought an internal instinct to protect.

Kygoss went around Cerial, away from Darius putting some much needed distance between them before squaring off against Aydan's back. He let the whip fly. He went for a methodical pace and on the fifth strike he was glad that Aydan hadn't thrashed. His fist had tightened against the chains, blessedly that was the extent.

Rayner smiled back at Kygoss only after Darius walked away back to the wall. "Very nice. Old bird you may keep your freedom for now but don't assume you aren't being watched. I expect you to be here when I call."

Kygoss bowed, turning away, careful to drop the whip on the table. He chose a space of wall that would give him the ability to study Rayner. He intended to learn all he could to better aid those who wanted to resist in future.

twenty-four

KYGOSS

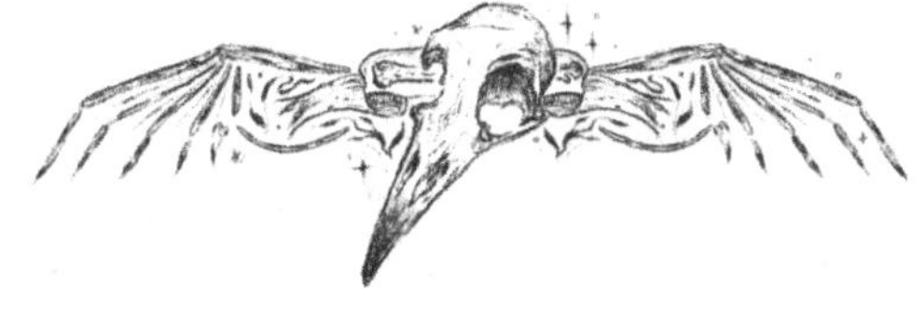

DRAKORE - TIX - YEAR 7557

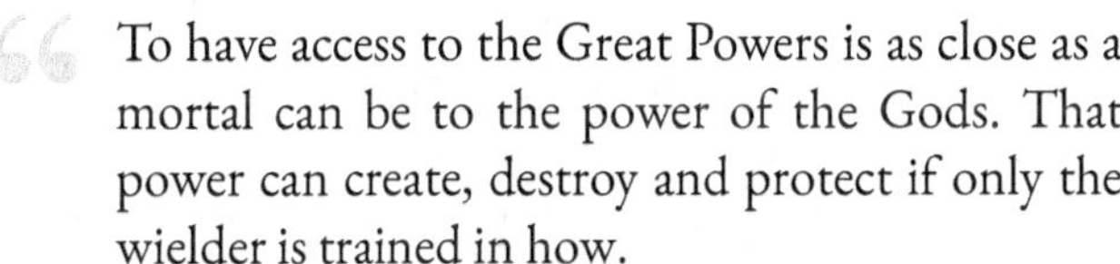

> To have access to the Great Powers is as close as a mortal can be to the power of the Gods. That power can create, destroy and protect if only the wielder is trained in how.
>
> ~Archives of Drakore

It didn't take long for things to escalate once more. Rayner hadn't forgotten Darius' misstep with Kygoss and it became obvious as to just how much danger Darius was in. Kygoss watched as the General stalked up to his son, his face a mask of indifference.

"Seems like we need to teach my boy here that he's been brainwashed all these years by the Berrids. There's no such thing as a Soulbond and that bitch over there used him." Rayner pointed a finger in Cerial's direction.

Kygoss felt his blood begin to thrum as he watched Aydan hang his head in defeat, while a groggy Cerial pulled half heartedly against the chains. She screamed in terror causing her voice to spike to a higher pitch than Kygoss was used to, "Darius please. We were supposed to do this together! What is happening?"

Darius took a menacing step toward his father and glowered as he backed up Cerial's claims. "You told her you would help us. You convinced her to help you take the throne. Why is she getting punished?"

"My boy she's getting punished because she's been using you all these years. I can't stand to see my precious boy taken advantage of." Kygoss felt a shiver of terror radiate through him as he noted the look of madness that rested on Rayner's face.

Rayner clapped a hand on Darius' shoulder so hard the boy stumbled forward. Cerial began a litany of denials that went relatively ignored, the only person seeming to listen being Darius as he glanced her way most often. "Prove that you are not under their mental magics. Prove that you are on my side." The arm that hung around Darius' shoulders was tense, the exertion to steer his son seemingly toward the table of tools obvious to all in the room. The men around Kygoss were whispering with excitement at the potential of blood and gore. Kygoss' stomach rolled knowing that whatever Rayner wanted Darius to do to prove his loyalty would have lasting consequences.

"Here we are." Rayner had walked Darius just behind Aydan, with the perfect view of Cerial's face. Rayner left Darius there, a challenge gleaming behind his eyes. He casually grabbed the whip from the table of atrocious tools as he walked past, taking his final place behind Cerial. "Hmm. I will need two volunteers, strong ones mind."

Two of the largest avian shifters Kygoss had ever seen

walked out to the center of the room causing Rayner to grin manically, predatory intent obvious. "Excellent, you both need to stand just next to Darius. You are to ensure he doesn't leave. No matter what. Don't physically restrain him unless he makes it necessary though, this is a test after all we would hate for him to claim I interfered in some way." Kygoss shifted his position preparing himself for the worst, he didn't want to watch his niece in pain, someone relatively innocent if misguided, so he focused his attention solely on Darius.

"Alright, soulbond partners are all a trick of the mind my son. I shall prove it to you. I will whip her, if the bond was real your back would feel the pain. Yet as we all know you won't feel a thing only she will. If your back hurts though, if you show pain in any way it will be proof that you are still under the spell of the Berrid witches. Which as I am sure you will agree can't be allowed to continue."

Darius had clenched his fists seemingly waiting. The tension of the moment caused a lump to form in Kygoss' throat, fear and anxiety building there without the ability to release them.

Rayner let the whip fly, the impact had to be hard as it echoed through the audience chamber. Kygoss did his best to hide his own flinch, pain echoing in his soul at the idea of someone he loved being hurt without a way to save them. Cerial howled and Darius grunted his back and shoulders clearly twitching in the rhythm of the hits.

A loud tsking sound came from Rayner. "See you must still be under their spell. I killed the witch who we knew had mind magic, and I know you've been in this bitches company far too often. Perhaps she inherited some of that mind magic from her bitch mother, she must have put you under a spell directly." Kygoss spared a glance at the General turned madman, his eyes dancing over Cerial's panting and bleeding form as the man paced twirling the whips handle. "I see two options. One we bleed her until she reaches the brink of death which may be enough to break the magical spell on you, or I bleed you until you're at the brink removing the tainted blood from your system."

He pivoted and stared hard at Darius tapping his chin with the end of the whip. "That does pose an interesting idea. I have missed smelling your blood being smeared about."

Kygoss watched as Darius saw the obvious answer and winced, already guessing the true motives behind Rayner's statements. Darius, unsuspecting, began to untuck his shirt walking around Aydan bypassing one of the beefy volunteers, toward his father. "Take me. I want this unholy bespelled blood out of me. Help me Father." Kygoss did all he could to keep from shaking his head, Darius walked right into the trap blinded by the bond he clearly had for Cerial.

Rayner burst out laughing, he motioned to the two large fighters indicating they should take hold of Darius by the arms. "Make sure he's back where I put him. You see son, a man not under a spell would never volunteer to bleed himself." Kygoss saw the blood drain out of Darius' face going ghost white. Not even putting up a fight as the warriors dragged him back to his position where he could see Cerial's face. "A man that isn't spelled would want the witch bled dry to aid anyone else she may have cursed in this life. Yet, you tried to sacrifice yourself, proving once and for all that you are indeed under her thumb. I knew it the minute you started spouting nonsense about soulbonds." Kygoss closed his eyes, tears threatening at the back of his eyes. He tucked a hand into his pants pocket and began to pinch himself drawing his attention and pain response away from the scene in front of him. He couldn't cry, he couldn't show emotion or sympathy over the death that was coming or his would be next.

Darius wasn't giving up though, "So this is how you treat those loyal to you? She helped you get this far. She gave you the plans to the palace and told you all about the different routines of her parents. She ensured you would be safe by telling you to get inside before her mother could kill you with lightning." Aydan's head shot up anger radiating from deep in the depths of his eyes. Darius turned attempting to meet everyone's eyes who stood around the room. "You see what he does to those loyal to him. He carves them up all because she claims to love me and I to love her."

Darius sucked back and spit as hard as he could on the ground. "You are not a leader. If you do this you are a murderer. Cerial is innocent."

Rayner's face was livid. He unleashed the whip on Cerial's already bleeding back. The blood running in small rivulets down to the ground. Darius roared and pushed against his captors attempting to get free to get to his soulbond. The warriors struggled to maintain their grasp. Rayner stopped his onslaught and watched the struggle before him.

Cerial was gasping for breath, her screaming causing her to go hoarse and the tears cleaning the grime decorating her face. "Darius?" The question was innocent enough and spoken in nothing more than a rasping whisper but the room went silent as Rayner glowered.

Darius roared again. "CERIAL."

Kygoss watched Rayner's face and realized this would be the moment. He purposefully turned his attention to Darius and Aydan not wanting to watch the death of his niece, his misguided and naive goddaughter. His mind suddenly very grateful to whoever managed to get Aurelia out.

A keening came from Aydan as he watched his eldest daughter die, Darius became more and more erratic. Shoving and pushing against those who held him. Suddenly his entire frame went slack and a noise of otherworldly moaning came from the man. As his frame lost the ability to hold itself up the warriors merely let him slump to the ground laughing at the sight of the great son in a puddle over nothing more than a woman.

Kygoss stared pointedly just beyond Darius' slumped form, the reality that Cerial Berrid no longer lived ringing in his head. A fact that couldn't be fixed. His mind thrown back to his explanation to Aurelia that she would be able to repair her relationship with her sister while they traversed to the manor in Slana. Guilt flowed heavy in his veins as he realized that would never happen now.

Kygoss was more than likely the first one to notice Darius begin to move. At first it appeared as if he merely stumbled in the process of regaining his feet, but then he saw the glint as Darius deftly palmed a dagger. Kygoss shifted his stance, ready for what was bound to be chaos. Though if he had taken a guess at Darius' intentions he would have been wrong. Darius crouched behind Aydan and then after a deep breath he launched himself grabbing Aydan around the neck from behind.

All Aydan did in acknowledgement was grunt at the impact. He didn't beg or bargain. Death incoming. What mattered now became who gave the death blow. Only that person would have access to the Great Sky Power through the throne. Only the killer of the monarch could truly take the throne.

The pieces fell into place for Kygoss. Cerial and Darius had undoubtedly planned to take the throne from her father. They wouldn't have had to kill him in that instance because she had been the natural born heir. Cerial's death meant that someone would have to kill Aydan to take the throne. Who would do it was now called into question.

Darius, his crazed gaze on his father, held the palmed dagger to Aydan's throat. "Wouldn't it be such a shame if you went to all this trouble and then you don't get what you want either?" Darius' voice had reached a deeper octave, hoarse from the emotions that raged. Kygoss shuddered at the darkness that oozed from Darius where once there had been sparks of light.

Rayner stood straight, shock and mild confusion lacing his face. He pulled up on Cerial's hair as if double checking that he had in fact killed her. Kygoss couldn't tell definitively but it was a safe bet that if she wasn't dead yet she would be soon.

"Son, you need to get off him this instant."

"Or what?" spit Darius. "You just removed any motivation I may have had to do what you wanted. You stole from me the one thing I wanted. All I wanted out of this was to end up with her. I helped you because you told me you would pave the way for that. You told me the Berrids wouldn't let me have her because I was a stupid fosterling and she a royal Princess. Yet, they would have honored the bond. The bond that you are wrong, and does exist." Darius' dark eyes latched on Cerial's slackened form. "Had you just let me have her you could have had the power. I didn't care about that. I didn't want to be King, I wanted to be hers. Yet you couldn't let me have even an ounce of joy could you."

Darius must have seen the men moving along the side trying to get close enough to wrestle him off of Aydan because he growled to the room. "No one else moves." He pushed the knife harder against Aydans throat causing a trickle of blood to begin to drizzle down. It didn't bleed for long, the Great Power healing it up rather quickly, but the point had been made.

Rayner dropped the whip into the puddle of Cerial's life blood and raised his hands in supplication. He took a few steps back from Cerial's body before a sneer adorned his face. "You're incapable of making such a grand move. You're weak, you always have been and you always will be. There's no point pretending now."

Kygoss watched as Darius turned into a man before their eyes, a cruel vindictive one who had no concept of kindness. He gave his father a haunted look a split second before his hand began to move. Kygoss almost wondered if Darius even knew his hand was moving because his eyes didn't leave his father's. The knife dug deep, blood pouring down at a shocking rate.

Kygoss glanced at Aydan's face and watched as his eyes grew glassy, his mouth slackening as his friend bled out faster than the Great Power could heal him. The only outward sign became a slight tremor and the gurgling of his blood coming out of his throat. He didn't fight and he didn't beg. Kygoss guessed that Aydan felt more relieved to be reunited with Cerial and Hesper. The need to find Aurelia surged within him, he didn't want his own son to lose his grip on his own morality as Darius seemed to be doing before his eyes.

Rayner unsheathed his sword and glared at his wayward son. "If you want to be with your slut so badly come over here and I shall reunite you. That throne is supposed to be mine. I should have known you would ruin this! You ruin everything."

Darius closed his eyes momentarily; the only indication that he may be experiencing something deeper appearing as his arms seemed to tighten involuntarily around Aydan's dying form.

No other warning came before a scream erupted out of Darius' mouth which halted Rayner in his tracks, observing his son trying to figure out what had caused the scream of pain. Leathery bat-like wings erupted out of Darius' back causing his shirt to tear and shred. His breathing got harder and his body seemed suspended behind the wayward wings as they began to flap.

"What in the Gods name?" Rayner looked shocked, his sword hanging loosely from one hand as he observed his now airborne son.

Darius' body wobbled between the wings that flapped, urging him upwards out of the way of Rayner's blade. Kygoss watched as a plan formed within Darius. His face morphing from shock. As far as Kygoss knew Darius and Rayner were from the Flightless clan, the hope of wind in their wings beyond them. The shock dissolved into determination as he sneered down at his father.

"What do you think of me now father? Still weak? You are a bastard and you shall die having never felt the wind beneath you or seen the ground from above." He laughed maniacally, "You look rather like ants from up here. Small and insignificant."

Kygoss saw him palm another dagger, as the wing beats became more sure and steady. He knew that it would be a terrible thing if they both died, leaving Drakore completely devoid of leadership.

He closed his eyes, fearful for his family and the state of the kingdom. He cracked open a lid as he heard Darius' wings flap suddenly. Darius nosedived at Rayner and with precision that seemed otherworldly. He kicked himself for not taking more of an interest in the broken boy that had been accepted into the Royal house. *Who had trained him? Why?*

Rayner dropped his sword in shock, his arms rising to block his face from Darius. Kygoss knew the aim was true however as Rayner gave a strangled cry blood spurting from his neck at an unmanageable rate. Darius got close to his father's face and growled. "In your next life try not to take what doesn't belong to you. She belonged to me."

Rayner answered with a gurgle, his hands reaching up to clasp his neck, the blood leaking between his fingers. Darius pushed Rayner to the ground, not receiving any resistance, and turned towards the men. "Everyone out. Scour the grounds. I want the tiny one. Aurelia. Where is she? Bring her here or meet his fate." He pointed a bloody finger at Rayner, who rasped out the remains of his lifeblood.

The room filled with the sound of shuffling feet and shocked whispers but Kygoss ignored all of that, his eyes glued to Darius. Darius lowered his body next to Cerial's, pulling the chains out of the ground with a strength that proved Kygoss had a lot to learn about this new ruler.

Using a care that seemed impossible from one as blood-thirsty as Darius had been he pulled Cerial's body into his lap, rocking her and humming as he gently pushed her matted, blood soaked hair away from her face. "I am sorry. I miss you already, my love. Perhaps I should just find someone to take my place and join you now. Please don't be gone." Tears were running down his face. Kygoss walked up to them slowly and with care.

"Darius. We need you now."

"Go away bird. I need her. I've always needed her. Yet, I won't ever have her again."

"I am so very sorry Darius. I would give her back to you if it was in my power to do so. Drakore needs a leader though and because you took the power from Aydan you are it. I will go in search of Aurelia while you prepare Cerial for the Rite of Tixdarr. Tomorrow I shall return to help you prepare for your Rite of Inheritance with the Oba. I will do whatever is needed to smooth the way. Please stay focused, Drakore needs you."

Darius glared at him with his blood shot eyes, "If you betray me you will end like he did." He pointed at Rayner.

Kygoss nodded and shifted into his crow form soaring out of the window.

KYGOSS

DRAKORE - TIX - YEAR 7557

Kygoss did a cursory look through the palace grounds though deep down he knew that she wasn't there. Once Darius saw her blue eyes so like Cerial's he would be loath to end her, meaning there was time to warn Maie and check on Mal. He had a feeling that Maledic may have a way of finding Aurelia.

He flew straight and true arrowing for his home study, surprise filled him as his eyes landed on Maie pacing, wringing her hands the panic clearly setting in. He shifted mid air, landing with a large thump that radiated through the floorboards. "What's happened to Mal?" Kygoss struggled to settle his own panic that surged within him echoing Maie's distress.

"He.. I.. I had no choice." Her head fell as she stared at the floor. After a pause Maie brought her eyes to meet his and his heart lurched at the tears welling within hers. "I had to sedate him to keep him in the manor. He became frantic around midnight, desperate to get to Aurelia. He's convinced something happened."

Kygoss sighed heavily. "Something did happen. It's bad

Maie. Aurelia is missing. I suspect someone from Palion snuck her out but I haven't been able to confirm that." He held up his hand to stem the questions he could see begging to be let out on Maie's face.

"Ayden and Hesper are gone." A sob welled up sticking in his throat. Kygoss swallowed it back down, tears gathering in the corner of his eyes. "I managed to sit with Hesper while she died but Aydan was no longer himself by the time he, left. Then Cerial," The sob he thought he had swallowed came out, causing him to stumble across his words.

"She was tortured to death for her soulbond partnership with Darius. Rayner led the coup but it's a very long story and for now I have to focus. I need to see Mal. He may be able to tell me if Aurelia is still alive."

Kygoss left the room leading Maie down the hall and up the central staircase toward Maledic's room. The door swung open, and Kygoss' heart rate ratcheted up as he saw Maledic's body laying atop the bedding, his legs twitching and his eyes racing beneath his closed lids.

"What did you give him?" He turned toward Maie, accusing eyes glaring into hers.

"A sleeping draft. It should be wearing off now though. I debated giving him another round to keep him calm."

Kygoss shook his head. "No Maie he needs to stay awake, we need to know what if anything he's feeling from her. You yourself explained that he is the foundation of the soulbond and therefore he would feel what his partner did. We know his partner is Aurelia. We need to be stronger for him."

Maie scrunched her face but nodded.

Mal's body began to thrash around violently on the bed, a deep moaning groan coming from him. His upper body shot up his eyes wild and panicked as he scanned the room. "Pops?"

"Mal. What's happening to Aurelia? Can you see?" Mal

scrunched his face, confusion emanating through him, as he took a deep breath.

"I can't see anything, just darkness. Coldness, bone deep ice. Fear fills her, there's never any calm. Pain, radiating through her feet with every step. Hunger."

Kygoss sucked in his breath and stared down at his son, his very soul heartsick. "The good news is she's alive to feel those things."

Mal's empty eyes deadened almost unrecognizable. Kygoss took a steadying breath, "There are things you need to know. Darius has taken charge of Drakore. Aydan, Hesper and Cerial are dead. This means it falls on us to fortify Slana against the possibility of invasion while playing the games of politics. Quite simply I can not be both the spymaster and the Lord of Crows." He saw Maie open her mouth to argue, but Kygoss shook his head.

"I am in hot water, not trusted and having to prove myself to Darius to keep him from killing me for my association with the Berrids." He turned to Mal, and his haunted eyes. "I have to give the power of the Crow Clan to Mal which will help distract until we can find Aurelia and get her to safety."

Kygoss placed a finger over Maie's mouth stopping her impending arguments. "We don't have time to argue it out. I need you to accept that it's safer for our people to be led by Maledic so he can form a new relationship with this new leadership. I will work on surviving and walking the delicate balance that comes with it, while spending time searching for Aurelia."

Maledic crawled to the edge of the bed, his legs shaking, "I will go find her, I can feel her fear, perhaps it will aid in pinpointing where she is. We have to move now, it can't wait."

Kygoss reached into his boot and pulled out a small concealed knife, slashing down across his palm. "No Maledic.

You are going to be Lord here and you need to stay put as the pillar of strength for our people."

He gripped his son's hand and cut down his palm, clasping them together. A white hot magic sliced through him before going into Mal, Mal shuddered at the impact. Kygoss repeated the words his own father had told him. "I, Kygoss Corvus gift the power of the Crow Clan on to you. I entrust their safety and wellbeing to you Maledic Corvus. Do you accept?"

"I, Maledic Corvus accept the responsibility of the Crow Clan." Maledic's grip tightened as Kygoss' was loosening preparing to let go. "Do you accept the responsibility in locating and protecting my fated soulbond Aurelia Berrid?"

Shock rippled through Kygoss at his own son. The haunted gaze held a glimmer of anger and retribution. Kygoss marveled at the audacity as they were performing an Oath, whatever was promised during it had to be upheld or risk the Gods' wrath. Maledic's mouth took on a determined slant as his fingers tightened despite the blood flowing between the two of them. Kygoss cleared the lump in his throat, "I swear to do my best by Aurelia."

Maie gasped but didn't interrupt the Oath. Maledic nodded once exhaling as the magic swirled around him. They released hands, the cuts closing up, time would tell what the visual reminders would look like. It normally took a few hours for the oaths to solidify under the skin, visual proof for the Gods to reference.

He stood and took Maie's arm pulling her into the hallway. "You need to rearrange the house. Make this look as official as possible. Pick whichever guest room you want and move our things in there and get Mal's essentials into the master bedroom. When the Crown comes to assess the loyalty of the crows it needs to appear that you are disowning me, just in case. Lock up Mal's room until Aurelia is returned, it's just going to drag him down into memories. My Gods it still smells of her."

Kygoss paced the small hallway before nodding to himself, "Yes, you need to warn everyone within Slana, no talks of soulbonds. I don't think it will end well with how Darius lost Cerial. Best to keep it silent. We are just married as is any other soulbonded pairing that appears while Darius is on the throne."

Maie nodded fear evident in the lines gathering around her usually smile filled face. "Kygi how will you stay safe? Our friends are gone. Stay here."

"Someone needs to take charge in the palace. It would be best if I can maintain a foothold of power at least until Aurelia is found and can take her place as Queen." He watched as Maie's eyes hardened in determination but he shook his head, negating her argument before she could even make it. "No you can't come with me. Maledic will need your help in creating a strong leadership foundation while struggling with the confusion of where Aurelia may be."

Tears formed in her eyes as Maie nodded slowly. "I hate when you're right."

Kygoss pulled her hard against his chest. "I know my love. I promise that next time you can be right."

She laughed, a sound that sounded so completely at odds with everything around them but also soothed the internal burns of watching his closest friends die gruesome deaths. He kissed her temple before murmuring. "I wish I could stay longer my love, but I must go find her. Then I have to repair what's broken or at least try. I shall send daily check-ins if I can."

He felt the heat of her tears as she finally gave in to the emotions. He just held her tighter, kissing the top of her head and murmuring loving words, stroking her back.

Once the tears had begun to stop he extricated himself

from her grip and took her hand kissing the top of it. "I will be back here next week and I shall send notes every day. I love you more than you could imagine Maie. Stay safe and prepare our son for the battles ahead. He will need the strength you carry."

She sniffled and nodded.

He turned and shifted, flapping out of the window once more. His purpose clear.

twenty-six

AURELIA

DODSFELL - TIX - YEAR 7557

As Aurelia ventured in the land of the dead she took care to stay next to the barrier, it being the only ground that seemed to be free of prickly plants. It took a few mishaps of stumbling into the sharp plants for her to learn her lesson. The prickly thorns seemed to dig their way deeper into her feet despite barely skimming the surface with the soft pad of her foot. One deeply embedded prickle thorn had required her to sit on the ground using her teeth to pull it out. Worry danced within her mind about infection, yet it truly wouldn't matter if she never left.

Merely existing within the realm seemed to be having an effect on her mental strength. Thoughts of dread infiltrated everything. It seemed as if her magic had fled, taking with it her joy, and positivity. Each step brought darker thoughts. Her body oddly empty, a peculiar echo where her magic had once been. *No magic will lead to no life. There has never been life without magic.*

Time didn't make sense. Her usual method using the sun and moon to dictate the hours didn't exist here in the gray haze that made up Dodsfell. She only realized that hours had indeed been passing due to the growing hunger taking root within her stomach, the growl getting louder with each step. In an effort to distract herself, her mind began to review what the Acolytes from Slana had taught her about Dodsfell.

Unfortunately all she remembered were that demons resided here. Her heart rate soared with each step, the idea that a demon could appear out of the blue to harm or worse made the steps halting and slow. The Acolyte had never mentioned if a mortal had ever been stuck inside the land of the dead, let alone if they had survived the trials. *Would she die? Would she be fine? How was she supposed to survive?*

Her mind became so entrenched, swirling through the possibilities that her tender foot contacted another prickle bush. Her howl of anguish echoed out amongst the dead trees, the noise radiating off the wall. Her foot had grown more sensitive from the previous prickles she had removed before. A glance behind confirmed that she was leaving a trail of blood speckled footprints. It wouldn't be a good thing if something dwelling here liked blood.

Relief filled her as she began to realize that the ground seemed to be flattening out. She hoped to see some evidence of the gate that the Palion stranger told her about. In front a path of cobbled stone, old and broken wound its way among gnarled twisted trees. She inched her way toward them looking around cautiously scared something would step into her path.

She leaned against a trunk and cautiously peered up and down the path, waiting to see if anything would happen. A loud grating squeak echoed throughout this section of Dodsfell causing goosebumps to spring up her arms as she waited. The eerie lack of animal sounds made her hair stand on end. She eased around the tree cautiously, immediately noticing that the broken path ended at the gate, as if at one point the demons could walk freely between the two realms. The twisted wrought iron gate hung open inviting her to step through toward her new life in the Mortal Realm. As she neared the iron came into sharper focus and she realized that it was twisted into the shape of demons dancing grotesquely. There seemed to be a breeze coming through from Baelia creating the squeaking sound that cut the air like a knife.

She ran full tilt toward the opening. Happiness radiated so deep she couldn't articulate it, her joy filling her mind bubbling up filling her every cell. Her entire being felt lightweight as if she could float on the very air itself.

Her mind shattered as her body slammed at full speed into the invisible barrier of magic that existed in the opening. The joy and happiness of moments before peeled away from her as her body flew through the air, ricocheting off the magic. She slammed into the ground all oxygen knocked out from her lungs. Her eyes widened as she clawed at the ground trying to get the air back. Shock and panic began to twine their way up her spine as her mind cataloged her injuries. Pain. She did her best to coax her lungs to accept the oxygen her body desperately needed to continue functioning.

Suddenly as if a switch had flipped in her mind she began to suck in air, the sounds emerging like a gasping choke. She rolled on her side trying her best to get her body to regulate its basic functions. Slowly with great care she leveraged her body up to a standing position. She limped forward placing her hand on the invisible barrier, tears pricking at the corners of her eyes, loneliness swamping her.

She looked beyond her hand and saw the wolf bounding toward her, shifting on the go and walking up to the gate with a wide smile on his face. "Come on Pip. Let's go."

She slammed her hand on the barrier making it evident that the magic prevented her. The magic rippled but stayed strong. An impenetrable force. The man's face screwed up, confusion evident.

"What the hell! It let you in, why won't it let you out?!" The man became frantic pummeling the barrier putting his strength into the hits. The ripples came faster but the barrier remained steadfastly solid.

Aurelia took a step back shaking her head, despair filling her, the tears beginning to fall in earnest. She returned to the barrier once she was sure that he couldn't fall through. She beat on the magic with both her fists in tandem to her sobs. "You can't leave me here! You can't leave me alone! What's going to happen to me? You made me do this. Why!?"

She collapsed into a heap at the base of the magical barrier. Her hand gently touching it, hoping that Dodsfell would take pity on her and let her out, to rejoin the mortals of Baelia where she belonged.

The man pulled a sword and aimed around her, placing the tip of the blade on the magic barrier. Slowly he pushed, pressing his body weight against the blade. A whirring buzz filled the air, earsplitting before a booming thunder emerged and the man was spit into the air by the magic of the barrier, his sword soaring and landing point down next to him.

Slowly he came up to the gate in front of Aurelia and sank onto his knees, placing his hand on the magic over hers. "I am sorry Pip. I shall do what I can to fix this. I will try to get King Harold here. Perhaps he can tunnel under and get you out. Stay strong little one. Stay safe."

Aurelia shot him a glare that scorched the sadness and desolation quickly morphing to anger. "Safe." She spat the word out as if it was poison. "There is no 'safe' here and you know that. How do I stay safe? I am stuck here unarmed, no magic. It would have been better to be slaughtered with everyone else in Drakore than this. You cursed me."

The man looked down, shame washing over his face. "I

shall make it up to you Aurelia. Someday somehow a boon will be yours. I shall fight for you, I won't let you just disappear."

Aurelia stood slowly, her face full of unmasked fury. "Whatever helps you sleep tonight you bastard."

twenty-seven

KYGOSS

DRAKORE - TIX - YEAR 7557

Kygoss flew from Slana intent on finding Aurelia, determination pumping through him to ensure that Maledic kept hold of his mortality. This first required him to ensure that the area around the palace was indeed free of any signs of Aurelia, the chance that someone found her while he was in Slana was negligible but not nonexistent. He studied the movements of the guards below him as he circled the palace. It took no time at all to determine that guards were still scouring the grounds, overturning carts and disassembling the bales of hay.

Kygoss expanded his search to the outlying city curious to see what the behaviors of the city watch were. Even there he noticed similar actions, tossing of buckets, emptying every barrel, searching every house and hovel that they came across. He lighted onto a branch his mind processing the evidence he knew. *A Palion mutt broke into her room, and they haven't found her yet.*

Where would someone take her when Drakore was

crawling with the enemy? The mutt would want to take her to Palion in the end and the only way to do that was to go west. Kygoss leapt back into the sky and turned toward the main Drakore gate.

An instinct he didn't quite understand pushed him to stay near the barrier between Drakore and Dodsfell as he flew toward the gate. If he flew high enough he could just barely make out the land on the Dodsfell side. His wings seized as he noticed a black and white blur moving slowly in Dodsfell. As he began to fall his brain kicked back on and he flapped back up enabling him to see once more the hunched form of the most wanted girl in Baelia, Aurelia.

She suddenly stopped and seemed to be pulling something out of her foot. He approached the barrier and tried to fly through it, desperate to reach her. Yet he kept bouncing off the magical wall, feathers falling off the more often he bounced. Desperation surged through his blood, he needed to save her to save Mal. Part of his mind knew that it would be impossible for him to cross the boundary yet it was clear that she had. *Why would Dodsfell welcome her and not him?* He flew alongside the barrier following her plodding process through Dodsfell lands.

As they went farther and farther west it occurred to him that she must be headed to the gate near the Tixdarr Temple. It grew larger the farther Aurelia walked. He winged his way to a tree standing tall near the gate. He waited, preparing to shift when the sounds of a wolf's padded feet became apparent. He stayed in his crow form watching and waiting.

A piece of him broke inside as he watched her come to terms with her new reality. Pride laced with fear and anger filled him as he watched her turn away from the barrier staring into the realm of the dead, her shoulders back, the dirty and tangled nightgown lifting on an inhumane breeze.

He let out a caw of farewell hoping she could hear him.

Hoping she knew that she wasn't actually alone. He stayed in the tree watching until she made it too far within Dodsfell to tell her from the broken trees that lined the broken path.

His hatred solidified for Palion, somehow they had gotten Aurelia through the barrier. Their intentions may have been pure but they would now be responsible for any pain that Aurelia and Maledic experienced. He flapped back to the palace, mentally preparing to do what he must in order to secure what little peace could be found from Darius as a ruler.

Once he arrived he headed to Aurelia's room, his heart hardening, refusing to give into the sadness that he may never see her again. Faziel still sat in the corner, propped against the wall in her stinking stench, it boggled his mind that she had been able to sleep in the filth and the smell. Flies had even begun to gather in the room, lighting on her.

He rustled in the drawers and found her a set of clean clothes before waking her. Once done he reached down and poked the sleeping girl awake. "Faziel, I need you to wake up now."

She opened a bleary eye squinting up, her face swollen from all the crying. "What? Mister Corvus? What's happening now?"

Kygoss smiled kindly hoping she felt calmer seeing his ease. "My dear you have been chosen to help bring Drakore back from the brink of chaos. You will be perfect in aiding His Lord Darius in ruling our fair kingdom. It will require you to clean yourself up though." He put out his hand, a mask of pleasure affixed to his face, as she placed her hand in his.

He led her to the bedside where the clean clothes rested. He reached over and poured the old cold water into the wash basin grabbing Aurelias old sheets in lieu of a wash towel.

"Quick now child! Go ahead and get cleaned up. Soon you'll not be a mere Princess but you will be a Queen."

Faziel watched him, her eyes looking hauntingly empty. She nodded but her movements were stunted and stuttered. He sighed heavily as he stepped into the hall and waited. It took a long while before she tentatively stepped into the hall. His heart broke for this tiny girl, only fourteen, the sacrifice for a nation's peace. His mind slammed down a shield keeping his internal feelings safe within himself.

He escorted her down to the throne room past the guards who glared at Kygoss. "You stay out here. I don't want you to see what may be inside. I shall be right back." Faziel tucked herself into the corner far from the guard, her expression closed off as she nodded mutely to Kygoss.

Kygoss opened the throne room door just wide enough to admit him, careful to hide what he suspected may still be lying on the ground. Shock rippled through him as he noticed that the bodies had indeed been removed. Unsurprisingly the blood remained puddled on the ground. Darius however sat on the throne, his bat-like wings spread open, staring into the distance, his face dark and glowering. Kygoss stepped back into the hall and beckoned Faziel forward.

Faziel followed behind him reluctance oozing out of her every pore. He got to the throne and bowed low, "My lord."

Darius started as if coming out of a trance staring at Kygoss and then at Faziel confusion on his face. "What is it old bird?"

"Sire. I have scoured from Slana to the Western Gate and can assure you that Aurelia is gone. Where I don't know, perhaps someone has killed her. Right now we need to turn our attention to something of higher importance, we need to cement your rule of Drakore now while we still have the upper hand. You need to marry before the Inheritance Rite, thus Faziel. She is an acceptable female and already in the palace."

He could see the refusal on Darius' face. He rushed on. "If we go forth and try to find an alternative it will alert the masses of the instability. While she is still too young to finish the ceremony, that will take a few years, she can be the face of your rule. Eventually she will also be attached to the Great Sky Power and create joy in the kingdom in the wake of this less than ideal way to gain the throne."

Darius paled, considering. "Why can I not just take the Rite without a bride?"

Kygoss nodded, aiming to keep Darius in a neutral state. "You can. However the kingdom will suffer if only one person is tied to the power. There could be weaknesses in your protection from Dodsfell.

Faziel will be unable to complete the Rite until she is at least seventeen better yet eighteen. Her being tied to the power would be in effect regardless. It will protect her and the kingdom, she just can't manipulate the power until it's completed. She can be raised from here on out to learn whatever you want, how to do the political dance, how to take care of the palace, whatever. You will have your own rooms and so will she. This will be an easy marriage."

Darius nodded slowly, "You make great arguments but how do I know you aren't going to betray me?"

"We can exchange oaths if that would suit you. Otherwise time will tell." Kygoss sucked in a breath, an oath was a heavy bargain but if that is what is needed he would do it.

Darius stared at him, twirling a dagger between his fingers. "An oath would be interesting." Darius muttered more but Kygoss couldn't hear it.

Kygoss approached the throne and held out his hand. Darius deeply scored it causing Kygoss to wince as Darius scored his own palm. He grasped Kygoss' outstretched hand with a grip that could break, raising his dark brow at Kygoss challenging him to make the oath.

Before he could think too heavily on it he let out a deep sigh, "I Kygoss Corvus vow to do whatever lies within my power to secure leadership within Drakore."

Darius tightened his grip, "I see you fail to be specific in who that leadership is."

Kygoss shot Darius a crooked smile, "The tide does change from time to time, however while you are in power you would be the one who has my support." He gave a small shrug.

Darius nodded along. "I understand old bird. I shall watch you carefully but for now I agree." Power filled them as the oath took effect.

They released hands, sickness welling up within him. It would take a long time to pave the path for a strong leadership within Drakore but the work had officially begun.

twenty-eight

AURELIA

DODSFELL ~ REALM OF THE DEAD - TIX - YEAR 7557

> Oaths are powerful magic. When one of the oath makers dies the promise is still expected to be upheld, unless of course that becomes impossible with the death. The Oath marks remain until the promises are fulfilled, thus creating promises that can last lifetimes isn't advised.
> ~Archives of Tiva's Temple

Aurelia turned away from the gate, her mind going numb as she faced her future, however long that may be. She had no idea where the path would lead, no Acolyte had ever spoken of it, yet it seemed to be the only option. She had to find somewhere to shelter, and find some sort of food.

As she got farther from Baelia, Dodsfell got darker and colder. Her skin began to numb, her toes and fingers losing sensation entirely. The broken path turned toward the left and in the distance it became clear that there were larger nondescript objects. She moved slower, sticking nearer to the trees trying to ease down the path without being noticed. As she neared the objects came into clearer view showing stone buildings, inscribed with names.

She stepped inside the first building not hearing anything suspicious. *Perhaps this could work.* She walked around the small building, her eyes skimming the names that were listed on the walls. Everyone listed all shared a surname. She had never heard of buildings dedicated to particular families.

In her land, the only acceptable way to handle someone who died was to clean the body before delivering it to Tixdarr's temple. There the Acolytes of Tixdarr took the body and wrapped it in linen and left them at the gate for the guardians within Dodsfell to take them to the land of the dead. The rumor being that the soul was offered a choice when their body entered Dodsfell; to walk Dodsfell for eternity or to allow the Gods to take their soul into the void to live a new life at a time of their choosing. *But why the buildings?*

She was so absorbed with trying to decipher the etched names, some worn with age when a large shadow darkened the doorway. Her blood ran cold as she slowly turned, taking in the sight of a large blue demon. She had never seen a demon in real life, only ever portraits within the temples. Yet the artists had done an excellent job capturing the likeness. His scale-like skin gleamed as if water dripped down even though no water was present. His face held no softness, the angles sharp and intimidating with horns twisting toward the sky out of his head. His eyes glowed yellow, exuding a malice that made her very soul quake.

"Hello there. Who do we have here." He took a huge inhale, his slit like nostrils flaring. "You are alive."

Aurelia took a few steps backward, her back hitting the wall. "Yes."

"That will make this even more entertaining."

He rushed her a cackle leaving his throat as she screamed.

twenty-nine

MALEDIC

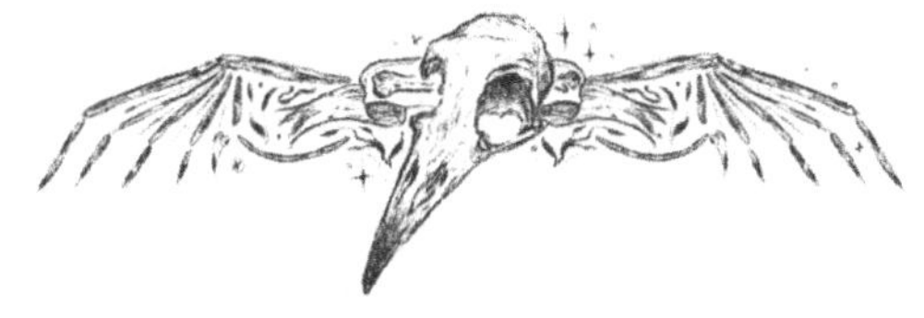

SLANA - TIX - YEAR 7557

The earth shook, a deep groaning rocking the Falrath Mountains setting trees to dance. Shifters and non-shifters alike took flight struggling to stay attached to the swaying branches jumping in tempo to the creaking ground.

He had never known a greater struggle than the one he presently faced in lifting his head. The pain of constant exhaustion coupled with the rippling agony that roiled through him on a near constant basis made it impossible to leave his bed. As his eyes lifted to look out the large window something implausible appeared to be happening. The trees were dancing. Perhaps the pain of losing *her*, the echoing remnants of her own pain finally caused him to lose his grip on reality. He had heard his mother's frantic questions to the medics on that very possibility often enough. The time finally arrived after all, trees shouldn't be dancing.

Slow beyond his eighteen years he leveraged himself out of the bed, his eyes never leaving the jumping trees. If his mind was slipping, *her* end must have come to pass. Ever since *her*

211

disappearance he imagined that when she died he would feel the passing of *her* soul. Yet perhaps this was the way it went, slowly degrading into madness.

What more did he have to fight for? Why not just end it all on his own terms?

He stood on shaky legs, his clothes hanging from his too lean frame. Closing his eyes he pushed at his magic demanding it to shift him. What should have happened as naturally as blinking didn't. He tried again. Envisioning his favored form. The sleek feathers, the long pointed beak, the strong powerful wings capable of carrying him wherever he wanted to go except the one place he needed to be.

The process had once been smooth, as natural as donning a shirt. Now pain graced the process, feathers poking through his skin, haphazardly scattered across his body. He half turned, catching sight of his body in the mirror and couldn't help a small chuckle despite his misery. He looked worse than he did when he had started to learn how to shift as a child. Feathers sticking through his skin oddly bent, the feathers themselves sparse and illkempt.

Watching himself in the mirror he visualized in his mind's eye the image of his crow form. It took a lot more fortitude than Maledic had prepared to use but slowly his arms shrank into himself and became wings, his torso shrinking a little faster. One by one his legs became the spindly legs of the crow, talons visible where once his feet were. His head shifted last, shrinking down to match his familiar avian body. He flapped his wings sore from disuse, studying his figure for what could be the last time. His favored form did not look nearly as bedraggled as his mortal shell had, a sight which made him feel slightly better.

Within this form he could feel his bond to Aurelia a bit stronger than when in his mortal shell. Perhaps because he had first felt the bond solidify in his crow form. The memory fresh in his mind, finding the flowers to make her smile, scattering them across her saddle. He turned back to the window watching the trees continuing to jump and dance while the wailing from below grew louder.

Before the madness took him he may as well find the cause of the rolling ground, perhaps he could spread any needed awareness to his parents before the bond took him back to *her*. He followed the sound, flying right to the Baelian and Dodsfell barrier toward the cave system on the eastern outer edge of Drakore. He could feel the barrier between realms thinning, not quite feeling firm and concrete. It crossed his mind that it may be possible that the noise could be demons breaking through such a thin barrier.

Perhaps he could go through to the demonic realm if they could get into the Mortal Realm. Hope sparked through him at the potential of finding Aurelia and saving her from whatever she endured.

He neared a cave opening where the noise had reached deafening qualities. He swooped into the cave system staying high and out of sight as he scanned for an answer to the noise. An answer to the very dirt awakening.

As Maledic flew further into the cave, far past where the barrier should have been he began to see rivulets of fire on the ground. The cave began to get hotter and hotter, squeezing him from all sides. The feeling was foreign and uncomfortable but his curiosity outweighed reason, so onward he flew.

It soon got far too hot for him to go further. He stopped watching the recesses of the cave as the fire continued to flow past.

A deep growling grimace echoed out from the depths. *Perhaps a new style of demon. One that had never ventured into Baelia finally awakened due to Aurelias presence in Dodsfell. After all the Gods demanded balance.*

Yet as he perched atop a stalagmite he watched as the

pebbles began to bounce up off the ground. He cocked his head, the madness worsening.

Without the sun gauging how much time passed became impossible, the pebbles bouncing higher and higher. A sound of ungraceful lumbering echoed growing closer. His attention honed in on the dark hole further into the heat, curious as to what creature his madness could think up.

His imagination reeled as the creature finally came into view.

A large, even overly large reptilian head slithered out of the opening, a long tongue tasting the air around it. Golden slits of eyes narrowed lit by an unseen fire within. Maledic struggled to understand how such a gargantuan creature fit within such an average sized cave system.

A hissing emerged as the creature came closer. "Shifter. I can smell you. You taste of wind and trees. Show me your mortal shell before I verify your flavors and make a tasty feathered treat from your crow body."

Mal hopped onto the ground dodging the molten tracks embedded into the stone. His mind tired, the ordeal of the past weeks wearing on him along with the effort it had taken to shift in the first place.

He closed his beady crow eyes and concentrated. The reptilian creature rested its large head onto the stone ground, the slitted eye watching carefully.

Slowly he shifted back into his mortal self not allowing the feeling of being watched cause him any more stress.

His throat ran dry as the heat swelled. He croaked. "Does this version make you happier?"

The scaled creature's skin seemed to ripple as it sighed heavily. "Why is it that the last of my house is stuck in the Realm of the Dead, and you her soulbond is here?"

Maledic debated if he was going to play dumb or if he was going give the scary creature what it wanted. He opted for one last round of mischief. "Which house is that? Given your size I am not sure I have seen a house big enough to encompass you."

The scales which were a dark dingy gray began to change color, as it absorbed his words the scales undulated in color not stopping on one. "This is why the last time I flew I ate crows. Birds intent on riling feathers and gathering mischief as one would gather sustenance."

Maledic gave a half shrug, reminiscent of the bird of his blood. A smirk unfurling on his face. "I can't see how she's related to a great one of your size. However, it is my understanding that my soulbond was sent to Dodsfell to escape the fate of her family." He ended his statement with a small bow of respect, not exactly enjoying the idea of being eaten.

The reptile huffed a puff of smoke showering him with ash. Mal coughed, covering his mouth with his tunic to protect his airways, his eyes stinging and watering. The creature in front of him closed its eyes and breathed deep. As this happened the ground quieted, seeming to calm. The eyes snapped open. "She will return and she will need you so do better boy. Be warned she will not be the same girl who last bid you goodbye. Take heart that the dragon will fly again."

The reptile rubbed its great head against the cave wall, the ground protesting in response. Maledic watched as two large scales fell from the dragon's face, nearest its eye. "The Gods caged me when they realized how little influence they truly had. So steps were taken. The Great Powers of Baelia were split, and I the embodiment of the power, found myself locked away to keep the mortals from my influence. Nevertheless the wings have come, the male who died carried them and his heir will have a much stronger connection. Her body already bares the wings, but more will be given when the time is right. They will see. They created a false necklace to indicate the true passing of the throne. Yet here is the real one." The dragon tilted its head at the scales that fell.

Maledic limped closer, careful to not touch the head of the creature blinking at him. The lips curled up, smoke escaping through clenched teeth. Teeth that looked entirely too sharp. Mal leaned down slowly, grasping the first scale with merely his fingertips. He slipped the scale into his pocket without investigating it more. Then he reached again for the next scale. Mal realized that this one felt much heavier than the first. As he pulled it up he walked backwards, careful to step slowly and never turn away from the creature's head. Once at a safer distance Mal glanced down at the scale, a gorgeous multi-colored rainbow shimmering as he tilted it from side to side. Slowly he flipped the scale over to the back, and gasped. There nestled inside was a necklace almost indistinguishable to the necklace that his Auntie Hesper wore as Queen of Drakore, similar but at the same time different. The gem on Hesper's necklace was red and orange, the color reminiscent of fire. Yet this one was a tiny rainbow dragon scale implanted in the dragon's claws.

"The age of cages is coming to an end. Be ready, young feathered friend." The words echoed through the cave.

Mal's mouth gaped open, shock shimmering through him yet before he could speak, the creature pulled its head back into the deep recesses of the cave, a flicker of flame escaping its mouth. Maledic leaned up against the wall of the cave breathing hard as his mind reeled. Finally after a millennia the fabled dragon, the one that Drakore got its name from was awakened.

A flicker of hope, the flame of righteousness began to burn deep within him. Aurelia would survive, the dragon of legend couldn't be wrong, could it?

THE LOST YEARS OF DODSFELL

Partially recovered by Maledic, Aurelia and Kygoss.

The Ancient Dragon of Drakore Legend

The rumors say that centuries ago a dragon ruled Baelia. The people loved her, the demons hated her. The job of protecting the mortals within the lands of the living kept the dragon strong and motivated despite being the last of her kind.

According to the rumors the Gods developed a jealous streak over the fawning that followed the dragon from place to place. A plan was hatched to limit her influence and weaken her natural power. Goddess Tiva aided by the six other strongest Gods of the Pantheon came together and destroyed the dragon's ability to wield magic. Once that was neutralized they ensnared the dragon below the ground in an open cavern system believed to exist beneath the mountains bordering Dodsfell.

The belief is that when the world is in its greatest need the dragon will be released once more bringing with it prosperity to the land and people once more.

~ Tiva Temple Archives

Dodsfell created by the Lord of the Dead, Tixdarr in an effort to quell the boredom that came within the Void where the Gods reside. In his own world, power quickly went to his head creating a haven for the nightmares of mortals.

 ~ The Lost Archives of Tixdarr's Temple

thirty

MALEDIC

SLANA - ANIT - YEAR 7558

It took many months for his full strength to return. Yet he pushed through, determined to make it happen. He would be prepared.

His mother became an invaluable resource, having stepped up for him as he recovered. She never blinked an eye at the need, having done the same for his father whenever he had been stationed at the palace. The time had come for Maledic to take up the mantle fully, allowing the enormity of the task to distract him. Distraction became necessary as his connection with *her* consisted of an ever present pulsing pain that varied in intensity.

The first step in dealing with his pain resulted in banning *her* name. Every time he heard it uttered a fresh wave crested within him, sometimes so sharp he doubled over gasping, internally clutching at his own consciousness trying to stay grounded in himself. The day *her* name had to be banned within the manor house stuck out in his memory like a blistering sore.

His mother Maie had been bustling in and out of his new rooms, her old ones, a physician in toe. "Aurelia's disappearance has caused him such weakness of the body. Is there nothing to be done? Surely there are individuals who survive the loss of their soulbond. What do you suggest?"

The use of Aurelia's name in the same conversation as a loss of a soulbond had been too much. The pain had crested within his mind, overwhelming his entire being. He had surged to a seated position gasping for breath desperate for his own sense of self to crest the wave of pain, the effort depleting his energy reserves to a dangerous level.

"NO more." He had rasped. "Never again use her name."

His mother had blanched. Her skin paling to an off yellow as she processed his words. She had opened her mouth to argue but a glare from him caused her to merely swallow hard and nod once.

That had happened just a few days before he had met the dragon.

Thoughts of the dragon caused him to spin the cuff at his wrist. He had taken the dragon's scales to the blacksmith's apprentice, his best friend Stulten and together they had determined that the scales were in fact what Drakore was. The ancient weaponry made with the famous material, said to be mined by long gone dwarves in the mountains of the Falrath Range were in fact made of smelted scales poured into molds. It took both scales, but he had created a dagger and an outward facing cuff, inlaid with the crest of the crows. Fanciful jewelry but easily explained by his new office. It didn't need to matter to anyone else that it held a secondary purpose, an outward connection to his soulbond.

He glanced toward the Dodsfell barrier, the feeling of suffocation and pain rising within him. Separating *her* experiences from his own body's reactions had become harder and harder.

A sigh rent through him as he turned his attention to the stack of papers on his desk. His mother had an organizational system that made little sense to him. Before him sat five stacks of papers that ranged in height. He took the first page from the middle stack, perusing it for the contents. He managed to internalize that something to do with the economy of their farthest village before a gut clenching shock of pain radiated through him. He curled his upper body onto the top of the desk clutching his stomach with one hand.

His other hand clutched the paper, well it had been a paper now it resembled more of a ball. Taking deep breaths forcing his mind to push the pain to the back, refusing to let it take over. After it had receded enough he sat up once more, his face glowering at the towering papers. An impulsive thought flickered through his head, the idea of throwing all the papers onto the ground screaming with the unfair reality he had to endure. Yet, he couldn't, instead he took another shuddering inhale. The task of organizing the papers and collating notes for his meeting in the morning would be simple. It would also aid him in the practice of keeping his cool, he couldn't be doubled over in pain at Darius' first official council meeting, it would be his first as Lord of the Crows and Darius' first as King of Drakore. A lot of interest and expectation rode on the meeting and he needed to be in his best mindset possible.

thirty-one

KYGOSS

DRAKORE - BYR - YEAR 7558

The wedding to Faziel haunted him. Images of the quivering girl no more than a child being forced to slit her palm and recite the words that Oba Aewenna issued flitted through his mind at the worst of times, causing nausea to roil in his gut.

Surprisingly, Darius had been almost gentlemanly in his actions since that day, never attempting or showing signs of interest in consummating the Rite. Luckily for all involved the Rite did not decree a specific timeline in order to fully complete it, so time remained in their favor for now. Kygoss had taken steps to ensure Darius' compliance, including an early warning system should her doors be forced open at night, yet it seemed overkill.

Kygoss paced his study debating what more could be done at this point. Aurelia had been missing for five months. While he knew where she currently resided, he could do nothing about it. From his most recent report from Maie, Maledic had somehow turned himself around, choosing to believe that she

225

would return despite the constant pain pointing to the contrary.

Gnawing on his thumb nail the reality that there was nothing more to do but wait settling upon his shoulders. His spy network did not extend into Palion to the level that would make him comfortable. If she showed up in Palion he needed to have the infrastructure in place to alert him. His intel network still hadn't managed to infiltrate the inner circle of the Prince, but from what he had gathered it appeared that Lucian and Harold were both convinced that she died. Lucian to his credit acted like a mourning love sick fool, opting to send search parties far and wide getting dangerously close to accusing Darius of her murder without actually muttering the words.

Today would prove to be a make or break moment for the new rulers, the first council meeting of Darius' reign. If the Lords of the Realm didn't respect his rule chaos could and more than likely would ensue. Darius had a hair trigger personality and a penchant for torture in the dungeons, especially without Cerial to ground him in reality. It would depend on Kygoss to walk the line and keep Darius centered on the meeting at hand and not on any potential insults given.

He shot a glance out the window, a curse leaving his mouth. His musings had left him with little time to reach the council chamber. His fear took shape as he crossed the threshold and saw everyone already seated. A burst of pride bloomed in his chest at the sight of Mal sitting among the Lords of the Kingdom, prepared to answer to their King. He bowed deeply, careful to keep his eyes down, taking his seat nearest the door.

He could make out across the table that Darius looked worse than he normally appeared. *Did the man sleep?* The dark black smudges under his dark eyes suggested he didn't. Kygoss flicked his gaze around, cataloging the Lords that represented each of the territories. No major changes besides Maledic which was best. The most shocking attendant to the table was Faziel, she had just turned fifteen. A child by anyones account yet here she appeared dressed in the highest fashion, a newly minted crown atop her head. Her appearance alone wasn't the shocking part, Hesper had spent her time in council meetings frequently enough. Faziel though sat at the head of the table, the place of honor while the leader of the rebellion sat behind her.

Faziel sat forward a small glare toward Kygoss undoubtedly over his slight tardiness. "Welcome Lord's of Drakore. My King and I are pleased to make your official acquaintances." Kygoss looked around at the men seated around the table as they all nervously squirmed in their seats, equally unsure how to address a child in the place of power.

A girlish giggle came from her as she batted her lashes, her eyes flitting from Lord to Lord. "I have never gotten the privilege of watching one of these meetings. Which of you strong men will explain the process to me."

Kygoss internally flinched a bit, she had taken her lessons from him and twisted them. Kindness, listening and care were the most important for Darius' Queen yet somehow she'd twisted it to be manipulative.

She leaned over to Gossek, the poor Sparrow Lord, seated nearest her. Kygoss clamped down on his urge to roll his eyes, he had given her a direct order to not approach Gossek. He had an unfortunate impediment commonly known to those within the room that he lost his ability to form complete sentences around females. "Sire." She pursed her pretty lips in concentration. "Oh yes. You're Gossek the Lord of the Sparrows. Perhaps you can enlighten me on the typical discussions held within these chambers."

Gossek nervously flipped through the papers and then stammered, "W-ell milady. Taxes, ti-tithes, fest-festiv-festivals."

His voice trailed off as he sat there swallowing hard as if trying to bring air into his deprived lungs. Kygoss watched in awe as Faziel reached over and squeezed the nervous Lord's hand.

"Thank you so much Gossek, your help has been invaluable." To his astonishment the praise was enough to have Gossek's cheeks flaming and nodding silently. *Why did she praise him? Why was she being nice?* The hair rose on the back of his head as he thought through the reasons she would have to be kind.

Kygoss' head whipped fast at the sound of the next voice, dread rising. *No, no keep your head down and unnoticed. Foolish boy.*

"What the Lord of Sparrows tried his best to impart to one so stunning, is that we cover an array of subjects important to the people within the Kingdom. Including anything that the crown may wish to impart to us as important. Perhaps today we could merely discuss where the kingdom is at, and next we meet we can all work to improve our general territories." Maledic's voice rang strong and true.

Faziel's eyes latched on to him and to Kygoss' dread her entire demeanor changed. "Oh my. I can see the familial resemblance you must be Maledic Corvus, the handsome, newly appointed Lord of the Crows. I must say we were grateful your father decided to dedicate his full attention to our rule rather than juggle responsibilities. Plus it gives us the enjoyment of seeing such a handsome face in front of us." She clapped her hands in joy, ignoring the slight growl that emitted from Darius behind her. "I think Lord Corvus," she threw him a wink. "Has the right idea. Let us go around the room, I want to hear all about your amazing territories. In honor of his brilliance let's have Lord Corvus please start us off."

She sent him a huge smile, her body leaning toward Mal to a degree that was practically obscene especially considering her husband sat behind her. Kygoss felt his breath catch in his throat as he waited to see just how much Mal would choose to reveal to his new King and Queen. Technically he could tell them as much or as little as he wanted, he alone held the title of guardian to Slana, though Kygoss hoped he would be wise.

"The people of the Crowlands are eager to celebrate the new Crown's authority. Our smithery is working on a gift to grace the Queen's gorgeous neck, along with the sharpest daggers to arm the King. The hunting is good, the people are happy and content."

Faziel clapped with joy and turned shining eyes on the Lord sitting next to Maledic, while Kygoss emitted the pent up breath. He tuned out the other lords staring at Faziel and Darius trying to interpret their minor movements, to see beneath their skin and learn what they weren't saying with their words.

His skill had become rusty during Hesper and Aydan's rule. He hadn't realized just how much he had come to rely on their open communication. The longer Darius and Faziel held their power the more Kygoss had to compartmentalize. His feelings, the confidences imparted to him by those who trusted him all while keeping the innocent as shielded as possible. A task better suited to someone with farther reaching wings but still he would continue to try.

Everything he had to do in order to salvage the Kingdom was done in Aurelia's name. She would return, that he fully believed and the task would rest with him until then. He just prayed it would be intact for her.

thirty-two

AURELIA

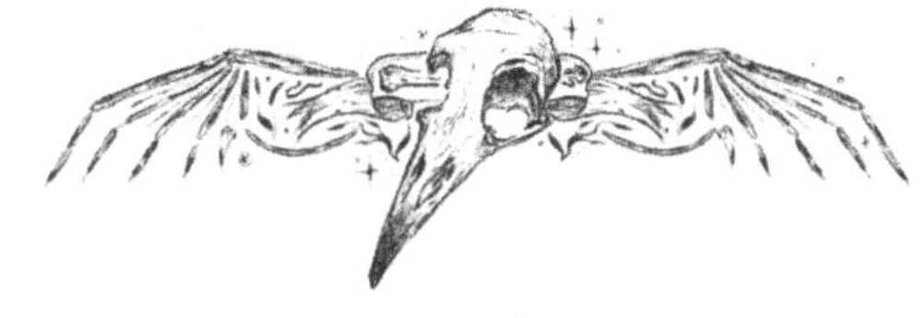

DODSFELL ~ THE REALM OF THE DEAD - DUELE - YEAR 7558

She huddled against the dark wall of her hovel. Her breath came out shakily as she mentally cataloged her newest hurts. Closing her eyes as the tears oozed out once more from beneath her lashes. Beneath her closed lids the image of her father danced in front of her from the last time she saw him. The likelihood that he still lived was laughable, her heart squeezing at the thought. He had been such a handsome strong man, always making sure she felt protected and safe.

She missed that feeling more than anything else. If presented with the choice between the feeling of safety or heat she would freeze to death feeling safe rather than be warm and in danger. He had come to her the night that everything changed.

A knock sounded on the door sharp and out of place given the time of day. Aurelia had walked opening the door a frown furrowing her brow as she came face to face with her father.

"Papa? What's going on?"

He had stood there an odd look on his face before ushering her into her own room. "My little warrior. I need to speak to you before you go to sleep, do you mind?"

She shook her head taking a seat on her bed, Faziel had already fallen asleep on her bed across the room. Her father had glanced in the direction and shrugged, lowering his voice. "We will keep it as quiet as possible."

Aurelia smiled and nodded.

"Things are gearing up to change for you little warrior. Do you think you're ready?"

She had frowned, "To be Queen? No. Don't I have a few years though? I thought I was able to wait until I was eighteen. Did something change?" Her questions poured out, unable to stop.

Her father had smiled indulgently. "No no not to be Queen. That may still be in the works in the future. I just think things may change before that. Do you remember our oath?"

"The one we made when I was thirteen? When you and Mother made me unofficially the heir in Drakore? Yeah. I am supposed to protect the people. Right?"

Her father frowned slightly. "At its most basic yes. However it's important to note one particular thing. In order to protect the people you must protect yourself. You have to fight whatever comes. No matter how scared you may find yourself, even if you are alone. Do you understand little warrior?"

"You and Mother will be with me though? I won't be alone." She had said it asking as much as stating.

He had remained silent waiting. "I will protect myself, papa. Never fear." He nodded and ruffled her head.

"Time for bed then. Climb in, I'll tuck you in." She had

hesitated. He never tucked her in, at least not since she was a small child.

It made sense now. Her father had known she had been destined for this hell hole. That she would be put through things that would break grown men in a blink. He expected her to weather it all because of the oath she had been tricked into taking at the age of thirteen.

Regardless she had fought. At the beginning she fought as hard as she could despite the repercussions. The days kept coming though, six months of being gone. Six months of pain. Pain became a tool for her compliance by her captors. More than once she found herself cursing her past self for not listening to her lessons about Dodsfell.

Along with learning how to stay alive she began to slowly learn how this new world worked. Scale color mattered, it dictated the social structure of the demons within Dodsfell. Greens seemed to be the basest of the creatures, stopping at nothing to attain what they desired. Blues appeared civilized. She had fallen for that trick early. No matter how civilized they appeared to be, they were bullies wearing nice clothes and fancy words. The other color purple seemed to be the upper elite but it didn't make a lot of sense to her how one could be upper class in a land of demons.

Red demons were a class unto themselves, rare, almost mythical in nature. From what Aurelia had pieced together from her eavesdropping it had to do with age and cunning. If a demon could live for centuries they would slowly begin to shift colors to a new station in life. Yet surviving couldn't be taken for granted as any little insult could and oftentimes did lead to riotous fights.

Her body shook as she shifted a leg in front of her, the

new cut across her thigh causing so much pain as to induce the tremor in the muscle. Her current captors were a part of a blue clan whose name she couldn't pronounce. Her duties were on the surface reasonable, cleaning and caring for the compound. However, the rooms never actually reached a cleanly state due to the rags that seemingly couldn't actually be cleaned. The pain only came at the end of the grey day, when the male demon who came calling more and more frequently found ways to corner her.

If it wasn't him it was the mistress of the house who frequently took out her frustrations on Aurelia, pummeling and punching until blood appeared. Today ended with a knife. The mistress had been preparing a creature of the night for a feast being held soon. She had inspected the room Aurelia had painstakingly cleaned and became unsatisfied so the knife found its home in Aurelia's thigh. She had to remove it herself which had actually been more tortuous than the stabbing. She did her best to keep her head down, choosing to believe that fighting took many forms, silence and survival being one. She just had to bide her time until she could find a way out of this monstrous place and back to the land of the living. Back to Mal, the one thought that kept her mind in a place of sanity amongst the insane.

Gods did not just appear from thin air. They are the products of dreams. The dreams of people hoping for a better life, for help with a particular problem, dreams of the lonely. Those all mixed together can oftentimes create a God. It takes a lot of dreams to amount to one though. Be warned a solitary moment in the dark will not equal a god to save you. It could in fact create a nightmare to run from.

~ The Lost Archives of Tiva's Temple.

thirty-three

AURELIA

DODSFELL ~ THE REALM OF THE DEAD - BURA - YEAR 7559

A dragon loomed above her. The scaly jaw clenching and moving, speaking. Yet she couldn't make out the words. Aurelia opened her mouth to ask but the dream shifted and she saw the dragon wasn't speaking to her. Maledic's tall lanky form stood next to the head conversing with the great beast. As fear spiked in one part of her mind the scene in front of her remained calm, free from terrors. Aurelia held her breath hoping to hear what was clearly being discussed.

Words floated through her mind as if on a phantom wind, Maledic's crisp tone caressing her comforting even though the words were not directed to her. *"You are keeping me alive. It is quite a small task for me to know the name of the one who has helped me."* Another voice gravely and foreign but no less comforting came through, *"My name is Feginth."*

The image swirled together causing panic to crest within her. She sat up suddenly, her breath coming in pants tears running down her face. The dream had seemed so real. His

237

voice had sounded just like it had the last time she had spoken to him all those months ago. Panic crawled up the back of her throat, panic that she would never see him again. Her eighteenth birthday would have been today but no one here would celebrate her, or make her feel loved.

Things were changing in Dodsfell, perhaps due to her being here for two years. Or perhaps the demons had something to do with it. The blue demon clan had begun to host more and more purple demons. Demons who appeared particularly interested in her. Every time she entered the common areas the eyes of purple demons in residence tracked her every movement. *Waiting.*

She made her way out of her hovel, ready to begin whatever hell this day would actually bring. She walked to the common room intent on gathering the cleaning supplies she regularly used. For the first time a purple female demon approached her pulling at the scraps of her nightgown. Speaking over her shoulder to the blue male responsible for the majority of her pain and issues. "Why is she clothed so?"

"She is naught but a maid and plaything who cares what she wears."

Aurelia glared at the male before remembering she would be far safer to just look to the ground. The female tutted low having seen the temper, cuffing her on the back of her head.

Aurelia swallowed her cringe and retort.

"We never treat our playthings this poorly. Perhaps that's why you still find yourself stuck in the diminished status of blue. If you want to climb the ranks as we of the Areth clan have you should perhaps direct your attention to how you treat others."

Aurelia wisely swallowed her smirk, pressing her lips so firmly together it hurt.

The female of the Areth clan turned her back to Aurelia. "We will take her off your hands. I want a price reduction since

I now have to clothe and feed her. You left her to be nothing but skin and bones, I must now fatten her up to be worthy of my clan. No one of my clan would dare to play with her in this state."

Fear rushed through her at the idea that they just wanted to fatten her up to play with her. *What would that even mean?*

The male hmmed and hawed. "I suppose 5 gold marks. No less than that."

Aurelia risked a glance at her new buyer. The purple female smirked in victory.

It didn't take long for her to be forced outside into a cart. The ride blurred the surroundings blending together until they reached another gated compound. The compound of the blue clan had merely been two large hodgepodge buildings on a piece of land surrounded by a gate. The purple clan's looked more organized and intense. The buildings were made of actual boards instead of what appeared to be sticks stacked together. There were also a lot more of them, at least ten from what she could see.

As the gates closed behind their cart and the female pulled the cart to a stop, Aurelia hunched in the back, uncertainty filling her. She glanced up at the demon waiting to see what would happen. *Would these demons do what the others did? Perhaps it's better if they ended it now, before she was found 'acceptable'.*

The female however blew out a deep breath and shook her head walking away from the cart and leaving Aurelia blessedly alone. At first her independence felt positive, something that hadn't happened in two years. Even now, her mind filled in the once calm places with fear. No one here would save her. No one here loved her. The only instance of safety came with the purple female. Yet now she had disappeared.

Aurelia sat up quickly scrambling to get out of the cart, scrapping her legs in the process. She had to find that female, the scraps of safety resided with her. A purple male stepped into the barren courtyard, glancing around. Aurelia stumbled until her back hit the cart. Putting as much room as she could between him and her. Yet the female had gone into the building whose door he stood next to. She feverishly glanced between him and the door.

The male followed her gaze and raised an eyebrow. Words emerged but they were in the demonic tongue. She shook her head, her breath coming in short bursts trying to stabilize her mind, she wasn't in the blue compound. There was no proof that he would act as the blue males did.

As the demon came up to her she shuffled to the side, aiming to put the cart between them. The male growled and began to get louder gesturing at the doorway she needed to get through.

Her mind stuttered, blanking as fear coated her insides. If she went near him he would grab her. *Hurt her.* She had been hurt enough for many lifetimes why must she continue to be? Were the Gods not satisfied? Her limbs felt heavier than normal, her feet going numb. Her brain didn't know where to look, her feet to stay upright, or the threatening male. He took a step forward and she involuntarily whimpered.

Inwardly she begged her body to move, to give in to her demands to move above a snail's pace, but her muscles merely locked harder. As her breaths came faster her vision began to tunnel and spot. It would only take a few moments before she would end up on the ground unconscious and at the mercy of this male.

He took another step forward and her vocal chords finally began to work as she screamed. Long and sharp, painful to every demon's ears. The female demon stormed through the doorway, her face angry and determined. She took a minute to decipher the scene before she spoke to the male in the demonic tongue.

He grunted and turned on his heel shaking his head. The female came to her and crouched so they were on the same eye level. "You are relatively safe for now, human. Gather your wits if you have any left and let's get you some actual clothes. Perhaps some hot food."

All Aurelia could do was nod and hope her muscles finally released their hold.

thirty-four

KYGOSS

DRAKORE - ANIT - YEAR 7559

Kygoss took a deep breath outside of Darius' chambers. The first year of his reign had gone about as well as Kygoss could have hoped. The Lords were silently accepting to his face but spewing hate and vitriol behind Darius' back.

Darius however had not adjusted. Kygoss had yet to see even a glimmer of the young man that had been raised with the Berrid girls. Kygoss held a small hope that after enough time had passed Darius would find his way out of the darkness. Yet, that didn't seem to be the case.

Kygoss knocked twice before pushing open the door and stepping into the room. Darius sat on the floor, rocking back and forth anger rolling off of him in clouds. Kygoss crouched down, getting on the same level.

"Sire, I have ideas that may help you conquer this cloud of darkness you live in."

Darius met his gaze. The fire of pent up rage burning hot in the depths. "What?"

"Come with me."

Kygoss stood and walked to the door, waiting for Darius to join him. "This better be worth it old bird."

Darius stalked toward Kygoss, the anger unwavering, instead seeming to grow. Kygoss straightened his shoulders and led Darius to the dungeons. He had arranged with the guards to bring all imprisoned individuals into the cavern. The Cavern was the deepest dungeon, set up with an arena that held a 12 foot tall cage in the center. It had been built by Aydan's father and retired during Aydan's rule. The intention had been to use fights to the death to prove innocence. The belief being that the Gods would back the innocent person.

Kygoss hoped that bringing back this archaic tradition would bring a sliver of sick joy to Darius. Darius looked around and arched an eyebrow at Kygoss. "What is this place?"

"This place was created by your predecessor's father, a place for ceremonial fights to determine if someone was innocent or not. I figured it would be something you would enjoy as well."

Darius prowled around the space walking the edges of the arena. A crank stood next to the door of the caged space. "What is this for?"

Kygoss smiled at him. "Give it a crank milord."

Darius rolled his eyes and moved the crank. A creaking groan echoed through the apparatus. The farther he cranked the lever the chains on the cage got closer together. This caused the cage to get a bit smaller and would obviously prevent smaller sized birds from escaping. Darius began to move the crank in the opposite direction. The cage grew a bit bigger, which would give prisoners a glimmer of hope yet not quite big enough for any but the smallest to escape.

A sickening grin spread across Darius' face. "This is an interesting concept." Kygoss watched as Darius stalked to the cages set into the walls. And pointed a shaking finger into the first cage, where a huddled middle aged man sat on the ground. "Him. Put him in the cage."

Kygoss stepped back, leaning against the benches that were set up for spectators. He expected that Darius would stalk around and pick another prisoner but instead Darius followed the guard who dragged the bound man into the cage. The guard shoved the prisoner in hard enough that the man fell to his hands and knees. Darius put out a hand, "Keys."

The guard flicked a glance to Kygoss and back to Darius before handing off the keys. Darius growled and slammed the door of the cage closed, closing himself in with the prisoner. Kygoss stood straighter. Concern flicking through him. *If the prisoner killed Darius the crown would once more be in flux.*

Darius knelt down and unfastened the chains from the prisoner's wrists and ankles. As the last chain slid free the prisoner shifted. He was a sparrow shifter, and the guard stationed outside the cage quickly cranked the lever closing the cage preventing the escape. Darius flapped his own wings, his eyes on the shifter.

Kygoss groaned to himself, this shouldn't be happening, he had a plan. Darius should be watching violence between two prisoners not participating in it. Yet here he was. Darius flew high following the shifter, pulling lightning from nowhere zapping just ahead of the shifter. Causing the sparrow to veer and undoubtedly panic.

Kygoss took an involuntary step forward wanting to step in and save the poor man trapped with the monster. However, the repercussions would be too costly. Darius in the meantime had captured the poor bird. A strangled cry escaped from the bird's mouth, almost human as the shifter tried to shift into its mortal form once more. Darius saw that coming and forced lightning into the birds body, preventing the magic from working.

Mania danced across Darius' face. It dawned on Kygoss

that the good that had been growing within Darius during his time with Cerial had truly died with her. This experience illuminated the monster he had been left with. A new plan must be created to handle and shield what was left of Drakore to preserve what he could for Aurelias return.

His plan to coax Darius into a more even mental space could not have backfired more spectacularly than it had. The monster in the arena could not be denied, nor could it ever have an even mental space, instead doomed to bounce from one extreme to another and the kingdom cursed to follow him.

MALEDIC

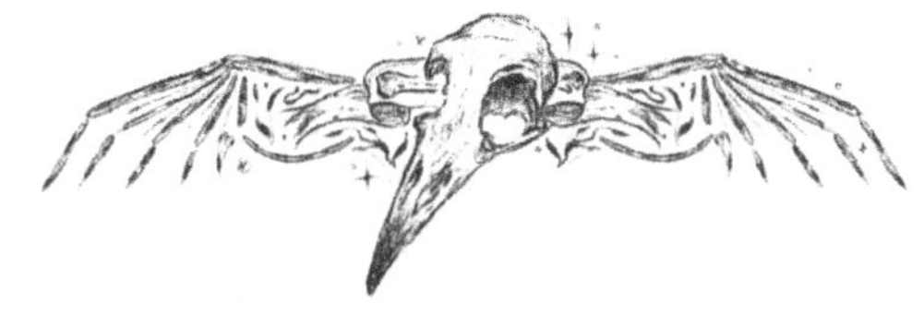

SLANA - XITA - YEAR 7559

Maledic flew in circles around Slana. Almost two years had passed since he had met the legendary dragon. The day that he had met the dragon his life had been close to the end and delirium had been in the forefront of his mind. Today curiosity drove him, he needed to verify that it hadn't been a delirious dream.

The cave entrance proved to be much harder to find than it had been the first time. His own anxiety spiking as a voice in his mind confirmed his fears. *It was all a dream created to protect you to force you to live.* However, he did have the scales and the necklace, for which the pessimistic voice had no answer. It took three passes for him to lose momentum and be forced to rest in a large tree.

He really wanted to check with the dragon, check to see if *she* still lived. *Her* pain had lessened and with that being his only indication *she* still fought his fear and anxiety had ratcheted up. The only answer his brain could come up with was that she had finally died.

There. As if his thoughts of the dragon called forth the entrance to the cave, through the leaves he could make out the darkness that beckoned him deeper. He couldn't point out what told him that it was the same cave, after all the Falrath range was known to be riddled with cave systems. Yet something pulled him toward this entrance. Taking a deep breath into his crow self he hopped from the limb and glided down toward the awaiting darkness.

As he glided into the cave, he noted that the heat that sparked his memory still raged within the cave. He shifted at once aiming to walk the rest of the way, hoping he could find more traces of how the large dragon had become imprisoned within its cage of rock. Perhaps there would be claw marks or pictures.

Disappointment took hold as he strode deeper into the cave. Picking his way across deep rivulets in the stone floor currently dark and empty but his memory filled them with molten rock and fire.

As he neared the spot where the Dragon had appeared he noticed deep cracks, they looked oddly like when he dug his talons into soft mud except these marks were embedded within cold rock. He ran his fingers over the spot, a shudder rolling through him at the power that those claws held.

He cleared his throat but realized he didn't have a name to call out. He didn't know what to say, just knew he needed to hear the words that *she* would be okay.

"Dragon? Are you there?"

He angled his head into the deep dark hole that the dragon's head had popped out of last, next to the deep claw marks.

His breath caught in his throat as he heard an echoing rumble. *Was that the dragon? Was there a cave in the hole that went deeper still?* Then the sound distinct and undeniable of claws tapping across stone occurred. Mal took a few hurried steps back, not wanting to get accidentally flattened by the large beast making its way to the hole.

Yet after a few minutes silence settled. "Dragon?"

A rumble greeted his ears. "Dragon if you are speaking I cannot make it out. Perhaps you could come back up here?"

The rumble got louder and as it neared he could finally make out the words. "Tiny mortals and their puny ears. Always shouting and yet incapable of making out perfectly reasonable words. Seems like a design flaw if you ask me."

A smirk curled across Mal's face in spite of the fear clutching his gut. "A design flaw for sure, great creature."

As the dragon's head came through the hole he bowed low. "Ah it's you. The soulbond to my blood. What exactly do you want now boy?"

Mal straightened. "I want to know that *she's* still alive. I can't feel her."

The dragon lifted a brow, on a low grumble that seemed to shudder through the great beast as it closed its eyes. Mal waited with bated breath as his fate lay within the words the dragon spoke next.

Warmth sulfur ridden air escaped its nostrils, "She lives. She is weakened but still capable of surviving as I have seen. All is moving along as foretold young one."

Mal clenched his hands pressing his fingernails into his palm the bite of pain holding the tears of relief at bay. He nodded instead. "What is your name?"

The dragon looked surprised, "My name? What good is knowing my name?"

"You are keeping me alive. It is quite a small task for me to know the name of the one who has helped me."

A grumble rumbled through the dragon. "My name is Feginth."

"Mistress Feginth." he bowed deeper. "I would love to

know your story. I will do what I can to help you as you have helped me."

A chuckle came from Feginth. "You, my mortal friend, are not capable of helping me. My story is long and sad but with the return of my blood things will change. Never fear."

Mal furrowed his brow. "How did you get here? You are trapped under the ground."

Feginth laughed darkly, "I had no idea, mortal pup. Let me ask you a question. If you encountered a creature that held great power, most of which you didn't truly understand but you wanted to keep control of, what would you do? Would you let them wander free? Or would you ensure they were locked down, capable of being found if you had need?"

Mal raised a brow. "I wouldn't imprison someone with no access to the air, no matter the reasons."

Feginth raised her brow, "We shall see."

Feginth pulled back her head into the shadows disappearing from sight.

> Magic exists for all within Baelia. One only has to know how to access it. Each culture has different beliefs on how that occurs throughout the world of Baelia, humans for instance live in fear of magic and all it can do, while shifters are able to access growing levels dependent on the Gods' favor.
>
> ~ Palion Library

thirty-six

KYGOSS

DRAKORE - DRAK - YEAR 7560

The process of protecting Drakore with the wild hope that Aurelia would return was beginning to wear thin. The disconnect between him and the people prevented the majority of them from maintaining hope she would ever return. Darius and his cronies had spread rumors far and wide that Aurelia had died with the rest of her family.

Darius had even gone so far as to hold a Dodsfell ceremony over lumpy rocks wrapped together with linen in a resemblance of her form. Kygoss knew from his spying that Palion had not believed it. They were currently enduring their own set of problems and were unable to make any solid advances against Darius

Lucian the slip of a boy had been nominated Alpha of the Wolf clan and with the aid of his demonic friend usurped the throne out from under Harold. The timing of the coup had Kygoss concerned that there was more to the story than the world at large knew. He had two distinct possibilities thanks to his meager birdie network. The most outlandish of which claimed that Lucian had slipped into madness, somehow unlocking his own demonic persona. The other more reasonable set of whispers claimed Harold still lived, bearing the Power of the Land, locked away and kept under a spell.

Ascertaining the truth seemed impossible, Kygoss kept running from place to place, coordinating his birdies. Hand selecting what bits of truth could be relied upon enough to filter down to Darius and Faziel.

Faziel, herself, had become an additional headache to the entire process. Kygoss should have anticipated it and at nights alone in his room he frequently berated himself about it. He had been far too consumed with his own survival to aid in someone else's. Faziel suffered from an inconsolable need to be with someone at all times. Yet, she drove every female companion away that Kygoss paid to take up the position, leaving him guessing at what would satisfy her.

He had personally trained her to be a subservient wife and Queen to Darius, aiming to give her all the information she would need to survive. How to talk to certain courtiers, how to address and shy away from the violent nature of Darius. Even so, somehow she had taken the lessons and twisted them to fit her own narrative, a puzzle he, himself hadn't quite figured out.

The last thing he could really suggest to take up the job of companion would be a guard, yet due to ancient rules guards were always male. When Kygoss had approached Darius about assigning a guard to help Faziel settle, Darius had put his foot down due to the fact that they had yet to solidify their union. Kygoss remained impressed with Darius that he had shown such unnatural kindness, understanding that she remained too young.

He shoved thoughts of the continual headache surrounding Faziel aside turning instead to his next plan. This involved planting someone next to Darius so he would know what continued to happen at all times even if Darius got into one of his moods.

He rounded the corner of the hall and almost smacked face first into Gerard. Gerard was a tall lanky man of the raven clan, who came highly recommended as being capable of maintaining his own identity while surrounded by those who were highly influential.

"There you are. Best hurry. We must get to him before the council meeting begins." Kygoss sidestepped the lanky man and led the way down the hall.

"Does he know I am coming?"

"Nope you are going to be my present on this fine spring day. Proof of my loyalty." He shot a sly smile back at Gerard who returned it shaking his head slightly at the audacity.

They neared the council chamber and after he determined they were in fact the first ones present he relaxed lounging against the wall to wait. Gerard took up a similar pose neither willing to discuss more on the off chance there were listening ears that they couldn't see.

Mere minutes passed and then they heard Darius coming through the hallway, his steps echoing down the way. He stopped abruptly, his eyes landing on Kygoss and Gerard.

"What is this?"

Kygoss stepped forward and bowed low. "Sire. I have vetted this man, Gerard. I am gifting him to you as an assistant, bodyguard or whatever you may need. His salary and all benefits will be coordinated by me so there's no concern for you at all."

Out of the corner of his eye he saw Gerard bow keeping his head low. Darius glowered and glanced around the hall. "I don't need an assistant."

"Sire if I am to maintain the information pouring in on our enemies and keep those within the kingdom happy he may be necessary. He can keep your dungeons full and coordinate the times you need to utilize it. While I handle the borders."

Darius looked between the two of them they both kept their head low in deference waiting. Footsteps sounded behind Darius and he rubbed his temple. "Yes, fine, fine. But you better step up your duties if you are pawning some of them off on Gerard."

Kygoss nodded briskly standing and opening the council room door gesturing Darius into his usual seat in the back away from the table. Inwardly pleased to see that a chair had been set next to the door for Gerard.

The entire room began to fill, no one acknowledging the new person. Gerard quietly settled into his seat, not a word out of place, sending a knowing look to Kygoss as Faziel brought the meeting into order.

AURELIA

DODSFELL ~ THE REALM OF THE DEAD - OSI - YEAR 7560

Aurelia found her chambers with the Areth Clan bland but more comfortable than any other ones she had experienced thus far within Dodsfell. The walls were made of stone and the place was kept clean despite the incessant layers of dirt that seemed to cover every dwelling she had entered before. Regardless of her relative comfort she had yet to feel the warm buzz of magic she had become so accustomed to in the mortal realms, she had assumed her terror had kept the magic at bay but that didn't seem to be the case any longer.

The female who had saved her had been kind in the beginning, making sure she ate and had actual clothes upon her person. There still weren't any shoes but it seemed demons didn't always wear them. The female must have notified everyone within the Clan that Aurelia was off limits because she rarely saw another demon except the younglings, whom she attended when she wasn't catching up on much needed sleep. As the months dragged on she began to feel almost safe, like the worst had passed and given some more time she would be able to discuss her release back to the Mortal Realm.

She even began to have fun with the younglings, attending the smaller children instead of just the helpless babes, and playing with them. Teaching them games from her childhood with Cerial. Her favorite activity had been teaching them hide and seek, it had the added benefit of warming her soul with thoughts of Mal and the crow children in Slana. The demon younglings had the game devolving into chaos especially when she realized a few of them could turn invisible at will.

As she had grown closer to the matriarch of the Areth clan, her rescuer, she often gained the added interest of being overlooked in places of importance. It made it easier for her to observe the mid level demons and ascertain how important hierarchy actually was in this hellscape. It became clear the more meetings she overheard that acts of service to fellow demons were used as ways to climb the ranks. Often times this involved oaths or bargains between the two parties as no one truly trusted a demon, even demons.

As her shift watching the younglings ended one afternoon she realized quickly that the trickier of the young lads had gone missing. Absol apparently had taken their game of hide and seek far more seriously than his friends. Aurelia laughed to herself as she began to go room to room combing for the young boy. He would be a handful as he aged, always in trouble. The order to leave her be had been rescinded but seeing how well she dealt with the young ones most left her be regardless. Aurelia however, determinedly avoided unmated males despite the kindness the Areth clan as a whole had shown her. Her experiences with the blue clan were burned too deeply into her soul for her to be naive again.

Aurelia walked into the matriarchs study without concern. The room could easily be called the pride and joy of the clan full of ancient text that Aurelia was sure many

Acolytes in Baelia would kill to read, and she was trusted to be in it. That was not the case for the younglings but Absol had a tendency of not listening or honoring those boundaries.

"Absol? Are you in here?" She didn't know why she felt the need to whisper but apprehension and fear filled her.

She took a few more tentative steps into the room, her eyes roving through the shelves, the couches and chairs. She stepped turning toward the right and found herself face to face with a large fully red demon, seated at the desk staring quizzically at her.

"Oh." She whispered as she whirled, grabbing desperately at the door that oddly shut and sealed behind her the handle seeming to meld into the wood.

She backed up against the rough wood, her breath coming faster.

"Who are you?" He spoke deliberately slow as if she wouldn't understand him.

Aurelia blinked her instincts of survival slower than her tongue. "I am Aurelia Berrid. Who the hell are you?" Her face flushed as her words filtered into her panicked brain. "I mean. I am a member of the Areth Clan and I am searching for the youngling Absol. I demand you release me to locate him as is proper."

"So that was his name. Rest assured Aurelia he is safe with his parents once more." The demon stood at an impressive height and walked toward her. "I found him in here about an hour ago."

Aurelia did her best to appear cowed, knowing that it would mean her life in most instances with a demon male. She had to be silent, she had to do as he said no matter the consequences. She had to survive.

"To answer your quite impertinent question. I am Balthor." He stopped in front of her and using a taloned finger he lifted her chin forcing her to meet his gaze. "You are a mortal."

She blinked, surprised it mattered. No one else seemed to make a big deal about it. "Yes I am."

"How did you get here? No wait, that is a question for another time." He looked at her carefully as if he was carefully calculating the hidden hurts beneath her skin.

Surprise bloomed inside as he took a large exaggerated step backwards putting the space she desperately hoped for between them. She wasn't sure what to say instead she just froze not wanting to insult him, his superior power obvious.

Balthor appeared to be equally frozen, unsure what he wanted to do. "Are you happy here?"

She nodded her head jerking quickly. Her mouth dry and unable to elaborate.

"I can see what you have endured to get to this point."

A flush crept up her skin and her head filled with a buzzing the pit where she stored the memories of those actions bubbling over in answer to his words. Flashes of demons hitting, beating and more filled her.

She closed her eyes, shaking her head sharply.

"GET.

OUT.

OF.

MY.

HEAD!"

She screamed the words sure that should the matriarch find her now she would help once more.

Balthor blinked, "Well that's interesting. My apologies."

Aurelia panted, "Apologies?" It came out as a croak unsure what he meant.

"It shall be explained in time. I have some arrangements to make. I shall see you again, Aurelia."

Before she could react he had vanished. She whirled back

to the door desperately yanking. It opened easily and she ran to her chambers.

Once safely ensconced in the familiar walls she began to hyperventilate in earnest. Looking at the marks etched into the stone she realized she had only been with the Areth clan for a year. Only a year of safety and relative calm. Bound to be disrupted now that a high level demon had found her interesting.

Tears splattered down her face, she didn't even bother to wipe them away. Perhaps surviving was pointless, after all there still was no clear indication she could even return.

thirty-eight

MALEDIC

SLANA - BENE - YEAR 7560

The note had come in the middle of the night without preamble waking Mal from a sleep he had barely attained.

Darius is coming on the morrow with the court. He is testing the loyalty of the Crows. Be prepared.

The night had been long as Mal and his mother worked hard to prepare proper guest rooms and ensure that the manor house sparkled to within an inch of its life. Mal also had to take a few precious hours and review the accounts of the Crow's tax contributions to the crown. The note had been a blessing otherwise they would have risked Darius' wrath.

The unfortunate aspect of this visit was there had been no time to acquire new formal attire. Maie had to break the seal on the door to his old rooms, the rooms that hadn't been entered since *she* had gone missing.

Due to the magic used to seal the room the leftover scent

of the only person he wanted to be around, pervaded everything within. Now even his formal clothes that had been in a chest smelled of *her* jasmine and honey sweetness. Every move caused the fabric to release more wafts of *her*, which caused his heart to ache deeply. The effort he exerted to swallow the tears that beat against his mind was immense, the sorrow threatening to swamp him.

He stood silent and stoic waiting for the group to arrive. Suddenly a flicker of movement drew his eye toward a group of shifters landing and changing into their mortal forms. He nodded at the anxious servant standing near the door, clearing him to open it just in time as Darius strode through the entrance, his black bat-like wings grazing the door frames.

Maledic bowed low as Darius grunted his greeting, "Maledic. I am here to assess the crows' readiness. I need to ensure loyalty with all."

Maledic didn't trust himself with words, so he gestured them further into the manor, the fakest smile plastered on his face. Inwardly he groaned at the sight of Faziel who slunk in just behind Darius, her limpid eyes latching onto him.

She sneered at him, "My, my Lord Corvus. How have you kept such glorious lands to yourself for so long? I must say I want to create a secondary palace here. It's so peaceful and quiet. Darius my love, what do you think of that?" She called out loudly at Darius' back as he moved farther into the manor.

Darius halted and whipped his head back at her. "I am not your love and you well know that. You are merely my wife. The last thing the crows want is your pestering presence day in and day out."

Mal swallowed his retort, his urge to come to her defense because it was the right thing to do. "Perhaps you would like a tour? I can show Your Highness' your rooms that have been created for this visit."

Darius grunted nodding once, Faziel remained quiet at his

side. Her only sign of defiance a small step away from the growly countenance.

Maledic took the lead forcing himself to ignore the smells that reminded him of *her*. He took them up the center staircase, past the room that would go unopened and made his way toward the best guest rooms available. Faziel however had other ideas, stopping in front of the closed dark room.

"What is this room Lord Corvus?"

Maie bringing up the rear arm in arm with Kygoss stepped up executing a quick curtsy. "Your Highness, this room is under construction. It sustained some damage during a late summer storm. It wouldn't be wise for you to stay within."

Faziel scrunched her nose looking between Mal and Maie. Maledic quickly fastened a look of sad reluctance. "My mother is correct, Your Highness but the rooms picked for you and the King are of our finest quality."

Faziel nodded distractedly. "Alright then."

Maledic wasn't surprised that Darius didn't want to relax after traveling for the few hours it took to get to Slana. Instead, Mal left his parents with the rest of the party to play hosts leading the King to his study. It used to be his fathers and honestly he hadn't taken much time to customize it. There wasn't a point to it, deep in his soul he knew that his time as Lord of the Crows would be temporary. One way or another he would be reunited with *her*.

Darius flipped through the ledgers nodding to himself and grunting. Oddly the work seemed peaceful, no awkward conversations nor posturing just straight to business. Once completed he cleared his throat.

"I figured tomorrow we could do a tour of Slana for you and Her Highness. That way you can see your people that dwell within this minor area of the kingdom."

Darius met his gaze and nodded, "Then we can be off tomorrow evening. No need to continue to dwell here."

"Whatever you desire, Sire." Mal released the pent up breath the quicker he could get them out the better for them all.

The evening went well. The only awkwardness came in the form of Faziel. As the night progressed she got more and more clingy to Mal. Hinting over and over that she desired to further their relationship beyond professional. Darius took note, as she got bolder, growing more silent and reproachful.

Maledic made the decision that during the night, he would use magic to bar the entrance. He even went as far as warding the hallway leading to the royal rooms preventing anyone from entering or exiting, for their sake of course.

The next day dawned grey and cloudy, the gloom Maledic felt inwardly displayed for the world to see. The crowd at the breakfast table appearing somber and quiet as well. Faziel seemed to be favoring her right side for reasons Maledic couldn't bring himself to investigate.

As the dishes were cleared he led them out onto the terrace. He turned to face the royal couple and his parents. "If you will all follow me. I shall lead you into Slana proper. Once there we are free to shift back into these forms."

Darius grunted.

Maledic turned away and shifted on a breath hopping into the sky and allowing the breezes to carry him further and further into the forest. He didn't slow, assuming that the rest would keep up with him.

They reached central Slana in just a few minutes and reluctantly Mal shifted back. He looked around and noticed unsurprisingly that most of the residents were absent. The tree shaded lane suddenly abnormally quiet. Mal found some peace in it even though it looked poorly on the crows as a whole.

"Why is it that the crows are nowhere to be found, Lord Corvus?" Darius boomed out.

Maledic bowed deeply at Darius, keeping his eyes low. "It appears that something may have come up. I can not account for it but do know that they are pleased with the crown. Perhaps your glory has scared them, after all crows are known to be a bit skittish."

Faziel stepped forward a small smile on her face timid as her body language was. The hair rose on the back of Mal's neck as he watched her, the evidence of a sore side suddenly seemingly forgotten. "It's understandable that they are intimidated by King Darius' greatness. It does, after all, speak for itself. Perhaps you can at least walk us through this area even if its inhabitants are hiding."

Mal watched as she stepped tentatively forward clearly unsure if she was making the right moves. His suspicion's regarding her rose, her personality far to erratic for his liking. His father shot him a look from behind Darius, a look that demanded him accept her explanation.

He took a deep breath, sketching a smaller bow to Faziel. "You are correct, Your Highness. They are intimidated by your King's greatness. Let me walk you all through this well loved area of Slana. It is where the majority of our small shops are located and tends to be where citizens gather to gossip and connect."

They only had to travel a few trees down to reach the city center. The large magically hollowed trees turned into shops and dwellings stood eerily silent, vacant, completely at odds with how it normally operated.

"Slana was created originally just for crows, intended for us in our shifted forms only. Thus this area on the ground intended for the mortal beings is just a few generations old. The buildings were constructed using magic to keep our beloved trees alive while making room inside of their hulking trunks for us to live as well. The hope is that nothing draws the attention of an outsider and our people can blend when needed."

It truly worked too. The trunks looked like normal trees, nothing outwardly suggesting that they held shops and diners and the like. The residents had buttoned up the doors and shutters intent on showing their displeasure through silence and a refusal to comply. Mal shook his head wryly wondering how he would get them out of this obvious slight against the crown.

They neared the center of the tree lined circle, dodging around the small tables and chairs. "This is where the people gather to discuss community. There are shops, food stalls and they hold meetings to keep the community informed of important issues."

Darius walked the perimeter seemingly investigating before returning with a nod. Faziel smiled at Mal, "You truly have a gem of a territory, Lord Corvus. Perhaps one day I can visit again without intimidating the people. I bet they make all the difference."

Maledic gave her a noncommittal smile. "They are the best people I know, but some say I am rather biased."

They made their way back down the lane with Mal pointing out the other shops that were available. Once they reached the top of the lane Mal gazed back at the party. "Is there anything else you would like to see while you are here?"

Darius shook his head and before Maledic could do much more Darius had snatched Faziel around the waist and launched into the sky, his large black wings carrying them both high. His father squeezed his mother before shifting himself and heading up following the wayward couple into the clouds.

Maie stepped closer to Mal and gave his shoulder a squeeze. "You did amazing, son. We will survive this we always do."

Mal merely nodded numbly.

year four

7561

> The Gods are all knowing and powerful and should be treated with respect. There is a God for many different things though the five most powerful deities will answer most prayers in a pinch. Tiva the Mother; Oxius the Father; Tixdarr the God of the Dead; Riarin the Goddess of Healing; Duella Goddess of the Harvest.
>
> ~ The Lost Archives of Tiva's Temple

thirty-nine

AURELIA

DODSFELL - THE REALM OF THE DEAD - BURA - YEAR 7561

She should have known that her time with the Areth clan would end after her meeting with the Red Demon. A knock sounded on her door and there stood the matriarch holding new clothes. She entered and in the echoing silence sat awkwardly on the edge of Aurelia's bed, not quite meeting her eyes.

"It's time girl."

"Time?"

"You have been purchased. It's time for you to move on. I must thank you for your hard work with the younglings."

Aurelia's mind stumbled around the words, shock coursing through her. "You sold me?"

"I bargained. I did try to keep you, however, it couldn't be."

"Whhhy?" Fear spiked through her, what if she went back to blue demons or worse green. She barely survived the last time.

The woman rubbed her temples. "It's difficult to explain to a mortal. However the main point is that my clan is intent on moving through the ranks. A vote determined my actions you see, the goal is to make it to red. Once we reach that we will be unstoppable. You as a mortal in our care aided us in our goals. Yet, somehow a very powerful demon found out about you." The face of the red demon flashed through her mind. "His name is Balthor and he will now have custody over your care. As odd as it may sound, the higher level demons are the safer options for you."

Aurelia nodded slowly grasping at straws. "I'll still be safe?" She couldn't keep the tremor out of her voice.

"I make no promises but you should be." She patted the clothes once more "Get changed he shall be here soon."

Aurelia nodded stiffly, her neck feeling as if it had turned to rock. She shed the lightweight dress she had been living in for the past year and half, carefully donning the pants and overcoat that had been laid on the bed. The similarity to what she had worn when she had lived in the Mortal Realm tugged at her heart.

She dragged her feet as she made her way to the front of the compound. Her eyes found Balthor instantly as he leaned against a pillar facing away from her. His coloring gave away his identity, the only red demon she had seen in this compound. Her mind reeled at his size, easily reaching seven or eight feet in height. She felt small and insignificant. He held the power to end her based on his overwhelming size not taking into account his undoubtedly immense power.

Balthor turned, meeting her gaze. He straightened approaching her slowly, careful to keep a noticeable amount of distance between them.

"Looking quite regal, Aurelia. Though I will say the amount of embroidery you were wearing was over the top.

This is better, more subtle. Lesson one. Always disguise the true amount of power you wield, the best way to do that is to blend."

Aurelia blinked her mind, stuttering over the words. *He knew about the embroidered coats?* "What?"

Balthor raised an eyebrow as he guided her out to the horses waiting outside. "I thought I was pretty straight forward."

"Why are you helping me?"

They mounted up, Aurelia noted that Balthor held the reins of her mount, carefully navigating both horses through the hilly prickly terrain. Balthor remained quiet for a few minutes. "It's a long story. However, the part I can tell you is I am going to mentor you, make you stronger, a force to be reckoned with. In the future you will understand why."

"I can't comprehend why a random demon has any interest in a lost mortal within the Realm of the Dead. It's not like I can get out, I tried."

Balthor nodded. "You will see. I had intended for you to stay at the Areth clan's compound but there's a threat you need protection from until it can be removed. The Shadow Dancer problem has resurfaced despite my past interference. I have demons out attempting to fix it but I would hate for you to be kidnapped or killed by in the meantime."

"Right." She drew out the word as confusion filled her every pore.

They reached a very large compound sticking out amongst the shrubbery like a sore thumb. As they dismounted and entered Balthor snapped his fingers. A few well dressed demons appeared suddenly in front of them making Aurelia jump. "This is my guest Reli. I want her treated with respect in the best guest room we have. No tormenting her, no abusing her. Am I understood?"

Aurelia looked between them the nickname causing her mounting confusion to double. The blue demons nodded along not even assessing her. "Reli, follow them, get settled. Tomorrow the training begins in earnest."

forty

KYGOSS

DRAKORE - OSI - YEAR 7561

"The time has come."

Faziel blanched her face, going as white as parchment. "What do you mean?"

Kygoss sighed heavily. "I mean I have gotten the Council and the King to let you grow up. I made sure you were able to mature before you were forced to bear this mantle. Yet, you are now eighteen and grown. Grown and ready for *all* the pressures of the crown." He stressed the word all, tempering his glare to merely an emphatic eyebrow raise. Hoping he wouldn't have to spell it out to her explicitly.

"He doesn't even want me. What does it matter if we ever complete the Rite or the union?" Faziel demanded as she turned back to her mirror fixing her hair in preparation for the day ahead.

"He will do his duty because it strengthens your reign and right now the both of you are still trying to prove that you are the best choice for the kingdom. The military is being held off by fear and intimidation but if he doesn't finish the job with you that will morph and everyone knows it. You must do your job." He rubbed his temples desperate that she understand.

Faziel's face fell into a sad mask. "He will be rough, he's such a brute. Would you sacrifice your daughter to his bed if you had one?"

That thought stopped him. He swallowed hard but couldn't meet her eyes as he promised, "I will make sure he isn't. I will make him be nice."

She let out a sharp laugh of disbelief tears shimmering in her eyes. "You're forgetting old bird. I am no longer a child huddled in the corner covered in piss waiting to be saved. I am an adult. A Queen." She swiped some lip color across her plump bottom lip. "When will this happen?"

Kygoss observed her cautiously, a glint of something feral had lit behind her eyes which had him second guessing if gifting her the Great Power would be wise. "After the Festival Ball. He will be expecting you that night."

"Fine. That leaves me three nights to do as I wish. Speaking of the ball. Make sure all the Lords of the land are present." She dismissed him without a second glance.

He stumbled from the room scratching his head. Deep down he knew something would come from this yet he struggled to fully understand what she would do armed with this knowledge. *Perhaps it would have been better to just have thrust her upon the situation without warning.*

forty-one

MALEDIC

DRAKORE - OSI - YEAR 7561

Maledic rolled his shoulders, his back itching from the constraint of the formal clothes. All the lords were forced to come to the Palace in celebration of the founding of Drakore.

This would be the first time that the crown had decided to celebrate the founding of the city since the coup. If rumors were to be believed Faziel had taken the planning of the festival celebrations and had opted to completely separate her and Darius from the Berrid rule.

Faziel decided instead of celebrating the people the crown would throw a ball for the upper elite. When the Council delicately questioned how the crown would pay for such elaborate celebrations her answer had shocked them all. The citizens.

"The citizens will pay to celebrate their Lord. Otherwise why would we take the time to care for them without some reciprocation."

Her words echoed through his mind. The lords had then gathered secretly in Slana trying to come up with the most cost effective way to pull off her masquerade ball while shielding the citizens from the brunt pain of taxation.

Slana had the most resources having been shielded for so long from the general population so Maledic had supplied the majority of the monetary needs for the ball. He had made it clear this would only happen once. Hoping secretly he could stick to that, knowing that if he had to he would spend every coin in his coffers to shield the crows in Slana.

Maie had done her part, ensuring he would be properly attired with formal garments and a delicately sculpted wire crow mask. His entire plan consisted of making an appearance, shaking the hands that needed shaking before slinking off into the night. Back to Slana before the morning sun could cross the horizon.

His bond had remained relatively quiet despite the random spike last year, giving him hope that she had found somewhere safe and gathered strength to return. This belief had him wanting more and more to stick close to Slana, close to Feginth in case she set the mountain rumbling once more.

As the musicians struck up filling the ballroom Maledic straightened looking around the room hoping to find the royal couple to give them his regards before making his rounds to the council men.

He stiffened as a small hand touched his elbow. He glanced down at the feminine hand that now gripped his arm firmly, fingers curled possessively. He studied the female, a silver mask obscuring most of her face. His mind raced as he catalogued her size, knowing that the entire guest list involved only the upper elite of Drakore. He glanced around and realized who this had to be.

"Your Highness."

She giggled. "How did you know?" Her fingers dug into his jacket sleeve as if seeking a hole to be able to caress his arm.

He leaned away from her despite being trapped. "It's hard to disguise a Queen."

She nuzzled her head into his upper arm, bile rising within Maledic. "Tonight is a special night, did you know?"

He nodded jerkily. "It is the celebration of the founding of the city. The first celebrated during this reign which is quite momentous."

He noted a pause before she peered up into his face. "Did you know I turned eighteen two months past?"

He blinked unaware of the consequences. "Then I suppose this could also be a belated name-day party. Happiest of Birthdays to you, Your Highness."

Faziel's face fell a bit. "Yes I suppose."

He slyly tugged on his arm, hoping to ease it from her grip which merely resulted in her tightening around him like a vice. He swallowed the bile that kept bubbling within. "Where is His Highness?"

Faziel dropped his arm as if zapped by lightning. "He is on his way."

Maledic nodded. "You planned an excellent celebration." He scanned the room desperate for a distraction, "Oh, I see my father I must go check in with him. If you will excuse me." He bowed and strode with a purpose toward the other crow masked individual.

"Father." He bowed to him to a lesser degree than that of the Queen but no less respectful.

"Was that Faziel talking to you? She is watching us quite avidly."

"Yes."

"What did she want?"

"She didn't seem to want anything. She was just talking."

"Hmm. I see."

Maledic nodded and watched the room purposefully avoiding the hungry gaze of Faziel through her silver mask. The mated couples had taken to the floor dancing and enjoying the celebrations since they really had no choice but to attend.

Maie had been forced to stay in Slana, no one wanting to leave their people without a semblance of a leader on the off chance that Darius turned his malice toward them.

"You have to go keep her entertained."

Maledic whipped his head toward his father, alarm and disgust filling his entire being. "What in the world are you talking about?"

"She's become relatively unruly. Darius has lost all interest in her. I can barely keep him interested in fulfilling the Rite soon. Which will give our land full access to the Great Power. Which will help the farms, the hunting and generally aid in all areas. She needs to be kept happy."

Mal ground his teeth, "Why is that my responsibility?"

"She picked you and she is the Queen." His father shrugged his shoulders.

"We both know why I can't do this."

Kygoss shot him a raised eyebrow. "Do you have any new things to report on that front?"

Mal swallowed his growl of frustration, his father knew that his bond had gone quiet. He did not know that Mal stumbled upon the dragon. He probably didn't even know the dragon existed and Mal couldn't divulge the secret until Aurelia resided safely in Baelia once more.

"No."

"Then off you go. Entertain our Queen, give her what she wants, whatever that may entail. Hope that you can satisfy her to such an extent that she doesn't bring Darius to our door."

Mal stopped his turn meeting his fathers eyes. "What's to

say the act of me entertaining her won't bring Darius around?"

Kygoss let out a malice laden smile. "Darius will be occupied. If he happens to even notice her, I doubt he will. Instead, he will merely be grateful for the reprieve from her constant complaints."

The hopes of having a quiet escape into the dark night lay dashed on the floor as he slowly returned to the spot Faziel still stood. *His father was serving him up to her on a silver platter, caring not.* Mal ground his teeth, the feel of her eyes tracking his every step burning him.

The musicians had begun to play a slow paced ballad designed for the lovers in the room to gather close, enjoying the company. Faziel laid her hand imperiously on his arm. "Dance with me."

He could have interpreted it as a question but the idea of angering her and bringing the wrath of a vengeful Darius upon Slana had him leading her onto the floor. He bowed to her and placed his hands lightly upon her body, touching only where it was required to perform the dance, not an iota more. His muscles took over, the hours of dance lessons his mother had forced him to take telling his feet where to go. His back stayed ramrod straight and he worked hard at keeping a distance between them, hoping against hope that she would clue into his discomfort.

Faziel however merely took every opportunity she could to get closer and closer, her perfume clogging his nose and making breathing difficult. The smell of oranges turning sharp and painful. As he spun her, he noticed that a palace guard watched their dance, his face a mask of anger and possessiveness which sparked a glimmer of hope deep within him. He pulled her to a halt in the middle of the dance, her face falling in disappointment as Mal steered them to the edge of the floor. He left her sputtering making the lame excuse of needing refreshment. "I shall return to you with some lemonade."

Instead he headed straight for the guard. "She's yours isn't she?"

He didn't bother with preamble. There wasn't time and he had lost all patience. There would be no way he would be touching her any more than was socially required and he hoped even that would end sooner rather than later. The guard stepped back as if Mal had slapped him. "She can't be mine. She's a Queen."

Mal shook his head, disgust radiating through him. "Not what I asked. Is she or isn't she *yours*?" He emphasized the last word as the true term had been outlawed by Darius after Cerial's demise. To utter the term soulbond was a death sentence

The guard glanced at Faziel who Mal could hear making her way over, her ridiculous shoes announcing her imminent arrival. He looked Mal in the face, desperation evident and nodded once.

Mal smiled, one full of his own brand of malice. It wasn't a perfect plan but it would work. At the moment he didn't care what wrinkles it caused his father. He turned just as Faziel reached him. "Your Highness." He bowed, taking her hand in his he turned back to the guard directing her attention to him. "I got distracted from my quest for refreshment due to seeing him. My once great friend and I had to offer an introduction. I do hope you can forgive me."

Faziel fumbled with her words as she met the gaze of the guard, her face flushing fully. "I... I guess so. You are?"

The equally entranced guard bowed low in front of her stuttering, "I am Notus, Your Highness."

"Notus." She sounded the word out as if tasting each sound as it left her mouth.

Mal pointed beyond Notus to an empty tall table set into the darkened corner of the room. "Perhaps you all can get to know one another here. That way you are away from prying eyes and potential interruptions."

Faziel nodded half paying attention, her entire gaze taken up by the guard. Mal slyly placed her hand in Notus', a smile playing on his lips as he walked them both over to the secluded table.

It took merely a few minutes before Faziel began to spout non stop about seemingly random information at Notus who stood enraptured.

Maledic slowly backed away a few steps testing to see if either of them would notice his absence. When they didn't he strode to the nearest balcony quickly shifting and aiming for Slana.

The Great Powers lie with the Sky, Land and Water, each tied to a specific throne. The ruling family of any kingdom has a deeper access, giving them more ability to deal with their kingdoms. This is how it is to be described to the mortals. In keeping the dragon alive we ensure that the balance and more difficult powers stay hidden from the untrustworthy mortals. Fire, and Life are far too powerful to be released. Death was hidden away in Dodsfell. We shall pacify the curious by granting access to powers for all beings within Baelia even if only a small amount. The Gods will always be in charge of who has the most, of course.

~Edicts direct from Tiva found within the Lost Archives of Tiva's Temple

KYGOSS

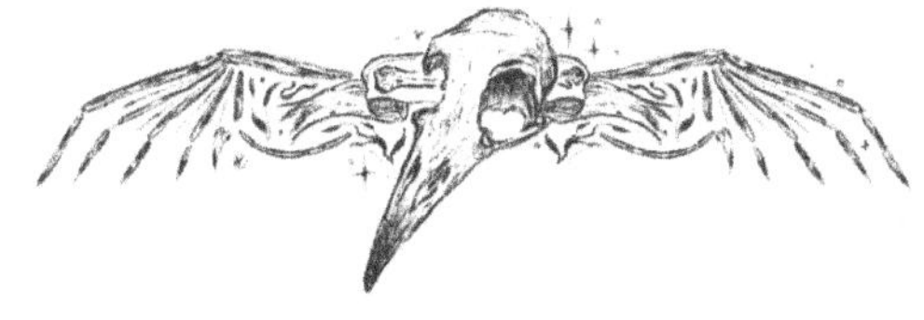

DRAKORE - DRAK - YEAR 7562

The fifth year since Aurelia had last been seen had begun and Kygoss grew tired of waiting for Maledic to collapse and cease functioning. Every day Kygoss could see the results when a Soulbond relationship severed, the survivor left with a tormented soul. It served as a glimpse into what he himself would become if Maie died before him. Yet, he knew Maledic's soulbond remained missing, presumed dead at this point, having spent all this time in the Realm of the Dead. Still he continued to function. According to Maie, Maledic didn't show any signs of adverse reactions. Perhaps a bit quieter but overall functioning, his relative personality intact.

Kygoss leaned back in his chair contemplating the next steps. Darius and Faziel remained on the throne despite the way they secured their rule. He had made sure that their Rite was complete thus protecting against those who opposed the rule. What else could he do?

The kingdom remained full of Berrid sympathizers. Full of individuals fantasizing about the youngest Berrid daughter hoping she would save them from the terror of Darius. After all Darius' reign revolved solely around what he found pleasurable. He hated the actual ruling aspect of it. The Lords had stepped up and made as many decisions as possible over their territories. Unfortunately the King didn't step in when the Lords grew greedy. The citizens of Drakore hoped against hope that a new rule would happen, that the youngest Berrid would appear and reinstate the open door policy on the palace. The safety that had existed for everyone regardless of which clan they belonged to. They needed unity.

Yes. There it is. The next step would have to involve the people. He needed to create more safe houses for the truest Berrid sympathizers. He stood stretching his joints releasing the stress he lived with on the daily. His first stop of the day would have to be Aewenna, the Oba of Tiva, the Godly leader on this side of Baelia. There were rumors that she had a counterpart in the farther reaches of the continent nearer the Meltem Isles but he couldn't worry about that now. He was stretched thin enough.

He shifted flapping out of his large window heading straight to the Temple, careful to look around as he did so. His head on a constant swivel never sure that anything was truly safe anymore.

He didn't bother stopping at the front door to ask permission for entrance. The times for niceties such as that were well and truly gone. He circled the temple's highest tower knowing that Aewenna's rooms resided there. Lucky for him he found the window open, gauzy purple curtains fluttering on the wind. He dropped suddenly, arrowing his small feathered body through the gap, shifting as he landed into the room with a small thud. His landing may have been graceful if he had been younger, now his creaking joints made nimbleness difficult. He only stumbled slightly however before righting himself taking a few precious moments to look around the feminine rooms.

Pinks and purples were everywhere, draped in the fabrics, on the wall hangings and even in the pillows. Softness and delicate beauty exuded from every inch of the quarters a stark difference from the palace he resided in. Blessedly empty. No screeching female noises echoing through the halls made that clear.

He walked through the room he landed in, a bedchamber, and into what had to be Aewenna's study. An oversized gleaming wood desk dominated the room, large bookshelves taking up the rest of the room full to bursting with rolled parchments, small trinkets and even parchments bound up as books. The sun bounced off the trinkets creating light rainbows throughout the room. *Interesting.* He could easily spend hours combing through just this room in the hopes that it would help him learn something useful in the fight he led. As he took a few steps toward the nearest bookshelf a throat cleared.

"I have killed men for less than this, you know."

A grin spread on Kygoss' face before he could stifle his reaction to the inherent challenge. He toned it down to a smirk as he turned his hands rising above his head in a sign that he held no weapons. "Aewenna, just the woman I was searching for."

Her face was obscured by her green hood, leaving only a gleam visible where her eyes were. "Most in search of my council use the front door."

"That would be ideal wouldn't it? I am however in a bit of a rush."

She waited, her arms hanging loosely at her sides. The lack of visibility of her face made it nearly impossible to read what lay in her mind, but he needed to sway her. He let the silence lengthen neither of them willing to move and give ground to the other.

"I can see you aren't a woman easily crossed. I shall be blunt. I came to ask a question."

She stepped toward him. He stepped back. There were still a few more steps before he found himself trapped against her behemoth desk. "What?" Her tone cold as ice.

"Why are you stationed in Drakore? There are temples to Tiva in every major Kingdom and even every major city within those kingdoms. Why are you the leader of all of Tiva's followers established here?"

She took another step. "That's not for you to know."

"It is though, as it determines the next step."

A low malice filled chuckle emerged. "The next step you say." Kygoss could only blink rapidly as she moved with such speed he couldn't track her. She had been directly in front of him and in the space of a blink she had a dagger to his throat and one it seemed at his belt. "The next step is you leave my private quarters before I deliver the *King*," the word sneered out disgust obvious "his faithful bird to his front step. Should I go to the trouble to deliver you, you'll be missing some key parts."

Kygoss swallowed hard. "Now, now that wouldn't do anyone any good. I am here for the Berrids not for him."

"The Berrids are dead. No thanks to you, their closest friend. Do you not know what is whispered of you." She forced him backwards again this time until his legs made contact with her desk. As she leaned in he could feel the heat of her breath as the dagger at his belt began to puncture through his clothes.

"Perception is an interesting thing." He sent a prayer up to Tiva that she would intercede on his behalf as he played his final card. "I think you are here because Kana has the Temple of Tixdarr and Palion has the pleasure of hosting them. All things being fair, we got to host the official Temple of Tiva. You are merely a political pawn."

A growl emanated from Aewenna. "I am no one's pawn but that of the Gods or are you forgetting who I answer to?"

"No, definitely not forgetting that. In fact I am hopeful she will step in at any moment to save me. While we wait though perhaps you want to hear my proposition which will in no way benefit the King."

This close together he could make out her eyes within the depths of her dark hood. She raised an eyebrow silently, waiting. "I want you to flee. I want you to seek asylum in Palion and make Palion's Temple to Tiva the official one."

"Why?" she grit out the grip on her daggers never lessening.

"It's for when Aurelia returns. She will go there. If not at first eventually. After all they won't kill her on sight, Darius will. I need to create safe spaces within Palion and to do that I need someone I trust with power behind them. I also need someone there to catch her if she appears, preferably before she marries the Pup." He knew he gave her enough information that if she felt moved to she could hang him with.

"Why do you even think she's alive? No one has even heard from her in four full years. We are entering the fifth! There's no proof."

"I know who her Soulbond is. He knows she's alive."

The shock filled her face. She stumbled backwards, her arms falling to her sides, blades forgotten. "You don't know that she was only sixteen when she disappeared."

"I understand the impossibility. The bond wasn't cemented which is probably the only reason Darius hasn't tried to kill him. Yet, we know, he and I, that he is her soulbond. He was over eighteen when they met and could feel the bond on his end cement. I know at the very least that she is currently alive. I am trying to pave the way for her to protect her when she is finally allowed to return."

Aewenna shoved back her hood. "I need to meet him and confirm the bond."

Kygoss breathing a bit easier now that the knives had been removed, "How would you confirm it? She's not here."

"That is a gift of being Tiva's representative in Baelia. I always know bonds, which are real and which are not and in this case most importantly I will be able to name the individuals of the bond."

Kygoss sighed heavily. "This will take time. I have to get him to trust this. He struggles to trust right now for obvious reasons. While I get him to agree, you must prepare to flee."

"If I can confirm the bond I will work with you from Palion. I will help to save the people who loved the Berrids and are being systematically slaughtered for that love. I will not, however, go blindly into another kingdom and a potential den of snakes without a good reason."

Kygoss nodded. "I shall go get him. In the meantime," He pulled a dagger. "An oath that you will hold your tongue."

Aewenna laughed, a cold cruel sound. "No. I do not do oaths. You forget yourself bird, I am an Oba of the Mother Goddess not a mere courtier. You chose to impart your story and you shall live with the consequences. You have one day to get her bonded here and we shall see what the next step truly is."

Kygoss glowered before shifting flapping out of her window, aiming straight for Slana.

forty-three

MALEDIC

SLANA - BURA - YEAR 7562

The dawn rays fell over his face, causing sleep to ease softly away. In that restful place between dreams and wakefulness Mal saw her. Dressed in her usual breeches and overcoat, though something about it felt different. Her dark hair had been pulled harshly away from her face revealing striking angles that hadn't been there the last time he saw her.

She held a staff moving through combat practice, the steps repeated over and over methodically. Her face drawn, her emotions locked behind her gorgeous blue eyes. A large bare chested red demon stepped up behind her, readjusting her stance, his taloned hands touching and maneuvering her. Mal felt a flare of jealousy surge within him. His mind fighting to get to her, to save her. Yet, she didn't appear disgruntled in the least. A smirk rested on her lips, not a look of fury at the audacity of this demon to lay talons on her.

Maledic's body and mind finally caught up to one another his eyes opening. His soul tore a bit more, the sadness suffocating him at the thought that she truly lived without him. Seemingly without a second thought.

Perhaps the vision had been a gift from Tiva now that his bond had been clearly verified by Aewenna, putting to rest any lingering doubts. He pulled his legs over the edge of his bed rubbing his head trying to see the point of it all. Five years felt like an eon. He needed her. He needed to see her, feel her, smell her, the urges of his heart and soul were getting louder while his brain and body were stuck in the realities that they were separated by an entire realm of existence.

He stood striding to the wardrobe. He had to continue on even though he sorely wanted to just bury himself in his bed on the off chance that he was granted another vision of her.

Despite his deepest desires he made his way to the study bypassing the too cheerful kitchen wanting to get the tasks for day done and over with. Perhaps then he could visit Feginth a journey that always made him feel closer to *her*.

His mother must have sensed his mood because she arrived in his study shortly after he settled behind the desk, her arms full of a breakfast tray teeming with food. Mal rolled his eyes standing abruptly, as he gathered the various parchments they would need and made his way to the larger table designed for meetings.

Maie didn't bother giving voice to her disapproval, merely snatching the parchments out of his hand when he neared trading them for the tray. Her face shown with triumph as his fingers closed on the handles.

"While you eat I shall review the latest from the villages."

He couldn't stop the grumble in his throat. Slathering some butter atop the fresh bread, before layering on eggs. He took an exaggerated bite, meeting her eyes before laying it back down on the plate.

Once his mouth was emptied he glared at her. "Happy now?"

"No, but it's a start I suppose. Now on to these." She waved the papers in front of him. "We seem to have quite a few issues to contend with."

Mal rubbed at his eyes once more, "I noticed." It came out dry, a bit meaner than he had meant to.

True to form his mother had no patience for it. "Maledic Mercer. I am here to help you. If you would rather tackle these mounting issues yourself I will gladly head to the palace to aid your father in his tasks."

"No, no I meant no offense mother." *Plus his father would scalp him if his mother left the safety of Slana for the snake den of the palace.* "What are your suggestions for these?"

"The most pressing issue is food. We need to organize a food system to ensure that everyone survives the hardships as they will continue to grow the longer that couple holds the throne."

Mal nodded. "Perhaps we could create a safe place where families could seek food assistance without the stigma of poverty. Plus as it becomes a more prevalent problem we could orchestrate a central kitchen in each area that everyone contributes time, money or food to depending on what they have available to them."

Mal looked up and met Maie's eyes and noticed her smiling face. She nodded encouraging. "Yes! That is perfect; perhaps Recin can be in charge of organizing and smoothing the feathers in the various villages."

Mal nodded, Recin had the personality to smooth the way for whatever they may need from the overseers in each village. Pleasure unfurled at the ease of which they seemingly solved one of the more daunting tasks he had been avoiding. The afternoon soon faded away with similar problems that seemed small but the longer Darius and his Queen stayed in power the larger the problems would grow.

One thing he knew by the end of the day was that his

mother had a head for the business of ruling. She often steered him to the correct answer, never allowing her personal feelings to affect her, staying neutral for the betterment of Slana. A skill he would never have no matter how long he was forced to maintain this position.

forty-four

AURELIA

DODSFELL - THE REALM OF THE DEAD - ANIT - YEAR 7562

The days in Balthor's compound were some of the most relaxing ones she had yet to experience while in Dodsfell. Yet it left her with a constant feeling that something else was coming. If everything bad had happened she would be safely back in the Mortal Realm, perhaps reunited with Mal if he even remembered her. Her heart seared with pain at the thought of her friend. She turned her mind away from him, knowing such emotions wasted her energy here.

As her time increased at Balthor's an interesting side effect seemed to be happening. The void where her powers had been when she lived in the Mortal Realm had begun to fill, with what she wasn't sure but as she became more secure, that void felt full with an inky haze. It felt foreign and dangerous which kept her from speaking to Balthor about it directly. Especially since she wasn't even sure what it could be. It wasn't like she could wield it.

Instead, she tried to ignore the growing darkness, focusing

on the combat and strength training Balthor insisted upon. The initial conversation when he informed her she would be learning these skills had been confusing. Months later and many training sessions under her belt, she still felt confused about why he would need to train a measly mortal stuck in the Realm of the Dead.

Balthor strode into the practice ring a sword in hand. "It's time to see what you've managed to retain these months. Let's see how good mortals can be."

She withdrew her practice sword from its sheath grimacing, sword was not where her strengths lay. She was much better at hand to hand or even staff fighting. They bowed, Balthor throwing her a mocking grin, knowing that this would be a quick fight.

Quick would be an understatement. She managed to block one good hit but as she lifted her sword to counter strike, he snuck in his blade resting it on her throat. She swallowed hard, unable to withhold the groan from escaping.

"Perhaps it's best if we just focus on the skills I have. It's not likely I will ever be given a sword of my own, here or in the Mortal Realm. I doubt society has changed its mind and suddenly decided swordplay is a ladylike pursuit."

Balthor removed his blade, sticking it point down into the soft practice mat. "When it's time for you to leave you will be given a sword, a dagger and a staff. There's no reason to think that they will be taken from you especially because you will now be trained to prevent that from happening."

She sheathed her blade and glared up at him. "You don't understand because you are both male and a demon. It's so far from reality to assume I will be allowed weapons of any kind or caliber when not in the safety of this particular villa."

"Why are you letting everyone else around you decide your life?"

Aurelia stopped her mouth gaping. *Is that what she was*

doing? "I'm not," her mind absolutely refused to accept the possibility that all this could be laid at her own feet. That somewhere along her past she could have just fought harder to get what she truly wanted versus what had been thrust upon her.

Balthor ruffled her hair, loosening it from its braid. "You have. If you don't fix up here," tapping his own head, "you will continue to do so. There is very little that *has* to happen to you. Sometimes it's easier to deal with the consequences of just allowing someone to dictate to you rather than burn your own world down to forge your own path. Are you a world burner? Or are you the mouse ready to accept the scraps offered to her?"

Aurelia took a step back, her mind reeling. Balthor stepped forward, matching her, "It's a lot to consider, luckily you have time. You have to reach your peak fitness before I can let you go home. I won't send you off to burn the world without the matches to light the flame." He shot her a cheeky grin and a wink. Yet Aurelia still couldn't process the words he was saying. *Burn the world? What does that even mean?*

She flinched away from him as he laid a hand on her shoulder. "What?"

He squeezed gently. "There's time, Reli. Focus on your breathing. In and out." He demonstrated. Coaching her waiting for her to match her breaths with his. Her body fought her commands, insistent on following its own rhythm. Slowly though the oxygen once more stabilized into her lungs, with it her mind cleared.

"Some hand to hand and then training will be done for the day. Your mind will feel better and more clear after you punch me a few dozen times."

Aurelia couldn't help the small smile that broke. "If I punch you, you mean."

"Hey. You claim you're good. I am giving you the benefit of the doubt. Show me all that pent up rage and emotion."

She strode away from him shaking out her arms and legs before dropping into her guard stance waiting for him to make his first move. He waited though. Impatience crested inside her, forcing her to move first. She lunged in getting close and delivering a rapid fire set of blows. She aimed them at his abdomen but being Balthor he easily blocked them with his meaty arms. She skittered back reevaluating while he just stood there waiting. She growled low in her throat as she charged again, focusing this time on kicks. She threw a feint front kick followed quickly by a roundhouse to his knee. Success had very little time to filter through her fight muddled brain before Balthor finally deigned to move.

She backed away. Keeping her feet moving forcing Balthor to match her. She rushed him again, this time aiming for the lower ribs with her knuckles. Her fists made contact and she let loose, feeding some of the evil fog that rose within her, answering her emotional state into her fists. For the first time ever Balthor took a step back, his face a mask of confusion as he maneuvered away from her fists.

Yet she wouldn't be stopped; she had to have more so she followed. Kicking and punching whenever she got close enough. Her lungs were on fire by the time she stopped leaning on her knees to breathe. Balthor approached his steps hesitating as if she elicited some type of fear within him.

She glanced up and her mind blanked at the sight. He had black marks where her fists made contact. She glanced at her knuckles which were bloody and beginning to sting. She stood slowly, her whole body stiff and wiped the sweat from her face.

Balthor shot her a grin, "Well that's new."

She grimaced at him "Yeah I don't really know what that was, but I am going to pay for it tomorrow."

He looked at her a frown dipping in his forehead. "We have a kit to clean you up. I'll go get it."

He was only gone for a few minutes, before he practically pushed her onto the nearby bench.

She wrapped her bruised knuckles and looked at Balthor debating how to ask about the tendrils of darkness she had utilized against him.

"B? Is there magic in Dodsfell?" Balthor scratched his horn and looked thoughtfully at her. "It depends on what you mean when you say magic."

"In the Mortal Realm I could feel things and interact with wind, and sometimes fire and water. Once I even grew flowers. Is there anything like that here for the demons? I know they have powers. I've seen you go invisible and others like Absol."

He nodded, "Magic here is -for lack of a better term- twisted. In the mortal realms it's tied to elements and living. Everyone can tap into the Great Power of Life, although now I hear it's been split between the sky, land and water which is odd."

He waved his hand dismissively, "That aside. Every mortal can access it and to varying degrees depending on the Gods favor. Or at least that's how it's advertised. The finer details are a bit murky."

Aurelia chewed on her thumb, curiosity peaked fully, her mind racing with a million little questions.

"In Dodsfell magic doesn't have anything living to latch onto. Not truly. Demons are technically alive, we bleed we have a heart beat and a brain but we were created to embody nightmares. Which is an intangible so we fall somewhere just outside of the idea of what constitutes living. Our magic is directly gifted to us by Tixdarr the Lord of the Dead. We have a Rite at our coming of age where he deems how useful our potential may be to him and gives us magic accordingly. As we move up in rank we can petition for more access and make bargains for even more. We after all survive on dirty deals and death just as he does."

Aurelia nodded her brain working through the information that had been given her. "I never knew there were degrees to being alive."

"Not a commonly known fact but for one as old as I, it is glaringly obvious. Does that answer your questions?"

"Umm. Yeah. Yeah it does. I think I am going to head to my room. It's a lot to think about." In fact Aurelia felt like her brain had exploded and was in the process of putting itself back together around the new information that there were degrees to being alive.

year six

7563

> If you are going to rule a people you must be prepared. Prepared to protect them but also prepared to feed them just enough power so they feel powerful without them having the ability to mutiny against you. Such is the way the demons exist within Dodsfell, relying heavily on Tixdarr for their magic but unable to freely manipulate the magic of nature.
>
> ~ Notes from the Oba Journals found in the Lost Archives of Tixdarr's Temple

forty-five

KYGOSS

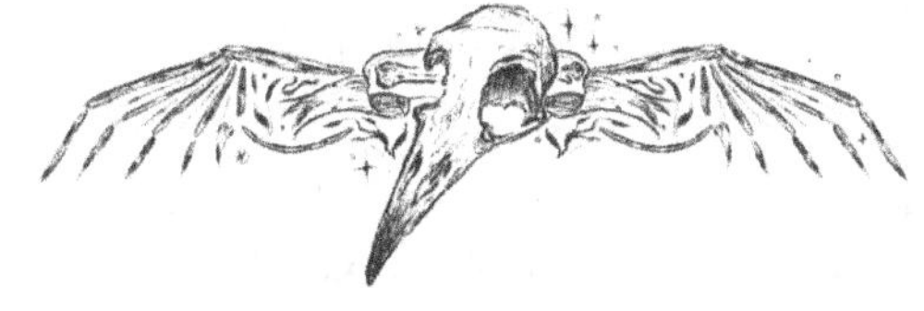

DRAKORE - BURA - YEAR 7563

Kygoss watched closely as Faziel went about her gardening project in the courtyard. Since her completion of the Rite she had taken to gardening as a way to meditate, the results were hilarious and far from productive. It took only a few minutes before magic would burst from her fingertips causing her to scream in frustration.

The rumor mill had begun to churn out more threats against her, perhaps sensing weakness. It had been so long since they were wed till when they completed the Rite, the consequence seemingly being Faziel's inability to manifest wings. Kygoss remained concerned even though they had done what was required. Perhaps the Great Sky Power withheld her wings as punishment for the deaths of the Berrids, or perhaps Faziel needed to actually train and hone her power.

It was a toss up, the only way to know would be for her to admit that a problem existed, so far her stubbornness won out. Which meant he would have to take extra precautions. He sighed as he turned away from the window and made his way down to the dungeons where Darius held court.

As he cleared the dank stairway he could hear the rumbles of the crowd gathered to watch Darius perform what had become known as the 'Cleansing'. Citizens believed to be sympathizers or were accused of romanticizing the time of the Berrids were captured and the Gods would tell him who was guilty. Then he would take them into the Arena, made bigger since he took the throne and perform a ritualistic plucking, accompanied by killing them.

Kygoss hated watching it, seeing his family in place of whomever was the latest capture. Kygoss knew he played a dangerous game and ultimately his family would be the price he would pay, it was just a matter of time. He waited until the cheering indicated the Cleansing had been completed before rounding the corner into the main area locating Darius amongst the crowd of his courtiers.

He walked up and bowed low. "Sire I must discuss something of great import with you if you have a minute?"

Darius covered in the blood of his latest victim grimaced at Kygoss. "Old Bird." His grunted reply was accompanied by a jut of his head toward a private corner, away from his adoring fans. Kygoss internally marveled at how far Darius had slipped into the hole that had been his fathers disturbing existence. He avoided the task of governing, leaving most of it to Faziel and Kygoss, striving to pull people to their cause through intimidation and fear. The farther they got from Cerial's death the more blood Darius seemed to require to quiet the monster within. Kygoss knew the exact depth he had sunk thanks to Gerard.

Kygoss followed faithfully behind careful to avoid staring at the freshest corpse in the pile. The smell had begun to be nauseating, all the bodies rotting in the corner of the Arena. Darius refused to let anyone remove them and send them to be processed by Tixdarr's temple. The lack of a Tixdarr ceremony a post death punishment for their misplaced loyalties.

Part of Kygoss grew more afraid of the retribution the kingdom would have to endure due to the lack of decorum to the Gods. He took care to keep his breathing shallow, despite his eyes watering. Once they were far enough away from the crowd to not be overheard, Kygoss orchestrated another bow. "Sire, I need you to hire more personal guards to be appointed to the Queen's personal care."

"Why?"

"There are rumors. Highly volatile ones claiming that she is useless to the kingdom without the wings promised by the Great Sky Power. While she continues to abstain from training, I can't protect her. If she were to train it's possible that the wings would appear, quieting the rabble. At the moment she's a liability and needs protection." Kygoss swallowed in the remaining words, hoping his carefully rehearsed ramble had just enough of the pertinent information to push Darius to act.

"You are telling me my wife, the one you forced me to take is now a liability to my rule? How exactly should I take that information?"

Kygoss swallowed. "She won't always be such a hindrance sire. We just have to convince her to cooperate."

A look of pure menace one Kygoss had only truly seen on his face in the arena settled on Darius. "Understood. Where is my wife?"

Kygoss swallowed hard. "She is in the garden last I checked sire."

Darius strode off leaving Kygoss little choice but to follow along behind him. Dread mixed with curiosity filling him as his footsteps echoed along the floor. Darius didn't bother cleaning himself, striding upwards toward the corridor leading to the courtyard where Faziel had chosen to place her garden covered in blood and grime.

Kygoss glimpsed her form still hunched over the dirt plucking at various green things before Darius closed the distance. Kygoss stifled his gasp trying hard not to openly stare as Darius gripped her neck from behind and pulled her upright. Faziel screamed, blood oozing from her neck as apparent claws emerged from Darius' fingers sinking deep into her flesh.

"Quit your screaming wench. I hear you aren't doing your duty. I am here to change your mind." He didn't have to yell at her, his voice holding enough coldness to chill her screams.

"I...I did my duty. You were there. What are you talking about?!" She squirmed but only a small amount, any more and she likely would have broken her own neck on his iron grip.

"The old bird here tells me you aren't studying your power. You must be at full strength to support this throne if not." He leaned in close to her ear, "Why am I keeping you alive?"

Kygoss could hear her audible swallow as she groaned. He glanced up and met her eyes. "I don't want the power. I want to help where I can but I don't need the power. It, it hurts Darius. It burns."

Darius let out a harsh laugh. "Let it burn wench. If you don't practice your magic you don't get to stay alive. The choice is simple. Remember I have eyes and ears everywhere and as much as you may think they love you I am the one ensuring they all stay safe. Me and my strength hold this throne. If you want more of a say, prove your worthiness. As it stands you're not worthy of shit."

He threw her roughly to the ground as she began to cry. Darius looked at Kygoss, meeting his gaze. "Get her lessons with the top tier magic specialist. I will assign one extra guard but if she continues to refuse, that guard will get different orders."

Kygoss nodded stiffly. He waited until Darius was gone before dropping in front of Faziel. "You really are a stupid girl aren't you. Get over your stubborn pride and learn what you can so he doesn't kill you instead. You seem to be forgetting he doesn't have the emotions you do."

Faziel sniffled and glared at him. Proof her spirit had not yet died. "You told him!"

"I had no choice in order to keep you alive. You need more guards or the kingdom's enemies will kill you themselves. Choose the way you die, Faziel. By the enemy's hands, or Darius' or possibly old age if you can find a way around your pride." A flicker of regret flamed to life in his gut, quickly snuffed by the reality they all existed in, had he not offered her to Darius as a solution she would have been removed as a child.

She snarled at him. "I am surrounded by nothing but enemies."

She pulled herself up refusing his help, striding out of the corridor leaving Kygoss rubbing his temple in frustration.

forty-six

AURELIA

DODSFELL - THE REALM OF THE DEAD - TIV - YEAR 7563

Balthor had begun to entrust her training to various other high level purple demons. There were safeguards in place and training never happened without him within earshot should one of the demons take too many liberties, no matter how odd she still felt rather safe. It probably helped that now she could actually begin to see improvements in her own strength.

Oftentimes she managed to throw the smaller demons she paired with. Granted she could barely budge Balthor and his immense size. If she someday managed to make him flinch she would think her job complete.

When not training Balthor had her helping the house-keeper with cleaning and the general upkeep of the villa. In the evenings he would counsel her on political problems. This involved a lot of 'what if' questions. Seemingly trying to ascertain her different philosophies and how she would rule if she ever got the chance.

Aurelia indulged him, though she knew it was a pipe

dream. She would never rule in the mortal realms. There was no ruler in Dodsfell so to her the entire process seemed like busy work. It made no sense why he took such time to care for her and make sure she would be ready for a future that no longer existed for her.

One day as she straightened up the study, a parchment caught her eye.

TIXDARR OATH REQUIREMENTS

- Demons must care for a mortal.
- Lower level demons must freely release a mortal back to the realm.
- A ruler must be chosen to ensure that demons follow the laws put forth by said ruler, laws that protect the civilians.
- Tixdarr will provide the mortal when the destined presents itself.
- Under no circumstance can the proposed ruler of Dodsfell release the mortal to ensure compliance to the Oath.

Aurelia traced the edges of the parchment, her mind reeling. *This can't be about me? Can it?*

Aurelia finished straightening up the study, her mind racing with the different possibilities. *What would Tixdarr know of her?* When she entered Dodsfell she had been convinced the Gods didn't exist. The longer she lived here however made it abundantly clear that Tixdarr at the very least was real. It remained to be seen if the other Gods of the Pantheon existed. *If they did, where were they?*

Over the next few days she stewed, not wanting to confront Balthor without proof. If she accused him of using her as a pawn in his own ambitions she had to be certain. A voice in her head unhelpfully stoked the inner turmoil, after all why would she be any different she wasn't special, just a mortal stuck in the Realm of the Dead. *What good could she ever offer a demon who was so high in the social structure?*

Balthor broke the stalemate during training after knocking her unceremoniously on her ass. "You gonna tell me what's got you distracted or are we going to continue to pretend you aren't?"

Aurelia leveraged herself up massaging her lower back. "I don't know what you're talking about."

He cocked his head to the side and stared unblinkingly at her. It was unnerving as if he could see beneath her skin but she was fairly certain that he did not possess the powers of mind reading or speaking. There had been a moment when it seemed like he might when she met him at the Areth compound but his lack of such powers since had her doubting that interaction. It would have come out before now. Balthor shook his head, "Until you are ready to speak go run through your sword dances. I don't want you to get hurt while you're 'not' distracted." He pointed off to the edge of the arena mats and she unsheathed her sword and began the steps that had begun to be second nature. She caught sight of a large demon looming in the doorway.

He stood a bit smaller than Balthor but she couldn't say for sure due to the distance. What stood out was that his skin was purple from the chest up and red from the chest down. *A social climber apparently.* She shrugged and continued working on her steps. It wasn't unusual for demons to come and spar with Balthor or to come to discuss demon policies.

It wasn't until a wet slap sounded on the mat that she tuned back into her surroundings. She stood stock still taking in the scene in front of her. Balthor in the process of standing up, the newcomer standing over him a snarl in place. Balthor groaned or perhaps growled a bit as he reached his full height. "Reli. Return to your room. Lock the door and don't trust anyone but me. I shall attend to you shortly."

She opened her mouth to argue but before she could form the words he risked a glance over his shoulder and glared with enough menace there that fear bloomed within her. "NOW."

She didn't even take the time to sheath her sword, instead jogged out of the arena and down the hall heading toward her quarters. As she reached her door she stopped her hand on the knob. *Why am I running? All this training and I can't try? He's the closest thing I have to a friend.*

Groaning at her stupidity of leaving, hope clogging her throat that he still fought, she sprinted back to the arena.

Balthor was on all fours spitting blood while the newcomer, appearing more red then he had when he showed up grinned down. *Fuck this.*

She walked around the dueling demons, her grip on the sword tight, waiting for her moment. It came when the newcomer delivered a shot to Balthor's face, his eyes rolling up clearly incapacitated.

Not allowing herself to think more she moved, she leapt between them placing her sword at the unsuspecting demon's throat. "I don't believe you were invited."

The demon's laugh sounded like a manic cackle. "This villa along with everything in it will soon belong to me, mortal scum. Don't pretend you can actually deliver any meaningful damage."

She growled her blood hot in her veins, the darkness that filled her magical void bubbling to be released. She opened herself up allowing it to leave. The black ooze came out through her very pores it seemed, falling to the ground heavy in the atmosphere. Gathering together it coalesced into a blanket of dark fog. As she stepped further forcing the demon back with her blade the fog moved forward as well.

The demon looked at her anew his head cocked to the side. "What good do shadows do against a demon you little witch. Put the blade down you'll look much better writhing beneath me then standing here pretending to fight."

She spat on the ground, her disgust roiling. "Let's see what these shadows can accomplish, shall we?"

She silently ordered this mysterious magic to envelope the demon. As it crested his feet the demon's face grew tight, his eyes widening as he looked down and then back to her. "It's not possible."

She raised an eyebrow. "Are you sure about that? Seems pretty possible to me." She had no idea what he was talking about but his shock could be used to her advantage.

She pulled her sword back and swung, aiming for his neck. The evil fog growing, reaching his knees. The demon teetered. An ear splitting scream escaping his lips as he collapsed clutching his neck. "You are not worthy of the Lord's gifts. What did scum such as you do?!"

Luckily that was the last cryptic thought to come from his mouth as the dense cloud of inky black fully covered the now twitching body. She held her hand out beckoning the darkness back, missing the feel of it in her body.

A wet cough sounded from behind her, she whirled dropping her blade and hunched over Balthor's prone form. "Are you okay?"

"You were supposed to be in your room."

"If that had happened you would be dead right now."

He groaned as he leveraged himself up to a sitting position. "Probably. When did you start to manipulate the magic of the dead?"

She blanched. "It's been growing for the past six years. I

never got to use it until now. I didn't even know if it would do anything useful. I just had to help my... friend."

Balthor gave her a look, "friend." He said it slowly, feeling the word. "I have never had a friend before. It's an interesting feeling."

She shot him a small smile. "Lets get you some help."

forty-seven

MALEDIC

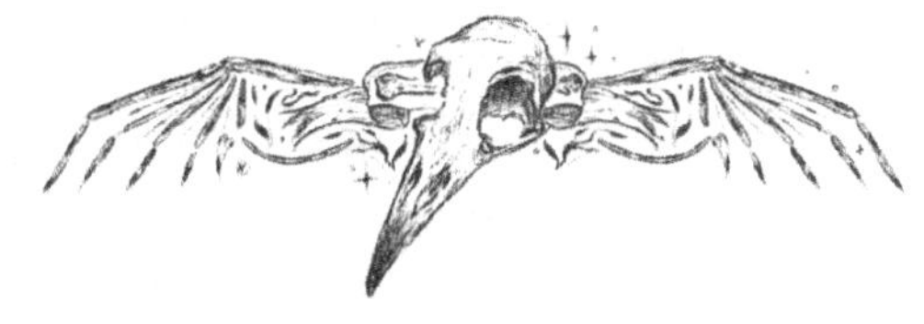

SLANA - OSI - YEAR 7563

Maledic whipped his head up as the door to his study opened without a knock, nondescript noise getting louder from the hallway. He began to rise, his hand landing on the hilt of his dagger, eyes locked on the doorway. *Perhaps his father had been found out. Perhaps Darius had come to exact vengeance.*

He let out a deep sigh, his eyes rolling back in his head in relief as Stulten strode in arguing hotly with Recin completely oblivious to the stress they had just caused him. Mal threw himself back into this chair and closed his eyes, his ears drinking in the familiar sounds of his friends' endless squabbling. Stulten and Recin frequently went toe to toe over the most random of topics yet the three of them had been steadfast friends since they were hatchlings.

Once his heart rate had returned to normal he looked at his bickering friends and raised an eyebrow, his mask of Lord of the Crows firmly in place. "What exactly brings you here to fight in front of me? Don't tell me I am meant to choose a side? You both know better than that after all these years."

Stulten and Recin halted their squabble to finally look directly at him. "We were actually arguing about you brother." Stulten walked around the large desk and held his hand out, Mal grinned, gripping it and allowing his best friend to pull him up into a hug.

"Me? Why are you both at each other's throats over little old me?" He made his way over to Recin and clapped a friendly hand on the slightly taller man's shoulder.

"Well." Recin threw a glare at Stulten. "I think it's about time we wet your whistle, so to speak." He threw a sly grin at Mal. "You know the tavern in the village nearest here hosts a fine variety of libations and other wet treats."

Mal groaned. "You did not seriously attempt that heinous of a joke. Do I need to send you to the housekeeper to clean your mouth out with soap?"

Stulten folded his arms in front of his chest. "I keep telling the rake that you have more important things to do than worrying about wetting your prick in the nearest weeping hole. You never have been a male seeking flesh for pleasure, there's no reason to start now."

Mal turned and studied Stulten. He had always suspected that Stulten knew of Mal's connection with *her* especially after the waterfall incident. Yet, Stulten had never directly accused him or demanded an explanation for his behavior since their separation. In fact it would appear Stulten had been going to great lengths to protect him from their rakish friend's bad decisions.

"I appreciate your concern about my reputation but perhaps it is time to let loose for once." Stulten stood there his mouth agape as Recin cheered in excitement.

"I knew it! Let's go tonight. I will send word and Thalia will have only the best for us. I bet she will even have someone for the prudish Stulten." Stulten snarled his lip curling back in disgust, undoubtedly a harsh word at the ready.

Mal intercepted him with a hand on his shoulder, subtly squeezing in warning. "We appreciate the attention, Recin. I would hate to take up the time you need to make it happen. We will be sure to meet you at the tavern this evening ready for some fun."

Recin grinned ear to ear as he nodded along. "Whatever you say milord."

Mal waited until Recin had left the study closing the door behind him, before he turned to Stulten an eyebrow raised. "What's gotten into you brother?"

"I know what *she* was to you. You can't go off and replace her, it wont work. In fact it will result in some terrible behaviors that I don't want to have to explain to those around you."

Mal couldn't hide his grin. "How do you know anything about it?"

Stulten flushed. "I can't explain."

Mal cocked his head to the side considering. "Can't explain? Or won't?"

Stulten swallowed hard, "Both."

"Interesting." He tapped his chin thinking. "I can't have rumors swirling as to why I don't have a Lady of the Crows. Despite what my personal feelings may be about the topic. I am surprised this is the first time Recin has brought it up."

Stulten looked down at the ground as his face flushed a deeper red. "I may have been the reason why it's been so long."

"What have you been doing?"

"I don't know what you mean."

"I see." His curiosity was fully piqued. "Tonight then, you shall aid me in pretending that I am at least slightly interested in whatever woman Recin foists upon me. Since there isn't a reason for you to not help me."

Stulten rubbed his face and groaned deeply. "I swore I wouldn't speak of it but I may have met someone. Someone extremely special leading me to understand exactly what it is you have felt. To insult the bond you have created is to spit on the God's favor. No matter what Recin says. He will never have a bond, he's far too much of a rake..." Mal held up his hand with a grin blooming across his face.

"Now, now. Let's not insult our friend. I am overjoyed for you my friend. I hope she has accepted the bond and we can arrange a wedding soon! As for tonight, never fear I will endure Recin on my own."

Stulten sent a small smile at him. "She does but she is afraid of the ruling couple. She doesn't want to bring eyes on our union."

Mal nodded understanding. Those who found their soul-bonds during the time of Darius and his decrees against even the term led to a lot of couples living in secret without their bonds being formally recognized. Slana was a bit better off due to their remoteness but fear knew no boundaries. "My mother and I can keep a secret if you both want to certify your union. We would be honored Stulten. You are my brother even if we don't share blood, and family is everything. Let me celebrate my new sister!"

Stulten smiled and nodded as he walked away. "I will speak to her but I shall still be there tonight to aid in the nonsense Recin will subject you to."

———

The day went by in a flash, Maledic rather looking forward to spending the evening with his friends. As the sun set he cleaned up his desk and headed to the kitchen to kiss his mother goodnight. He found her making wedding bread. His smile grew.

"Is that for Stulten?"

Maie looked back, meeting his gaze. She echoed his smile and nodded once. "Yes dear he stopped in and told me what happened. I am overjoyed for them, another couple off to begin their lives together. It's always a time of joy regardless of the laws and nonsense."

He leaned over her shoulder and kissed her temple lightly, careful to avoid the ample amount of flour that coated his mother. "You have fun. I am going out with Stulten and Recin. Celebrations and all."

Her smile grew wider and she threw her hands up. He narrowly avoided the cascade of flour through the air. "Oh my son! That's amazing, it's been too long since you relaxed and enjoyed your time with your friends." He merely nodded and turned toward the front hall. Once safely outside he shifted and made his way to the tavern where the boys undoubtedly waited.

The night quickly became a disaster. He had no idea why he thought he would be able to pretend that *she* didn't matter. Anytime a female got to close or dared to put their hands on him Mal had a visceral physical reaction. After the fifth one caressed his arm he ducked out of the room entirely to puke in the potted bush in front of the tavern.

Stulten thankfully kept any righteous bragging to himself and merely shot him sympathetic looks as he rejoined the group. Mal couldn't believe just how much his body couldn't stand the idea of another female touching him or being near him.

Recin became more and more suspicious as Mal's agitation grew. After the second attack of his stomach Recin dragged him outside toward a secluded grove Stulten following hot on their heels.

"You are bonded!" he hissed at Mal, accusation shooting through the words like fire.

"Not officially." It wasn't a lie but it wouldn't satisfy. Recin narrowed his eyes and then they widened comprehension, sinking into his alcohol laced mind.

"It's that girl. The one from the waterfall. Oh what was her name?!"

"DO NOT" Mal shouted.

He couldn't stand it. He wouldn't hear her name again until she stood before him, in reach.

Recin nodded slowly as his mind caught up to the years of subtle evidence. Mal had enjoyed the time where Recin had been blissfully ignorant, it lent to a feeling that his life hadn't been paused with *her* disappearance. "You love her though don't you."

"Honestly? I couldn't tell you because I don't know. The bond never formalized; she was too young and now she's gone." He shrugged helplessly watching as the pieces of his broken life finally fell into place for Recin. "Look, I'm gonna go home. You two have a great night. Stulten come by tomorrow for that help you need."

Stulten nodded. Recin appeared for the first time in all the years he had known him as lost. "I'm sorry Mal. I didn't realize."

"It's fine."

But it wasn't.

year seven

7564

Dragons were once so common one had but to look into the sky to see one. They were the source of all magic and protection. We still had Gods but dragons held a special sway. They were revered especially when it became known that they could create lifelong connections to mortals. It was rare but needed to keep the dragons focused. The Gods became an afterthought.

~ Slana's Library

forty-eight

AURELIA

DODSFELL - THE REALM OF THE DEAD - TIV - YEAR 7564

Balthor had healed but it had taken a few months for him to be back to full strength. She continued to work hard training her mind and body. Since the incident at the training room she had been very disappointed in her mind's response. *Why had she run? Running was a weakened mind set.*

Balthor had only tried talking about her magic once and that hadn't been productive. It seemed he didn't even really understand what happened. She wanted to make sense of it, magic was a mythical mystical beast that she hadn't even managed in Baelia. Now it appeared that she had somehow tapped into Dodsfell's innate magic. She needed someone who could explain it.

The day began just as normal, getting dressed and heading to the training yard. As she began to warm up Balthor came in and hit the wall loudly, interrupting her calm meditative movements, the sound jolting her.

"Come with me."

Aurelia raised an eyebrow as she straightened, tossing her long braid over a shoulder. "What's going on?"

"There's news. Come along."

"I see." She followed along after checking that all her weapons were fastened securely.

They walked through the Manor silence blanketing the entire place, entering the study. Balthor closed the door behind himself. "Things are going to change after today."

Fear crawled up Aurelias spine. "What?" She was proud that her voice remained steady.

"You will be joining the blue Dulvak clan starting tomorrow. Their emissary will be here in the morning." Balthor didn't meet her piercing gaze, keeping his fixed on the floor.

"What the fuck? What is the purpose of that? Why?"

Balthor finally met her gaze. His eyes lit with an inner fire she didn't understand. "You will go home. It's time, you are ready. The Dulvak clan will facilitate that. Then you will go and rule over the mortals just as you were destined to."

Aurelia blanched her mind racing through all the possibilities. "What? Why can't you take me? I don't know them."

Balthor's jaw clenched. "It's fine. They are a trusted clan moving up the ranks and this task will secure their place in the rank they want. It is a favor from me to do it this way. While you are destined to rule the mortals I must find a way to keep the Demons in line here."

His words ceased being words, instead her brain filled with buzzing. "Are you done?" She demanded.

Balthor stopped talking abruptly, returning her glare. "You leave in the morning. Be ready."

"Fine." She turned on her heel and stomped back to her room. Her brain wouldn't process what was happening. Her feelings raging through her uncontrolled. The darkness brewing within her, growing and pressing against her skin. She plucked a dagger out of a sheath, and flicked it through the air as she tried to understand what came next. Besides coming to Balthor's, change had yet to be positive.

She couldn't settle, her time with the last blue clan had been the worst experience in her life. How could she put herself in the care of another blue clan? Could they actually be trusted to take her home? No. In short she couldn't trust anything.

She paced throughout the night, plans roaming through her mind, her skin tight due to the magic swelling within her.

As the brief light that existed within Dodsfell began to appear showing the dawning of a new day someone knocked on her door. She sheathed her knives, having repeatedly embedded them into the wooden door of her room. Once she had them securely back in their sheaths she yanked the door open, her eyes dry due to lack of sleep.

Balthor stood leaning against the wall across from her doorway. "You ready?"

"Do I have a choice?"

He rolled his eyes and led her out to the front of the compound. There was a cart and a blue female lounging lazily next to it, her face twisted with malice.

Fear filled Aurelia, instinctually knowing that this blue woman would not help her. She took a step backward not wanting to enter the cart or the care of this clan. Balthor placed a hand on the small of her back halting her backwards trek. "Reli, this is the matriarch of the Clan Dulvak, Estrez. She is going to take you to the Dodsfell gate leading to the Mortal Realm. You will be released. The magic will allow it. She knows what to tell the gate to let you out."

Aurelia stiffened and shot a glare at him.

Estrez smiled at her, the smile more a sneer. "Yes dear but

it's important you take all those weapons off. The mortal's wont accept a queen that's armed."

It was Balthor's turn to stiffen. Aurelia turned back to him, an eyebrow raised in silent question.

"She has a point, Reli. They will accept you better if you appear more feminine at first. Arm up after they put you on the throne."

Her face flushed.

Demonic Liar.

"Fine."

She stripped off all the visible weapons. Keeping the hidden daggers tucked tightly to her corset and in her boots. The woman smiled indulgently.

"What a good little pet. Are you sure she needs to be released now? Perhaps in a couple days." Her eyes lingered too long on Aurelia.

Balthor growled menacingly. "If you want me to fulfill your favor and locate the Shadow Dancer. Thus protecting your clan you will do me the favor of returning my friend to the gate and release her into Baelia. Do you understand me?"

The woman bowed with deference. "Of course Your Mightiness."

Balthor snarled, turning and grabbing Aurelia by the elbow, steering her away from the woman. Once they were far enough away Balthor hissed in a lower tone. "You have the skills to protect yourself. While they have agreed to release you, you shouldn't let your guard down around them."

Aurelia scoffed loudly. "You think! I have been with the blues before and you are naive and stupid if you think they are going to hold to your agreement. Whatever that is, I hope it was worth my life."

She yanked her arm away from Balthor and stalked toward the cart climbing onto the driving bench. The female climbed in beside her giving Balthor a toothy grin.

MALEDIC

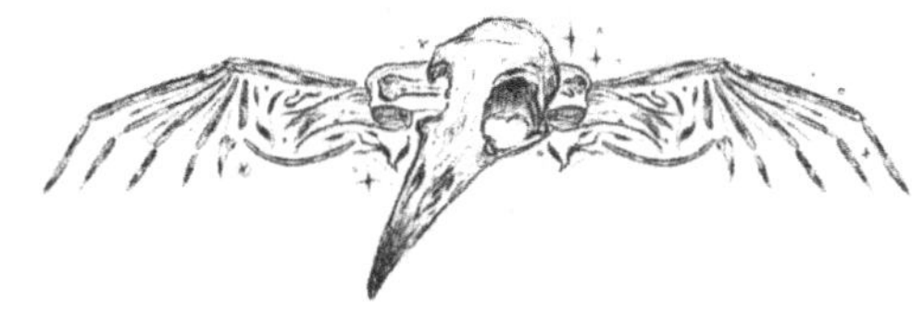

SLANA - ANIT - YEAR 7564

Aurelia contorted in pain. Chained to a stone wall receiving lashing upon lashing administered by a faceless blue demon. Her head tipped back, a scream tearing from her throat. The vision cut off abruptly as Maledic sat up. His sheets soaked in sweat, breath coming fast and uneven. *What was that?*

Years had gone by with no feelings from her, only for this vision to yank him from a dreamless sleep. Throughout the peaceful time he had gotten a few random visions in his sleep showing her practicing with a large red demon. Looking healthy and safe.

Yet, now she was back to being tortured. *Why? What changed?*

He cleaned up, heading outside toward the waterfall. Since *she* had disappeared, the waterfall held a special place in his heart. A place that had been important to her and to him. He sat on the rocks, watching the water rain down, feeling jealous of the rocks being cleansed. He just wanted his soul to feel clean for once.

Existing felt heavy. The connection between Aurelia and himself felt nothing but pain, how could they be destined to love one another when all that existed did so bathed in pain. The predawn light began to brighten and awe began to fill him. As the light filtered through the water falling down small rainbows of light bounced on the rocks around him. As often as he had come here throughout his entire life he had never really taken notice of the rainbows.

This must have been what had fascinated her so much. Her joy at the small things bitter sweet in his mind. He could only hope that when she returned she would continue to have that joy. Yet, he already knew she wouldn't be the same girl he had fallen for so quickly all those years ago.

fifty

KYGOSS

DRAKORE - RIARI - YEAR 7564

He stared at the creased note on his desk. How would this be explained? Aewenna had sent a missive by way of his more trusted operatives.

> *"They are amassing the wolves within the palace grounds. This is being done under the guise of palace guards presently it is only wolves entering service. No other shifter has been employed since the King disappeared."*

Kygoss groaned. He didn't need this kind of change to happen. There were far too many consequences to this sort of thing. It hinted at a coup of their own within Palion. How would Baelia survive such an atrocity? Eventually someone would alert the Gods or worse the demons. If it was a misunderstanding. If perhaps Harold was sickly and Lucian merely trying to appear strong in the face of the unknown. He had to tread carefully. If he told Darius too soon he would unleash Drakore's sizable force on an unsuspecting Palion.

If he believed Mal's behavior, something of a grander nature was changing. Kygoss had been keeping close tabs on his son through his wife, the nightly nightmares had begun again, increasing in frequency. Mal also spent more and more time at that blasted waterfall. Kygoss couldn't have Aurelia come home to a war. She needed to come back prepared to secure Drakore and bring it back to glory, not mop up a war cleaning up after the madness of men.

He crumpled the note having long memorized the contents tossing it into the fire. He reached high over his head stretching the muscles in his back, preparing for the coming mental battle. This would be the most delicate of political dances.

He found Darius where he always found him. In the arena plucking the feathers of some poor unsuspecting civilian under the guise that they had been a Berrid sympathizer when in reality they had been more than likely in the wrong place at the wrong time. He waited in the corridor hoping to avoid watching the death blow, hating the sickening flop that sounded when the body fell onto the pile of decomposing flesh and bones.

He took five deep breaths carefully breathing through his mouth so as not to smell the remnants of the king's pastime. "Sire. When you are available we need to have a private discussion."

Darius met his gaze and grunted, making Kygoss wonder not for the first time if he had stepped so far into madness as to lose his power over speech. It took a few minutes until Darius finally willingly left the arena. "What is it, old bird?" He growled.

"There may be an issue in Palion that needs the attention of the Council."

"What good can the Council do that I cannot accomplish on my own?"

Kygoss cleared his throat toeing the dirt. "War is something that must be decided by the council. If you want to decide war yourself you will have to disassemble many laws in order to ensure your people's backing."

Darius glared daggers at Kygoss, and for a moment concern that he had crossed the line flitted through him. After a few tense moments he nodded. "Send out the call."

Kygoss retreated back to his study to do just that. After each note was written he spent a precious minute thinking hard on the recipient before his wind magic rushed in whisking the paper to the Lord in question.

MEETING TONIGHT ATTENDANCE REQUIRED URGENT.

The wind picked up the scraps and sent them off to the various lands they were needed in. He hoped everyone showed. It would be worse if someone abstained. While technically they could, it would undoubtedly cause an eruption from Darius.

***

The Council members assembled without fuss in the large meeting chamber. Darius the last to settle into the chair, even Faziel taking her seat before him. Kygoss stood awkwardly at the foot of the table, all eyes upon him. "I have news. This news is something we can not take lightly nor should we jump to conclusions so I am praying that the Gods will guide our choice moving forward."

No one said anything, no one even moved. Instead they all

seemed to lean in closer to Kygoss as if holding their breath for his declaration.

"I have received a notification that Palion is amassing the wolven shifters in the palace. At the very least in the palace grounds. King Harold is missing and Lucian and his inner court seemingly have taken control."

The silence was deafening. The Lords fidgeted avoiding the eyes of the royal couple who were only on the throne due to their own coup. "There is a concern that they will be moving toward Drakore."

The Lords sat straighter, expressions darkening. Lord Gossek tapped the table nervously before piping up. "What proof do we have that they are moving to us? Perhaps he is merely securing his actual rule. I did hear he is the Alpha of the Wolves now."

Kygoss nodded. "Yes. He is the Alpha. Meaning he has the power to utilize their manpower."

Maledic nodded in understanding, "We all know that it takes some time to secure a throne after a coup. Successful or not. I don't think we should make any official moves until they cross into the Neutral Land. We will have a three day lead and our troops have the benefit of wings."

The other lords nodded before turning toward Darius and Faziel to see their opinion. Faziel smiled warmly at the Lords, her mask of reassurance firmly in place. "Lord Gossek and Lord Rayik will be our eyes and ears on the situation. I trust that they will send patrols into the neutral lands to verify if the Palion dogs are actually making moves this way."

Gossek and Rayik nodded along agreements pouring from their lips.

Darius merely glared at everyone. Faziel sighed heavily, "If that is all for this particular meeting I shall dismiss the Council. Please send any news directly to us Gossek and Rayik. We are relying on you."

year eight & year nine

7565 - 7566

When the Gods turned on the Dragon of Legend imprisoning her in the ground hidden from mortals, a caretaking group had to be entrusted with her wellbeing. The crows charmed their way into the position, using cunning and mischief to convince Tiva that only they would be able to trick the world into forgetting about the Dragon. The crows however had other plans. Plans to stay in the good graces of the most powerful creature. For when she returned it would be with vengeance in her heart.

~Slana's Library

fifty-one

KYGOSS

DRAKORE - TIX - YEAR 7565

Kygoss paced the temple's altar room, his mind blanking on ideas to make it better. Three years ago he had felt the desperation to send Aewenna to Palion to have an insider within the Palion court. While that had come to fruition beautifully it had disastrous consequences he hadn't foreseen.

Slowly one and two at a time over the course of the three years the temple of Tiva had emptied. Today the last acolyte had visited him in garb to disguise her identity and handed him the key. The people of Drakore had been upset to learn Aewenna had seemingly abandoned them. The rumors of a curse however had shocked them all. The origin of the rumor remained a mystery. Some claimed that a prophecy locked deep in Tiva's temple foretold the day it would stand empty proclaiming doom to the kingdom that housed it. While others merely gossiped that the Acolytes and the Oba herself could tell the evil that lay within Darius and could not deign to live within his presence. He had betrayed the Gods' favor by becoming a central part of the coup.

Now he had to navigate the delicate balance that had become their court; Faziel and Darius. If they weren't aware of the rumors of a curse yet, he knew they wouldn't take kindly to the idea. The people could in theory rise up and place someone else on the throne. There was already an issue with Darius capturing civilians and needlessly killing them in the name of halting Berrid sympathizers in their tracks.

Kygoss had done what he could to release the younger and innocent civilians held within the dungeons but as the years had gone on, the guards more often than not, worshiped Darius for his physical prowess. The price to free a prisoner had quickly become too high except for the most extreme cases. In the beginning a simple silver mark or an adjustment to a guard's rank and they would turn a blind eye to him sneaking away with a child or two. Now however they had begun to threaten him, claiming turning him into Darius would net them a bigger reward than helping him ever had.

He wrote up a pamphlet explaining that the Temple of Tiva had been abandoned because of a fake incentive offered from Palion. Perhaps this would do. They had just been manipulated and pulled to another court. If he ignored the rumors of a curse the court would be forced to ignore it as well.

The Palion Court requested the appointment of the true Tivan Oba. Once she left the temple. The delicate balance of the temple fell into disarray. No Abbess or Abbott had been selected and the Acolytes were unable to continue to keep the temple functioning.

He crumpled the paper, rubbed some dirt on it and let the edge burn a bit. Carefully he took pains to make sure the back looked just as old and torn up as the front, a common issue that fakes had. Once satisfied he headed out to hand off the missive to Faziel. Relying on her ability to manipulate the council to keep them on her side, more often than not forcing Darius' hand.

His mind slogged through the possible repercussions but his instincts pointed to this being the safest option for them. The longer Aurelia remained away the more fatal any mistakes would be.

fifty-two

AURELIA

DODSFELL - THE REALM OF THE DEAD - BURA - YEAR 7566

The dankness of the dungeon had begun to sink into her bones. Causing her to feel stiff and creaky. Her wrists burned in the manacles that held them above her head. She wasn't even sure how much time she had been held. The Dulvak it seemed were more conniving than anyone would have guessed. They had been kind in the beginning. Forcing her to pay for her exit by caring for their younglings.

It became clear they were waiting to see if Balthor held up his end of their bargain. In her time working with the younglings she had befriended a few of the mothers. They snuck her food, knowing Estrez withheld the necessary nutrients, only giving enough to ensure she wouldn't pass out. It put her in an interesting dilemma; she couldn't hate those who cared for her, who put their own lives on the line to ensure she was taken care of. All the same, she did hate the Dulvak; those who were making decisions were truly corrupted.

Balthor had failed to meet their timeline. Aurelia had no

knowledge of why. Perhaps his friendship had been an act. They had tortured her for that information. Once it became clear that she didn't know why he withheld his promise they routinely brought her down here to torture and abuse as the mood struck them.

She had fought in the beginning, using the skills Balthor had taught her. It had seemed so easy since they didn't bother with manacles the first time they brought her to the dungeons. Her body had been the first to betray her, the stiffness of disuse causing her reactions to be slower than she needed. Balthor would have grumbled and growled at her. Luckily Estrez didn't want her dead because that first fight would have been an easy moment to accomplish it.

After that when they decided to punish her they manacled her before they went very far. She fought each time but as her bruises grew it became harder and harder to even pretend she stood a chance. She would still watch the younglings and the mothers would sneak her ointments to care for her bruises at least the visible ones. The bruises to her soul however were getting too deep to manage.

All she felt was tendrils of evil. Even the tiny thread of connection she liked to pretend existed between her and Mal faded indistinguishable from the black cloud that brewed within. Yet she couldn't release the power like she did at Balthor's compound. Try as she might, it just grew darker and more solid. Something here had to be blocking her but she couldn't tell what. The only item she could see that was unfamiliar to her were rocks that appeared to jut all around the compound.

No one had ever spoken of rocks being able to block powers. She would have to ask one of the mothers who was kind to her. Her time in the dungeon apparently fulfilled the punishment because before her brain could wander much farther Estrez came in twirling the key around her finger.

"How's my little pet doing?"

Aurelia resisted the growl which threatened. She was no one's pet, not any longer. She clamped her lips shut and waited knowing from past experience that silence worked better than her urge to snark.

"That's what I thought." Estrez sneered. "The younglings need to be watched today while the clan and I attend some very important business. I expect them all to be cared for when we return or we shall add to your punishments." The evil woman attached a slave collar onto Aurelias neck before releasing her hands. The leash, a tattered rope, added humiliation.

She allowed Estrez to lead her up the stairs to the main living area where the normal assortment of ten younglings were gathered. The oldest of which was probably fourteen. When you took into account that demons could live indefinitely if undisturbed fourteen was very young.

Estrez handed her leash off to the fourteen year old with a sneer. "Keep the pet from killing our young. She is to ensure that you all are safe. I'm told Balthor the Great," she chuckled, "taught her. We shall see."

Aurelia silently snarled her lip curling at her back. Dalro shrugged, barely holding the leash. A look torn between disgust and sadness on his face.

Once the adults had filed out of the compound Aurelia heaved a sigh of relief. Gingerly she began to assess her various bruises and cuts.

Dalro dropped the leash as if it burned him. "Are you okay? My mom sent me with some balm once she realized where you had been taken." He toed the ground not meeting her eyes. Aurelia sent him a small smile, waiting for him to meet her gaze.

"It's okay. I would love some of the balm. Then let's make sure all these younglings get some food."

Dalro nodded along and handed over the small tin of balm his mother had sent, before heading into the kitchen. Aurelia looped the leash around her throat like a scratchy scarf and began rounding up the smallest of the demons.

After they were all arranged around the table she and Dalro began doling out the food for the children to eat. These younglings were surprisingly kind for demons, especially after Aurelia had gotten to know the adults that managed the clans affairs. Sadness seeped in when she considered that these children would be forced to grow into a semblance of their parents.

She released the younglings into the play room full of toys and activities to entertain them and stood off to the side monitoring them. Dalro walked up looking everywhere but in her eye, uncertainty flowing off of him in waves.

"What's going on Dalro?"

"My mom told me to ask if you wanted to leave."

Aurelia scrunched up her face, *leave*? "What do you mean by leave?"

"We know Auntie Estrez is not holding to her side of the bargain with Balthor." He whispered Balthor's name as if afraid of calling the demon to the compound.

Aurelia nodded a bit trying to keep up with his reasoning. "I know she isn't maintaining the bargain. It was clear the first day."

"Well mom says that is unforgivable and that the clan had agreed to follow the agreement in order to climb to purple. You are the quickest way to achieve that goal. She wants to help you."

Aurelia's body froze. She wanted to help. "This will take some planning. Dalro will you help me understand some things?"

Dalro nodded solemnly. "I won't tell. Neither will mom.

She's really worried about when Balthor comes looking for you. He has to know you haven't been released."

"He knows?"

"Undoubtedly. He's far enough up the social ladder that he's gonna have some sort of system set up on the gate."

Aurelia nodded along considering what that may mean. She paused rifling through what she wanted to ask of a child regardless of what kind of child. It didn't matter to her that he was a demon, innocence should be gifted to every child. "Do you know how long I've been here?"

His eyes grew wide. "About two years."

Interesting she'd been away from him for a year, supposedly he knew she never made it back and yet here she was enduring torture after torture. If she couldn't rely on her friends.

It may be time to rely on some enemies and be the creator of her own destiny.

fifty-three

MALEDIC

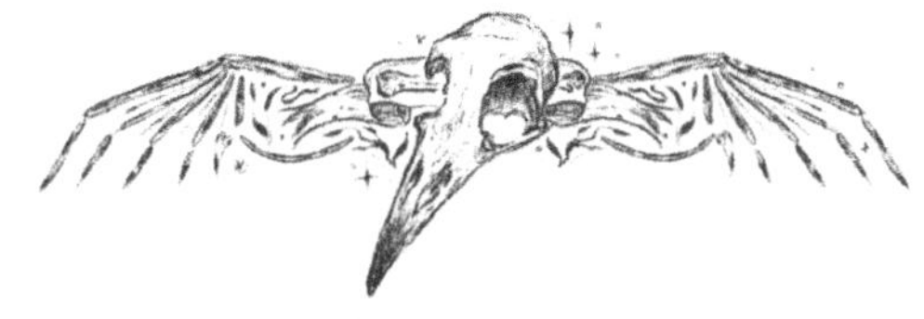

SLANA - ANIT - YEAR 7566

Frustration swelled as the feelings coming from *her* bond got increasingly murky. He had to find a way to get to her. Enough was enough and practically nine years far exceeded anyone's patience.

He walked into the kitchen looking for his mother. She would need to know his location in the off chance the crown came looking for him. As he walked into the kitchen he noticed that she wasn't making anything. *Odd.* Instead he found her sitting holding her head in one hand while idly stirring her cup of tea.

He halted in the doorway torn by how to approach her. She looked forlorn, lost and a bit sad. Regardless he had endured enough of his own torment these past years, things had to begin to change. While he hated that he would be adding to this there was no other way.

Taking a deep breath he cleared his throat before making his way to the table to sit across from his mother. She looked at him and smiled, a broken rather forced one but one none-theless. "Hello my darling son. I hope today is going better."

She knew the pain he experienced, the nightmares that made sleep difficult, he had begun to suspect that she experienced her own version due to his father. "I came to talk to you about that actually. I think it's time I make a more serious stand. I am going to go get *her*."

Maie looked him in the eye, calculation apparent. "You can't."

"I shouldn't perhaps. But I guarantee you I can." His voice took on steel unbending his patience fully expended

"No Mal. You don't know the extent of it. You can not leave Slana except for the palace and occasional visits around Drakore but even those have a time limit." She looked even sadder, tears gathering in her eyes. "I wish you could."

Mal tightened his fist on the table. "Why can't I leave Slana?"

She dropped her head not meeting his eye. "It's part of the lordship. It ties you to Slana and the Capital. She sighed, finally looking up at him. "It's why your father made you Lord to begin with. To protect you."

Mal stood and began to pace. "You're saying I am a prisoner here? I am stuck being the Lord of these people but unable to make decisions that benefit myself?"

She sighed heavily. "Does it truly matter Mal? You can't go to the Realm of the Dead to get her out. I know you tried that first year, and your father tried after she was taken. It's hopeless. You just have to keep pushing past the feelings."

He pulled his hair in frustration. "You have got to be kidding me mother. I can't keep doing this. I cant. I refuse. I either go get *her*. Or I cease living in limbo. I made my choice. Are you going to sit here and deny me access to it?!"

"How would you get her Mal? How will you cross the realms of magic?"

"I have a plan for that. One that can't be discussed for fear of someone listening. Trust that it is something not even father knows is an option." He paced the kitchen a few more times before glaring at her accusingly. "Will you help me get free of Slana?"

She straightened. "At the end of the day I am your mother Mal. I will do what is needed to keep you healthy. Even if I am afraid of the consequences. We need to have Recin help us plan all the intricacies of the transfer. He's become quite good at navigating the delicate dance of politics, and we can't have the crown negating it for some reason. He's the best we have."

Mal stopped in front of the table. "I shall see to it all. For now keep this quiet even from father. I don't want his schemes to ruin this moment. Something is happening." he rubbed his chest hard right above his heart. "Something bad. I need to do what I can to save whatever is left."

Maie's face blanched but she nodded. "I love you Maledic and I shall do what I can to help you. Whatever that is."

Mal nodded as he left the kitchen still rubbing the spot on his chest. True sadness flowed through him at all that had to be done. This would not be easy or fast.

Kingdoms are passed down through inheritance most commonly through blood. It matters not if the inheritor is male or female just that their bloodline is correct. However there are times when a ruling couple has no direct descendants. In that case inheritance can be tricky. If uncontested it goes to the throne's direct bloodline, whomever is next in line; be that a sibling or a cousin. However in times of strife thrones are taken in coups. The person who kills the bloodline will be granted access to the Great Power from the Gods, having shown mightier strength than the current ruling family. After all Kingdoms should be ruled with strength not weakness.

~The Lost Archives of Tiva's Temple

fifty-four

AURELIA

DODSFELL - THE REALM OF THE DEAD - TIX - YEAR 7567

Her time with the Dulvak was going to end. The plans had been contrived by the parents of the younglings all determined to uphold their clans' promises to Balthor. Aurelia didn't care why they wanted to help her just that they followed through with the promises that had been given. She had reached the end of promises going unanswered.

Estrez had assigned her once more to watch the younglings, while she and the hunters of the clan went in search of the Shadow Dancer. Little did they know that Aurelia would never actually watch the younglings again. Instead, the compound flooded with various elderly clan members, all intent on taking that burden and freeing Aurelia for her next move.

She busied herself in the kitchen preparing the final step to the escape; jars of various sizes filled with oils. Any oil it didn't really matter to her but she filled them all half way. Then she placed old rags of hers and other slaves' old clothes inside the oil jars, just enough sticking out that fire could take hold. She walked around the compound starting in the dungeons, the home of her torture and pain distributing the oil jars.

Ten jars later she wandered around the main living floor positioning the jars near the edges of the rooms. She avoided the room where the younglings still played not wanting to endanger them. Part of her knew that once the fire did take hold it would be unlikely any of her tormentors would actually be affected yet she wanted the impact of her loss to be felt regardless. Her ire was hot enough to burn the world but she would have to settle for this small portion, for now.

Allith, Dalro's mother, approached her. "It's time. We will need to head to the hills and hide you in the outbuildings. Once they are on the hunt for the burning we will move you out and bring you to the wall. We can't have her find you too soon."

Aurelia nodded her agreement. It would be fine to wait a few days, after all once she was away from the compound she could theoretically pull more power from Dodsfell to protect herself in future.

Allith handed her the weapons she remembered quite clearly leaving at Balthor's compound. "She had them sent for in order to give to you when you were released to the Mortal Realm and Balthor eagerly sent them. He wanted you to have them so now you will. I just," She paused looking down at the floor before meeting Aurelia's gaze. "hope you concentrate your retribution and vengeance on those who did you wrong. Though I will understand if you choose to unleash your fury on us all."

Aurelia took a deep breath centering herself. "I will do my best to protect the truly innocent in the times to come."

"That's all we can ask."

The next hour passed in a blur of activity. The first priority became getting the younglings and their new caretakers, to a larger outbuilding far from the impending inferno. Once Allith felt they were safely away she returned to Aurelia, panting slightly at the exertion.

"We are going to the mausoleum at the farthest part of the grounds. There we will wait to see her return. Then we shall burn it."

Aurelia met her gaze unblinkingly. "No. We burn it now."

A gasp went through the crowd of demons who had pledged allegiance to Allith, looking to her for guidance. It was clear she would be placed as matriarch once the old died.

"Why?" She gritted out.

"To kill her outright, with flame ensuring a swift end to such a nasty individual. I think not. She hasn't earned a swift death. Instead she shall see her home burn to the ground, she shall sit and stew over who could be responsible. Dread will sink in once they scour the ashes and don't find my body. I shall have her jumping at shadows before I feast on her. Then and only then will she die. After all, I have all the time in the world."

Allith ground her teeth. "You seem to be forgetting the deal we have with Balthor. There is in fact a timeline. As quick as possible. The longer you are here the more danger you bring to me and mine."

"I am failing to see how your problems have become mine. I didn't get a choice in any of this, from Balthor's deal to your current issue with Estrez." She looked at her nails flicking invisible dirt from beneath them. "In fact I thought you were grateful I wasn't going to target the entirety of the Dulvak clan. Should I change my plans? I did hear a rumor of an assassin targeting your people. Perhaps I should find that individual and aid them in their mission."

"You wouldn't dare. She has targeted everyone young and old alike!"

Aurelia stepped into Allith's space, getting right in her

scaly face. "You have no idea what I am now capable of. If you would care to find out, keep pushing." Aurelia could feel the evil fog of magic swamping begging to be released after so long stuck within her. Her head swam with it. She kept her grip on it by the skin of her teeth, clamping down on her strength of will.

Allith actually took a small step back, that in and of itself was a win with a potential clan leader. Aurelia hadn't even had to draw a blade to be intimidating. "We do things my way or our agreement to protect the innocent goes up in smoke with this building."

Allith swallowed hard before nodding once. They all filed out leaving Aurelia alone with her last scrap of rag. She walked to the roaring fire in the hearth and lit the end carefully. She strode quickly to the doorway everyone had exited and draped the smoldering fabric carefully against an oil soaked rag next to the door.

It quickly caught fire and Aurelia stepped into the perpetual gray of the outdoors walking quickly, knowing the straw and wooden furnishings wouldn't last long against the oil bombs spread throughout. She didn't even flinch as the explosions began. Instead she led the way into the trees lining the property toward the mausoleum that would be her base as she slowly dismantled the upper structure of the clan Dulvak.

fifty-five

MALEDIC

SLANA - TIX - YEAR 7567

He awoke in the middle of the night sweating and struggling to breath. All he could smell was smoke, his body feeling the harsh lick of flames. *What in the world?*

Part of his mind demanded he ignore it, a remnant of a nightmare nothing more. A calm voice from deep within spoke *her* name. It echoed within his chest and he knew somehow the fire he had felt, connected with *her*. Yet he couldn't feel *her* enough while awake anymore to know if she had perished in a fire. The nightmare could merely be remnants of his mind catching up to that reality, or perhaps he somehow received a vision of what she had witnessed.

Something was changing though. The air felt heavier and his magic jumped under his skin ready to leap to his command in a seconds notice. He sighed pulling himself from the bed. The only one who could assure him that he should keep fighting was Feginth locked within the ground. It had been many years since he had bothered her, concerned if he made it a continual habit someone else might happen across her, or she may make good on her threat of eating him.

Once dressed he wrote a quick note leaving it for his mother to find when she came looking for him. Then he shifted winging his way out the window just as the first rays of the sun made themselves known. He focused on Feginths essence, her fiery presence in his mind and in doing so the entrance to her prison seemed to jump out from the mountain that Slana called home. He didn't hesitate just winged further into the cave only shifting back into his mortal form once he reached the furthest cavern. The hole her head came out of was dark, looming and creepy but he stepped to the edge and called, "Feginth are you available for a small chat?"

A grumble almost immediately followed his words bringing forth a sly grin. She could pretend not to like him but he suspected he was slowly bringing her around to love crows for more than their flavor. His heart thundered in his ears as her great maw made itself seen through the hole. Her scales and skin sagging on her bones, as if all nourishment and vitality had been sucked from her. He drew in a sharp breath unsure how that was even possible.

A grumble came from the once strong throat and she exhaled a breath of sulfurous air in his face, his shock locking his legs in place. "You will have to come down here crow boy. I am too tired to bother coming to you."

He nodded jerkily, unsure if she even saw his movements. He shifted once more into his crow form and took flight, waiting patiently while she cleared the way for him. Once her great maw was out of the way he flew down and shock shattered through his soul at what he saw.

Her prison consisted of a gigantic cavern. Larger than should be physically possible considering she was being held under the ground. Yet it appeared the mountain peak that housed Slana was in fact hollow, and this entire time a dragon lived beneath them. His mind buzzed with questions as he glided down to the floor of her cavern and shifted back to his mortal form.

Did his father know? Did his mother? How could they all exist above an immortal creature and not know she's there?

He finally got a good look at Feginth in her entirety and her size even as shriveled as she now appeared still astonished. In her prime she would have spanned the length of Drakore's kingdom. Yet, how she appeared as if her life had been sucked away. Gone was the imposing threatening force and in its place a scaly skeleton with wings remained.

He sketched a bow. "Feginth what has happened?"

Feginth collapsed into a non delicate heap on the floor. Her face tilted in his direction. "Your soulbond, she's alive. That's why you came, isn't it?"

Mal swallowed back the momentary relief flooding his body. "That's not what I asked Feginth. What has happened to you? I can feel in the air that something is disastrously wrong and now I think it has to do with you. How can I fix it?"

Feginth opened one slitted eye and observed him silently. "What do you know about dragons boy?"

"You're immortal. Never to die. Rich in magic and influence."

Feginth let out a crackly chuckle. "That is a very mortal way of looking at something."

"Is it wrong?"

"Yes. Every world in existence survives on balance. The balance of life and death, the balance of magic between everyone. Nothing is truly immortal though my species has no true predator. Or at least we didn't before I got locked up here." She let out a sigh, an inner flame licking up inside of her, visible by the glow in her throat.

"Balance. So how do you die? I know the Gods locked you up and theoretically could kill you. Yet, you look like you've been drained of your life force."

Another sigh escaped. "Aurelia must have stumbled into something dark. I am her balance if she needs it. Apparently she does."

Mal sucked in a heavy breath. "You look like this so she can be healthy?"

"It's not entirely all because of that. I am the last dragon in this world. Because of that I have been holding a secret but I fear my time is coming to a close so I must share the secret with someone. Will you hold my secret Maledic Corvus fated soulbond to Aurelia Berrid?"

Mal stood taller, swallowing his fears. "Yes."

"Depending on what comes back from Dodsfell in her body, you may have to keep this from even Aurelia."

Mal swallowed again. Fear lancing through his chest. "I understand."

She studied him for a long minute. "Alright." Feginth shuffled away, revealing a pile of what appeared to be rocks behind her. "Come look at this."

Maledic walked closer, stepping carefully one eye on the large dragon staring at him. As he neared the pile of rocks his jaw dropped and he turned to Feginth. "What do I need to do?" All fear he had felt disappeared with that one glance, his purpose clearly shown before him regardless of the outcome with Aurelia.

"I fear her return will be soon, I will be the price of it. If that's the case, come back and hide this."

Mal nodded vigorously. "Absolutely." His mind was already whirling with ideas and possibilities.

"Careful though, the Gods themselves if made aware will come hunting."

Mal's mouth formed a sneer. "They can try."

Feginth's mouth formed a snarl of satisfaction as she curled around the rock pile. "Away with you birdy boy. The world will be changing soon enough."

fifty-six

KYGOSS

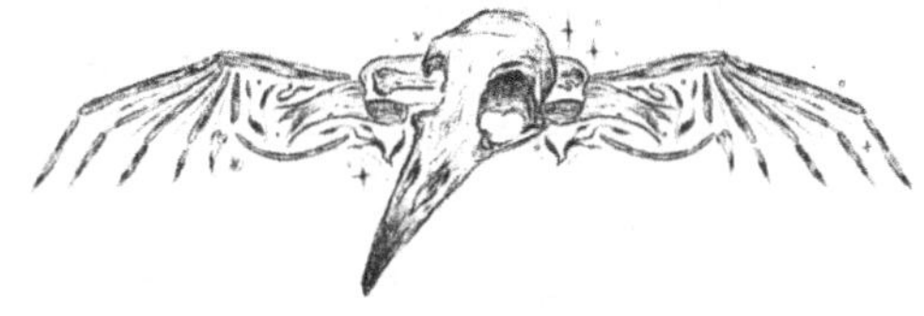

DRAKORE - LATE TIX - YEAR 7567

Wind tugged at his collar, insistent and nagging. Kygoss looked to see a note floating on the breeze. He snatched it and the breeze drifted up to caress his face leaving with it the smell of baking bread. He smiled to himself knowing this would be a note from his love. As he unfolded it the world around him faded away, replaced by terror for his family.

'Mal is acting odder than his normal levels. You need to come home. He leaves the manor periodically for hours at a time yet no one can vouch for his whereabouts. Something is happening. I can feel it in the air.'

Kygoss straightened looking around the crowded dining hall and breathed out a sigh of relief that no one was paying particular attention to him. He walked over to the hot hearth at the back of the room cheerily burning, and threw in the missive. He didn't love burning his notes from home but there was no telling what they could twist to fit their narrative.

He looked to the head of the room where Faziel held court with her treasured few. Those who put up with her volatile emotional swings. Darius stood against a wall watching the room unperturbed at the courtiers wandering around the dining hall.

Kygoss approached him discreetly. "Sire. Is it possible to take a few days to return to the Crowland's. My wife misses me and my son is apparently sick."

Darius looked him over and raised a skeptical eyebrow. "Lord Corvus is ill enough to bring his father home. Interesting."

Kygoss shrugged a noncommittal shoulder. "My wife is tenderhearted. I am mainly returning to make sure she is stable. I have no doubt Mal is fine."

Darius grunted. "Women are rather weak. It still amazes me that the throne rests more securely on the heads of couples that consist of both a male and a female. He shook his head in disgust before meeting Kygoss' gaze. "Go comfort your woman. But be back in two days time."

Kygoss sketched a low bow. "Of course my lord."

year eleven

7568

> Baelia used to be a land where it mattered not what you looked like. Creatures small and large alike would mingle together living in peace and harmony, working together to fulfill their dreams. Then the Gods changed things. They started to insist on specific worshipers, shifters only worshiping shifters, dwarfs the dwarven Gods and so on. Thus the world became fractured, split along the lines of race. War followed swiftly, the lack of understanding of each other echoing throughout the lands.
>
> ~Drakore's Library.

fifty-seven

AURELIA

DODSFELL - THE REALM OF THE DEAD - DRAK - YEAR 7568

It took days before Aurelia made her next move. The outcast Dulvak all glaring and grumping at her as they waited. Estrez had spent that time scouring the local area searching for the assassin known to have a grudge against them assuming it was them that had blown the compound to ash. According to reports Allith received, Estrez was deeply concerned about where the majority of her clan had disappeared to. Aurelia shielded herself in the shadows with the aid of her Dodsfell magic watching as Estrez got the news that her body had not been among the ashes.

Estrez had gone pale. She immediately relocated what faithful demons she had to what should have been a secure building. Aurelia knew that it wouldn't be secure from her. She stalked Estrez locating the building nestled into the mountains of Dodsfell. Estrez tried to be smart by setting a guard. Little did she realize that all she successfully had done was make it easier for Aurelia to gain entrance. Everytime a guard exited the building. Aurelia sent her now vast magic of Dodsfell at them.

The magic had grown so much in scope that she wasn't even sure of its capabilities. So far it had only taken her thinking what she wanted for it to be done. Each victim gagged before she seared them alive, leaving nothing but dust behind. It took the loss of ten guards before Estrez seemingly wised up. Aurelia smirked. It wouldn't matter in the long run. She had the bitch right where she wanted.

Withdrawing her blade she walked through the front door, glad that she had sent the outlawed clan members to all outbuildings belonging to the Dulvak, removing the pesky stones that dampened her powers. She sent her dark power through the halls ahead of her and any demon she encountered met the same fate as the guards. She knew where Estrez would be hiding and Aurelia would ensure she paid.

Aurelia's grip on her Dodsfell powers had strengthened far beyond where it had been at Balthor's compound, spiking due to lack of training. Born from the death and evil that existed within the Realm of the Dead, killing was obvious. Could it do more?

There was no time like the present to find out. The demon standing guard in front of the door she knew housed Estrez pulled his sword and leered at her. She still wore little more than rags but she didn't let that stand in her way. She reigned in her darkness sending only a small tendril toward him. She willed it to wrap around his ankle, doing no more than surface level damage and knock him off his balance.

A thrill shot through her as the tendril of fog secured itself around the ankle. The demon exhaled a hiss of pain. She sent another tendril toward his other ankle unable to contain the grin that filled her face.

She twirled her sword, lowering herself into an attack position, relying heavily on muscle memory. The demon growled slashing at her magic first. Dismay filtered through her success as the tendril of dark fog broke into wisps of clouds. She kept her smile, as her plan really didn't hinge on the experiment. She attacked shifting into one of the more complex sword dances Balthor had ground into her mind and body. The demons face filled with shocked horror as it struggled to keep up with her moves, his blocks coming a tad slower the longer the dance continued. He began to groan as his blocks barely met her blade. It only took a few more moments of fighting before she ended him, her sword drinking in his blood. She had broken a bit of a sweat but had managed to not get injured in the process.

She straightened and opened the door to the main chamber where she knew she would find Estrez. Aurelias eyes darted around verifying that the room was clear. Estrez sat at a small table with a bottle of liquor open in front of her.

"I should have guessed this was due to you, pet. I should have slit your throat long ago."

"Yes. That would have been much smarter. Instead you left me to your men to play with, or you saved me so you could cut me up yourself when you were feeling feisty." Aurelia sheathed her blade across her back as she sent out four tendrils of power grasping the ankles and wrists of Estrez.

Estrez gasped as she watched the tendrils come towards her and let out a scream of shock as the inky substance touched her skin. Aurelia merely smiled in satisfaction. She pulled her dagger from her borrowed boots. Closing the distance between them in a few steps.

"How does it feel to see all that you worked for go up in flames. To know that your decisions brought down your clan?"

Estrez spat on the floor a look of derision and disgust evident. "You don't deserve the power you've been given, nor do you deserve to live long enough to go to the Mortal Realm. I hope Allith figures it out and kills you before you gain more opportunities to kill us all."

Aurelia laughed. "We shall see. Either way I won't be seeing you again now will I. Demons don't get the choice between Dodsfell or the Void. Instead they just cease to exist. Poof. All that work, done and gone." A maniacal cackle left her as she dragged the dagger down Estrez's chest. She stabbed it into her side, letting blood pour out of the wound. She sliced low on her abdomen letting Estrez's guts spill from their fleshy cage. Estrez screamed. Loud and long. Something inside Aurelia's chest lightened. A burden finally released.

"There's no one within hearing distance, and with this wound you will die soon. It will be slow and painful. But just in case." She sliced behind Estrez's knees preventing her from any use of her legs.

Aurelia stood wiping the blood from her blade and left. Not bothering to stay long enough to watch her die. There were pressing matters in the mortal realms to deal with, too many years had passed.

She reunited with Allith and the outcast Dulvak now willingly walking in the open. They escorted her to the closest hole in the wall. "May your journey on the other side be fruitful." Allith met her eyes. Aurelia startled, unsure what to say in response.

"I hope Balthor upholds his end of the bargain finally." She turned to the hole, the entrance into her old life, or whatever tattered remains still existed.

Part of her was sure the magic would hold her in, but as she climbed up, placing her feet at the hole sitting on the edge, Allith leaned in and whispered to the wall. "She is free."

A quake shook the ground. Pebbles bouncing up and the rocks of the wall creaking around her. She glanced at the demons accompanying her and with tear filled eyes she pushed her feet through the barrier. Her feet broke through the magic, sunlight touching her skin, a feeling foreign after ten years of darkness. Her feet landed on hot cobblestones and a sob escaped as her mind reeled.

Freedom.

fifty-eight

MALEDIC

SLANA - DRAK - YEAR 7568

He stared at his father, eyes narrowing. "You no longer get a vote. You gave this responsibility to me and now I am getting to choose what to do with it. I am giving it to the one person who is consistently available. You do not qualify under that requirement."

Kygoss glowered. "You are making a mockery of the crows and putting us in the direct crosswinds of the royals. I won't let you do that to my soulbond. I don't care that you are my son. For fucks sake she's your mother."

Maie stomped her foot. "I am right here. You both have to stop talking about me like I am not here." Mal watched as she turned to Kygoss, meeting his gaze. "I know you are worried about me, and about the reception we will get from the Council. We have consulted Recin, we know the consequences. Maledic and I have created contingencies, the time is now we can no longer shield him. We have to let him live his life as he sees fit. It's been long enough, Kygi. You can't protect us from them forever." Her tone which had started out harsh gentled as she stroked his face lovingly before turning toward Mal.

"Let's do this Mal." She held out her hand. After scoring his own palm he scored hers as well. "I, Maledic Corvus gift the power of the Crow Clan on to you. I entrust their safety and wellbeing to you Maie Corvus. Do you accept becoming the first official Lady of Slana?"

She smiled widely as she nodded. "I do"

The trees around them shook slightly as magic swarmed up both their arms.

Out of the corner of his eye Mal saw his father lower his head in his hands, the oaths finished, despair clear. A flicker of guilt swarmed him, but he stomped on it. It was time for his life his way.

"Now you two get to reorganize the house once more. I am off. I shall return eventually, I hope." Mal stood shucking off his formal robe of Lordom handing it off to his mother. He strode from the room without a backward glance.

He went to his chambers grabbing a rucksack and filling it with the essentials. The current plan was to hide the bag in the forest close to Palion for when the time was right. He couldn't control the eye roll as he heard his fathers hurried footsteps. "Mal!"

He stopped and turned glaring at his father. "Yes?"

"Is it her? Where is she? Where are you going?"

Mal assessed his father, debating how much to share. "It's best for all involved, father, if you wait to see just like everyone else. After everything I have seen you do I don't know who you truly work for. It was you who tried to serve me to the Queen to keep her happy after all." He turned on his heel and left.

After packing his bag he shifted heading not to Palion or the Dodsfell barrier but instead to Feginth. His heart knew the time would be now. But he had to follow through on his promise first.

He flew in circles careful to track to see if he had been followed but it didn't appear so. He headed down to her cavernous home not bothering to announce his presence. He had been by so much in the last few weeks that she was used to him popping in and out.

He shifted and swallowed a well of tears that began at the sight of his scaly friend. His one connection to Aurelia. At first sight she appeared dead, frozen in place but then her eyelids fluttered open.

He sucked in a deep breath. "Feginth."

She grumbled. "Bird boy."

"Is she back? Is that why you're almost gone." He oddly couldn't feel his connection with Aurelia as if their connection had been eroded with all the time apart.

Feginth focused one of her great eyes on him. "Not yet but very soon boy. Are you ready to fight for her? She will need it. The evil of what she's been through will overpower her. You are her link to the living. Don't let her scare you. She needs you."

Mal swallowed his questions knowing there wasn't time, managing a small nod. Then, as if a bell had been struck, the ground shook all around them. He had one more second of looking at Feginth in her scaly magnificence before she let out the largest sigh possible and dissolved into a thousand butter-flies. They were a rainbow of colors and they swarmed him, swirling around him some lighting on his nose. His soul screamed, doubling him over in pain both physical and mental anguish washing through him.

She was back. But Feginth was dead, the reality of what that meant shocked his core, crushing down on him. Feginth wouldn't have been taken if Aurelia had stayed herself, she had returned as something unknown. He hoped their connection had survived, yet how could it.

He sighed. The only way to know was to find her. He blew out a breath wiping the tears that fell from his eyes. He made his way to the precious pile in the center of the room. His first task was to ensure these were safe. He looked around the cavern and found a few deep pockets that would work perfectly to store and hide Fengith's secret, until the time was right for more to happen.

epilogue

TIXDARR

THE VOID

Our existence has been exceedingly dull as one can imagine being locked up for a mortal century. I am never one to sit still and let things just happen. After all I am the only God to create his own Realm dedicated to all the things I love. After many experiments it was clear that I can still exercise some of my powers.

After reaching the demons back in Dodsfell it felt appropriate to expand the reach past that of my own realm. Prove to the weaker Gods that I am above them all, even that holier than thou Tiva and her mate Oxius. I focused on the kingdoms closest to Dodsfell to see just how far it could go. Thus I found Drakore and the curious relationships that existed there. All it took was a small twist. One person changing their mind, and boom Aurelia was delivered into my realm like a tasty present wrapped in nothing but her nightgown.

I watched eagerly as my pets had their way with her. Yet, she kept enduring, proving again and again that her strength was unmatched, and I got hungry. Hesper and Aydan slipped my net, their souls safely off to their next life. Not every soul is as lucky though, Cerial is still mine and I plan to use her while I can.

Palion will prove an interesting experiment indeed. Little do you know dear readers I released my toy two years before I started to play with Aurelia. The problem is that Kingdom is heavily guarded by my godly brother Culgan. Should you want to find out, come back to read just how my beloved toy saw himself around that little obstacle. I am quite proud.

Death of the Wolf - The companion novel to The Breaking - releases Fall of 2025.

author bio

Mave Hathaway is a writer of fantasy fiction. She contributes to BETA and ARC editing for fellow Indie authors as time allows, eager to aid in supporting fellow authors achieve their dreams of publishing. A prolific writer, she has two different fantasy series in progress, one for adults and one for kids. The biggest hope for her writing is to challenge the preconceived notions we have on who is and who is not a villain.

When not writing she is learning how to kick ass in martial arts, and watching movies with her family.

 instagram.com/mavehathaway

acknowledgments

This book and the ones that come next are how I have survived the darkest days in my life. It's been in production for five long years and I can't believe it's here for others to consume. I wouldn't have had the strength to write this if not for the following people.

My husband: In the darkest times of our life together he is the one who encouraged me to write adventures. The specific adventures he has requested are still in production but without his belief I don't think I would have picked up the pen. I am beyond grateful to have had you to ramble bits of this book to.

To my chaos gremlin: You won't read this for MANY years. But I hope I do you proud.

My mom: You raised me. You taught me all the ways to survive and without you I simply wouldn't be. I am lucky to have you as my best friend and helper to get this out into the world.

To my sister: You are my biggest cheerleaders and have been there for every plot hole and twist. I hope you enjoy this.

To my amazing editors; SplitLeafSaturday! You were the first people to read this that aren't included in my family. Though you may as well be my book family. I claim you!

To my one faithful BETA reader. Your comments made me brave enough to push through this process.

To my ARC readers. Thank you for taking a chance on this Indie Author!!